FOR THE ONE

A GAMING THE SYSTEM NOVEL

Brenna Aubrey

Silver Griffon Associates
Orange, CA

Silver Griffon Associates
P.O. Box 7383
Orange, CA 92863

Publisher's Note: This is a work of fiction. Names, characters, places, and incidents are a product of the author's imagination. Locales and public names are sometimes used for atmospheric purposes. Any resemblance to actual people, living or dead, or to businesses, companies, events, institutions, or locales is completely coincidental.

Trademarked names appear throughout this book. Rather than use a trademark symbol with every occurrence of a trademarked name, names are used in an editorial fashion, with no intention of infringement of the respective owner's trademark.

Book Layout ©2016 BookDesignTemplates.com
Cover Art ©2016 Sarah Hansen, Okay Creations
Cover Photography: (c) Lindee Robinson Photography
Cover Models: Madison Wayne and Chad Feyrer
Content professionally edited by Eliza Dee, Clio Editing.
Line and copy professionally edited by S.G. Thomas

For The One/ Brenna Aubrey. – 1st ed.
First Printing 2016
Printed in the USA
ISBN 978-1-940951-18-8

For Kate, the Lucy to my Ethel (and sometimes vice versa, depending on the day)

ACKNOWLEDGEMENTS

It takes a village to write a book. It truly does. And my village is full of super smart, helpful and caring people whom I am fortunate enough to know or make the acquaintance of during the process of writing it.

Huge thanks to my earliest readers, Kate McKinley and Sabrina Darby who kick my butt daily (because I ask them to!) and make the book so much better.

This book required more research than any other that I've written. Aside from reading and viewing lots of material, I've also had the benefit of consulting experts. Thank you hugely to: Peter McGonigle, Olivia Devon, Elizabeth Varlet (and her mister), Aleksandra Adamovic, Adnan Nurkanovic, Carey Baldwin, Laney Jordan, Lyra Marlowe, Cindy Kinnard, Sabyna Aydon, and Temple Grandin (who is definitely an expert deserving of thanks even though I didn't directly consult her!).

To my production team, who take the lump of clay and make it into a shiny, pretty story: S.G. Thomas, Eliza Dee, Sarah Hansen, Lindee Robinson.

The invaluable moral support department: Tessa Dare, Kate McKinley, Sabrina Darby, Natasha Boyd, Bria Quinlan, Cora Seton, Julia Kent, Bev Kendall, Zoe York. The Novel Spot Lounge on

Facebook. Members of my own reader group, Brenna Aubrey Books on Facebook. The Selfpub Warriors, the Chatzy authors, Romance Divas forum and Romance Writers of America.

Major gratitude for all of you who blog, review, post, share and chat about my books. You make it possible for me to bring you these stories. To all my amazing readers: thank you for your reviews, your messages, your posts, your tweets, your shares and your squees. Thanks for loving these characters and stories so much.

That brings us to the last but most: Those dear sweet people who share my daily life. I love you more than words can say (and I'm an author, so that's saying a lot!), to the moon and back again, to the second star to the right, to infinity and beyond. I know it's not easy living with a writer--not by a long shot. But thank you for making it possible for me to do what I do and live with the insanity and love me anyway. xoxo

1
JENNA

SOMETIMES THERE WAS NO OTHER WORD TO DESCRIBE MY LIFE besides *absurd*. It's a good word, actually. It rolled off the tongue easily. Sounded better when you said it aloud than when you heard it in your mind. And sometimes, in the middle of a situation where you're outside of your own body looking at events taking place around you, it just fit so well.

That was the word that popped into my mind that sweltering Saturday morning in March. I sat in the front row of an outdoor amphitheater at a local park watching two grown men in full medieval-style armor hack at each other with long swords. The reflection of the slanted morning sunlight glinted off the metal and stung my eyes as they faced off against each other. The shorter man was Doug, the guy I'd been seeing for the past few months. The tabard draped over his breastplate was brilliant scarlet trimmed with gold. The other man was taller, and though his head was hidden beneath a metal helmet and visor, I knew him to be William Drake.

"Huzzah, Sir William! You can do it!" Shannon called. She was one of a group of women I liked to refer to as his fangirls. William seemed to have obliviously acquired his own little collection, and they alternated between trying to date him and trying to mother him, almost always failing on both counts.

However, he didn't seem to show much interest in the women in the group, no matter how many times they threw themselves at him. I could see why they did it though. He was, in fact, almost too handsome to be real—tall and strong, with dark hair, a square jaw and excellent bone structure. His features were marred only by a tiny scar across his chin, which only lent ruggedness to his beauty.

Armor clanked as swords crashed against each other with surprising speed. These weren't padded or wooden swords, the typical weapons of choice for medieval battle reenactments. No, this was the real deal.

The rules of Historical Medieval Recreation Combat—as the formal organization was called—required real but blunted weapons. The injuries, however, could be all too real. Given the way Doug's left shoulder sagged where William savaged it in the first bout, I was certain he was feeling just how real it was.

Currently, Doug was down by one, and they were fighting the second bout out of three now. I looked on with only mild interest. I had no dog in this fight.

Well no, that wasn't *exactly* correct. I had one dog in this fight— Doug. I wanted him to win so that when I broke up with him later today, it wouldn't be as big a blow to his already enormous ego.

Clang! William's weapon landed on Doug's armor, followed by a series of aggressive blows. He appeared to be overwhelming Doug, who clearly had not expected him to be this good. Actually, Doug had said as much to me this morning before the duel. He'd even laughed and made some disparaging remarks about the competition—"who could barely be called that," he'd sneered.

Doug was an ass sometimes, but that was only part of the reason I was done with him. The winds had changed, and I had that familiar aching feeling that I needed to cut ties and move on. It was my fate to never be tied down, especially by a mediocre relationship.

Behind me, another group of people also cheered for William. They were friends of mine as well and most definitely *not* fangirls. Mia, one of my best friends, was whooping and hollering over the crowd, and Alejandra, my roommate, had started a chant while clapping in rhythm. "Sir William! Sir William!"

I inhaled a breath and let it go. It would serve Doug right to learn some humility at William's hands. But I couldn't really break up with him on the same day he'd been defeated in battle, could I? What would a medieval lady do?

Thank goddess, I'd never actually know the answer to that question. Being a woman of the twenty-first century, I had a lot more choices than that proverbial medieval lady.

Doug straightened after being driven back by William's blows and began swinging his good arm wildly, causing William to retreat. He cut in at the waist, and when William went to block with his buckler, Doug smashed his own buckler into William's helmeted face. A perfectly legal move, if an assholish one. Doug was clearly pissed that not only had the "easy competition" wounded him in the shoulder, he'd also won the first bout.

In minutes, the second bout was over, Doug declared the winner by the judge. It was a tie, with one bout to go. The first combatant to score three hits on his opponent would be declared the winner of the final bout and thus, the entire duel.

William and Doug were given a few minutes to catch their breath. With purpose, Doug strode right over to the railing, stopping in front of me. He bowed with a loud clank and then lifted the visor on his helmet. *Absurd.*

"My lady," he called, still breathing heavily. "Your favor, if you please."

I raised my brow. He did not actually believe that my hair ribbon or a scarf would help him, did he? I pressed my lips together when Caitlyn, at my right side, jabbed me in the rib cage with her elbow, giggling. "You lucky wench. Give him something!"

I pulled the ribbon off my head, which promptly caused my long hair to fall over my eyes, and held it, dangling between my thumb and forefinger, toward Doug. He extended his sword, hilt first.

"Tie it around the pommel, *my love*," he said again in a loud, sing-songy voice.

Acid filled my stomach at the term of endearment—and at his stupid grandstanding. My cheeks burned in embarrassment. He'd been calling me that for the last few days—loudly, and in public only. It was about fifty percent of the reason that I'd decided to cut and run now instead of later.

My gaze flicked to the other figure in the arena. William had switched out his small, round buckler for a tall shield, which was always used in the third round of a duel. He stood still as a stone as he silently watched us through his lowered face guard.

I rose from my seat and quickly tied the ribbon in a bow around the pommel of Doug's weapon. Then I sat back down before he got really obnoxious and asked for a kiss or something.

Doug then held up his sword, facing the crowd. A loud cheer erupted. "Louder! We can't hear you through our helmets."

William had not moved, and his helmeted head was still aimed in my direction. Disquieted, I demurely clapped my hands, my applause lost in the clamor behind me. People were stamping their feet on the wooden bleachers and whistling. William's helmeted head swung in the direction of the bleachers, his shield lowering a fraction. Then, he spun and turned his back on the crowd, his head drooping.

Doug had turned to look at William as he waited for the referee's call to battle. I squinted as I watched him. He seemed to be studying William, too. An intimidation tactic?

After swapping out his shield, Doug strode to the center of the battlefield where the referee stood. Haltingly, William turned toward them, stumbling as he took his place. I frowned. What was up with that? He'd seemed so confident during the first bout. Maybe the defeat in the second bout had shaken him.

The two knights faced off again, swords poised as they awaited the signal to begin. The moment the yellow flag lifted between them, they began pounding each other. It was so surreal to watch these grown men playacting their war games when I had lived through an actual war. In fact, I'd been born in the middle of a war zone and survived for years in a city under siege.

I shuddered, forcing the horrible memories from my mind.

William was heading toward Doug again, but his movements were halting and haphazard. He swung and hit only the air, and his shield was cocked at an awkward angle, almost as if to block the spectators from watching him fight. The crowd cheered louder and stomped harder.

William stumbled within striking distance and his sword came down hard on Doug's injured shoulder. Doug let loose a loud string of curses that could be heard over the din of the crowd. The referee blew a whistle and called for them to separate. Both knights lowered their weapons and raised their visors.

"Foul, Black and Silver, for attacking a previously injured portion of the opponent's body in an unchivalrous manner. Black and Silver, this is a yellow card warning! One more such penalty will disqualify you. And you—Red and Gold. You are hereby warned about your unchivalrous language. Have a care, sir."

William nodded, his eyes fixed on the ground, but Doug was staring at William through narrowed eyes. I couldn't tell whether he was angry or plotting. His lips thinned as he turned to the crowd and raised his sword to drum up more noise. The crowd happily complied.

William's entire body stiffened—if such a thing could be detected under all that armor. I wondered what the hell Doug was up to. Earlier, he said something about knowing an opponent's weakness being the key to winning a duel. Until a few minutes ago, William hadn't displayed any weaknesses.

The crowd was clearly bothering William. I hadn't noticed it until Doug approached me and asked for my favor, then roused the crowd to cheer. Had that been a calculated move on Doug's part? It sure as heck hadn't been sentimental. Doug didn't work like that. He'd had a reason for asking me for that favor when he did and making such a production of it.

Doug pushed forward the minute he was given the signal by the ref. He landed two direct hits in quick succession. William was forced to retreat without making a single attempt to block. The crowd roared. With one more hit, the bout—and the duel—would be Doug's.

And though I'd originally felt it would be good for my purposes if he won today, I suddenly wished he wouldn't.

William readjusted his large shield against his side. Doug raised his sword again, but this time as a signal to the crowd to cheer louder. They did so in earnest by stomping, yelling and whistling with even greater fervor. I, however, was focused on William. It was hard to read body language under a layer of steel, but with his shield sagging and his sword jutting at a strange angle, he clearly looked uncomfortable.

Doug moved toward him and William suddenly charged, moving faster than he had before. William snuck a hit in on Doug before fending off what would have been the final blow. The crowd was on its feet now, including me. It was *so close.*

The ref stopped play again and William paced in circles, his gauntleted fist opening and closing at his side, his helmet turning as if he was shaking his head inside there. Doug turned to the crowd, raising his hand as if to get the crowd to shout louder. A shudder passed through William's whole body.

When the flag between them was lifted, William lunged almost too soon and started chopping away at Doug randomly. Gone was the precise, staid style of fighting that had worn Doug down during the first bout. Now William's energy almost seemed chaotic and Doug fended him off easily.

Until William's sword landed on him once again...at the juncture of his breastplate and helmet. We all jumped up and down, screaming. William had gotten his last hit.

And yeah, I was probably happier about it than I should have been. Everyone was cheering so loudly that no one heard the ref's whistle until both contenders raised their visors. It took a few minutes, but the crowd quieted down.

Something was wrong. The ref was not declaring William the winner.

"Due to another yellow card violation—a strike against the neck piece—I hereby declare the Knight of Black and Silver disqualified. Red and Gold, you are the winner of this duel."

The group of people behind me—William's friends and family—were questioning each other in tight voices. I turned around to look at them. Mia was watching William carefully, her pretty face creased in a frown. Alex was complaining loudly, and Adam and Heath had their heads together, conversing. Others were in a similar state of confusion. Doug's friends, of course, were ecstatic, and Caitlyn and Ann, who sat on either side of me, cheered. "He won! Your man won!"

Doug raised his visor to reveal the grim smile on his face. He appeared supremely satisfied. A chant went up. "Sir Douglas! Sir Douglas!" Inexplicably, my stomach bunched in a knot. I couldn't help but feel bad for William. He had fought such a good fight with quick and powerful hits.

Within minutes, there was a crowd around Doug, and William took off in the direction of the camping site where the sleeping tents were set up. As a group, we had camped the night before in preparation for the weekend's events. Beyond watching the duels, we non-fighters also had work to do. After lunch, there would be a yearly planning meeting for our club, traditionally held at the beginning of every spring.

Two more knights filed into the ring for a practice duel. I let out a deep breath. Might as well get this over with. Perhaps he wouldn't take it too hard on the tail end of his "great victory."

My two closest friends in our clan, Caitlyn and Ann, walked with me. Ann chatted amiably about the duel while Caitlyn called and waved to people along the way, sometimes peeling off to go hug or greet someone.

I, on the other hand, was quiet, already mentally practicing my breakup dialogue.

"Are you happy that your man won?" Ann asked suddenly.

I sent her a look out of the corner of my eye. In the past, Ann had been quite frank in telling me she was not a fan of Doug and that he "didn't deserve" me. I took a few steps in silence before I answered. "Sure."

I didn't meet her gaze, afraid she might figure things out. I hadn't yet shared with either of them my waning interest in Doug.

"It's too bad," she said in her mellifluous Somali accent that I so enjoyed listening to. "About Sir William. He's a kind man."

"He is..." I shrugged. "But every battle needs a winner and a loser." I frowned. That had sounded a lot better in my head than it did out loud. William was no loser.

Caitlyn fell into step beside us again, calming her usual boisterous tendencies in order to catch up on our conversation.

Ann stole another glance at me and sucked in her cheeks, emphasizing her already exquisite bone structure. "He has a thing for you."

"Doug? Of course he does," Caitlyn said.

My eyebrows shot up, and though I knew Ann had meant William, I stayed silent, hoping Caitlyn would steer the conversation in a different direction. She didn't get the chance.

"I meant William," Ann explained to her. "I catch him looking at Jenna all the time."

"Sir Hottie MacFine has the hots for Jenna?" Caitlyn said, far louder than I would have liked.

I shushed her. "He does not. We argue all the time. The guy is constantly contradicting everything I say."

Ann shrugged. "Sexual tension. It's not that far beyond reason, honey. He *did* challenge Doug to the duel, remember."

I shook my head. "That was a male dick-measuring contest, nothing more."

Caitlyn erupted into loud peals of laughter. "So it was a physical manifestation of an argument about who has the longest—uh—sword?"

I nodded, grinning. "Exactly. A man thing. They think very highly of their *swords.*"

"What is *with* that, anyway?" Ann asked. As usual, I found her naiveté endearing. She and I had bonded over similar backgrounds; we're both immigrants to the US. In fact, we met while working together at the International Refugee Support Center.

"Who knows? We aren't men. We just keep them around to pleasure us," I said.

If a blush could be detected under Ann's smooth, dark skin, then I surmised she would be blushing right now.

Caitlyn leaned in and tapped her arm. "When Rodrigo finally gets his head out of his ass and asks you out, you'll see."

Ann's hand shot to her mouth. "Caitlyn! Don't say such things!"

I continued what Caitlyn had started, relieved that the heat was off me. "He lurves you, Ann. He's just too shy."

"He loves me in the same way that William loves you?" Ann shot back. Damn. So much for that plan. Now *my* face was burning, the image of a perfect, tall man—a literal knight in shining armor—floating before my eyes.

"She has Doug. She doesn't need *another* man. Save some of them for us homely girls." Caitlyn gestured to herself with a laugh.

"You're doing it again. Stop it," I lightly reprimanded, referring to her tendency to indulge in self-deprecation.

But Ann could not be deterred. "I know you don't like Doug. Not *really.*"

"Is that your all-powerful African intuition talking?" Caitlyn teased.

"It's called perception," Ann countered. "You should try it some time."

Caitlin shrugged and deferred to me. "What does *your* intuition say?"

"I never trust my intuition. I'll stick to my Tarot cards," I said.

Ann turned to me. "Why haven't you broken up with Doug? He doesn't deserve you."

My right brow shot up in a perfect imitation of Mr. Spock, but I refrained from pointing out that her intuition—all powerful or not—seemed to be right on the mark this time.

Caitlyn nudged her. "Don't. Not everyone dislikes Doug."

Ann shrugged. "I'm sorry. I just hate that he won. He's going to be more obnoxious than he normally is."

My mouth quirked. "I can guarantee that Doug isn't going to crow too loudly about this particular victory. He won on a technicality, after all."

Ann appeared to think about that for a moment. "William seemed uneasy out there."

"Maybe he doesn't like crowds?" Caitlyn said.

Ann nodded. "He is very reserved. Maybe that was it. He got distracted."

I frowned, reflecting on that. It was more than mere distraction, though. William had Asperger's Syndrome, which meant he was on the autistic spectrum. It made sense that crowds would bother him—from what little I knew of the condition, anyway.

Ann looked at me with a knowing grin. "I think he challenged Doug to the duel because he has feelings for you. And don't roll your eyes at me!"

"You think everyone has feelings for me," I told her. "I think it's hormones and my trusty push-up corset." I gestured to my noticeable rack that only appeared while in period garb. Maybe that was why I loved dressing the part so much. "I wasn't even there the day that William issued the challenge."

"Yes, but—"

But I rode over her. "I think that William got sick of listening to Doug constantly brag about being the best fighter in our clan. He just decided to school him."

Caitlyn called across the compound to a friend. Then she turned back to us. "So do you wish he'd won?"

I shrugged. William not winning was going to make my impending breakup with Doug easier—or at least I hoped it would.

When we reached Doug's tent, I told them I was going to get my stuff together. They dispersed, saying they'd see me at the planning meeting after lunch.

I slipped inside and pulled off my medieval garb—my laced outer corset, frilly blouse and two layers of brightly colored skirts. I was ready to transform back into a woman of the twenty-first century, and I was doing it fast, before the tent's other occupant arrived.

In fact, I'd just pulled on my jeans and buttoned them up when Doug entered the tent. He'd already removed his armor and the padding that went underneath it. Like most of the group's warriors, he wore period-authentic under-armor garments. And under all of the items he had been wearing, he appeared small, sweaty...sapped.

I gave him a tight smile as I bent to shove my stuff into my bag. "Congratulations on the win! That was an exciting fight."

Doug's eyes narrowed. "That was an *annoying* fight. That idiot has been working out. And training. He got a lot better practically overnight. Who the hell does that besides Captain America?"

"It wasn't exactly overnight. He's had months to work on it," I said in a mild voice to calm his ruffled feathers, in spite of my resentment at the 'idiot' remark. The mellower he was, the better this would go for me. "You were more than prepared. You won, after all."

"It was a technicality. I didn't *really* win. It was close. Too close for my comfort. And he took some cheap shots."

"I'm sure he didn't mean to hurt you. He seemed on edge."

"Yeah, I figured that out after the first bout. He's such a moron that he admitted to me that the crowd freaks him out. Naturally, I used that to my advantage."

My throat burned with bile. "Speaking of cheap shots..."

His eyes widened. "Hey, *I* followed the rules. He broke them. I won fair and square."

"On a *technicality*."

His face darkened and he pulled off his sweaty shirt, wiping his face with it. "Whatever." Shit. My mouth had gotten ahead of me and now he was annoyed. *Stupid move, Jenna.*

I buckled up my satchel. I'd been prepared to flee after the fight, so I was pretty much ready to go. All I had to do now was deliver the speech.

No big deal. I'd done this before...just change the specifics and convey the generic message I'd resorted to in the past.

"So, Doug...we need to talk, and I figure now is as good a time as any."

He dropped his shirt and looked at me. "That sounds kind of serious."

"Well, you know that I'm getting ready to travel with the Renaissance Faire when it starts up for the season. I thought...I thought it would be best if—"

He held out a hand to cut me off, green eyes glittering. "Wait...what? You aren't breaking up with me, are you?"

I hesitated, watching him.

His hand fell back to his side, tightening into a fist. "I can't believe this! I just won that duel. I was going to convince you *not* to leave with the Faire people. To stay with me."

I set my jaw. "Oh? And how were you going to do that?"

He started counting on his fingers. "I've helped you out a lot, Jen. Even when you didn't know I was. Every time we went out together, I've paid for everything. I've bought you stuff—"

Gross. I wasn't feeling so bad about doing this now. "Stop right there, okay? You can't buy me, and you can't *convince* me to do something by using your money."

He smirked. "Oh really? So I guess you wouldn't care if, say, I bought back a certain little bauble that you so callously hocked and decided to keep it instead of giving it to you as something nice that— you know—a *boyfriend* would do?"

My insides froze. The tiara? What the hell? He bought out my loan? Doug, as he was often quick to remind me, had a fantastic, secure job as an engineer and more money than he knew what to do with. Could he be telling the truth about this? And would he have the balls to hold the tiara over my head even if he *had* bought it back?

"You'd better be joking, and if you are, that's a goddamn awful joke."

He shook his head. "Not joking. I was going to give it to you tonight at dinner to celebrate my victory." He turned away from me to grab a towel. "But now I'm not so inclined."

Shock yanked the breath from my lungs and my blood roared in my ears. My fists tightened. "I want it back."

"Then maybe you shouldn't have hocked it to Tim."

Doug's uncaring words stabbed my heart. His judgment had been silent but obvious when he'd driven me to an acquaintance's shop. It was always easy to judge someone else's desperate measures where money was concerned when you had more than you needed yourself.

"You're lying," I huffed. "Tim wouldn't have sold it to you. *I* signed the papers, and he promised he'd give me six months to buy it back before anyone else could."

Doug shrugged. "You were late on your last payment and I figured I'd just buy it back. I was embarrassed enough that you were late. I didn't want you to default."

"I was four days late! I needed to wait 'til my paycheck—"

"I was doing you a favor." He sneered. " Some gratitude you have."

I wanted to howl in frustration. When I'd mentioned needing to hock the tiara, Doug had offered to lend me the money. Even then I'd known that was a bad idea, so I'd politely declined his offer. That was when he'd mentioned this jewelry broker he knew who could get me a better deal than a pawn shop—and who would hold on to the item for me until I could pay him off.

Stupid, stupid Jenna. Why did I do this to myself?

"Please..." I squeaked. "Do you really want things to end like this?"

Doug fumbled in his bag for a clean shirt and then straightened. "I don't want to end this at all. I told you, I was going to convince you to stay."

"By holding the tiara over my head?" That sick feeling in my stomach was increasing by the moment and tears poked the backs of my eyes. "You're a bastard. You don't even know what that tiara means to me. It's...it's..." I stopped myself. He didn't deserve to know those precious, private emotions attached to that inanimate object...memories of the hopes and fears of a scared little girl on a plane clutching it to her chest as she landed in a brand new country where she didn't even speak the language.

He shrugged. "You're the one who wants to break up. Like I said—"

"So you're saying if I don't break up with you, I'll get the tiara back."

"Sure...eventually."

I wanted to beat the shit out of him with his own weapon. "What do you mean *eventually?*"

"I mean that I *was* in the mood to celebrate tonight, and I *was* going to give it to you. I made reservations at La Terminale and everything. I take you nice places, Jen. You've got to admit—"

"That tiara is *my* property. A family heirloom. You'd *better* give it back, Doug."

"I believe I have a receipt that says it's currently *my* property."

I almost stomped my foot. "Don't be an asshole. I'm not going to stay with you because you are trying to blackmail me, okay? That tiara..." My voice gave out, succumbing to unexpected emotion. It was no use. The more upset I got, the smugger Doug looked.

He would *not* see me cry. If it were in my power, I wouldn't let him make me cry. The last man to ever make me cry was Brock, and then my very *soul* had poured out into the ocean of tears I'd shed for him. *Only* him. I could *never* let myself get that way again.

"Fuck you, Doug. You haven't heard the last of me. I'll take it to the clan council."

"Drama queen, much?" He rolled his eyes, and I burned with so much hatred that I wanted to slap him. "I'm sure the clan council will think you're as heartless as I do for selling some *priceless inheritance* your daddy gave to you."

I took a threatening step toward him, and for a split second there was fear in his eyes. But I couldn't say anything and the tears were clogging and blurring everything.

He'd pay. I'd *so* make him pay.

I scooped up my bag and, spinning on my heel, I stormed out of the tent and raced toward the edge of the encampment. The tears were coming fast and I couldn't let anyone see them. With my head down, my bag slung over my shoulder, I sped up, fists tightened at my sides. I was so close to escape—

Only to slam into a solid body as I rounded the very last tent in the row. I'd been moving so fast that I couldn't stop my momentum and thus landed flat on my ass.

I sat back in shock, taking a few seconds to gather my wits. When I looked up, it was straight into the face of Doug's nemesis. Despite my best efforts, there were tears on my cheeks and I was sure the expression on my face screamed helplessness.

For his part, he looked stunned, then bent immediately to help me up. My eyes fixed on the thick column of his throat rising up from his open tunic, which also exposed the very top of his chest. There was a thin patch of dark hair over solid muscle.

Doug was right. William had been working out for months—and it showed.

He looked...amazing. Especially with so few clothes on. William had always been a handsome guy, but his preparations for the fight had honed him. Now he was tall, dark, handsome *and* muscular. And where Doug had appeared small and tired, William looked vibrant and powerful.

He extended a hand, his bulging forearm peeking out from the cuff of his rolled-up sleeve. *Damn.* Even through my tears it was hard to ignore.

"Mistress Kovac. Pardon." He addressed me as most did while we were still roleplaying among our clan. Yeah, it was geeky as hell, but it was also fun. At least I thought so most of the time—like when I wasn't *ragingly* pissed off.

I quickly ducked my head to hide my face. "It's fine, William. You're fine." I grabbed his hand and let him pull me to my feet. Then I bent to get my bag, but he was faster, snatching it up for me. "I'll carry this for you."

As was his custom, he avoided looking directly at me. This suited my purposes, for I had no wish for anyone to see me like this. I reached to take the bag from him and kept my face down. "No need. Thanks. I'm very sorry for your defeat. You didn't deserve to lose." He handed me the bag slowly, reluctantly, and I hooked it over my shoulder.

With a big sniff, I turned to go, but his big hand landed on the top of my arm, just below my shoulder, and the warmth I felt through the thin fabric of my shirt did something to me. I swallowed, resisting the urge to shrug him off. I resolved not to be rude to him just because I was pissed off at another man.

"I beg your pardon," he said in that same stilted roleplaying mode. "But why would you say that?"

I shook my head, irritation gnawing at the edge of my mood. "What? Why would I say what?"

"That I deserved to win. I violated the rules..."

"You were tense."

His hand fell away from my arm. I chanced a glance at his face. He was staring at my shoulder—likely the closest he'd come to looking at my face—and frowning.

"How did you know?"

I shrugged. "Just an educated guess. You've been working hard. For months. I can tell..." My nose was starting to run from the tears I'd shed, so I sniffed—louder than I would have liked. Annoyed with myself again, I swiped my sleeve over my face like a preschooler.

"I gotta go." The hand was back on my arm again in a split second. "*What?*" I hissed.

"You're crying."

I suppressed a sigh and an eye roll. "Thank you, Captain Obvious," I huffed.

He frowned and ignored the snark—another habit of his. "Why?"

I wondered how much to tell him. "Um. Someone has something that belongs to me and won't give it back."

"Who stole from you?"

I sighed. "It's not stealing...exactly. Look, I know it's only late morning, but my day has already gotten off to a bad start and it's a really long story."

"So shorten it."

I gritted my teeth, considering. The clan elders liked William. He had sway with them, from what I could see. He was a stalwart member of the group, and with his handy blacksmithing skills, he commanded respect. Maybe telling him would be a good place to start. He could get them to make that jerk give me my tiara back.

"Doug has something of mine."

He stiffened, and I only belatedly remembered Ann's observation that William liked me. I still didn't believe it, but...in case he was going to take this personally, I needed to tread carefully. I bit my lip. What to do?

"What did Doug take from you?" His handsome face darkened.

"Well, he didn't take it from me. He...he bought it from a broker."

"But it belongs to you?"

"Yes." I coughed. "I needed some money quickly, and it was the only thing I owned that was valuable enough to secure a loan."

"He bought it from the broker..." he repeated, his voice lowering. I couldn't tell what he was implying. Maybe he was about to back up Doug's assertion that since Doug had bought it, it belonged to him.

"He...he was there the day I signed the papers. The guy is a friend of his and asked him to cosign my loan in case I defaulted—which I did *not*. Doug says he bought it back for me, but since I broke up with him, now he doesn't want to give it to me."

William chewed on that for a moment, his face stern. I was about to give up on this course of action when he finally spoke again. "How much was your loan for?"

"Two thousand dollars."

No change in that stern expression whatsoever, and he was still staring at my shoulder.

"And how much did Doug pay to buy it back?"

"The full buyback amount was...five thousand."

William's mouth dropped open. "A hundred and fifty percent markup?"

I rolled my eyes. "Please don't judge. I was desperate."

"No one should ever be that desperate."

My hackles rose. I couldn't help it. "That's easy for you to say."

His face clouded. "It's not easy and it's not hard. It's just a fact."

"It's your *opinion*."

His eyes narrowed. "I'll get your item back. What is it?"

Oh goddess, this was embarrassing. I was making a big deal out of a tiara. I could see the princess jokes coming, but no one knew what it *really* meant to me. It was a symbol of something I'd lost and could never get back. It was *mine* when so little else really was.

"It's a...it's jewelry," I hedged.

"Okay. I'll speak to Doug now."

"That's not going to help. He won't budge. I was hoping you might go to the clan elders."

William appeared to think that over. "I'll speak to Doug," he repeated, then turned on his heel and headed back the way I had come—straight for Doug's tent.

Oh shit.

2
WILLIAM

I'M WINDING MY WAY BETWEEN TENTS AND ENCAMPMENTS. ON my right, there's shiny cookware, all period authentic, set around a stone-ringed fire pit. Atop the ring is a metal spit that I worked on last year in my own smithy. On my left, there is a weapons rack with a boastful display of wares for sale. In the next camp over, Ginny is laying out her homemade jewelry, hoping customers will wander over from the battle ring.

I can smell the preparations for lunchtime wafting over from the eating area. The food is cooked traditionally and authentically to the period, as much as possible. Our weekend outing is just getting started, and I'll have blacksmith orders coming in the entire time. It will be a busy few weeks in my workshop.

But right now I'm not thinking about that. I'm thinking through the words I want to say to Doug. With each step I take that brings me closer to his tent, another phrase or sentence comes to me. It's always easier for me in conversations when I've prepared most or all of what

I need to say beforehand. Or with written notes. That's often best, but I have no time to do that now.

Jenna's been tagging behind me the whole way, interrupting my thoughts, trying to stop me from talking to Doug for some reason. I'm ten feet from his tent when she clamps both of her thin hands around my wrist in an attempt to yank me around to face her. If I were to train her how to fight, I could show her how to do that properly. My eyes dart to her hands—specifically, her wrists. She has the most delicate wrists. Elegant. Like a swallow's wings. I hesitate, but I don't look up.

I can't look in her eyes. And I hope she doesn't ask me to.

"Wil—stop."

She called me Wil. I'm not sure how I feel about that. I frown for a moment, still studying her hands. Her long fingers are digging into the muscles of my forearm. She holds me firmly, and I like that feeling. I usually don't like being called by nicknames, or being grabbed by people. But this is different. This feels...special. Like how holidays and birthdays are *supposed* to feel, yet how I *never* feel on those days.

"Jenna," I say quietly, though I'm confused and I don't know exactly what I want to say until the words are vocalized. That unsettles me. "Let me be your champion."

She's silent for a moment and I chance a look at her face. I'm relieved to see she's not looking at me. She's looking down and her mouth is open...like she's trying to breathe. Slowly, she lets up on the pressure on my arm, and I pull it back and away from her. I'm regretting it even as I'm doing it.

Something in my throat makes it hard to swallow. My eyes catch on the strands of Jenna's pale blonde hair trailing in the breeze. She's so beautiful.

"Be careful, okay?" she says.

I laugh. "I'm *not* afraid of Doug."

She blinks and looks up at me, and I barely have a second to avoid the entrapment of her stare. I know if she catches me, I won't be able to look away. I'm more afraid of that than I am facing Doug and his six best friends without my armor on. My heart is pounding. It's a narrow escape. *This* time.

I turn and head for the door of Doug's tent. It is poorly made to vaguely resemble something from the period, but it's nothing next to my pavilion-style tent. The fabrics he's used are not authentic, and it appears as if he does not care. I've noticed that the only thing he does care about is fighting—and winning. There is no other interest in the period for him. He spends very little time acting as part of the community or helping younger fighters rise up through the ranks.

I reach up and tug on the bell hanging from a string at the entrance.

"Come," says the voice from within.

I lift the flap of the canvas and enter with Jenna right behind me. Doug spins and looks at me, then at her, then back to me. "What do *you* want?"

"I've come to retrieve the item that belongs to Mistress Kovac."

His mouth curls up into a smile, but it looks more like an animal snarling. "I don't have anything that belongs to her. And if she's sicced you on me because of her little tiara, that's *mine*. I bought it."

Jenna steps forward to stand next to me. Her pale head of hair barely clears my shoulder. "You had no right to buy that back from Tim. I told you I didn't want to borrow money from you."

"It's *my* money, Jen," he says to her. His tone of voice and the way he shortens her name make me want to punch him. Right in the mouth. That way, he'll never use that mouth again to say anything that will hurt her.

I step forward. "I'll purchase it from you. Right now. With cash."

He looks me up and down. Maybe he's trying to figure out where I could be hiding the money.

"No." He crosses his arms over his chest.

So he's choosing to be difficult. I don't understand why. Doug and I have never had much to say to each other. Now isn't any different, apparently.

"I will pay you triple what you paid for it, then."

He just stares at me, and since I can't read faces—and don't do staring either—I avoid looking at his face. I have no idea what's going through his mind, but when I glance up again, he's staring at Jenna and smiling. A quick look at her confirms that she is not smiling at him.

I should be happy that she's angry at him and doesn't want to be his girlfriend anymore. I've liked her for so long and it's angered me all these months that she was with him. I have no claim on her now, but someday...I *will*.

But right now I'm worried that she's going to change her mind. That she's going to decide she wants to be with him after all, even if it is just to get her tiara back. Come to think of it, I've never seen Jenna wear a tiara—or any sort of expensive jewelry. This must be worth a good sum in order for her to pawn it for two thousand dollars.

Doug's now looking at me with his head tilted to the side. "I see why she brought you in here. You've got money. Isn't your brother a billionaire or something?"

I shake my head, annoyed now. "I don't have a brother. You mean my cousin. Yes, he's a billionaire, but I don't spend his money. I have my own job. Now, if I give you fifteen thousand dollars today, will you give her back the item?"

He holds his fist up in the air and makes a sound like a buzzer at a game show. I have no idea what that means. "Try again."

Jenna is tugging at my arm now. "Come on, Wil. We can take it to the clan council. They're meeting after lunch."

"Yeah, you do that, Jen," Doug taunts. "Go—and take your idiot with you. You know what they say, like attracts like."

I stiffen. There it is again...that word. *Idiot.* Just like the others I've heard throughout my life. *Moron. Retard.* But this is much worse. He called Jenna that name, too.

Her fists tighten at her sides. "How dare you—"

"Jenna," I interrupt, stepping forward and putting my arm out to block her from advancing on Doug. I can fight my own battles. To Doug I say, "I haven't insulted you. I don't care if you insult me because your opinion means nothing to me. But you won't insult her. Apologize."

"Not gonna happen."

I take another step toward him. His eyes get round, but when I think he's going to step back, he doesn't. We've just had a confrontation while both dressed in armor. This feels much more real, more immediate, just inches from each other and no metal between us. "Whatcha gonna do, retard?"

Suddenly, heat rushes up from the depths of my being and my skin is on fire. I reach out and grab a handful of Doug's t-shirt. "Stop trying to provoke me."

He pushes against my chest and I let him go. He takes two steps back, brushing himself off. "Back off, psycho."

"I don't need to back off. *You* just did. Now apologize."

Silence.

I'm getting ready to take another step toward him when he holds out his hand. "Fine. I'm sorry. Get the hell out of my tent."

"You should be ashamed of your unchivalrous behavior toward Jenna."

Doug's face scrunches up. "Get out."

Jenna tries to push past me again and I hold her back. "Let's follow the rules of the clan, Jenna. We can take this issue to the council."

She mutters under her breath, saying a lot of unchoice words about Doug. I won't argue with that opinion of him. He was never going to be a friend under the best of circumstances, but now, not ever...and *especially* not after the way he spoke to her.

And to think that they were together until today. He had called her his girlfriend, and yet he turned around and treated her this way. I can't understand how he could be so cruel to someone he once liked or even loved.

Doug is not a good person. And now I am even angrier with myself for having made such stupid mistakes during the duel. I could have won. I could have proved what I'd set out to prove all those months ago when I'd challenged him. All those hours I spent working out, and all that time and money spent with a private martial arts trainer. I could have been the better man...I could have been *worthy*.

But I hadn't proven myself. I'd failed. Yet again.

That same frustration stabs painfully in my chest. My fists tighten and I escort Jenna out of the tent. She has her head down and her skin is flushed.

"Are you all right?" I ask. I can't tell by looking at her—or anyone, really. These are things that come so easy to everyone else, but I have to study mannerisms, gestures and tone of voice. Even then, I rarely get it right.

Jenna doesn't say anything for a long time, but finally she nods. We are making our way up to the center of the park. There's a large main tent where the council will meet shortly. I turn to her. "You need to eat. And so do I. When the council meets after lunch, we can speak to them."

She reaches out for my hand, and before I can pull it away, she squeezes it. "Thank you so much. It was very kind of you to stand up for me. I..." Her voice trembles and fades away as she blinks rapidly. "It means a lot to have a friend with me for this."

She drops my hand, and I'm left confused as we make our way over to the cook fires to buy some lunch. What did that mean? That's the second time Jenna has taken hold of my arm. She likes to touch people. But I've never been able to understand exactly why and under what circumstances she touches them.

We are served bread and stew in wooden bowls, along with mugs of mulled beer. We're sitting down on opposite sides of a nearby picnic table when my knee brushes against hers. She doesn't pull away. I look up and she's staring right at me.

Oh crap. My eyes drop to her hands on either side of her plate. She wears a plethora of rings—one on almost every finger, even her thumbs. Some are made from semi-precious stones. I recognize hematite and tiger-eye. And the fingers themselves are long and slender, half the size of mine. I'd like to know what it would feel like to wrap my hand around hers, to hold it tight.

She looks away and begins fiddling with her rings. "I could go to small claims court," Jenna was muttering. "I could win that case."

I frown, shifting my eyes to her. "Would it be rude to ask you why you put the tiara up to secure a loan?"

She's still for a moment, but then she reaches over, breaks the roll in half and dips it into the gravy of her stew. "It's not rude to ask, no. I told you. I needed the money."

I puzzle this for a moment, rubbing at the whiskers on my chin. I usually don't shave while I'm at an overnight outing. It bothers me to have itchy whiskers, but it's more tolerable than trying to shave in ice-cold water while we are camping.

"You're not in some kind of trouble, are you? Because I'd help you if you are."

Her hand pauses, the bread immersed in the gravy. Then she slowly begins moving it again, and I follow the path of that drenched morsel of bread from the bowl to her mouth. Jenna has lovely pale pink lips, as elegant and refined as the rest of her. She presses the piece of bread to those lips and opens her mouth to take it in.

A familiar buzz of heat and excitement runs through me, and now I'm thinking about what it would be like to kiss her. I've kissed other women. It was all right. But I think it might be different to kiss Jenna.

"I'm not in trouble." She grimaces. "Not how you're thinking, anyway."

"Hey, kids!" Someone plops down suddenly beside Jenna, and I turn to see that it's her best friend and roommate, Alex. "That smells good. I'm 'a get me some of that."

"Here, have the rest of mine. I'm not super hungry." Jenna pushes the bowl toward Alex after only three bites.

Alex turns to me, speaking between scooping up spoonfuls of the stew and swallowing. "Hey, William. That was such a good fight. I'm sorry you didn't win."

I shrug. "You needn't apologize. You are not responsible for my loss."

Her spoon pauses on its way to her mouth. "No—I...uh, I mean I feel bad that you didn't win."

I don't know how to respond to that comment. Should I thank her or nod? Instead, I move on in the conversation. "It was unfortunate. I didn't follow the rules. I was distracted by the crowd. I've been training a great deal and I judged that Doug and I were equals in skill level, but the distraction caused me to make an error and injure Doug's shoulder. I apologized to him during the bout and explained my difficulty with the crowd, but he still seems quite angry, even though he won."

"Wil, why did you tell Doug that the crowd was bothering you?" Jenna asked.

"To explain my reasons for breaching the rules."

"He used that against you to win." I frown, failing to understand her logic. She sighs. "I purposely agitated the crowd in the second and third bouts, trying to get us to cheer louder. When he came over to ask for my favor, he said he was having trouble hearing us through his helmet."

"What he did was not against the rules," I observe.

Jenna's open palm slaps the table. "But he was exploiting your weakness."

"Also not against the rules."

"But the jerk wouldn't have known if you hadn't been so open with him."

"That is a dick move." Alex pushes a lock of dark, curly hair behind her ear and looks between Jenna and me a few times. Then she turns to Jenna. "You, uh, seem pretty unhappy with Doug. Did you two have a fight?"

Jenna glances at me and then away. "I broke it off with Doug."

Alex's mouth twists and she rubs her jaw. She looks like she's thinking, but Jenna appears irritated—well, I think that's her irritated look, anyway. I've seen that look often enough that I should probably know it by now.

"Don't say it, Alex." Jenna stares at her roommate between narrowed eyes.

"You *know* I'm going to say it." Alex laughs. "What's the date? That's three months on the dot, right?"

Jenna rolls her eyes. "I'm not in the mood."

I'm completely confused—not at all an alien feeling. There is subtext between these two that I am not picking up. And since I often have difficulty with regular text, subtext is far beyond my meager abilities.

As she often does, Alex picks up on my bewilderment. I'm grateful. I've observed that Alex has a keen knack for social behavior and perceives a great deal that isn't being said with words.

"I'm just teasing Jenna because of her pattern," Alex says.

"Her pattern?" I ask.

"Shut up, Alex," Jenna says with a sigh.

"She doesn't go out with guys for very long, and I've taken to graphing them. Six weeks here, three months there. Her longest was five-and-a-half months, because I guess six would have been considered too long-term."

"I don't like to settle down." Jenna shrugs, her cheeks and neck turning a very becoming shade of pink. "Drop it, okay?"

Alex and Jenna share a long look filled with more unspoken words. If they were touching, I might assume it was some kind of Vulcan mind meld between roommates. But Vulcans can't read minds out of nowhere. They need to have skin contact in order to share the thoughts of another.

Sometimes I wonder if everyone has the ability to read thoughts except for me. It feels like I'm deaf in some ways, missing half of what's going on around me. I can't tell what people's faces and gestures are trying to say, what words they're using that aren't coming out of their mouth. It seems like another language, one I'm not familiar with.

"So if you broke up with Doug, then do you want to head home with me this afternoon? I'm sure you won't be sharing his tent tonight."

Jenna looks away, fidgeting. "I have my sleep roll. I can just camp out next to the fire tonight. I'd like to stay and participate in the evening activities."

"It'll be too cold for you to camp outside tonight," I say. Both heads turn toward me.

Alex's mouth stretches into a wide smile. "Do you have room in *your* tent for her, William?"

Jenna blushes and punches Alex in the arm. "Ow!"

"I can't allow you to sleep out by the fire tonight, Jenna," I say. "That would be unchivalrous of me. There is room in my tent, and I have a comfortable bedroll mattress that I made myself. It's period authentic and it's comfortable. You can sleep there and I'll take the floor."

Jenna hesitates. Then she opens her mouth as if to answer, but we are interrupted again, this time by my cousin Adam and his fiancée.

Mia is also my new stepsister, but she doesn't like it when I call her that so I just think of her as Adam's future wife instead.

The two of them sit down on my side of the bench, but I'm still looking at Jenna, waiting for her to answer.

3
JENNA

I WAS *SO* GOING TO KILL ALEX WHEN I GOT HER ALONE. SHE thought she was hilarious, putting me in this position. But she knew damn well that I didn't get mad, I got even. Perhaps it had been too long since I'd demonstrated that. Instead of answering William's generous offer, the wheels were turning inside my head as I plotted my revenge on my mischievous roommate.

William was hot. Everyone knew it. And it was obvious he took this chivalry stuff *very* seriously. That made him even more appealing, really. But I had just barely broken up with Doug the Douchebag, and whether or not this was a romantic overture on William's part, there was no way I could follow through. Not now.

Yet there he was, watching me, waiting for me to answer when Adam and Mia appeared—as if it were timed that way. *Fuck. My. Life.*

"Hey, William," Mia said, putting a hand on his shoulder. "That was an intense fight. You did an amazing job."

William hesitated for a moment, as if in answering Mia he'd miss my reply to his question. I knew I shouldn't just let it slide, but it was so much easier that way. So I went along with it.

"He would have won, I think," I said.

"Sure he would have. What happened, William?" Mia asked.

"I violated the rules," he said, and the obviousness of his answer would have made me laugh if it wasn't said so solemnly.

"So what's the plan?" Adam asked his cousin. "Are you going to keep fighting duels?"

"I don't know," replied William, who was still staring at me, then pulling his eyes away whenever I looked at his face. My face was starting to warm from the attention.

Perhaps Ann was right. And if I wasn't having such a crappy day, I'd be more than a little flattered that he seemed interested. Or maybe he just felt sorry for me. It was so hard to tell with him. With his aloof and stoic manners, he kept everything close to the vest.

Minutes later—and smack in the middle of Mia's story about working on a cadaver in her first year of medical school—William checked his watch and then abruptly stood. Her voice faded out as her eyes followed his movement. Thank the goddess for William's interruption, albeit a rude one, because I was squeamish about stuff like that. Mia didn't seem upset, so I guess he was excused because they were family.

"I need to go to the Clan Council." William stepped over the bench and gathered our dishes. "Jenna has to come too," he said and then left the table.

I popped up and followed him, but not before noting how Mia's dark eyebrows arched upward. After quickly catching up to William, I fell into step beside him as we made our way to the large pavilion tent that belonged to our organization, the Barony of Anaya. It was named after two different cities in Orange County, Anaheim and Santa Ana. Above the doorway of the tent hung the heraldic banner, designed ages ago. It bore a white unicorn on a silver shield against a backdrop of deep purple—*purpure* in heraldric terminology.

Divisions of the Renaissance and Medieval Reenactment Alliance were patterned after feudalism. Territories called "baronies" grouped together under duchies and then under a kingdom, which represented a quarter of the country.

Kingdom leaders were usually chosen by combat competition. In fact, Doug had let me know it was his ambition to rule our kingdom. *Goddess forbid.* Thankfully, our local leadership had been chosen by consensus, and I was confident that they'd treat this situation in a fair and intelligent manner.

William and I stepped into the war tent, and I was relieved to find it empty except for the five people sitting at a table at the very back. One of the things I loved most about these weekend campouts was the feeling of living in another time period. We weren't completely authentic, but we tried, wearing clothes that imitated medieval fashions and trading goods and skills in order to help each other out. I felt wildly inappropriate standing here in my jeans, but a girl had to do what a girl had to do.

I glanced at William, wondering if he enjoyed the club for the same reasons I did. That feeling of belonging and a comforting sense of community. Especially for a person as reserved as he was. In many ways, it was the perfect place for misfits like us.

William approached the table where the council elders sat. Lord Richard de Bricasse, our baron, was known in real life as Derek Richardson, a fifty-something businessman. His wife, the baroness, sat beside him, and along with three others, they ran the business of the clan, setting up meetings and making sure everyone followed the bylaws—all that boring stuff that the rest of us didn't want to worry about when there was fun to be had.

"Sir William. Have you a petition to bring before us?" Lord de Bricasse began formally, as he usually did during the meetings.

William bowed at the waist, as was custom. "My lord and lady, gentlemen, I'd like to let Mistress Kovac speak for herself."

William waved a hand toward me and I dipped in an awkward curtsy, made even more so because I had no skirt to grab. Then I faced the council table to find all of them looking at me.

"Mistress Kovac, do you have a complaint against Sir William?"

My mouth dropped open, then I quickly recovered. "Not against Sir William, no. He's here to support me. My complaint is against Doug—I mean, Sir Douglas."

Doug picked that moment to show up, striding in with his chest puffed up. He halted on the other side of William, like he was more scared of me than he was of the guy who had injured him with a big-ass longsword not an hour ago. I noted that he now had his arm in a sling and he threw a stinging glare at William, who either ignored him or didn't notice.

"This ought to be good," Doug mumbled, turning that glare on me.

I cleared my throat and once again faced the council, explaining my plight as quickly as I could while giving as few details as possible.

Lady de Bricasse cleared her throat and adjusted her seat. "This might be out of the purview of our council if Sir Douglas does not choose to follow our arbitration, but it would seem that the item belongs to Mistress Kovac. What say you, Sir Douglas?"

"It's true that I was with Mistress Kovac on the day in question when she chose to hock her supposedly precious tiara in exchange for money."

Lady de Bricasse raised her brow. "But you weren't willing to lend it to her?"

He shrugged. "I offered. She said she didn't take money from friends."

Her gaze narrowed and my hopes soared. Getting the lady on my side was a coup. This might work yet. "Yet you spent even more money to buy the item back."

Doug shrugged with his good shoulder. "I was trying to do something nice."

I stiffened. "He wanted something to hold over my head." I folded my arms over my chest, unwilling to go into the details. I'd tried to talk to Doug about breaking up weeks ago, told him that I didn't think we were right for each other. But he'd begged me to give it another chance. I should have gone with my gut, but I suspected that Doug saw the tiara as a bargaining chip. *Jerk.*

I scowled at him. What had I even seen in him in the first place? He wasn't a bad-looking guy, and sure he'd been charming and effusive when we first started seeing each other. It had even been sweet at first, and then...it became needy and weird. Three months with him had been way too long.

Doug's face contorted into a facsimile of sadness. "Mistress Kovac is being unnecessarily cruel and throwing my kind deed back in my face."

I turned to him, fists clenched at my sides. "It *would* have been a kind deed had you chosen to give me the tiara and let me pay you back. Instead, you are claiming it's yours."

"Would you allow her to buy it back from you?" asked Lord de Bricasse.

"Hmm..." Doug put his hand to his chin as if this was the first he'd heard of the idea. *Ass.*

"I offered to buy it back at triple what he paid," intoned William. "He refused."

Doug made a show of lowering his head, emphasizing his "heartbreak." I almost groaned.

"I'm willing to give it back, but I don't want money attached to it. It will sully my memory of my time with Mistress Kovac." His voice trailed off, and this time I did audibly scoff.

The council all turned to look at me. "You aren't sympathetic, Mistress Kovac?"

"*No.* I'm not. That item..." My voice faltered for a minute and I swallowed. I didn't want to go into it—not now, not here.

How could I explain this tight ball of panic in my chest at the thought of losing yet another part of my past? Before I could stop it, the memory of my dad placing it my hands with sorrow in his eyes overwhelmed me. "*Kci,*" he'd said—the Bosnian term for "little daughter"—"*You have to be brave...be brave for Mama and Papa.*"

My fists tightened at my sides and I was tempted to stomp my foot. I gave Doug major side-eye. "If not money, then what do you want?"

Doug got that look in his eye again, as if he were contemplating the answer to that question. But he'd already figured out what he wanted. Either I'd have to undo the breakup or.... Goddess, I had no idea, actually. He *knew* I was planning to follow the Renaissance Faire in a few months. I would *not* leave without that tiara any more than

I'd leave without my right arm. Maybe he was using it to keep me here?

"If Sir William is willing to stand in as her champion, then I challenge him to a duel of honor at the Beltane Festival in May."

I opened my mouth to protest, but William was faster. "I accept that challenge. As the prize, I will accept Mistress Kovac's tiara."

"*If* you win." He sneered and then turned back to the council. "And as *my* prize, Sir William will agree to exile himself permanently from our community."

The silence was so solid in that tent, you could have set a full table on it. People had been filing in and taking seats on benches and floor cushions in preparation for the formal meeting to take place in a few minutes. Usually there was a great deal of chatter before meetings, but no one so much as whispered.

Lord de Bricasse's jaw had gone slack and his wife was biting her lip, glaring at Doug. It was then I remembered that William was a favorite of hers.

After a few beats of awkward silence, William cleared his throat to speak. But before he could get a word out, Lord de Bricasse held up his hand. "This is highly irregular, Sir Douglas. What you demand of a member in good standing is unreasonable—"

"I can demand what terms I want." Doug jerked his head toward William. "It is for Sir William to decide whether or not he will agree to them. I offer him a chance to recover his *besmirched* honor from the dishonorable defeat—"

"It was not dishonorable—" Lord de Bricasse countered.

Doug shrugged again in that profusely exaggerated way. "Whatever. I'd rather defeat him without having won on a *technicality.*" He turned and glowered at me, making sure I understood that this punishment of William was about me.

Or maybe not...

Maybe he saw William as a threat to his bid to win the kingdom someday. William had just proved himself as good a fighter as he was. Maybe this was Doug's way of eliminating the competition.

Doug cleared his throat and continued. "Sir William has a chance to win her bauble back if he wants to. But only if he accepts *my* terms if he loses."

All eyes shifted to William, but it was my turn to speak up. "No. I won't allow William to do that."

William turned his head toward me with a scowl on his face. "I don't need your permission."

I ignored him and continued. "That item is legally *mine,* and I'll go to small claims court to get it back." Then I turned to taunt Doug. "You *obviously* aren't a man of your word."

William looked at me, shocked. "You don't question a knight's honor...*ever.*"

Clearly outraged, Doug turned dark red and jerkily grabbed one of the leather gloves hanging off his belt before slapping it on the floor at my feet.

Everyone one around us gasped.

And I was completely at a loss for what had just happened.

I looked up at William and he was staring at the glove, then he bent and swept it off the ground. Holding it up, he said loudly, "Sir Douglas has thrown down his gauntlet at Mistress Kovac's feet. I accept this challenge on her behalf and fight as her champion."

Lord de Bricasse raised his brows. "Well, I assumed you would say that even before his histrionics. Really, Doug...." he said, slipping from his role for a second.

Doug puffed his chest out even further. "This is within the rules. I've checked."

He'd obviously planned it this way and now appeared very pleased with himself. I turned to William. "You don't need to do this. It's my problem, not *yours*. Doug obviously has a problem with *me*. I can take this up with the guy who gave me the loan."

William shook his head. "I will fight as your champion. The challenge has been issued and I accepted it. These are the rules we abide by and they are very clear. There is nothing left to say."

I almost howled in frustration. What if he *lost?* Was I going to stake my most precious possession on a fight that he might not win?

Triumphant, Doug bowed dramatically and held out his hand to William for the glove. Then, without so much as a thank you, he turned, saluted the rest of the occupants of the tent and marched out. *Asshole to the nth degree.* I glared at his back the entire way out. What the hell had I ever seen in him?

William still stood before the elders, and Lord de Bricasse was asking him if he had any further business with the council. I stepped up to put a stop to this.

William held out his arm to hold me back. "No, we'll settle this the old-fashioned way. After all, it's what we're about."

"But..." None of them had any idea what that "bauble" meant to me. I wasn't about to leave my fate in someone else's hands. But I didn't say anything until we were outside the tent. "Wil..."

He stopped and turned to me, eyes fixed on my shoulder. "Yes?"

"I think it was very nice of you to offer to defend me, but..."

He waited while I summoned the courage to question his ability to do this.

"The Beltane Festival is only two months from now. How do you know that—that the same thing that happened today won't happen then?"

He continued to stare at my shoulder. At his sides, his fists opened and closed several times. Then he rubbed his palms across his thighs. Following the motion, I studied his muscular physique, wondering what he'd look like in a fitted pair of jeans. Probably hot as hell...

I shook my head to reorient myself, since he was answering me. "I'll practice every day. I'll work out and train. I'll get better."

I shifted my weight from one leg to the other, only now realizing that my hands were gripping each other tightly. "But will that help? What if you still stress out and violate the rules? Then he wins on a technicality—again."

He frowned. "It wasn't stress. It was..."

"What?"

"More like...dread."

Dread...I knew about that. Being born in the middle of one of the bloodiest wars in recent history would do that to a kid. Then being torn away from half your family and shipped to the other side of the world to be "safe?" Yeah, I knew all about dread.

I took a deep breath and relaxed my grip on my hands, letting them fall to my sides. "If you want, I could help with that. Like...we could make it part of your training."

His brows rose. "You can help?"

"Yeah, uh...I've had some experience with dread."

That really seemed to shock him.

"Let's just leave it at that, okay?" I said before he asked the question.

"Okay," he said slowly, as if he didn't completely understand what I was saying.

"You know, we could have avoided this whole thing if I'd just gone to the police. I still could, in fact."

"You could. But I still have to fight him."

I drew back, stunned. "Why?"

He looked as if that was the stupidest question ever. "Because I accepted his challenge. I won't back down now. I'll go to battle against him, and if I lose, I'll withdraw my membership in the clan."

I gasped. "You can't let him drive you away like that."

"Those are the terms of the duel," he said with a slight frown. "I'll accept those terms if it comes to that. But I don't intend to lose."

I thought for a moment before coming to a decision. "I want to help you win, William. Not just because I want the tiara back, but because someone needs to take Doug down a few notches."

William's frown deepened. "Take him down from where?"

I wondered if he was pulling my leg. After noting his serious expression, I realized he wasn't. "It's a figure of speech... it means he needs to get off his high horse—"

William opened his mouth, and I could see the question on his face. He clearly didn't understand that one either.

"Um—it means he needs to be humbled."

He nodded. "Oh. Okay. Yes, I agree."

"So, do we have a deal? I help you with your issues with crowds, and you kick the—I mean, you win this duel like a boss."

"Like a boss," he repeated, grinning. "Deal." He reached out to clasp my hand and I returned his grip. Something electric sizzled up my arm from where his long fingers tickled my wrist. Suddenly, my body flushed with heat and the breath hissed out of my lungs.

I blinked, momentarily dazzled by his touch *and* his good looks. William didn't smile a lot, but when he did—*wow*. And though half the time his hair was in his eyes, when it wasn't...well, he just had the most beautiful dark brown eyes. Even if they never seemed to meet mine.

William was delish and he didn't even know it. That made him even tastier.

I bit my lip. *No boys for you, Jenna. Not now. Not when you're going to leave anyway...*

In the end, I politely declined William's offer to stay in his tent for the night. Ann, Caitlyn and their friend, Fiona, one of William's biggest fangirls, squished their bedrolls closer together to make room for me in theirs. William, thankfully, did not seem offended. He was probably relieved that my virtue was intact, or some other old-fashioned notion like that.

I noticed that he took a lot of his social cues from our organization, often acting as if he was roleplaying even while having both feet planted in the twenty-first century. I imagined that for a socially inept person, the stricter codes from an earlier time served as a comfort. There were rules for everything, whereas in modern times, you just had to instinctively navigate your way around situations as best you could, often inadvertently offending people.

Overall, the weekend with the clan went well—after the duel and the affair of the tiara, that is. Even better, Doug had left soon after the council meeting, so I didn't run into him again after our awkward breakup.

Now if only I could hire a cat burglar to get my tiara back from him. But as I was eternally broke, it looked like I was going to have to rely on William.

***

Several days later, I was awakened early—after having gone to bed too late—when my phone rang. Blinking in the darkness, I fumbled around my nightstand when I caught a glimpse of the clock: *five a.m.* This had better be an international call or I'd be pissed.

Glancing at the caller ID, I confirmed that the call was indeed coming from Bosnia. What was Maja thinking? She knew damn well the time difference between LA and Sarajevo. I cleared my throat but still croaked into the phone. "Hello?"

"Janja." The familiar voice in my ear called me by my childhood name, as only members of my immediate family or friends from my younger years ever did.

My head fell back against the pillow. "Maja. You know what time it is here, right?"

She answered me in Bosnian, our first language, and we carried on like that—as we always did—with her speaking in one language and me answering her in the other. The two of us were fluent in both, but this strange practice reflected our adopted nationalities. We may have both been born in Yugoslavia and we both came to the US as young girls, but now she was Bosnian and I was American.

"I'm sorry about the time, but I wanted to call before Mama gets home from work."

I frowned. "Why? What's wrong?"

"Nothing. Everything's great. In fact, it's amazing. Sanjin and I are getting married!"

I sat up, unable to suppress the sleepy smile curving my lips. "I'm so happy."

"It's all thanks to you. I don't know what I would have done without the money you sent. His family has finally agreed to let us marry."

Sanjin's family was ridiculously old-fashioned, insisting on the bride's family footing the bill for the wedding. Even in the old country, that was straight out of the nineteenth century. But as usual, I bit my tongue about that. No need to upset my sister from thousands of miles away.

"Oh Maja, that's wonderful. *Čestitke*," I said, conceding to congratulate her in our mother tongue.

"We're getting married in June, here in the city, but then we'll honeymoon on the coast. You remember that old town in Croatia where Mama's family is from?"

"No...I'm sorry. I don't remember. I was only five."

"I'm sorry, I forgot you don't remember as much as I do."

Maja, five years older than me, had much more substantial memories of our childhood there. And since she'd returned nine years ago, her knowledge of the country was immediate, whereas mine was full of faded memories from early childhood and occasional summer trips back to see Mama and the rest of the relatives.

"You can come, right?" she asked and my gut tightened.

I mentally ran through the possibilities and what it would involve to raise the money to purchase a plane ticket. I'd already sent the last of my designated-for-tuition money, sold the car and hocked the tiara. What else could I spare?

My mind scrambled for something to say that wasn't either a lie, an excuse or a promise I knew I couldn't keep. "Um. I'll try. It's...I've got a lot going on here. And the job. I'll try to see if I can get away."

A June wedding. Right in the middle of high Renaissance Faire season. The Faire traveled all over the western United States throughout the year, beginning and ending its cycle in Southern California for two months in May and June.

My plan was to join up for the next year, travel and see new places while making a tidy sum from reading Tarot cards for Faire goers. It was all part of the plan to replenish my savings and eventually finish college—if that's where the wind took me.

The only way I could afford a plane ticket to Bosnia was if I stopped paying my rent, and that would be screwing over my roomie, Alex. On top of everything, I owed *her* money, too.

Maja was like a schoolgirl as she regaled me with her wedding plans, going on about the cake, the flowers, the gowns and how her dream was to have me as her maid of honor. I listened, nodding and asking questions where appropriate.

My body really wanted to go back to sleep, but my mind was racing. What the hell could I do? My family had no idea that I'd spent the last few years slowly impoverishing myself in order to send them money. Mama worked at an insurance agency as a secretary and Maja was a nurse, but their income just covered their basic needs. The money I sent helped them with extras—emergency repairs, birthdays, holidays...and now, a wedding.

I'd managed, for the most part, to keep my head above water. Until this wedding. Months ago, Maja had tearfully told me that she and Sanjin were probably never going to be able to get married because they couldn't get the money together to pay for the wedding. I'd done everything I could to help, even giving up the tiara—temporarily.

"Janjica?" she said, and for a moment I was assailed by memories of hugs from Papa, of biting into Christmas cake and finding a silver coin, of sitting for long hours in church on Sundays when I wanted to run outside and play. "I know it's a lot to ask, but...can you bring Baba's tiara with you? I've dreamt of wearing it with my veil for my wedding day. My 'something old,' you know."

Guilt almost squeezed the breath right out of me and tears immediately stung the backs of my eyes. That day I'd taken the tiara in to have its value assessed, little pieces of my heart had died with each beat. The jewelry broker had dispassionately inspected every antique crystal, every tiny amber bead, even the quality of the gold while I'd burned with shame. *Kci, you must be brave...*

Right now, I wanted to curl into a ball and die.

"Janja? You still there?"

I cleared my throat a few times before speaking. "Yeah...yeah. I am. Definitely. Of course I'll bring her tiara. You must have it."

"Just to wear on that day. Papa gave it to *you*. And I know it's one of the few memories you have of him." Maja paused for a moment, and while I attempted to collect myself, she must have misunderstood my hesitation. "I'd never want to keep it. I just want to wear it. To have Baba's and Papa's blessings on our wedding."

Papa gave it to you...

Oh, the irony. I'd sacrificed the tiara to pay for her wedding and now she wanted to wear it at that same wedding. The last thing I had that connected me to that blurry, faded past, to those memories of Papa. And it was now out of my reach.

I had to continue leading them to believe that everything was all right. Because they never, *ever* would have taken the money if they'd known all that it cost me.

I hung up minutes later, then rolled over and sobbed into my pillow for a good fifteen minutes before I finally got hold of myself. But there was definitely no going back to sleep.

4
WILLIAM

MONDAY IS MY FAVORITE DAY OF THE WEEK. MOST FEEL that Friday should have that honor because they look forward to the weekend. They *live* for the weekend. But I prefer the comfort and structure that a weekday brings to my life. My days seem more difficult to fill on the weekends, even while participating in the Renaissance and Medieval Reenactment Alliance. Only so much time can be set aside for grocery shopping and meal preparation, for home organization and my various hobbies, and it's hard to occupy that eight-hour block most often consumed by work.

And since I do not care to watch television, that's a lot of time to fill.

Order is restored to my life on Mondays. I arrive at my station approximately five to ten minutes before the start of my shift. I don't punch a clock, but I've always been punctual—and not just because I work for my cousin's company. Things are easier when you are punctual. There's no stress, no rush. You feel the accomplishment of arriving on time, ready to begin your workday.

However, this Monday, no matter how good it started, takes an annoying turn not long before lunch. I'm at my drafting desk in the art department when I suddenly become aware of someone standing near me. And since I'm in the middle of focusing on what I need to be doing—a computer-assisted rendering of some 3D background models—I ignore whoever it is until they loudly clear their throat.

Taking another few minutes to save and back up the complex and detailed work, I remove my special glasses designed to help with this task and look up.

Jordan, the company's CFO, is standing across the desk from me, his hands in his pockets. "Hey, William. Sorry to interrupt."

No, he isn't, or he wouldn't be doing it. Irritation bubbles up immediately. Jordan is not one of my favorite people and hasn't been for some time. It's been a few months since his crap advice lost me the chance to ask Jenna out on a date.

I'd made the mistake of asking Jordan for guidance on how to approach Jenna, since approaching women is easy for him. I'd followed his suggestions by inviting Jenna to participate in the RMRA, which she'd loved, and it *had* given me the opportunity to see her more often. Before that, she had just been one of Mia's friends, but then she started to become one of mine. Just as I'd been designing my plan of attack, she'd met Doug, and *they* had begun their infuriating relationship instead.

As a practice, I still mentally curse out Jordan with words I don't usually like to say out loud. I've been told that I have a hard, unforgiving nature, and that may very well be the case with Jordan— which I'll admit could be awkward given our work situation. But he's done nothing to make my life easier, and I don't trust him.

Jenna might be single again, but she's still not mine. And nothing Jordan has advised me to do has helped that.

"Yes? What?" I say.

Jordan hesitates and then smiles. "Just checking in. I heard about the LARP duel. Adam filled me in."

I almost growl at him. "It's not LARPing."

He blinks. "Don't you guys, uh, roleplay and stuff? Isn't that was LARPing is?"

"LARP is live-action roleplay. That's not what we do. *We* reenact. We have personas, but we recreate history in an authentic way—we don't do fantasy roleplay. I save that for sitting around the table and playing D&D."

"Oh, uh. Sorry. I didn't mean to insult you. Actually, I wanted to be at your duel, but April had a family thing down in San Diego."

I try to stifle more bitterness. Sure, *he* is happily in love with a very pleasant and pretty girl, all while dispensing crap advice to those of us not born with his suave moves. He doesn't deserve her.

I don't reply and Jordan continues. "I'm sorry about the duel, man. I was really pulling for you."

"I didn't need any pulling," I reply, forcing away the mental image of him grabbing my arm and pulling it.

"No, I mean I was hoping you'd win."

I fold my arms across my chest and swivel on my workbench stool. "Why, so you won't feel guilty anymore?"

Jordan's lips thin and his eyes get squinty. "I see how it is. You're still pissed at me."

"I have a very good memory."

"Yes, I'm well aware. I've already offered to make it up to you. I could fix you up with someone—"

My jaw tightens and heat rushes to my face. I stand up stiffly from my stool. "Maybe women are interchangeable to you, but they are *not* to me!"

Jordan blinks. "William—dude, calm down. I'm serious. I want to make this up to you. Maybe I could show you how—"

I point at him with my index finger. "I'm not taking your advice! Do you think I'm stupid? Clearly, you think I'm stupid."

Jordan holds out a hand, palm out. "William, quiet down, okay? Let's go talk in the warehouse or my office. Or let me buy you a coffee."

"No. I don't even like coffee." I fold my arms across my chest again.

Jordan rubs his jaw and looks at me for a long, silent moment. "What can I do to make this up to you? Tell me..."

"Did Adam make you come here and talk to me? Why do you care?"

He glances up at the ceiling and blows out a breath. "Because I feel bad that you didn't get your girl."

My arms tense against my chest. "And you think something *you* can do will make up for that?"

He hunches his shoulders. "I don't know. Look...call me when you feel like talking about it."

"I deleted your number from my contacts," I say.

His gaze shifts to the ceiling again. I wonder if there's something up there—a bug or a spider. "Dude, throw me a bone here," he says.

Images zip through my mind—a pirate flag with skull and crossbones, a dog carrying a bone in his mouth, a pile of dinosaur bones. "*What?*"

He waves his hands, sighing. "Never mind. Look. Here's my number."

He bends, grabbing a pad of sticky notes from my desk and my favorite pencil. I'm about to shout at him to drop the pencil when I stop. The vivid image of facing Doug in the battle arena floods my mind. I'm staring through the grill of my helmet and I'm swinging fiercely at him. The swords clank, the flash of metal in the sunlight blinding me. I can taste the dust in my mouth. Doug's blocking me with his sword—held firmly in his left hand.

Jordan's using his left hand, cocked at weird angle, to scribble down his number in his typical messy writing. I study him as he does it. I've known that Jordan is left-handed, but before now, that information hasn't been important to me.

Jordan is saying something again, and I faintly hear it through the whirlwind of images flashing through my mind. Doug and I are on par, skill-wise. But his advantage is that he fights right-handed men far more often than I practice against left-handers. Practicing and sparring against a left-hander—even if not as skilled as Doug—might give me a competitive edge against him. Left-handed people only represent roughly twelve percent of the population. I know of no one who is physically fit enough to match my training regimen and who is also left-handed. *Until now, that is.*

Jordan straightens and turns to leave when I speak out. "Stop. I've just thought of how you can make it up to me."

Jordan's looking at me strangely, out of the side of his eyes. "Yeah? What's that?"

"You can come help me train during my sessions with the European martial arts trainer."

His brow scrunches together. "Martial arts? You mean like karate or tae kwon do?"

I sigh. Jordan is smart—most of the time—but sometimes he can be dense. "Those are Asian martial arts. I'm talking about European martial arts. Sword fighting, archery, fencing, et cetera. I'm specifically talking about fighting with sword and board."

"Sword and *what?*"

"It's the term for a shield, or buckler. I need a left-handed person to train against for those bouts."

"You're fighting another duel?"

"Yes. And it's very important I win. She's depending on me. If you want to make it up to me, this is what I want you to do. Maybe I'll forgive you after that."

His mouth purses for a minute like he just ate a lemon. "I'm not responsible if I beat the crap out of you, am I?"

"If you can manage it, no. But your overconfidence is your weakness," I say, repeating Luke Skywalker's line from *Return of the Jedi.*

"Your faith in your friends is yours," he quotes back. "Fine. I'll do it. Hell, I might even enjoy it."

"And if I win, I get to date April?" When he opens his mouth to protest, I start laughing. "Joke." By *far* a joke. April is very pretty, but she is nothing compared to Jenna. And as far as my mind is concerned, Jenna is the only one. Since I first laid eyes on her, I haven't thought about any other woman. Just her.

I am *not* about to let her down. I'll do whatever it takes to win this. For her.

***

Later that night, I continue my Monday routine. After dinner, I change into my workout clothes, ready for a short run. I complete five kilometers in about twenty minutes, and then after another forty minutes of planks, lunges and free weights, I begin to work on my fighting moves.

I look at my wall calendar. It's the latter half of March. The Beltane Festival, and thus the second duel, is exactly forty-one days away.

Along with my instructor-led martial arts training, I've been watching videos to study the strategy of swordplay. I've also color-coded my workout schedule and labeled the amount of time I should spend training at each activity. In the last few months, I've managed to fine-tune my fitness regimen. My body fat is at an optimal level, all calculated to the most precise evaluation of my BMI. Even my cousin, who is in very good shape, has noticed and complimented me on my efforts.

I'm about to start my sword routine when my phone trills. It's the least annoying of the signals available—I checked the settings.

With a deep breath, I get up to look at the caller ID. I have never yet managed to ignore a phone call, which is why I normally turn it off while in my workshop or art studio. I also prefer to answer after the second ring. This time, it almost rings for a third time before I'm able to pick it up, and I realize in my haste to stop the ringing that I did not glance at the caller ID. Both of these things unsettle me. I'm already two steps off my routine, and it's making my skin feel itchy.

"William Drake here," I snap.

"Uh...hey, William. How are you? It's Jenna."

Jenna. A feeling, like an entire ship sinking in my stomach, comes over me. My throat tightens.

For a moment, I blank on an appropriate response as I envision the first time I ever saw her. It was at a surprise party that Adam threw for Mia at his house over two years ago. They'd been celebrating her acceptance to medical school. I despise parties and had stayed close to the wall, as I usually do on such occasions. But that was when I saw her.

Beautiful.

So beautiful that everything froze when I looked at her. I see that vision now as if she is standing right in front of me again. She's wearing a turquoise and violet patterned shirt and a black skirt. Her legs are long and slender. She has pale skin, and her hair is so blond it's almost white. And her eyes…so blue. Pale, but with a purple undertone. Somewhere between the shades of cornflower and cerulean.

"Hello? William? You still there?"

"Yes. I haven't gone anywhere. Hello, Jenna." I force the almost overpowering image from my mind.

"Oh, okay. Good. I was…I was wondering if I could come over for a few so we can talk."

"We can talk now. We actually *are* talking now."

She laughs. Something I said must have been funny. Then I realize her asking if we could talk means that she wants to see me face to face.

"Well, I thought we could get started on some of those calming techniques to help with your unease with crowds. Would tonight be okay? After dinner?"

"I've eaten dinner, but you are welcome to come after you've eaten. I'm working out right now. Then I will be in my workshop. You can come during that time."

"Uh, okay…your workshop? Is that at your house?"

"Yes. Just ring the doorbell and come in. I'll be able to hear the doorbell in my workshop. I'll leave the front door unlocked, and the workshop is in the backyard."

"Hmm. Okay. I'll be over at seven-thirty."

I glance at the clock. "I'll see you in ninety-four minutes, then."

She laughs again. "Yeah…more or less."

When Jenna hangs up, I pace the floor of my workout room. What will I say to her? How will I talk to her? I've never been alone with her. *Ever.* I have no idea what to expect.

I pick up my phone and quickly dial my cousin's number. He answers on the third ring.

"Liam," Adam says, calling me by my childhood nickname. "What's up?"

"I need your help with a situation that has come up."

I continue to pace in tighter and tighter circles around my gym until I'm eventually rocking from one foot to the other.

"A situation? You okay? You need me to come over?"

"Are you still at work?" I say, glancing at the clock. "Mia will be upset with you."

"She's fine. She's at school late today, studying. What can I do for you?"

"I don't need you to come over, but I do need advice. Jenna just called me. She is coming to my house."

A pause. "You make it sound like that's a bad thing."

"It is neither a bad thing nor a good thing."

"So what do you need?" he asks.

"I need to figure out what to say to her. I can never tell what she's thinking."

Adam chuckles. "Well...in spite of my many impressive talents, I can't read the female mind. *Especially* the female that I live with. So I doubt I'll be able to shed any light on your situation." Though I understand that euphemism—Adam uses it a lot—I immediately picture him turning on the bright red desk lamp in his bedroom at the house we lived in together as teenagers.

"Okay, but I may need to call you back afterward. I'm sure I'll have a lot of questions."

"If I don't answer, I'll call you back as soon as I can. But whatever happens, please remember not to get worked up about it."

"I always remember not to get worked up, Adam. But that doesn't affect whether or not I do."

He sighs again. "Yeah, I know. Good luck."

I hang up. Why would I need luck? There is no such thing as luck. As a programmer, Adam knows that perfectly well. He uses the expression liberally anyway.

I check the clock—only a few minutes left of my workout session. I'm stiff with frustration as I realize I have no time to practice with my sword tonight.

After I change into a pair of jeans, I stop by the kitchen to load up on some ice water to quench my thirst while attempting my next project. Then, it's time to head out back.

My blacksmithing workshop is inside a big shed in the backyard. It's large enough to fit my forge, bellows and the other equipment I use. The moment I walk in, a wall of heat hits me from the forge. I'd started the fire when I got home from the office so the forge would be ready for me when it came time to work.

I pull the chain to turn on the overhead light and check my list of orders placed by members of our clan over the weekend. Fortunately,

I'd only planned on doing some minor work, so Jenna's visit won't be overwhelmingly disruptive to my schedule. That, at least, brings me a little comfort.

It's too late to completely abandon the plans to work here tonight, as I don't want to waste the fire and all the wood it took to attain the optimum temperature. And besides, it's a perfect night to work in the shop. Chilly, but not cold.

We've had a warm winter, and sometimes that makes it downright unpleasant in the workshop. But I do really love the work...the way I feel, the way it relaxes me.

Having already shed my workout clothes in favor of jeans, I throw on my goggles, a protective leather apron and thick gloves. Though hot, the fire is small, perfect for simple heating and hammering.

I pull out my tools and line them up near the anvil, fill my metal slack tub with water and I'm ready to work. Yes, this is much better. My forced concentration on the task at hand will keep me from obsessing over Jenna's impending visit.

I grab a flat shovelhead, commissioned by Goodman Meyer, a clan gardener. Holding it with a pair of tongs, I shove it into the fire, glancing at the clock to time myself. I'm deep in the middle of hammering—the rhythm and the force of the blows of metal against metal ringing through my arms—when I glance up at the clock again. I note that it's well after the time Jenna told me she would arrive.

Is she late? Is she not coming? Maybe she's changed her mind and doesn't want to help. My hammer falters, stuttering off the anvil, and I frown. I clench my teeth and try to focus, attempting to regain the concentration I've lost.

I start hammering again, trying to take my mind off of her, but with each hit I hear, *"Not. Here,"* like a voice in my head, mocking me. I find myself first growing frustrated, then angry.

Why would she tell me she was going to be here at seven-thirty and not come? Would she call back? I glance at my phone over on the workbench and see no updates on the lock screen. I'm positive I have not turned it off.

Moments later, I get that weird yet familiar weighted feeling on the back of my neck and shoulders. Someone is watching me.

I swallow and my back muscles tense. I straighten, but don't turn around.

5
JENNA

THANKS TO ALEX'S KIND OFFER OF A RIDE ON THE WAY TO HER mom's house, I arrived on William's doorstep. Glancing at my phone, I saw that it was almost eight o'clock.

I knocked, wondering if he'd mind that I was late. *Oh well.* I shrugged, then after standing there for minutes with no response, I remembered that he'd told me to go through the front door and into the backyard.

Following William's instructions, I headed through the house. He'd helpfully left the way lit all the way from the front door to the back—again, helpfully left ajar. He'd done just about everything for me besides lay down breadcrumbs.

His house was big but modest. A lot of the furniture was mismatched but comfortable-looking. For an artist, he sure had no sense of style for home decoration. Not that I was one to judge. I still used plastic-framed posters and hand-me-down furniture to decorate my rented place.

I was glad I'd worn my sweatshirt when I walked into the yard from the kitchen and felt a cool breeze. The path to William's work shed was accommodatingly lined with solar lamps, and I made my way toward the glowing open doorway. Something mischievous in me wanted to surprise him so I bounced up on the balls of my feet, tiptoeing along. In my sneakers, it wasn't hard to be silent on the brick path.

A hammer rang against metal with a rhythm so precise it might have been operated by machinery. I knew that William was a blacksmith for the RMRA. He'd been doing it for several years, as a matter of fact, and I'd admired the pieces he'd made. After the weekend, I imagined he had a lot of work to catch up on.

But there wouldn't be any more blacksmithing tonight. We had important work to do. William had a duel to win.

I entered the workshop through the open door and, as I'd hoped, I caught him unaware. He was bent over his anvil, tongs in one hand and hammer in the other. He had goggles on and jeans with a full leather apron. I was briefly reminded of Hephaestus, blacksmith to the gods of Greece. But he had been deformed, and from what I could see, there was nothing about William's body that could even be remotely described as deformed.

His arms and back were fully exposed, and seeing him like this hit like a punch to the gut. A pleasant punch, actually. I inhaled a deep breath and drank him in, watching as his biceps and triceps bunched and stretched with the rhythm of his hammering. His arms were sculpted, strong—superb. I hadn't noticed under all that armor what good physical shape William was in. He'd never been unfit, but with all the working out and training he'd been doing over the last four months...now he was downright scrumptious.

My mouth went dry as I imagined those shapely, solid arms wrapped around me. Distractedly, I licked my lips and looked away, startled and even a little unsettled by this powerful jolt of attraction. I'd always thought William was good-looking and knew I was attracted to him. But it was never in a lusting, gotta-have-him sort of way. At least not until now.

Suddenly, the hammering stopped—along with the attractive ripple in his back muscles that accompanied the motion. Without turning, William straightened and said, "You're thirty-three minutes late."

My jaw dropped. How the heck did he do *that?* Had I been breathing too heavily or something? *Damn.* "Oh, uh. I'm sorry."

He adjusted where his hammer rested against the piece he was working on, but he still didn't look at me. "And you didn't ring the doorbell."

Oh shit. I'd completely caught him off guard...and he sounded pissed off about it. Though honestly, it was always hard to tell with him. He was like a Vulcan on steroids most of the time.

"My bad," I said, trying to stifle a little heat—both from embarrassment and irritation.

"Your bad what?"

"Uh..." Okay, now I was completely lost. "Huh?"

He heaved a sigh. "I'll be right with you. This needs more work before the metal cools." He bent over his work again, then added, "Oh, good evening. I hope you are well." He recited the words as if he'd learned that that's how you greet a person. Like he actually was a Vulcan who had just landed on the planet wielding his trusty guide, *The Customs and Mores of Earthlings.*

I blinked, wondering what I'd gotten myself into.

While I watched William finish his piece, I continued to be disturbed by how much the movement in his back and arm muscles fascinated me. I finally forced my eyes away, turning to take in the shelves of his workshop. Atop each shelf were pieces—some finished and some still in progress—all meticulously labeled with their intended destination. They were mostly simple looking, garden implements and lots of metal buckles for period-style belts, armor straps, weapon sheaths and canvas tents. People who made these other items depended on William to supply them with the hardware.

There were also more complex pieces that he'd obviously been using for practice. I'd read somewhere that it took years and years of fulltime work to master blacksmithing. This was William's hobby, but from the looks of his workshop—fully tricked out with his own forge and bellows—it was a serious hobby.

I also spotted a full suit of armor on a stand in the corner. It did not resemble the armor he'd worn at the duel, and I moved to get a closer look. In the process, I stole a glance at him again, noticing the play of light on his sweat-coated upper body as he bent to drop his piece in the bucket of water. With a slight hiss, it sank to the bottom while he removed his goggles and pulled his apron from around his neck.

I stopped in my tracks. Now his chest was fully exposed and I had to suppress a gasp. Heat rose to my face. Holy Artemis, he was hot. His chest was all sharp planes and masculine angles, and it looked very, *very* hard. I stopped fantasizing about touching him—and maybe even licking him—when I realized that I was staring, and he, in turn, was watching me stare. I spun and my wandering eyes once again focused on the suit of armor.

"Don't touch that," he said as my hand was halfway extended toward the breastplate. I jerked it back, flustered.

"That piece is broken and needs to be fixed...it's too delicate to handle right now."

"Huh. I was just wondering where the Ark Reactor was..." I snarked, still staring at the wall. "It's obviously not, um, not on your chest—" I cut myself off, thankful that he couldn't see my face.

Damn it. Flash some fine muscles and a strong, male physique at me and I lost it like a schoolgirl. I swallowed the thick lump in my throat.

William pulled his piece from the water bucket—or at least that's what it sounded like. "That's not an Iron Man suit. Those don't actually exist."

I laughed. "Yeah, I knew that. I wasn't expecting you to go flying around or anything." I faced him again, forcing my eyes to stay on his face. "Are you finishing anytime soon? I haven't got all night, you know."

He blinked. "I'm finished. I just need to bank the fire. It won't take all night. Just a mere fraction of the night."

I would have laughed if I thought he was making a joke. But he wasn't, so that breath I let go was merely to help me blow off some steam. I was flustered and embarrassed—both at my reaction to him and at his lack of reaction to me.

If he were any other guy, he would have checked me out twice by now. Instead, he'd barely looked at me since I arrived.

In minutes, he was done and wiping his face on a towel that he'd pulled off his workbench. I took another gander at his chest...well developed and clearly defined pecs, firm abdomen, pale skin but not pasty with a light dusting of dark hair.

I took a deep breath and looked away, hoping I wouldn't have to ask him to put on a shirt. It was as if he read my mind. "I apologize for not wearing a shirt. The forge is very hot."

"Aren't you worried about getting burned?"

"Not with this kind of work. When doing big pieces, I wear better protective gear, but this was just a little shaping and finishing work."

"Did you make your armor?"

He shook his head. "I am only a beginner. I make simple pieces. That practice armor and my real battle armor were made especially for me by a master craftsman." I took a step toward him and he held up a hand. "Don't come any closer. I have a rule about visitors to my workshop. They are not allowed within fifteen feet of the forge."

"I'm typically a pretty big rule breaker. Give me a rule and I'll break it."

William frowned and then pointed to a sign posted above his workbench. It was hand-lettered perfectly in old-fashioned script with decorative scrollwork all around the edge. It stated that exact rule: *Visitors – please stay at least fifteen feet away from fire.*

"Don't break my rules," he said in a solemn voice.

I studied him for a long moment, not quite sure what I was expecting him to say. *Just kidding.* Or, *Got ya!* Either would have worked. But he was serious. Firm. And damned if it didn't make me want to take a few steps closer to him, just to see what he'd do. But that wouldn't get us off on the right foot.

"Well, I'll try to hold myself back, then. For your sake."

No reply. It was like I hadn't spoken at all. He was banking the fire, and once that was done, he began meticulously wiping down the tools before putting them in their exact spot. How did I know? Because there were *outlines* drawn on the wall behind the workbench.

I folded my arms over my chest and sighed loudly. I'd had about enough of William's workshop and his brusque manners.

As he continued, my eyes wandered back to that sign. I hadn't seen much of his work, but I knew he was an artist by profession. Mia had told me that he was incredibly talented. I wondered if he'd show me some of his other work if I asked him.

Twenty minutes later, he escorted me out of the workshop and said, "My gym is in the living room. We can work in there." He turned and locked the metal-lined door with three latches, all padlocked.

Without waiting for my reply, he spun on his heel to lead the way. Who had a gym in their living room? Apparently, a guy who lived alone and didn't do a lot of entertaining. *More power to him.*

William walked into the house and led me into a large living room, which looked fairly normal with a couch, game table and chairs. It was, however, conspicuously missing a television of any kind. Maybe he watched TV in the bedroom?

Along the wall in the gym area was a set of weights, a treadmill, a rowing machine and rolled-up mats. He bent and grabbed his previously discarded T-shirt and slipped it over his head. I was simultaneously dismayed and relieved, the former because he covered up the nice view, and the latter because I didn't have to studiously avoid getting lost in the manchest.

My reaction to his looks was a little over the top tonight. Was I having some kind of weird hormone rush, maybe? It wasn't like I'd been going through a dry spell, when I likely would get turned on by anything and everything.

It's just that I'd never really thought of William this way before. Tall and handsome, yes. That was obvious to anyone with a pair of eyes. But maybe his epic reserve had previously discouraged me from viewing him as an object of lust.

I cleared my throat, attempting to clear my mind of sexy thoughts. "So…have you ever done any meditation exercises, or do you know of any calming techniques?"

William walked over to the wall, unfolded a big mat and laid it across the floor. He sank down on one end, sitting cross-legged without saying a word. I sat down facing him.

"No," he finally answered.

"Okay… So you want to tell me what happened at the duel?"

"Weren't you there?"

"I was. But I wasn't in your shoes."

He frowned. "I wasn't wearing shoes. I was wearing my armored boots."

Was he joking? William had never struck me as stupid—quite the opposite, actually. Maybe he was teasing in his usual deadpan way that made me think he was serious. "Well, I mean, walk me through it…"

"Walk you through what?"

I blew out a breath, my frustration level rising. "Are you bullshitting me with this?"

His dark brows pushed together. "You're aggravated. I probably should explain that I have issues with language. NTs are always using figures of speech instead of just speaking plainly."

"NTs? Is that like ETs?"

"No. ET means extra-terrestrial. NT means neurotypical."

"Neuro-what-ical?"

"It means that your brain behaves typically. Mine doesn't. English is not my first language."

I smiled, happy to find *something* I could relate to. "It's not mine, either. My first language is Bosnian-Croatian-Serbian. What's yours?"

"Pictures. Images. Other types of sensory input. But not words. Words came later." He shrugged, his eyes drifting down to the mat just below my knee.

"Huh...that's interesting. That's something you never really think about...the way you process thoughts inside of your brain."

"It's something I *have* to think about. All the time."

"I think in English when I'm speaking English and in Bosnian when I'm speaking Bosnian. But I don't have to worry about it. I guess that's the big advantage NTs have without really knowing they have that advantage."

He appeared to be concentrating on that spot on the ground while he listened to me. "When you think in the same language you are speaking, you don't have to translate. But everything comes to me in pictures first. So, for example, when you said filling my shoes, my first reaction was to see you wearing my shoes." He shook his head, shifting his gaze to my feet. "My shoes wouldn't fit you. It's a very funny image."

I couldn't help it...I started laughing. William was adorable in spite of the aggravation.

His dark brown eyes moved up my body slowly, stopping just above my chest, and where his gaze touched, my skin warmed. *Damn, Jenna...you're out of control tonight.*

"Anyway..." I said, steering the conversation back on course. I willed myself to not think about how much William was intriguing me with each passing minute. "I want to know what went on inside your head while you were fighting the duel. What exactly was it that caused the distress?"

He took a deep breath and then released it. "It was the crowd. I hadn't counted on that. I knew exactly what I was doing out there. I had a plan and I would have won, but..." He shook his head. "I hadn't planned on all the faces and the noise."

"And Doug made it worse once he found out."

He nodded but didn't say anything. His hands fidgeted as they rested on his knees.

"So does that mean you don't do crowds at all? Theaters? Sporting events? Concerts?"

"No."

"Really? How do you see movies?"

"I wait until they come out on Blu-ray, or I go see them at Adam's house. He has his own theater."

"Wow. But what about big movies that you don't want to wait for? Like what about the new Star Wars movie?"

He shook his head. "I can't. Even if it's a movie I really want to see."

I frowned, wondering what that must be like. "Oh, that's rough. But maybe going to some places like that and exposing you to larger groups of people would help get you used to it?"

He seemed to think about that and then shook his head as if dreading the thought.

"Okay...well, there are techniques you can use to help calm you down. Visualization, breathing. When I was younger, I had really bad panic attacks. They were usually brought on by loud noises, so I had problems with certain types of movies, too."

He looked up from the floor, appearing surprised. "You're afraid of loud noises? Why?"

I hesitated. "Because...when I was little, the city I lived in was bombed pretty much constantly." His gaze rose slowly from my chin to my nose before it stopped.

"You lived in Sarajevo?"

"Yes. That's where my family is from. How'd you guess?"

"It wasn't difficult. You said you spoke Bosnian as your first language. Sarajevo is the capital of Bosnia and Herzegovina, in what used to be Yugoslavia."

"And you know more about it than ninety percent of Americans."

"The city was under siege for almost four years. Your family came here to escape that war?"

I sidestepped the small pang that I'd long since grown accustomed to. It was only like a distant shadow in the background now. "Yes—well, only my sister and I. We lived there 'til I was five, and then we were able to leave to go to Croatia before ultimately coming here with my aunt. But...my parents stayed there. My grandma was sick and elderly, and they didn't want to leave her. But at the same time, they wanted us kids to be safe so they made a difficult choice."

William rubbed at the stubble on his jaw and I tracked the motion, noting how square and masculine his features were. His perfect cleft chin was crisscrossed by a prominent scar that made me wonder what it tasted like. I swallowed, barely listening to his words as he continued. "It was a terrible war. I read a lot about it and watched documentaries. I didn't know that you were from there."

I nodded. "I was little when I came here. I didn't speak English, but I was only five so I picked it up fast."

"And these techniques you've learned? Have you ever taught them to someone before?"

I smiled. "Trying to test if I'm legit?" His features clouded, so before he could ask, I continued. "Yes. I work with other war refugees. You know that's my job, right? Ann and I both work at the International Refugee Support Center." At least until I began traveling with the Faire in June. The thought of leaving the RSC was one shadow over that bright spot of moving on. "We help refugees from places like Iran, China, Cambodia and now Syria, with all that's going on there."

"I'm not a refugee."

"You don't have to be for these techniques to work for you. You have a trigger—something that stirs panic. For me, it was loud noises...anything that sounded like bombs or rifle fire. For you, it's crowds. We can work on that."

I scooted across the mat until our knees were almost touching. "Here...let me show you. This is simple breathing."

"I already know how to do that."

I laughed. "Okay, true. Everyone knows how to breathe, or we wouldn't be here. But there is a *right* way to breathe."

He looked skeptical. His eyes flicked to mine and then immediately darted away. "I didn't know there was a 'right' way to breathe."

"Well, there is. It's the way that's healthy for your diaphragm and your abdominal muscles. It's probably counter to what you've always thought. When you breathe in, your chest expands, and when you breathe out, it contracts. But it should actually be the reverse. If you breathe correctly, it will trigger a sense of calming in your nervous system. Here...give me your hand."

William tentatively held out a big hand and I took it. Placing it on my stomach, I took a deep breath in and then exhaled it. "Do you see what I mean?"

His fingers moved ever so slightly against my abdomen, and through the thin cloth of my baby tee, my skin reacted to his touch— *really* reacted to his touch. Tingles everywhere, like I'd been shocked by static electricity. I resisted the urge to move away and chanced a glance at his face to see if he understood what I was demonstrating.

He frowned. "Do it again."

I did and he paused. I waited.

"One more time."

I complied and he didn't say anything, just moved his fingers again then splayed them across my stomach. His fingers were so long that his hand covered most of my belly. After another moment of no commentary from him, I looked up. He had the biggest grin on his face.

Well, he might not think his brain behaved typically, but right now he was acting just like a typical man.

I batted his hand away. "You get the point."

He blinked. "I might need a refresher course later."

"Don't make me smack you, Wil." His face clouded briefly, and it occurred to me that he might not realize I was joking. I immediately felt like a jerk. "I'm kidding."

He nodded. "Now you tell me if I'm breathing correctly."

He inhaled and exhaled. I leaned forward to get a better look at his abdomen. "Again?"

"Maybe you should put your hand here." He gestured to his firm, sculpted abdomen, which was now, thankfully, covered by his t-shirt. "So you can tell."

I peered at his face to see if he was pulling a fast one on me, but he appeared deadly serious. I tentatively reached out my hand and, with the lightest of touches, placed my fingertips on the area just below his sternum. He inhaled and exhaled, and the feel of his rock-hard, muscled chest under my fingertips made them tingle. *Again.*

I jerked my hand back. "That's good."

"So we've established that I know how to breathe. Now what?"

I smiled. "Now we ground and center."

"Ground and center? That sounds like baseball."

"It's a visualization technique that should work well with your style of thinking. So time to put your image-centric mind to the test. Close your eyes and rest the backs of your open hands on your knees, palms up." Hesitantly, he complied, closing his eyes last, as if he had no concept of how to move or place his hands unless he was watching them.

I began to speak in a low voice, keeping it calm and even. "Okay. Now you are going to relax every part of your body. With each breath you take in and expel, you are going to become *more* relaxed. Your muscles easing. Your heartbeat slowing. Your breaths becoming further and further apart."

A long pause. "You're using a Jedi mind trick to get me to stop breathing, aren't you?"

"Wil! Be serious. Do as I say."

"I'll do as you say."

"Good."

"It is very good."

I opened one eye and peered at him, but he had his eyes closed and was sitting exactly how I'd left him. *Hmm.* Was he joking around? It was so hard to tell!

I decided to test him. "Clear your mind."

"My mind is clear."

"These aren't the droids you're looking for."

"These aren't the droids I'm looking for...."

I tapped his leg with the back of my hand. "Stop goofing around. This is important!" The smile melted from his face and I immediately felt bad. I cleared my throat, continuing in a less waspish tone. "You need to take this seriously. You *have* to win. You have my honor to defend, remember?"

I said it lightly, but he nodded soberly. "Your honor, your tiara, my place in the clan and...my worthiness. A lot depends on this. I won't joke around again."

He'd mystified me. "Um...your *worthiness?*"

"Yes."

I blinked. "What exactly do you mean by that? You think you lost because you weren't worthy?"

His gaze met mine and fled just as quickly. "I lost because of my shortcomings."

"We all have shortcomings. You're no different. It has nothing to do with your worth."

He didn't appear convinced. "In the medieval era, disputes were solved by duel. The worthy knight was the one who won the duel."

"Well, this is the twenty-first century, not the medieval period, and you aren't unworthy. Who on earth ever gave you the idea you were unworthy?"

Something flashed in his eyes—a deep, dark hurt. His lips pressed together so hard they whitened, but he didn't answer. I'd hit a nerve and the Vulcan veneer had cracked just a little.

I held out a placating hand. "Um, I'm sorry. I didn't mean to pry. If you want to believe that this battle is for your worthiness—if that's what motivates you—then you should be allowed to believe that."

"I believe it because it's true," he asserted.

And he said it in such a somber way that something inside my chest twisted and then tightened. I could tell he was using those words to say something else. Those words had weight. They fell like coins, rattling on the floor between us until they were motionless and their echoes had faded.

"You don't think that because of Doug, do you?"

He looked profoundly puzzled. "Doug?"

"I mean, because Doug was mean to you and talked shit about you?"

He chewed on his lip. "I never think about Doug. He's not worth my time."

"Oh…I'm just confused, I guess." I *so* wanted to argue with him. If not because of Doug, then why would he think himself unworthy?

"Doug can't tear me down because I don't respect him. Why would I believe his opinion of me or let it define my opinion of myself?"

I nodded. "Good point. That's a healthy attitude to have. But why believe yourself unworthy, then?" The pain that had passed through his eyes went deeper into his past. I immediately wanted to know what it was.

He looked away. "I have reasons."

So that was that.

I clenched my teeth, fighting the urge to pursue the issue. But I couldn't allow myself to get involved. I was moving on soon and I couldn't be anchored down. I'd help William because I had a stake in this, but that was where this had to end.

I took a deep breath and lifted my chin, ready to begin. "Time for us to get back to this breathing business, okay? No more talk about being worthy or not."

He glanced up at me and nodded, but what I caught in his eyes startled me. Because it looked a lot like fear.

6
WILLIAM

"**N**ow," SHE SAYS, AND I TRY TO NOT LOOK AT THE WAY her lips form the words, the way she brushes her pale hair back from her shoulders. I try to ignore that tight, tense feeling I experience whenever I'm around her. I wipe my palms on my jeans again and she leans forward to correct me. "No. Palms up. Rest them on your knees."

She grasps my wrists in her small hands—her fingers aren't even long enough to close around my wrists—and turns my hands upward.

I do that sometimes. Rubbing my palms across my pant legs calms me. I turn my palms back over again, brushing them across my jeans a few more times. It's already starting to work.

She folds her arms across her chest. "What's going on? You don't want to do this?"

"I like to know what's ahead and be in control of it." I brush my hands across my thighs again, the friction soothing me.

Her eyes follow my movement. "Should I go?"

I freeze. "No."

"I don't want to make you uncomfortable by being here, William."

My back straightens and my muscles tense. Though I'm unsettled by her nearness, I'm suddenly afraid that she'll leave. She smells so good—like freshly ground cinnamon. But it's all I can smell, and she's all I can think about. And I really don't give a crap about breathing correctly. I just want to please her.

I force myself to stop rubbing my hands on my jeans by closing them into fists. "Let's continue."

"So do you do that to calm yourself?"

I nod.

"Then you've found a way to cope when you're stressed out. That's a lot like what we're trying to do—using a coping mechanism for dealing with crowds."

"This isn't something I can do when I'm in a full suit of armor. And it wouldn't help even if I could."

She thinks for a minute, her eyes wandering to the left while she catches her top lip between her even, white teeth. Her dark pink tongue darts out to wet her lips, and I'm suddenly flush with warm arousal. I wonder if she has any idea how lovely she is. How much I want to kiss her, touch her…

Her head jerks back to me. As she speaks, she begins fiddling with the rings on her fingers. "How do you feel when you're wearing the armor?"

"I like wearing the armor. It has a calming effect."

She cocks her head to the side. "Really? I would think it would make you feel stressed or uneasy, since putting on armor is like preparing to go out and kill."

"I don't kill anyone in my armor."

She blows out a breath, eyes wandering to the ceiling. "Of course not, but...you're getting ready to fight. That doesn't stress you out?"

"No, the armor weighs me down." She doesn't seem to understand, and I don't really have any idea how to explain it to her. I wish I could draw a picture to make her understand—to convey the message straight from my brain to hers.

There's silence between us and she flops back onto the mat. With a long sigh, she stares up at the ceiling. "You've got to be willing to work with me here."

"I am willing."

"No, you're resisting me at every turn. Meet me halfway, would you please?"

I picture about five different possibilities for 'half way'—half of a pumpkin pie at family dinner at my dad's house, a half-empty glass of water I left on the kitchen counter beside the sink before going to my workshop, half way to—

Jenna sits up again so suddenly that I'm startled from that train of thought. "You're pissing me off, Wil. I'm sorry. I just have to say this. I *need* that tiara back."

"Why?"

Her pale brows bunch together. "It doesn't matter why. It's important to me."

I nod. "I understand."

"No. You don't. I don't meant to be mean, but...well, my sister is getting married in June and she wants to wear it at her wedding."

I have a feeling that's not the entire story, but I don't know what to say in the face of her obvious anger.

She sighs again. "Don't you care that you won't be able to associate with the clan if Doug wins? He says you'll have to exile yourself."

My eyes lower to the floor, her words flowing over me in a strong current. They pull at me and steal my breath like I'm trapped under quickly rushing rapids. "I care about my friends. I don't have that many."

She doesn't say anything, so I lean back on my arms and watch her.

"Why did you challenge Doug to the first duel? You weren't even into fighting when you challenged him. It surprised everyone."

I swallow what feels like a large lump in my throat. I can't tell her the real reason. I have no idea how she'd react to, *"Because Doug had you and I wanted you to be mine."*

But I don't want to lie, either. "Doug is arrogant and insulting to people. I was tired of it." That's the truth...part of it, anyway.

She appears to think about that for a moment before looking up. "Is—is that the only reason?"

My face heats. Should I lie? *Can* I lie?

"To prove to myself that I could do it." I throw that out there because, yes, it was a reason, too. It's probably the biggest reason I initiate and excel at mostly everything I try to do. My art, the blacksmithing, the sword fighting. All of it.

Have I not been setting up these standards of personal worthiness my whole life? *If I just get better grades in school, she'll be proud of me. She'll love me. If I become an accomplished artist, she'll brag to her friends that I'm her son. She won't stay away anymore...*

When I breathe in again, it actually hurts. But I shove that old pain aside, willing it to go away.

Jenna's shoulders hunch. "We need to get you used to crowds. Like a sporting event. Do you like baseball?"

"No."

"Well, it's just as well—there's no baseball in March anyway. But hockey...we could go to a Ducks game?"

I shake my head.

"Come on. It will be fun. Hockey players are a lot like modern-day knights. They, um, wear their own sort of armor, they carry big sticks—like lances—and they fight a lot."

I laugh at the thought of likening hockey players to knights. I've seen portions of hockey games before, and I would never view them that way. I chance a look at Jenna's eyes and see that she's not looking at my face. She's staring at my chest. So I take this opportunity to study that dark circle of blue around those cornflower irises fringed with pale lashes. She's fresh-faced and wearing hardly any make-up, and I think she's more beautiful that way. I feel warm, like when the sun comes out on a cloudy day.

Her eyes meet mine without warning and I jerk my gaze away. I can't look too hard or deep. It feels like I'm seeing things that I shouldn't see.

"Do you trust me, William?" I hesitate to answer that. In all honesty, Jenna has given me no reason to trust her. She waits and then sighs. "If you go with me, we can practice. I can't think of another way to acclimate you to crowds otherwise."

"Did you do that? For your fear of loud noises?"

She nods. "Yes...I went to see some movies. About war. And"—she shudders as she continues—"I went to a rifle range. *That* was hard. I freaked out pretty bad."

I look up, suddenly wanting to know more about her—about when she struggled with panic like I do.

"How did you get through it?"

"I reminded myself that it's mind over matter."

Again she's speaking in the language of metaphors. I've heard this expression before, but I still don't get it and it's even hard to envision. She seems to pick this up from my reaction.

"It means that I had to remind myself that I'm stronger than the fear."

I nod, looking down, thinking about her words. How incredibly brave it was to force herself to confront that fear. Just the thought of her "freaking out" at a rifle range stirs something in me—a fierce protective instinct, I think. I imagine myself there with her, wrapping my arms around her, whispering that it will be okay, protecting her.

If she's brave enough to do that...then I can be, too.

"And if I want to leave?"

"Then we'll leave," she says simply.

"Why did you freak out at the rifle range?"

"It brought back...memories. They took me by surprise."

"What memories?"

Her face changes, along with her entire posture. "Bad memories. I'd rather not depress you with them." She's laughing as she says this and waving a hand in front of her. She doesn't want to go into detail because, whatever it is, it's dark. I remember the pictures and film I saw of that war. Horrible images come to mind.

And when she was little, she was there...in the middle of that. I'm marveling that she chose to expose herself to gunfire in spite of the terror.

I clear my throat. "I'll go, then. If you come with me. But—"

"We'll leave if you have to. The minute it becomes unbearable. No judgments. Okay?"

I nod, but my heart is racing. I'm not sure if it's the idea of putting myself out there, or if it's the fact that I'll get to spend more time with Jenna.

***

I've purchased the tickets to the hockey game, and we are going after I leave work. I'd expressed doubts—via text message—about navigating the traffic around the hockey arena. She had the idea of parking at a nearby movie theater and walking. So that's our plan.

I'm waiting at the curb outside her apartment. I've texted her twice now to tell her I'm here, and she's finally just let me know that she's on her way down. Minutes later, she appears wearing jeans and a long-sleeved sweater that accentuates the curves of her body. She smiles when she catches a glimpse of my car, her pale hair spilling out under a dark knit beanie. The more I focus on her, the harder it is to focus on anything else, so I blink and tear my eyes away.

"Right on time. Sorry I was late..." she says as she gets in.

"Again."

As I reach over to adjust the temperature in the car, I note that her brows twitch, but she doesn't respond. I pull away from the curb while she remains silent.

Her cinnamon smell assaults my senses the minute she's settled beside me. It's so distracting that I can barely keep my mind on the road.

I clear my throat. "I'm always on time. Or when I'm not, I have a good reason for it."

She shifts in her seat. "Somehow I already knew that about you." I puzzle over her words, wondering how she could know that about me. "So how are you feeling about this?" she asks.

I shrug. "I'll have more information for you when we get there."

"Are you nervous?"

"I'm trying not to think about it. When I think about it, I keep picturing massive crowds of people all shoving up against each other—" And again that image fills my mind. I can practically feel the press of bodies, and I can't see anything but heads and arms all around me. I shake my head to rid my mind of the image.

"Don't think about that." She places her hand on my upper arm. "Try not to picture it that way." I shrug my shoulder, causing her hand to slip away, but she doesn't comment on it.

"I can't help it. It's how I think. *Everything* is in pictures."

"But there are other ways to be in a crowd—controlled ways. Like a hockey game where everyone has their own seat and more or less stays in their own space. It doesn't all have to be like a mosh pit at a rock concert. You could imagine yourself at a museum, looking at pretty art, everyone respecting their own space."

She watches me for a long time, but my hands are on the wheel and my eyes are on the road. I try to ignore that feeling I get when she's near. It can be so overwhelming that it's distracting, and I have to fight that in order to stay focused on my driving.

Minutes later we are in Anaheim, and I park the car. We make our way to the sidewalk along the busy, crowded Katella Avenue. The Santa Ana River, which, despite it being winter, is barely a trickle as we cross over the bridge. I glance over my right shoulder toward the mountains and see that there is very little white on them.

Meteorologists are predicting one of the worst droughts ever this year, and I think they are correct.

When I think of droughts, suddenly I picture the empty high desert along Interstate 15 on the way to Las Vegas. But that picture is yanked from me the moment I feel someone take my hand and squeeze it. I jerk my head to look.

Jenna's hand is holding mine, and everything speeds up—the pounding of my heart, the speed of my blood through my veins, the rate at which I'm breathing. I have no idea what this gesture means. I bring our hands up to stare at them.

"Sorry—do you not like that? I was just offering some moral support."

"Support? Like...holding me up?"

"Figuratively, yeah."

I ponder that. "Is that what holding hands means?"

"Sometimes. But sometimes it's more. It depends on the context...on the relationship."

I realize that I'm focusing more on comprehending her than I am on the orderly file of human beings who are making their way toward the entrance of the towering Honda Center, home of the Anaheim Ducks. So I squeeze her hand back.

"Thank you for your show of support. So far it's working."

"We should have a code word."

"A code word?"

"So you can tell me when you aren't feeling so great."

"Can't I just tell you I'm not feeling so great?"

She shrugs. "Yeah. But a code word could be more fun. We could make it a game. Like...when you aren't feeling great, you can say 'pickles.' And when you really, *really* feel like you need to leave, you can say 'relish.'"

"I like relish."

"It doesn't matter what the word is. We can pick something else if you like."

By this time, we are at the glass doors that lead inside. Sadly, I have to let go of her hand to pull the tickets out of my wallet and hand them to the ticket taker.

The building looms above us as we walk in. It's big—really big. I'm trying hard to breathe the way she showed me, but I'm not sure it helps. I'll keep trying though, because she showed me and she seems to believe in it. What does help is that we are headed in a direction that most are not taking. I bought the more costly tickets, hoping that would be the case.

Jenna looks down at our tickets stubs to determine where our seats are. "Wow, you spent the big bucks. I've never sat in the good seats before."

"You come to hockey games often?"

She shrugs. "I dated a guy who was into hockey. He shared season tickets, so I came with him a lot."

As we walk to the other side of the arena in search of our section, I'm overwhelmed with unpleasant feelings about what she just said. I can't help but wonder who the guy was that she dated. It wasn't Doug. As far as I know, he isn't into hockey, and she didn't date him for very long.

Suddenly, I'm furious as memories of seeing them together flit through my mind—sitting next to each other at RMRA meetings, holding hands, even kissing. That heated feeling inside me is jealousy, and it's not rational because she's no longer with Doug. But I hate those memories because they remind me that she was with Doug and not me. It makes no sense, but I'm angry anyway.

"You've had a lot of boyfriends?" I ask. It surprises me the way I blurted it out. I've learned over the years to keep my mouth shut and to force myself to think about what I say before it comes out of my mouth. About half the time, the words are left unspoken. But these words slip through when my guard is otherwise occupied with fighting off irrational jealousy.

"Um. I've had a few."

"Alex says you don't date people for very long."

Her eyes fix on the ceiling. "Alex is overly critical of my dating habits. She doesn't really understand."

Well, that makes two of us. *I* don't understand, either.

She stops and turns to me. "This is our section. Are you ready?"

I stop beside her and glance around us as people are heading toward our door. We are fairly early, so it's not busy yet. "Yes."

When we step inside, I'm immediately overwhelmed by the massive arena around and above us—so much so that it's dizzying. But some people are already seated and it doesn't feel as oppressive as I'd anticipated, so I'm relieved. Jenna is watching me closely as we walk down the stairs to find our seats. "Wow, William. You must have paid a fortune for these. I'm used to sitting up in the nosebleed seats."

I look up at the top of the arena toward the seats she's pointing to. "People get nosebleeds up there?"

She laughs. "Sorry, no. It's an expression. It means the seats are so high in altitude that you *could* get a nosebleed."

I picture the last time I had a bloody nose. I was jumped in high school and some kid head-butted me right in the nose while calling me a 'hopeless retard.' The blood was hot and tasted like metal.

I look back at Jenna, whose eyes are on my face. I jerk my gaze away.

"You're picturing having a nosebleed, aren't you?"

"Yes."

"I think I'm getting the hang of how you think. I'll try to be more literal."

She sinks into her seat with a small smile. "Want to work on some stuff while we wait for the game?"

"More visualizing?"

She shrugs. "If you want. Or we can just talk."

"What would we talk about?"

"Well…I was wondering about your armor. You said that wearing armor calms you because of the weight."

I nod. "The pressure feels good."

"I think I get that. It's like when you're at the dentist and they put that weighted blanket on you for X-rays. That makes me feel relaxed."

I picture my last visit to the dentist. The hygienist, Nancy, told me she likes me because I don't try to talk while my teeth are being cleaned. She has short, blond hair and her hairspray smells awful. "Yes. Not exactly, but that's approximately it."

People are filing in, talking loudly, laughing even more loudly. Odors of the food they are carrying from the vendors overpowers me. I'm hungry, but I am in no mood to eat.

All the while, Jenna is talking to me. I try to focus on what's she saying, but I only pick up some of it. Shifting in my seat, I turn my ear toward her, but all I can hear are the people coming in, pressing around us, filling up the arena. The Ducks have been doing well, so she tells me, and it's late in the season. Lots of people are coming to watch these final games.

"How are you doing? Are we getting close to pickles yet?"

I give her a look and then remember it's a code word. "I'll be fine if I can get my sketch book out. It's something I do in public that helps."

I pull out a small sketchpad from my back pocket and a retractable pencil I use when I'm on the go. She tilts her head and looks at me out of the side of her eyes. I look up and meet her gaze.

It's a lot easier when she's looking at me like that—less intense. Less like staring into a bright headlight or the sun. Jenna is definitely the sun to everyone else's bright headlight.

"What are you sketching?"

I flip open my pad—naturally, it's to the wrong page. There's already a sketch on that page, but before I can flip it to the next blank page, she stops me, angling the paper so she can look at it. "Whoa, you drew that? It's so good."

I look down at the hand I've drawn. It's one of my quicker sketches—from memory instead of a sitting model. It's a strength of mine. In those few formal art classes that I did take, all I needed was to study the model for a few minutes from several different angles. Afterward, I could bring up the picture in my mind whenever I needed. It allowed me to take my time with my renderings.

"Whose hand is this? Every single detail is so..." Then she holds up her hand and positions it next to the drawing. I figure she's guessing right now that she is the model.

"This is my hand?"

"Well..." I'm not sure how she will take that, so I don't answer.

She points to the middle finger in the drawing, noting the chipped nail. "I chipped that the other day...the day I went to your house. When did you draw this?"

"This morning."

She sits up, hunching over the drawing while tucking a strand of golden hair behind her ear. And now I can't take my eyes off that ear...the shape, the texture. It looks soft and delicate like the rest of her. I'll draw that ear next.

"How the hell did you do that, Wil? It's such a minute detail for you to remember."

"When I'm in the right frame of mind, I can recall anything I see. If I concentrate, I can see the details, too."

She's shaking her head as if she doesn't believe me. I swallow, my throat feeling tight. She'll challenge me, call me a liar.

"That's just...unbelievable."

I blink. "It's true."

She looks at me sideways again. "Yeah, I believe you, William. That's just so fascinating. Amazing, really. I wish I could do that. My memories of some things seem to fade so easily. Things I wish I could remember better."

"Like what?"

She sucks her bottom lip into her mouth to bite it. Her lips are light pink and a little shiny from the product she's put there. It occurs to me that I'd like to know what it feels like to press my lips against hers. I've never wanted to kiss a woman as much as I want to kiss Jenna.

Tonight. When we are alone. I'm going to kiss her.

I can't dwell on it, though, because then I'd actually be tempted to do it now instead of later. "What would you like to remember better?" I repeat the question.

She shrugs, looking away. Her leg is bouncing up and down in place. "My father."

"You haven't seen him in a long time?"

She licks her lips and brushes her hand across her jeans as if to remove something that isn't there. "Twenty years. He died in the war."

"And you were...small."

"I was five when I last saw him. Before we left to come to the US."

This troubles me. I'd be very, very sad if my dad was dead. He's a great dad—an excellent man. I'm suddenly lost in these miserable emotions, dreading the possibility of losing him. What must that be like to lose your dad? My dad...I'm lucky to have him. His brother died young. What if *he* died?

"I've depressed you. See...I should never talk about my childhood. It's a depressing subject."

I frown. "You grew up in a war. You can't help that it's a depressing subject."

She clears her throat and bounces her knee some more before focusing on my sketchpad again. "So, back to the sketch...why did you draw my hand? It's not a particularly remarkable hand."

I trace the lines of the drawing, taking care not to smudge the pencil marks. "Your wrists...they look delicate, but they're strong. Look here—" On my drawing, I point to the bump on the top of the outer wrist. "You have a prominent ulnar styloid, but a very thin distal radial-ulnar joint. And here—"

"You know the whole anatomy?"

I nod. "I draw people...it's necessary to understand anatomy."

"Wow, I bet Mia uses you as a study partner for medical school, doesn't she?"

"Sometimes. But my knowledge does not need to extend as deeply as hers."

She pushes back her long sleeve to study her wrist, then glances at the drawing as if comparing the two. "I would never have thought in a million years that my wrists are remarkable."

"Well, you won't live for a million years so—"

She holds up a hand, laughing, and I realize I did my usual. "Sorry, I wasn't being literal again. It just means I'm surprised."

I flip the page to a blank one and begin to sketch as we talk. I'm choosing a safer subject to draw this time—the scoreboard that hangs centered over the ice rink. For a while, this helps. With Jenna beside me, I make it through the rest of the time that people file in—past us in our row, in the seats in front of us and behind—and even to the introduction of the players as they skate onto the ice when their jersey numbers and names are being called. I'm okay as long as I can focus on my pad and only look up occasionally.

It's harder to block out the bright lights, the smell of food, the sound of feet shuffling all around us. It's loud and Jenna has to lean close when she wants to tell me anything. I want her to keep doing it though. I like the way it feels when her hair brushes against my cheek. I like how she smells tonight... like rain on grass. Like ripe pears.

But after a while, it's too hard—and the arena too dark—to concentrate on my sketchpad, so I'm forced to tuck it away in my back pocket. The noise is distracting and so is the presence of the crowd. It feels like ants crawling across my skin. I rub my hands along my thighs to calm myself, but that's not working either.

Jenna, however, is keeping a close watch on me. She leans over again and says, "You okay?"

"Um..."

"Feeling a little...pickles?"

Her phrase is complete nonsense, but I remember that's because it's our code. So I nod. "Yes. Pickles. Sour dill pickles."

Her brows rise. "We don't want sour dill pickles. I, um, have an idea. Maybe it will help you take your mind off of things so you can watch the game."

"Okay."

"Well, it's not going to be as good as a suit of armor or even a weighted blanket at the dentist."

She stands up and then just as quickly sinks onto my lap. Then she settles herself gingerly on my thighs. I freeze, completely at a loss for what to do. In fact, I'm so confused right now that I forget to worry about the crowd around us or even the sounds of the hockey game.

She turns and says, "Is this okay? Are you okay?"

I lean forward a little so she can hear my answer. "Yes."

A beautiful woman is sitting on my lap. As Jordan would say, *What's not to like?*

Slowly, she leans back, settling against my chest. We are now touching from her ankles up through her legs to her hips, which rest against my upper thighs, and her back is pressed to my chest. Her head is tilted to the side so that I can still see past her if I want to watch the game. I don't. Right now, I couldn't concentrate on it if I tried.

My heart is racing. The feel of her and that smell—it's even stronger now. Is it her shampoo? Her soap? Or is that *her* that I'm smelling?

"You comfortable?" she asks, turning her head again, her silky hair brushing against my face. I close my eyes, relishing it. *Relish.* The good kind of relish. Not 'relish' the code word.

Now would be a bad time to use that code word. I could sit with her like this all night.

My hands are gripping the armrests, but slowly I release my death grip. Jenna lays her arms along mine, resting her hands on my hands. Hers are so much smaller, but her fingers fit in the crevices between mine. I can feel my heartbeat in every inch of my body that is pressed against hers.

Her neck is three centimeters from my mouth. It looks soft...succulent. I want to taste it. Would she taste as good as she smells? What would her skin feel like under my hands?

She might not like me doing that. My hands have callouses on them from the blacksmithing and my artwork. They would feel rough and hard on her smooth, supple skin.

Suddenly, I'm imagining tasting her *and* touching her, and my body is reacting. I'm getting hard right where she's sitting on me, and I don't want her to know.

So I say into her ear, "Relish."

I *really* didn't want to say that word, but I don't want her to feel my erection, either. She'll think I'm a pervert or something. But her reaction is slow and she's asking me to repeat myself. At the same time, the crowd jumps to its feet, cheering at the two players on the ice who are fighting.

I twist and slide my arm under her knees, pulling her up with me in one swift motion.

"What the—?" says the man next to me, but I'm not listening. I need to get out of here and she's coming with me.

"Wil!" she exclaims, but the rest of her words are lost in the crowd. I shoulder my way down the row and out to the aisle. Then it's up the stairs to the deserted concessions area, where I stop, finally able to breathe.

Jenna is staring at me with wide eyes but making no move to get out of my hold, so I don't let her down. "I thought that sitting on your lap was helping." She frowns.

"It was helping." In *some* ways. But making it more difficult in others.

"Well, you almost made it to the first intermission. That's good." She pauses, her face growing a shade of pink. "It's, uh, it's a good thing you're strong, so you could just pick me up and go like that." She licks her lips and looks up into my face. My eyes fly to the nearest door and I start walking toward it.

"I wouldn't have to be very strong in order to carry you. You can't weigh more than a hundred pounds."

"Women don't like to discuss their weight."

"Yes, I remember hearing that, but I don't understand it."

"Women are complicated, Wil. Like you shouldn't talk about how we look in our jeans, either."

My eyes shift to her legs, noticing how her jeans hug her feminine thighs. She looks really good in them. Should I not say that? She *did* warn me.

Her closeness, the feel of her body pressed against my chest, the smell of her and the tight sweater hugging the curves of her breasts...none of those are helping my current state of arousal. Not in the least.

Now that we are outside the glass doors, it's safe to let her go. I release her legs and she lands on her feet with a thump.

"Oh!" she exclaims and grabs onto my arm to steady herself. Not expecting her hold, I tense and jerk my arm away. I pull her with me and she almost falls before I catch her.

"You startled me," I tell her.

She huffs out a breath. "Well, *you* startled *me* first! You don't just scoop someone up in the middle of a crowd and then plop them unceremoniously in the parking lot without a word."

"I spoke words. More than one."

She throws her hands up. "I can't even. I can't!"

"You can't what?"

Her fists tighten at her sides and she's talking through her teeth now. "You're pissing me off."

I blink and pull away from her. "Oh."

She folds her arms across her chest, and all I can think about is how the material across her breasts tightens and I can see every curve. I'm obsessed with imagining what they look like underneath her shirt. It looks like she has very pretty breasts. As pretty as the rest of her. "Well...should I not be pissed off?"

I think about that question for a minute, but am startled when she hits me on the arm.

"Stop staring at my boobs!"

I rip my gaze away from that perfect chest.

Then she says it. That phrase I hate more than anything else. "Look me in the eyes, Wil."

My stomach drops and I feel nauseous. I hate it when people tell me that. I hate it more than when they call me retard or Rain Man or whatever else I've been called. Because the people who say this to me are not my enemies. They are people I care about—my friends, even my family. I swallow and stuff my hands in my pockets, but I'm still staring at the ground.

"Look at me!" she repeats.

I take a deep breath, and then, because I don't trust my voice, I shake my head, balling my fists inside my pockets.

7
JENNA

I WASN'T QUITE SURE WHAT WAS HAPPENING. IT HAD STARTED out as a fairly enjoyable trip to a hockey game, but things had deteriorated quickly. Now William and I were hashing it out in the parking lot of the Honda Center, getting quizzical looks from security personnel.

"Look up, Wil."

Instead, he rubbed his hands down the sides of his thighs, then turned on his heel and walked away.

Just like that. At full speed. Like he didn't even want or expect me to keep up.

I had to run to catch up to him, and by that time we were on a narrow sidewalk along a busy avenue. I stuck to his heels as we crossed the river and cut over into the theater parking lot.

He sped up once we reached the lot as if avoiding the possibility of me walking next to him. Heaven forbid *that* happen. "William Drake. Stop right now!"

He stopped but didn't turn around.

I caught up with him and moved into his line of sight. "Well?" I said.

"Well, what?"

"What the hell was that? Why did you storm off?"

"Because I didn't want to say anything rude, and you made me angry."

"Because I asked you to look me in the eye?"

"Yes."

"Well, maybe I'm just tired of you looking everywhere *but* my eyes."

He blinked. "It's difficult."

"Why?"

He shook his head. "Because when I'm looking in your eyes, I'm too distracted to hear what you are saying. It's intense."

"What's intense? I mean, I know I'm beautiful, but…" I joked in an effort to lighten the mood.

"Yes. You are beautiful. You're the most beautiful woman I've ever seen."

I sucked in a breath. *Wow.* He'd said it in a matter-of-fact tone as if stating that the sky was undeniably blue. There was no art to the words, no obvious attempt at flattery. *Why was my throat closing up like this?*

"I was joking." I laughed self-consciously. "I'm not really that full of myself."

"I don't know what that means. But you shouldn't joke about being beautiful. It's not a joke." He stuffed his hands into his pockets and waited.

I felt both uncomfortable and pleased at the same time. My cheeks were flaming hot and—ironically—I couldn't meet his gaze even if he wanted me to.

"I didn't realize," I suddenly blurted, my voice trembling with regret.

"What?"

"That it was so hard for you to look in my eyes. I thought that was a myth. I don't spend a lot of time around autistic people."

"It's hard to look in anyone's eyes, but easier if I know the person." I was flooded with relief that he seemed okay discussing this. "Mostly it keeps me from focusing on what is being said. It also makes me feel like I'm violating that person's privacy."

"By looking in their eyes?"

"Like I'm seeing things that I shouldn't see." He shakes his head. "I get tired of having to explain it to people. And you aren't going to get it so—"

"The eyes are the windows to the soul," I interrupted quietly.

"Eyes are not windows."

"It's a metaphor, Wil. It means that a person's eyes can show what's going on with them beneath the surface. So maybe you're feeling like a Peeping Tom?"

He was quiet for a long time, shifting from one leg to the other. "Yeah, so maybe if I make eye contact with you as long as you want, you'll let me peep through your window."

I opened my mouth, about to lodge a protest, when I saw the smile on his face. He was rather pleased with himself and his joke. "Ha ha. Then again, you do stare at my boobs enough."

"I like your breasts." His eyes darted to my chest, causing my nipples to tighten under my t-shirt.

I folded my arms to cover my unconscious reaction and laughed. "I can tell."

"And your butt. And your legs. And—"

"All right, all right. I get the picture. Let's get in your car," I said with an exasperated sigh. *Typical man.*

William opened the car door for me and then walked around before sliding in behind the wheel. As we headed out of the parking lot, I dared a glance at his chiseled profile.

I wasn't above feeling gratified when a hot guy noticed me. And evidently, William had. He thought I was the most beautiful woman he'd ever seen. His compliment—couched more like an observation of fact—made me feel more glorious and radiant than Aphrodite when Adonis chose to be with her over the goddess Persephone.

We grabbed some fast food from a drive-thru and ate it in the car to avoid the dinner crowd. Then William took me home and, taking his chivalrous duties seriously, insisted on walking me up two flights of stairs to my door.

I wasn't entirely sure why I wanted to kiss William so badly—well, maybe because he's freaking hot as hell—but if there was ever an opportunity, this was it. So I leaned in to kiss him goodnight. He was so much taller than me that I pushed up on my tiptoes, expecting him to lean in, too.

No such luck.

He must not have known what I was attempting to do, which would explain why he stepped back when he saw me leaning toward him. I lost my balance, but he caught me, and his strong arms stayed wrapped around me for a few moments longer than they needed to be. There was something electric in that embrace—a heaviness in the air, like before a rainstorm.

"Are you all right?" he asked.

"Uh, yeah," I said, feeling my face burn. Thank goddess it was dark outside. "I, uh, I just wanted to give you a goodnight kiss."

A pause. "Oh." He cleared his throat. "You should have told me."

Slowly, stiffly, he bent down, and I—now embarrassed beyond belief—turned my head and quickly landed a peck on his cheek. Then I reached for the knob to scurry off into my apartment and lick my wounds.

I was detained when William hooked a large hand around my arm.

"That's not a goodnight kiss," he said.

"Oh? So then—" And that's all I got out before his mouth pressed against mine. I barely had a chance to catch my breath before I was on the ride of my life...

I opened my lips and suddenly something inside of me jolted, like a rollercoaster hitting the track at full speed. The shock was such that I almost pulled back.

I was certainly glad I didn't when William reached up and slid his palms to the back of my head, his fingers weaving into my hair. I pressed my hands to his broad chest as he pinned my body against the cold metal door. Struggling for breath, I felt that kiss not just at the juncture of our lips but all over my body. From the top of my prickling scalp, where his fingers rested without ever relinquishing their hold, to the tingling in my toes.

It was almost *too* much. And yet I wanted *more*. Like the craving of an adrenaline high on a rollercoaster after the first breathless dip, I wouldn't stop until the ride had come to a screeching halt.

Almost as if hearing that thought, William's tongue slipped along my lips, slowly, seductively asking for permission to enter.

Goddess, the tingles suddenly transformed into aches. Now it was more than mere wanting. I *needed* more.

Permission granted.

Within seconds, the kiss intensified and the pressure from his mouth deepened. His tongue slipped into my mouth and was now dueling with mine, as if we faced each other on a field of battle. Against my will, a little sigh escaped my lips.

I hadn't had a kiss like this in ages. It was searing, bright and powerful—pure thrill. At once, I trembled with fear *and* craving. Wanting to pull away and end it while also willing it to never end.

William made the decision for me, and as he slowly pulled away, I felt just as jolted from the severance of our connection as I did when it began. After a long, silent moment, he cleared his throat. "Now *that* is a goodnight kiss."

I burst out laughing. I couldn't help it. As soon as I did, his grin widened and I felt a pang at how adorable he was while still being incredibly sexy. My throat tightened and my heart rate sped up as a distant fear nibbled at the back of my thoughts.

I couldn't get involved with William for so many reasons, not the least of which was that I was leaving soon. And though I *needed* that tiara back, I couldn't let feelings get involved. I—I couldn't go there with him. I could never go there with *anyone.* My heart had been killed and buried long ago.

But it hadn't taken me long to realize that William was different than the others. And if Ann was right and he did have a thing for me, then this couldn't go any further.

I stepped back to move into the doorway, only to bang my head loudly on the closed door. "Ow! Shit." I'd forgotten to open the door, and in my dazzled state had tried to walk through solid matter. It didn't take a physics student to know that you couldn't do that.

William asked if I was okay, and I barely muttered enough to alleviate his concern before telling him goodbye as quickly as possible. Then I unlocked the door and moved inside before he could say another word.

No, I couldn't open this drawbridge and let him in. I had to keep everything shut up tight inside—man my watchtowers, bar the city gates. He could assemble his siege, lay in wait outside the moat, but I wouldn't be around long enough for him to wait it out. Unlike a medieval fortress, Jenna Kovac was a movable, transient being.

And I always would be.

I didn't fall asleep until the sun was almost up because I may have spent a few hours reliving that kiss. I tossed and turned and told myself I was being an idiot. It wasn't the first time a handsome guy had kissed me, after all.

When I woke up on Saturday morning, it was almost noon. *No thanks to my roommate.* There should be a law against running a vacuum before nine o'clock on weekends. And if there were such a law, I'd have been the first one calling the cops on Alex.

Fortunately for her, she was gone by the time I got up, having left me a note on the fridge to explain that she was spending the day helping her mom with a garage sale. I was slurping up a bowl of cereal when my phone rang.

I checked the ID and answered immediately. There was no way I was missing this call—bleary-eyed or not.

"Ćao, Helena," I said with a smile on my face.

"Janja! How are you? Are you free this afternoon? I'm going to be in Orange County this evening to meet some friends. I thought I'd come early and take you out to lunch. Are you busy?"

"I am now. I haven't seen you in forever."

"Yes, it's been over a month and it's all my fault. But we'll catch up over lunch, yes?"

"Of course."

"Okay, I'll pick you up in hour."

After I hung up, I pressed the button on my phone and noted the date. The twenty-eighth of March. It was no accident that Helena wanted to see me today—the anniversary date was less than a week away.

Seven years. I blinked the sting out of my eyes and swallowed, determined to dig out my finest outfit to wear when I saw Helena. She was always so elegant, so put together. For years, I'd wanted to grow up to be just like her.

A flash of a memory invaded my thoughts. The night I'd met her it had been the homecoming dance of my freshman year in high school. My third date with Brock. He'd brought me over to the house to take photos and meet his parents, and they'd been so thrilled that he was dating a girl from "the old country."

I reflected on that night as I spent twice the amount of time that I normally did on my hair and make-up. I pulled my hair back into a French braid and tied it with an embroidered ribbon that Caitlyn had given me at the last regional market. She'd been so happy to hear that I'd agreed to travel with the Ren Faire as their fortune card reader that she'd given me the ribbon to celebrate.

Helena arrived on time, and I was waiting at the curb for her...in the exact same spot where William had picked me up the night before.

He'd probably be both shocked and thrilled at my punctuality. I smiled at the thought.

Helena, as always, looked perfect. A forty-nine-year-old woman who looked at least a decade—possibly two—younger than her actual age, she had dark hair and olive skin, and she always reminded me of a sophisticated movie actress from the eighties.

She had high cheekbones and an elegantly constructed face, with a neck like a swan and a beautiful figure. The clothes she wore were expensive but understated, and she attracted admiring looks wherever she went.

There was no doubt she'd passed her beauty on to her son. With his dark curly hair and deep blue eyes, he'd been the most handsome boy at our high school. And he'd picked me. Or rather, he'd listened when the Fates had picked us out for each other.

"Janja!" As always, Helena greeted me by kissing me on both cheeks, keeping alive old country traditions. Like me, Helena had been born in the former Yugoslavia. Unlike me, Helena was ethnically a Serb, while I was Bosnian-Croatian. But we'd met here, in California, and now she and her husband were like family.

Neither of us had found a Balkan-style restaurant in the area that satisfied our cravings for our native homeland, so this afternoon she took me to one of the trendy bistros in downtown Fullerton.

"How is Vuk?" I asked as we were handed our menus and served ice water. "Is he feeling better?"

"This last scare has really changed him," she said, speaking of her husband's recent diabetes diagnosis. "We exercise together every day, and he's finally watching what he eats. Did I tell you we are going to Belgrade in June to see his mom? He wants to lose weight before she sees him."

"Oh, I'm so happy for you. I just found out that Maja is getting married in June."

Her fork paused on the way to her mouth and she looked up, brows raised. "Where? In Sarajevo?"

I nodded.

"When? Maybe we can fly out together. Vuk and I don't have our plane tickets yet."

I poked around my salad for a while and cleared my throat as I tried to figure out how to change the subject. I had no desire to go there with her, yet it was my fault for bringing it up in the first place.

"Early June, I think."

"Are you going out early?"

More silence and salad picking from me.

"Janja..."

I sighed and looked away. "I don't really have the money to buy a ticket right now. I'm trying to figure out how I'm going to do it."

"It's simple. You come with Vuk and me to Belgrade, and then take the bus to Sarajevo to be with your family."

I suppressed a smile. "Thanks. I'll see what I can do."

"No, there is no *seeing*. Vuk has loads of air miles from all the business traveling he does. It will cost us nothing to get another ticket."

I was almost speechless with gratitude. This was so generous of her to offer, but it was in no way out of character. I only ached at the thought of sitting next to her on that plane with no tiara on my lap.

I had to get it back. There was no way I could show up to the wedding empty-handed. Disappointing Maja would be just like the time I'd disappointed Mama all those years ago.

We finished our meal, and I was using a piece of my roll to sop up the gravy from the plate. Helena teased me about my old world manners and I laughed, blaming her son for the habit.

Our smiles faded just a little bit at the mention of the ghost between us. Without looking at her, I reached for my goblet of ice water. "I can't believe that next week it'll be seven years..."

Helena's elegant dark brows were untroubled, but I could read the pain in the back of her blue eyes. That unique, sharp pain that, I imagined, could only be truly understood by other parents cursed with the most horrible of fates—to have outlived their child. But Helena was no mythical Queen Niobe, who wept unceasingly for her lost children. Helena, in fact, was the picture of dignified strength. I admired her greatly for that—among other things.

She rolled her lips into her mouth and then smoothed her napkin across her lap. "I'm going to the cemetery tomorrow. I'll be out of town next week," she declared in a flat voice.

I straightened in my chair. "I'll be there next week. I'll make sure there are fresh flowers on his grave."

"You go often," she said. It wasn't a question.

I nodded. "His birthday. The holidays. The anniversary of our first date. And..." I left the last one unspoken. The anniversary of his death. Next week. Seven years. Seven years since my heart had followed him into that grave.

Her dark brows twitched together. "What does that work out to be? Every month? More?"

I shrugged. "Something like that."

She frowned, studying the uneaten food on her plate, picking at it with a fork. "Jenna, we've had this talk before," she said, switching to English.

"I know what you're going to say."

"Do you? But you're still going to ignore it? You're twenty-five years old. You have your whole life ahead of you. I *know* he wouldn't want you living like this."

"Like what? My life hasn't ended. I've seen other guys."

"Yes, how is that going with the new one? Douglas, right?"

I grimaced, aware that this would only serve to reinforce her argument. "I broke up with Doug last weekend."

"Hmm," she said, her gaze on me sharpening. Heat rose to my cheeks. It was like she and Alex were psychically connected. "Braco wasn't perfect. You just remember him that way."

I swallowed, my throat suddenly clogged. Helena watched me as I blinked my tears away. "I know he wasn't perfect. He was just—"

"Perfect for you, I know. But you were both children. How do you know you wouldn't have grown apart as you grew up? Jenna...he wouldn't want you ending your life when his ended. I say this bluntly because I'm talking to a girl who I've thought of as my adopted daughter for ten years now."

I reached over and covered Helena's hand with mine. "Thank you. I understand what you're trying to do."

"Then you must listen to me. Somewhere out there, there is someone for you. This belief you have of one true soulmate...it's not true. It can't be."

I shook my head, unable to give her words credence. "So you don't think Vuk is your soulmate?"

"*No*, I don't. He's my friend and my lover and my partner, but there is no soulmate."

"You think you could be just as happy with someone else as you are with him?"

She shrugged. "Maybe even happier. Maybe somewhere out there is a Vuk who doesn't leave his socks all over the floor or likes to do the dishes once in a while. Or who can dance." At that, we both laughed.

We turned down dessert when the waiter returned and Helena asked for the bill. As always, I wished I were in a position to offer to pay, vowing that someday I'd take her out to a nice eatery and proudly pay the bill myself.

After driving me back to the apartment, Helena gave me a long hug and called me *srce moje*, which meant, "my heart." A name a mother called her child. She held me tight, and when I pulled away, she clamped on tighter.

"For me, Janja, and for *him*. Fall in love again. You must free yourself before it will even be possible."

I kissed her cheeks, not allowing my tears to fall until she turned away. I didn't have the heart to tell her that I couldn't allow it—that it wasn't only myself I was protecting, but those around me. Too many of my relationships had ended with people being hurt or even killed.

I was a wanderer, never meant to set down roots. I'd been torn from my home soil at the tender age of five and had been drifting ever since. In so many ways, it was my destiny.

8
WILLIAM

I T'S MONDAY MORNING AGAIN, AND I'M AT MY DESK WORKING ON the three-dimensional rendering—again. Mostly I'm checking the work of artists under me, but I'm also cleaning up details and fine-tuning textures. Many have called it tedious, but I enjoy focusing my attention on minutia.

Especially today. I've been unable to think of anything besides Jenna since the moment I kissed her—and she kissed me back.

I spent hours last night thinking about that kiss. I couldn't sleep. I could only remember the way our mouths fused together, the feeling of her body pressed against mine. Now I try to force that image out of my mind as I adjust my goggles. There are lots of things to do today. Things that don't involve my fixation on Jenna.

And just like the previous Monday, I'm aware of someone standing at my desk. But unlike Jordan, there is no waiting until I'm done with what I'm working on before he speaks.

"Liam," my cousin says. I should have realized it was him when my nearby coworkers all went silent. Adam doesn't appear in the art department very often, and though our office is pretty casual, people still get intimidated by the CEO showing up unannounced.

Sometimes I do too, even though I was the one always picking up his shorts off the bathroom floor throughout our adolescence. He also ate up all my favorite breakfast cereal on a consistent basis. In fact, Adam annoyed me greatly when he first came to live with us. Fortunately, it didn't take long for that to change.

I straighten and look at him. "What?"

"I need you for a sec. Let's take a walk."

Let's take a walk. That's his favorite way to have a short, discreet conversation with an employee. There may even be a meme of it floating around here somewhere. Or a funny little cartoon drawing of my cousin standing at some employee's desk asking to take a walk.

When Adam wants to take a walk, it's usually not a good thing. It *is* a logical way to get some privacy in an open-concept office, I suppose. But if Adam needs to speak to me, he knows exactly where I live and is well acquainted with my phone number, too.

Without a word, I save and close my work, remove my glasses and set up my desk so that it's perfectly arranged for me to pick up where I left off after the lunch break. I trail behind him off the floor of the art department, ignoring the gazes following us. None of them will dare to ask me the details later, so I ignore them.

We're walking down a back hall on the way to R&D when he stops for a minute and turns to me. "I don't have a lot of time, but I needed to have a quick conversation with you. Whatever the hell is going on between you and Jordan needs to stop."

I fold my arms across my chest and he seems to take great interest in that gesture. "Nothing's going on between me and him."

"That's not a good thing. I get that he pissed you off. He pisses me off a lot, too, but he's your friend. He's *my* friend, and most importantly, he's your boss."

I shrug. "So are you."

His eyes look up at the ceiling, then fly back down. "Yeah, we're family. That's different. We're stuck with each other, and if we ever did get like that, your dad would probably kick both our asses. Jordan is a good guy. He screwed up, but he genuinely feels bad about it. And I can't have another feud going on in my office, Liam."

He's referring to the dispute I had with Gene, a former co-director in the art department. We had artistic differences, and apparently those differences had been broadcast everywhere. We'd both been branded the "temperamental artists" by employees in other departments.

Things had been okay until the day that he blatantly took credit for my work. From then on, I refused to work with or even speak to him. Adam tried to do what he could to resolve the issue, but in the end, Gene found a job somewhere else. Adam ended up admitting that it was no great loss to have him gone.

"Look, you need to learn to separate the professional from the personal." Adam straightens. "Jordan didn't fuck you over—"

"He *did*. He gave me bad advice."

Adam takes a long breath and releases it. "But it was you who chose to take that advice. You need to work on what it means to forgive someone. In the end, this hard-ass attitude is only going to cost *you*, not others."

"My ass is not hard."

Adam looks away and laughs. "No, I mean...look, I love you, guy, but you *do* have a problem with this. In all the years that I've known you, you've never been the forgiving sort."

"Why should I be? If someone ruins their chance with me, then that's it. They're gone. I don't need people like that in my life."

Adam is rubbing the back of his neck now and looking down the hall in both directions. "So people can't be human and screw up? If they make a mistake, they're dead to you forever?"

I shake my head. "I'm not going to kill anyone."

"It's an idiom, Liam. It means you'll act like they are dead even if they aren't. You'll sever your relationship with them? It was one thing when it was Gene. He proved that he had no morals whatsoever and ended up going somewhere else—win-win for us. But that's *not* happening with Jordan, okay? He's not going anywhere, and you have to learn to get along with him."

When I say nothing, he sighs and looks at his watch. "I have to get going for a lunch meeting off campus, but dude, think about this. What if your first duel had been your only chance to beat that other guy? You got your second chance—give one to Jordan. That's all I'm asking."

I think about that for a moment. "I did."

He frowns. "You did? What do you mean?"

"I told him that he could make it up to me by helping me train against a left-hander."

Adam's expression changes. "That's great." He smiles. "You've made me happy."

I frown. "I wasn't doing it to make you happy, but I'm glad you are. I just hope Jordan comes to the training or else it *will* be like he's dead to me."

"I'll make sure he does. I'll come too."

"Good," I say. "I don't have as long to prepare this time."

Adam nods. "We'll help you all we can, and just...think about this, all right? Sometimes the moral high ground isn't always the best place to stake your claim."

"Huh?" I say, completely confused. Was he even speaking English? All I can picture is a bunch of gold miners rushing around driving stakes into high, hilly ground.

He sighs. "I just mean that being stubborn and holding onto grudges isn't always the best way to go. But I can sit here and explain that to you until I'm blue in the face and you probably won't listen. Maybe when you get into a relationship, you'll figure it out. Or else you're just going to be lonely, because *no* one is perfect."

Perhaps he is referring to himself and Mia. They were far from perfect and had broken up several times before finally ending up happy together. Maybe those are the chances he's referring to. Did he have to forgive her for something, or did she have to forgive him?

Or maybe it was both? It makes me wonder if getting into a relationship means learning new things about yourself. And making changes. I don't like changes.

I mull over those thoughts as I finish up my workday. On the way home, I stop by a fruit stand. It's strawberry season in Southern California and the stands are everywhere, selling them freshly picked and packed in large boxes. They're dark red and almost the size of small apples. I end up buying a full box, even though I know I can't eat them all before they go bad. So I stop by my dad's house to leave some with him and his wife, Kim.

I ring the doorbell and enter, like I always do, and Kim comes around the corner. "Liam!" she says. It didn't take long before she picked up the habit from all of my other family members to call me by that nickname. Kim has been my stepmom for only a short time now—almost nine and a half months. And the fact that she is Mia's mom makes Mia my stepsister.

"I brought strawberries." Because I know she's going to invite me to eat dinner with them—she always does—I add, "But I can't stay long—"

"Yes, it's Monday. I understand...your workout routine. That's okay, but at least wait to say 'hi' to your dad. He just got home a few minutes before you pulled in."

After he's changed his clothes, Dad comes out and we talk for a few minutes. They thank me for the strawberries before I take my leave, mentioning that I'm already off my schedule. Fortunately, they know me well enough to not push it.

I'm almost out the door when I stop suddenly. It's seconds after I've passed through the front hall, but something has jumped out at me. Something is different. I turn around and move back to where I saw it... and there it is.

A newly framed painting is hanging in the hallway. My throat is inexplicably tight. So tight I can't swallow.

"What is it?" my dad asks. Kim quickly excuses herself, and I'm so stunned I can't tell her goodbye.

"That picture. Where did you get it?"

There's a long pause. My dad doesn't say anything. I turn back to study the art. I'm very familiar with it. I produced it when I was fourteen years old. It's a black line drawing with watercolor wash, a medium I haven't used in at least four years. It shows an autumn scene in the hills out by the historic town of Julian. They hold an annual apple festival there, and I'd visited the area shortly before painting this.

But I threw it away years ago. There was too much anger and pain associated with it. My fists tighten at my sides as I replay the scene in my mind. I can see every vivid detail and feel every feeling, including the cold anger and the hurt. Returning to my room after having been called into the kitchen to speak on the phone with my mother. Her excuses—there were always excuses—as to why we wouldn't go out to dinner, as she'd previously planned.

I'd grabbed that picture—intended as a gift for her—and shoved it in the trashcan. I didn't cry. And I refused every invitation to see her after that.

"Well?" I ask between clenched teeth.

"I have a big folder of your artwork, and I was showing it to Kim. She loved this and wanted to frame it and show it off in our front hallway."

"But I threw this away," I say quietly, glancing at him out of the side of my eye.

"Liam," Dad says.

I turn to him and he's not looking at my face. That's good, because I don't want him to see me like this, and I sure as hell don't want to look in his eyes while he lies to me.

"I threw this away, Dad. What is it doing on your wall?"

He takes in a deep breath and lets it go. "I saved it from your trash can. It was too beautiful to throw away."

I blink, confused. Not because he dug it out of the trash, but because I'm not sure how I feel. That hurt and anger are back, fresh as ever, resentment toward a mother who never cared enough. Those feelings are mixed with frustration and also admiration toward a father who cared almost too much.

"Does it bother you?" Dad's question interrupts my jumbled thoughts. "Kim really loved it. In fact, she loves all of your art."

My stepmother loves what my mother never saw. Never cared to see. I take a deep breath, and suddenly Dad's hand is on my shoulder. "Liam."

I stiffen. "I gotta go. I'm already thirty-eight minutes off my schedule."

His hand slides off. "Okay, son. Love you."

This time I don't recite the words back to him like I usually do. Instead, I say, "Goodbye."

As I go about my workout routine—putting extra vigor into it to make up for the lost time and as an escape vent for these confusing feelings—I think about the things that have happened today. Specifically, Adam's words about forgiveness and letting go. Later that night when Dad texts to ask me if I'm okay, I answer that I am and that he should keep the picture hanging on the wall.

9
JENNA

ARLY ON SATURDAY MORNING, I MADE IT TO THE CEMETERY as promised. Alex was kind enough to lend me her car, but because I didn't want to leave her stranded at home all day, I left at the asscrack of dawn.

I didn't have money for a professional bouquet, so I'd spent some time on a sunset walk the night before picking wildflowers along the side of the road. As I did so, I indulged in memories I usually preferred to keep buried...our first date, our first kiss. The time he spent all his savings from his part-time job at the pizza shop to take me out on a special date and buy me a necklace for our anniversary. I still had that necklace, though the clasp had broken and I couldn't wear it anymore.

I'd tied up the wildflowers with a pretty ribbon and took them with me to Brock's grave. There, I removed the wilted bouquet that Helena had set there the week before and replaced it with my fresh bundle.

I passed an hour in quiet contemplation before speaking out loud. Sometimes I did this—and not just when I was at his graveside. If anyone ever overheard me, they'd think I was insane for talking to my dead boyfriend. But I liked to think that, wherever he was, he could hear me. That he could still feel our connection the way I felt it. That he'd know that I missed him.

Indulging myself in self-pity, I cursed what a rotten fate it was to find your soulmate at a young age and then have your time together cut tragically short. I lamented having to live an entire lifetime with him only as a memory, and I mourned the fact that the closest I could get to Brock was a plaque in a green lawn where I lay flowers every so often.

My thoughts drifted to last night, when I did a Tarot reading for myself. I'd wanted to confirm that I was making the right decision by leaving to travel with the Faire at the end of June.

I drew the Fool. How appropriate. How *me.*

Not because I was foolish, but because of what the Fool represented—a wanderer, an adventurer. A person who listened to the wind and did not set down roots in any one place.

The card showed a man with his possessions in a bag over his shoulder, looking up toward the radiant sun. He was stepping precariously near the edge of a cliff, a happy dog clipping at his heels. Ready to start a brand new adventure.

I felt that also and tried to ignore any of the other pangs at the back of my mind—the thought of leaving Alex, my other friends. And for some reason, William and his surprising lips had popped up, too, before I'd forced the memory of our kiss from my mind.

But as I drove home, my mind kept returning to it—the feel of William's hands in my hair as they pressed against the back of my head, the way my body had heated instantly from the contact. I couldn't *not* think about it.

With a sigh of frustration, I turned on one of my favorite mythology podcasts to listen to on the way home.

A few hours later, I sat at the dining room table pouring over my daily calendar, making a to-do list for the week and checking my appointments. Despite my hesitation to get too close to William, I was determined to get that tiara back. Thus, I was figuring out when I could sandwich in more time to help him with his crowd problems. If I'd been highly motivated to get it back before, I was even more determined now that Helena had made a flight to Serbia possible.

Alex sank down in a chair opposite me and plopped a foil container of food in front of my face. The delicious aroma of Lupe's enchiladas swirled around my nose.

"Lunchtime. Eat up, girlfriend. I invited some of the gang tonight and we're watchin' Doctor Who and drinkin' tequila."

In spite of the siren's song—otherwise known as Alex's mom's wonderful food—I glanced over my daily agenda again. *7 p.m. – William: visualization & breathing practice.*

"I'm supposed to have William over this evening."

Her eyebrows rose. "Fun. He'll know everyone. Heath, Kat, Mia and Adam, and some of their work friends are coming over, too."

I forked a bite straight from the tin—meaty, cheesy goodness exploded on my tongue and my stomach rumbled for more. "So that's why you were cleaning like a madwoman when I got home. *Again.* I thought you'd lost your mind."

Alex grinned and pointed to her forehead. *"Loco como un zorro."*

"Crazy like Zorro?"

"Like a fox. And we both know I'm a fox."

I leered at her, taking in her smooth, bronze skin, her big, dark eyes and high cheekbones. She had a rebel stripe of pink running through her almost-black hair. Her oh-so-traditional mom had chewed her out for it, but I'd talked Alex into standing her ground and keeping it. "You are. If I swung that way, you'd be in trouble."

She stuck her tongue out at me. "So what's up with William? Are you dating *him* now? I bet the girls in the clan are pissed."

I laughed. "No. No, we're not dating." Just trading explosive kisses on the doorstep. My face flushed, remembering the way our tongues tangled. *Damn.* The dude knew how to kiss. What was it they said about the quiet ones? *Still waters run deep...*

"Hmm. First you drop in at his house, then a Ducks game last week. Drinking party tonight..."

"I had no idea you were planning that. We're supposed to work on visualization and breathing tonight."

She perked up with a sly smile. "*Heavy* breathing?"

I rolled my eyes. "Calm your libido, please."

She looked at me skeptically. "You don't think he's cute? Especially since he's been working out so much..."

"No, I don't think he's cute," I replied, keeping the rest of my thoughts to myself. William wasn't merely "cute," he was *hot.*

And he kissed like Eros himself. Those hands...the way they'd sifted through my hair. I swallowed and looked away.

He wasn't right for me. Or more accurately, *I* wasn't right for *him.*

I *couldn't* be right for him. I was leaving in just three months, and my intuition told me that, if I allowed it, my involvement with William would last longer than that.

We were merely working toward a common cause. We couldn't muddle it with anything else...fantastic kisses or not.

"You know what that tiara means to me." I kept my voice low to keep it from shaking with emotion. "He has to win the duel so he can get it back, and I need to help him."

"But kissing should be involved." She nodded enthusiastically and my face burned even hotter. I faked coughing into my hand, as if the food was too spicy for me. As it turned out, Alex wasn't paying that close of attention. "*I'd* date him if he was into me."

"So would half of the RMRA—the female half, anyway."

"True. But he's into someone else." She smirked at me.

I scoffed at her. "We're just friends."

"Friends can have benefits. You've done friends with benefits before."

I shrugged. "I'm leaving in a few months."

Her face darkened. "Yeah, I know. Time for you to move on like your gypsy ancestors."

I cursed myself. This was a sore subject with Alex.

"*Roma* ancestors. They don't like being called gypsies. And I have no idea if I actually have any Roma blood in me."

She shrugged and didn't meet my gaze. Now she was picking at *her* enchiladas. I ate a few more bites, watching her carefully.

"You okay?" I finally said in response to her silence.

She shrugged again. "I ran into Dr. Zweitberger the other day when I was in the science building."

I raised my brows. "*You* were in the science building? Doesn't that make you break out in a rash?"

She smiled. "There are some cute science nerds over there. Sometimes I hang out. Anyway, your professor recognized me. He asked me when you're coming back to the program."

Finished with my food, I busied myself with cleaning up while avoiding her searching gaze. "Probably not for a while...if ever."

Alex's face fell. "*Seriously?* You have like, what? Two semesters left?"

"Four classes. It's okay. What the hell was I going to do with a physics degree, anyway?"

"Teach, like you said you wanted to."

I laughed. "I said that on a whim."

She speared me with her gaze. "You're amazing with the kids at the refugee center, and you'd be a wonderful science teacher. I know it's your dream to get more girls to study science."

I shrugged. "It would have been nice, but I've moved on from that."

Her lips thinned. "Yeah, that's your specialty, isn't it?"

I took a deep breath in, willing myself not to be irritated with her. Alex wore her heart on her sleeve and always spoke her mind. It was one of the things I loved about her.

She shook her head. "*Jenna...*"

"*Alejandra,*" I mimicked.

She blinked. Oh shit. I could tell she was seconds away from tears.

"*Why* do you do this to yourself? Why do you punish yourself like this?"

I shook my head, folding the foil over the container to ready the leftovers for the fridge.

"It's survivor's guilt, you know." Her voice trembled. "You're always like this after you've gone to the cemetery. Are you afraid other people you love will die, too? So you move on?"

I dropped back into my seat again, letting out air like a tire that had been punctured. I reached up and rubbed my forehead.

Survivor's guilt. That wasn't the first time I'd heard that.

"Let's not fight, Alex."

She shook her head. "I don't want to, either. But I just have to say that I hate what you're doing. You're sabotaging yourself, you know."

"I'm moving on to experience life...to experience new things. That's not a punishment!"

"But what about everyone who cares about you here? Me, Mia, everyone else? *All* your friends. What about Helena?"

"I've moved on from Helena's house, and we're still close. It will be like that with you and me, too."

Her lips curled. "Yeah, sure." She stood up and snatched the container off the table then scurried into the kitchen. I grabbed our dishes and followed her.

"Can I help you get ready for the party?"

She answered quickly. "No, I'm fine. People aren't coming over 'til about eight or nine. I figure we could binge-watch reruns or do a drinking game or whatever. Just hang out." Alex hesitated before adding, "You're going to join us, right?"

I shrugged. "If I'm done with William by then. We'll see. You know I'm not a huge fan of this new Doctor. He's dark and moody."

"Hmmm. I love him. It must be the eyebrows!"

I laughed at her, relieved that the mood between us was a bit lighter. "You're a weirdo."

A couple hours later, William knocked at the apartment door at exactly seven. I raced to answer it, but Alex was quicker. "William! Hey, dude. How are you?"

He nodded. "Hi, Alex. I'm fine. How are you?" Again, he had that weird tone to his voice, as if reciting memorized lines.

"Just grand. Hope you are up for some drinking later because we are watching Doctor Who!"

He frowned. "Reruns? I've already seen every episode twice on Blu-ray."

"Not like this, you haven't. We are drinking and watching with beer goggles on!"

He looked at Alex as if she'd said everything in Spanish.

"Never mind that. Wil is here to work." I motioned to him to follow me back to my bedroom. "Come on, Alex is going to be noisy and disruptive out here."

"*Wil?*" said Alex quietly as I walked by her. I shushed her and led William to my room.

"Sorry, there's not a ton of furniture in here. I don't rent as nice a place as you do. Do you want the chair or the bed?"

"I own it," he answered in a quiet voice as he settled his large frame on the foot of my bed. Probably a good thing, because the wicker chair didn't look sturdy enough to support him. I concluded he had judged wisely to take the bed.

"I'm sorry—what?"

"My house. I own it. I paid off the mortgage last year."

"Oh...oh, that's awesome. It's a nice house. A very nice house, actually. I didn't know they paid artists so well at Draco."

As he stared at the cheap print on the wall, I took the opportunity to stare at *him*. He was wearing jeans tonight and a dark blue t-shirt almost the exact same color. It was a lot of blue, and typically he didn't match his clothes well, but it was more subdued tonight because pretty much anything matched jeans. Still, he filled those jeans well with his long, muscular legs. And his t-shirt looked damn fine, too, stretched over a solid chest and bulging biceps as he leaned back to continue solemnly studying that poster. I almost sighed and certainly could not stop my eyes from traveling over the thick column of his neck and across his broad shoulders.

Then my eyes shot to his mouth with memories of the taste of his lips. *That's not a goodnight kiss,* he'd said. And he was right. Heat invaded my body from my cheeks down my spine, settling in my gut.

I swallowed and forced my eyes away before he caught me ogling like a fool. Like Echo ogling the gorgeous Narcissus until it had become an obsession.

The poster he was currently fascinated with was a print I'd picked up at a flea market. It showed a young woman in a garden at nighttime, her brow crowned with flowers. She was bent over, surveying the party of fairies and other wee folk surrounding her, amidst glowing balls of colorful light. I loved it for its whimsical feel.

"It is the industry standard," he answered, and it took me a few seconds to realize he was responding to my comment about his artist's salary. "I wasn't always paid in money, though. At the start, when there wasn't a lot of money, Adam paid me with stock in the company."

My brows shot up. "Holy crap...for real? That must be worth a fortune now."

He was still staring at the print. I couldn't tell whether he liked it or was horrified by it. "It changes depending on the day and the value of the stock. I don't pay much attention to it. The last I heard from my accountant, my portfolio was worth a little more than fifty-six million dollars," he said as if he were talking hockey scores.

I almost fell off the chair. I knew his cousin had gone from millionaire to billionaire, having started the company on his own, but I had no idea that William himself was a millionaire.

"Uh...wow. Why are you still working?"

He finally pulled his eyes away from the poster and looked at my right shoulder. "What else would I do?"

I laughed. "I don't know…travel all year round? Sit on a different beach every week and read books? I could think of a lot of things."

"The colors in that print are extremely faded from what they should be." Clearly, talking money didn't interest William, given the way he blew off what I'd just said. "That is a famous painting by E. R. Hughes, an English painter of the pre-Raphaelite tradition," he said without looking at it again.

"It's an old poster I bought a few years back. I'm going to give it away when I move."

"When you leave with the Renaissance Faire?"

I shifted in my chair and crossed my legs. William's gaze followed the movement, his eyes settling on my exposed calves. I sat there for a moment, watching him watch me. He wasn't ogling. He was just…studying. Maybe he was memorizing how my legs looked in the shorts so he could draw them on his sketchpad later.

I remembered the drawing he'd shown me at the hockey game— the one of my hand. It was excellent…so realistic. And detailed. Almost lovingly so. I'd never really thought my hand was particularly beautiful, but he'd rendered it beautifully. He'd *made* it beautiful.

I blinked, wondering where that weird thought had come from.

"I've never really lived in one place for a long time. My friend says I have what she calls *želja za putovanjem*—wanderlust. Nothing can nail me down."

"Nails? Wouldn't that hurt?"

I laughed. "Sorry, no. I mean…it's hard for me to stay in one place. Nothing can keep me still."

"Nothing? And…no one?"

I frowned, thinking about that for a moment. I considered the hurt in Alex's eyes when I'd told her I was leaving. And Mia. In fact, most of my friends didn't understand. The people at the Faire got it though. A lot of them were like me. "I'm going to work the Faire for a while, reading Tarot cards."

His expression didn't change. "You believe in that? Fortune-telling?"

"I believe the cards can teach people to follow their own intuition. I'm just there to...help it along. My aunt used to read cards a lot. She taught me before she went back to Bosnia."

He spoke after some hesitation. "I would like you to do that for me sometime. I don't believe in it, though," he added quickly.

I nodded. "I'll read for you. But right now, we need to work on visualization and breathing. We can't have what happened at the hockey game happen at your next duel, right?"

He looked up at me briefly, caught my gaze and then yanked his eyes away. He looked almost...guilty.

"What's up, Wil?"

He shrugged. "I didn't leave because of the crowd."

I blinked. *Well, this was news to me.* "You picked me up and carried me out of the arena like the place was on fire. If I recall correctly, you seemed pretty darned determined to get out of there."

A smile hovered on his lips, and then his eyes flicked to my chest before shifting away just as quickly. Then he colored beautifully. Though William had dark hair and eyes, his skin was pale and it flushed a deep shade of red.

"You gonna tell me why you're blushing, or am I going to have to guess?"

William's jaw clenched and he looked off into the distance, over my shoulder.

"Hmm." I folded my arms. "I was sitting on your lap and..." I remembered the feel of his body underneath mine, the hardness of his chest against my back. It had been pretty darn pleasant for *me,* and maybe—"Oh, I get it. You got turned on."

"Turned on what?"

I mentally groaned. This language thing was a bit of a pain in the ass. "You got...aroused?"

His color deepened. He'd probably been worried what my reaction would be if I knew he'd gotten an erection.

It was both adorable and incredibly arousing. And funny. Because I'd been turned on, too. Feeling his strong arms under mine, his warm breath on the back of my neck. It had been almost impossible to concentrate on the game.

Suddenly, I started laughing.

"Why are you laughing?"

"Because it's funny. Did you think I was going to slap you?"

He frowned. "No. I just thought you'd call me a pervert."

"It was a natural reaction, Wil. I can't fault you for that. I was the one who volunteered to sit on your lap, remember? And I know how male anatomy works."

His eyes narrowed. "How well do you know?"

My eyes flicked meaningfully to his crotch. "I know enough. So *that's* why you bailed—I mean, left?"

He rubbed a hand down his thigh. "Yes."

"Well, next time just tell me. We're adults here. Don't be silly, okay?"

"I'm never silly."

I cleared my throat. "How about we work on visualization now before everyone gets here..."

I instructed him to sit cross-legged on the floor facing me, our knees touching. Or rather, my knees touched his shins, as his legs were longer than mine.

His whole focus seemed to be on where our legs touched each other. "You okay? No, um, sudden reactions?"

He scowled but didn't reply.

"Okay, so this should be easier for you because you naturally think in pictures. We're going to ground and center using a mental image..."

"What am I picturing? TIE fighters? Snow speeders? Imperial walkers?"

"A tree."

He raised his brows and smiled. "Ewoks?"

"Nope, no Ewoks. A tree. *You* are a tree."

"But—"

"It's pretend, Wil. Imagine you are a great oak tree and you are going to connect with the earth. You are going to be solid and sturdy and unflappable as a tree. You will be dug in so deeply that not even the strongest storm can blow you over. Because your roots run deep into the earth."

He was staring at me as if I'd sprouted a third eye on my forehead.

"No, I'm not crazy. Close your eyes and imagine roots extending from your body into the ground below us."

"But the ground isn't below us. We're two floors above the ground."

I sighed. "Just do it." His eyes snapped closed. "Good. Hold out your hands. It might help to connect with me." I rested my palms on his and clasped his hands.

"Now breathe in and send those roots down into the soil below you."

"Out of my butt?"

"What?"

"Are the roots coming out of my butt?"

"Come on! You aren't taking this seriously."

I moved to pull my hands back from his, but his fingers tightened around mine. In that moment, something startling happened. It felt like...a pulse of heat passed from him to me. If I were more new-agey than I actually was, I'd have called it an energy exchange or said that I'd felt his aura.

But no, this was something much more basic. I licked my lips, acknowledging this in-your-face physical attraction.

William was a handsome guy, and though he seemed to be a man of few—and sometimes exasperating—words, he was also accustomed to getting his way. I attempted to pull my hands back again, but he still didn't release them.

"I don't want to let go of you right now," he said in a low voice.

I took a deep breath through my nose and caught a whiff of him. He smelled like soap and clean goodness. And now the tension thickened as my gaze slid down the strong column of his neck to his chest. "Don't forget to breathe," I murmured.

"I won't forget that."

I didn't reply. I was talking to myself, not him.

"I don't want you to leave with the Faire, Jenna," he said quietly in that strange monotone of his.

"What about you?" I asked. "Don't you ever get wanderlust?"

He shook his head. "Lust, yes. Wanderlust, no."

Lust...there was plenty of that going on right now as I focused on William's broad chest. His t-shirt had a picture of a knight in a full suit of armor with the words '*Dressed To Kill*' beneath it. I wondered if he understood the play on words—or even the irony—and I surmised that someone had given him the shirt as a gift.

My grip on his hands loosened as I became aware of the rough calluses beneath my palms. William was a man who worked with his hands—all raw talent and masculinity. And the more I became aware of that, the warmer I felt—and the harder it was to breathe. His fingers squeezed, as if anticipating that I would pull away.

I began to fidget as he scrutinized my neck and then my shoulder, his gazing moving as high as my chin. "Why would I want to move on when everything and everyone I love most is where I am now?"

Longing. Loss. *Pain.* Something about his words made me ache, and I hated feeling this way, which is why I rarely allowed myself to wallow in those feelings.

"Can you—can you let go of my hands now?" I said in a tiny voice. And he did—slowly—but without pulling them away.

I removed my hands while I tried to analyze where this pang was coming from. My mind raced to figure out a way to make it stop.

As we continued to sit there, William's eyes drifted back to the poster, then over to the bulletin board hanging next to it. He gingerly rose to his feet and walked directly over to the board. Something must have caught his eye.

He reached up and traced the decorative scrollwork on the border of Maja's wedding invitation with a long index finger. "This is nice work. Hand drawn."

"That's my sister's wedding invitation. Apparently, her fiancé likes to draw as a hobby."

He nodded and moved to get a closer look, his eyes skimming over the text. They were lovingly handmade invitations instead of the fancy, mass-produced kind. And Maja had taken care to have some printed in English to send to her old friends in the US. "In June," he said quietly. "Will you be attending?"

I shrugged. "I thought I'd go back for a couple weeks...spend some time with my family before the Faire moves north at the end of the month."

He nodded but said nothing before turning back to me.

There was something so refreshing about William. So unassuming. He was comfortable in his own skin and didn't try to make himself out to be something he wasn't.

And he never boasted. The offhanded way he'd let on that he was beyond financially secure was evidence of that. The car he drove, the house he lived in...both were nice, but not over the top. Nothing about him screamed small-penised man trying desperately to overcompensate. He was Doug's polar opposite in practically every way.

I had to admit to myself, if to no one else, that I wanted William. Maybe the card I'd pulled last night really was calling me a fool. A sudden wave of sadness washed over me.

I leaned back on my hands. "I think I could use a drink. How about you? Do you drink?"

"Sometimes. But not to excess. And not when I'm driving."

"Let's get drunk, Wil." And before he could answer, I pushed up to stand and turned to leave the room. I didn't want to chance him detecting my melancholy—or that strong pull I was feeling toward him. With alcohol, I could convince myself that it was all about my vulnerable state and blind attraction to a handsome guy. Nothing more.

And as with everything else, this, too, would pass.

10
WILLIAM

I'D COME OVER TO SPEND TIME ALONE WITH JENNA—AND TO WORK on this crowd issue, too, I guess. I never imagined I'd be sitting in a circle of my friends playing drinking games and watching my cousin get inebriated while his fiancée laughed. In fact, I'd never seen Adam drunk before.

"Never have I ever...watched Star Wars in just my underwear," Mia says with a smirk while looking straight at Adam.

"Aw, shit," he says and then grabs his glass of beer and chugs it. "Half of this should count as a shot."

"Not according to the FDA's alcohol content guidelines. Drink up, son, or hit the hard stuff," says Heath, who holds up his shot glass and clinks it with Adam's beer mug. Heath downs his shot while the women laugh.

"Fine." Adam sighs, then holds his mug high in the air and lets out a huge belch. Everyone is laughing and teasing him, especially Mia.

"Damn, I'm gonna need to switch to light beer or donkey piss. They taste about the same," he mutters.

"Oh no, we're getting you wasted tonight. I plan to use every opportunity to make you drink," says Heath. "C'mon, everyone, who wants to see Adam Drake soused?"

Everyone raises their hands but Adam and me.

"Me! Me, definitely me!" Kat laughs, and Mia makes a face at her.

"The Force is with you, young Bowman, but you are not a Jedi yet," Adam says to Heath. I wonder what the quote has to do with the drinking game.

And this game is a strange one. We are supposed to make a statement about something we have never done, and if the other people in the room *have* done it, then they are supposed to drink. The object of the game, of course, is to get intoxicated. I wonder why we need a game to do that. Why don't we just sit around the table and drink?

"*My* turn, then," Adam says, and he gets a funny look on his face. I've seen him make that face before...when he's planning something devious. "Never have I ever sucked a dick."

"Ah, come on!" Heath and all the women clink glasses and drink. Adam looks extremely happy with himself.

Me, I'm not happy at all. As I watch Jenna laugh and drink, I feel that same tight curl of jealousy inside. Who is she thinking of? Doug? Another man? Other *men*? Suddenly, I want to hit something. I don't like imagining her with other men.

I only want to imagine her with *me*.

But I've trained myself not to go there. If I expect something, I don't handle the disappointment well when it doesn't happen. Suddenly, though, I *am* imagining it.

Her head is turned up to mine, her pale hair cascading over her shoulders. Her mouth is open and she's kissing me like she did last weekend…like the heroine in a movie. Like Arwen kissed Aragorn in *The Fellowship of the Ring*. Though we aren't standing by a giant waterfall and that annoying music isn't playing super loud in the background.

The others are continuing the game and I'm ignoring everything that's going on around me, caught up in that image.

"Earth to William!" Alex is saying. I haven't had to drink once tonight. I doubt it's going to change now.

"What?" I ask.

"I said, 'Never have I ever had sex with a woman,'" Alex repeats.

Everyone is looking at me, though I suspect Adam already knows the answer because he's talking now, saying let's just move on to the next one. He's trying to protect me. Since he came to live with us when he was thirteen and I was eleven, it's always been like that. We might genetically be cousins, but in many ways, he's my older brother.

But this time, instead of accepting his help, I shake my head. "Neither have I," I say. And I make it through another round without having to drink.

It's Heath's turn. He glares at Alex. "Well, since Alex stole mine, then I need to amend what I was going to say. So…never have I ever made out with a chick."

The other men drink and so does Jenna. Everyone makes noises of surprise. After she downs her shot, she looks up, eyes round and wide. "What?"

Alex starts laughing. "Don't mind the men, they are all just picturing it—and getting turned on."

"Yep. I kissed a girl—and I liked it!" She starts to sing the Katy Perry song and everyone else laughs.

Finally, I have a chance to drink, so I down a shot and immediately start coughing and sputtering. I've had tequila before, but I don't really like it. Beer is much better. Maybe I'll be like Adam and switch to beer.

"William!" Heath says, slurring his words. "You devil... Details! I need details."

I shake my head. "You aren't going to get them. Play your game. I guarantee that you aren't going to get me drunk before you pass out."

"Challenge accepted!" Heath says.

It's Mia's turn again. "Shit...this is getting hard!"

"That's what she said," replies Adam with a smirk.

Mia frowns, looking at him between narrowed eyes. "You'd better change that pronoun, mister. And quickly, unless you want damage to your most favorite body parts."

"Hey, they're *your* favorites, too. Okay, how about....that's what *you* said?"

Mia laughs, snorting through her nose. "Much better. All right, let's take this game in a nonsexual direction..."

"That's no fun," says Jordan, who is elbowed by his girlfriend, April. She still seems flushed and angry from the previous round, when Jordan was the only one who had to drink to, "Never have I ever been in a threesome."

We end up playing three more rounds. Jordan's challenge, "Never have I ever kissed my step-cousin," elicits a lot of swearing and rude gestures from a now fully intoxicated Adam.

Just as I'd predicted, I end up the only sober person at the end of the game. I'm silently gloating about it, and I don't even care.

Afterward, everyone sits around, either talking or continuing to drink until they pass out (Heath), or trying to sober up by making coffee (Adam). I end up going back into Jenna's room to get my shoes and stop short when I find her curled up on her bed, crying.

It's not loud sobbing. In fact, there's hardly any noise coming from her, and the noise that does come out sounds like a kitten. She doesn't even notice I'm here. Do I grab my shoes and leave, or do I try to comfort her? I have no idea how I can comfort her, and I could end up making it worse. I'm frozen with indecision until she wipes her cheeks with the back of her hand and sighs. I perceive that she's no longer actively crying.

I sit down on the bed next to her and, without understanding why I'm doing it, I stroke her hair...like I'm stroking a kitten. She rolls over and looks at me, then sniffs loudly. "Turn off the light and come back here," she whispers.

I do as she asks and then feel my way back to her bed. She reaches out, grasps my wrist and tugs. I think this means she wants me to sit on the bed again. I do so, but she tugs again. "Would you lie down next to me? I just need to be with someone right now."

Someone? Just anyone? Or...*me*?

In spite of those questions whirling around in my brain, I lie next to her. But I try not to touch her. In seconds, she has scooted over, resting her head on my shoulder, pulling my other arm around her.

I'm so tense that I'm sure she can feel it. She shifts her head, settling closer against me, and I can smell her hair again. That same smell. It fills me with...something. Makes it seem as if my blood is speeding up, rushing through my veins faster. And it's hard to swallow, too.

"Relax, Wil. Take a deep breath. Or does this bother you? Would you rather not be touched?"

I inhale a deep breath and let it go. She adjusts her head to look at my face, though it's dark so I can't imagine what she can see. I can't see her very well, either, but I can definitely smell her. The cloud of her scent enveloping me. It's enough to cause vertigo. And it really *does* feel like the room is spinning.

I clear my throat. "Why are you crying, Jenna? Are you sad about your tiara?"

She shakes her head and is silent for a long time, then she sniffs again and swipes a hand across her cheek before leaning into me. "I get like this sometimes when I drink too much."

"Drinking makes you sad?"

"Only if I'm sad before I start drinking. It just amplifies it." I picture a microphone echoing in a loud room, screeching, hurting my ears. Her sadness is hurting her like that?

"Then you shouldn't drink when you're sad."

She lets out a quiet, gentle laugh. "Impeccably logical, Wil. You should have been a Vulcan."

"I've been told that before. Why are you sad?"

She's suddenly still and very quiet, then she shrugs. "Just a long day…got off to a bad start. I'll be okay once I sleep it off."

I turn my head but just slightly. Her hair is tickling my nose, so my choices are to turn away so I no longer feel it or press my face more firmly into her hair. I chose the latter. I've heard of people talking about a "head rush" before—this must be what they're describing.

Jenna's hand is moving across my chest. It's a light, fluttery touch, and I hate that it makes me uncomfortable. I capture her hand under one of mine to stop it.

"Do you not like that?"

I take a moment to think about the question and how I want to answer it. "I don't like light touches. It feels like my skin is crawling."

"So you don't like to be touched at all, or...?"

"I don't like to be touched lightly."

Suddenly, the pressure from her hand increases as she presses harder. My heart starts to race directly under her hand, which rests firmly on my sternum.

"How's that?"

"Better," I answer, but my voice is a rasp. It's suddenly harder to speak and my mouth is dry. I'm almost obsessed with the thought of kissing her again.

It's a weird word, kiss. With so many different meanings, it confuses me sometimes. A kiss can be a kind of chocolate, it can be a kiss of death, it can be truelove's kiss. It can be the chaste pressure of lips against a cheek in greeting or a momentary show of affection. But that same word can also describe incredible, unfathomable passion. Like Jack and Rose's forbidden kisses in *Titanic,* though their love was a doomed one. Or that expression of undying love and a promise of self-sacrifice, like Arwen's promise to Aragorn when she declares she will give up the immortal life of an elf in order to be with him as a mortal.

"Was that true...what you said during the game?" she says in a quiet voice.

"I don't recall lying during that game."

"When you said you've never slept with someone—I mean...are you a virgin?"

I think about how I want to answer that question, and the silence stretches on.

She shifts, turning toward me. "I don't think less of you because of it, if that's why you aren't answering. In fact, it's just the opposite."

"Really?"

"I'm actually just surprised. You're very handsome. There are women in the clan who would jump at the chance to...jump you." All that does is produce images of people jumping in my mind—on a pogo stick, on a trampoline, off a cliff—though I'm vaguely aware that she's referring to sex and not actual jumping.

"I've had the opportunity. I chose not to."

Her head lifts from the pillow. "Really? You didn't want to?"

"I want to. With the right person." I wait for her to react in the number of ways I've heard before...disbelief or disgust or with questions about my sexuality.

"That means that sex means more to you than it does most guys."

She's right, and something inside of my chest twists at her words. It sounds as if she admires that difference, which has been both a blessing and a curse to me in my life. I *am* different.

But Jenna understands me. It's been a long time since anyone really has.

And I can no longer resist. I want more of what we shared last weekend. I turn to her and press my mouth to hers. She lets out a little gasp, and I might have pulled away if I wasn't already desperate for her.

11
JENNA

ILLIAM'S TONGUE BREACHED MY LIPS, SLIPPING IN effortlessly without asking permission this time. He'd assumed authority and I happily ceded it to him—even more happily when his hand slid from my head, down my back, to my hip and then slowly to my butt.

What the hell was this? My body was trembling like *I* was the virgin, not him. Suddenly, I couldn't catch my next breath. There was so much here in this moment, and I was almost overwhelmed by the swift rush of feelings.

I wasn't drunk on liquor anymore. I was drunk on *him*. His smell. His taste. The feel of his hard, masculine body beside mine.

Twenty minutes ago, I'd retreated into the dark, accompanied only by aching thoughts about today's visit to the cemetery and my potential lifetime of loneliness. I'd been licking my wounds when William had entered and immediately honed in on my emotional state. It was humbling to have him here, but impulse alone had driven me to ask for his comfort.

And he'd offered it with no aim to take it any further. He'd stroked my hair and held me in his arms, where I felt so safe. Like I could sleep for a decade wrapped in his iron embrace. Like I was Hera asking Hypnos, the god of sleep, for the blessings of peaceful, uninterrupted rest.

What did this mean? And why was it making me ache with even more longing than before? For the love of the goddess...

My heart raced, but it wasn't just from the pangs of desire. It was fear. Pure, screaming fear put me in fight-or-flight mode while playing tug-of-war with hungry, burning lust that wanted more, more, *more.*

When William's callused hand clasped the tender skin of my neck, desire won out. The rough feel of his fingers was maddening, ratcheting up the lust a few more notches from the already blazing level of our kisses.

I placed my hands on his firm chest, sliding over every plane. I itched to get under his shirt and vowed to have his clothes off in the next half hour. This hot hunk of man-virgin was not going to stay that way much longer if I had anything to say about it.

Needing to be even closer to him, I pushed my breasts hard against his chest.

He let out a long, hot breath against my mouth, which was cut short by a noise at the door. Another person in the room. "Hey Jenna, have you seen my—?"

I froze, only now realizing that William was lying completely on top of me at this point. In the dim light spilling in from the hallway, I could just make out Mia standing frozen in her spot.

Slowly, sluggishly, I straightened while my entire body protested being pulled away from William. He rolled back, freeing me from under him, and then he immediately sat up without looking directly at his cousin's fiancé. His eyes were on the floor like a chastened schoolboy, and that kind of annoyed me.

What on earth did either of us have to be ashamed of? We were both consenting adults who weren't in any sort of committed relationship with other people, for heaven's sake.

We sat next to each other on the bed and I adjusted my shirt, thinking that if he were any other guy, he would have had his hands up my shirt during the first minute of that kiss.

But instead, he'd gently cradled my head in his big hands. *How incredibly sweet.* I glanced at him and then at the doorway, where Mia was still standing with her mouth hanging open.

I met her gaze, raising my brows.

"Uh…oh, sorry. Adam's finally decided he's not going to be sober enough to drive home anytime soon, so he called for a car to come get us. Heath passed out, and we've been drawing all over him with a Sharpie to pass the time. He's probably spending the night on your living room floor. I came in here looking for my phone."

"It's on my desk. You plugged it into my charger, remember?"

Mia was staring fixedly at her stepbrother's bowed head and didn't respond right away. Finally, she roused herself. "Oh, yeah…um. That's right. Duh…losing my memory at the old age of twenty-four."

I looked away and William fidgeted beside me, folding his hands over the sizeable bulge in his jeans. *So awkward.*

Mia walked over to my desk and pulled her phone off the charger, then stuffed it into her back pocket. Turning back at me, she said, "Jenna, can I…talk to you for a sec?"

William stood from the bed, still conspicuously covering his crotch area. "Excuse me. I need to use the bathroom."

Mia watched him go with concerned eyes and then closed the door after him. I reached over and flipped on the desk lamp, blinking at the unwelcome light. My *friend* was staring at me like a reproachful mother who had found birth control pills in her teenage daughter's purse or something.

"Can I ask what's going on between you and William?"

I clenched my teeth. How was this any of her business, stepsister or not? "You can ask."

She tilted her head and grimaced at me.

I sighed. "Well, the only thing you saw was kissing, right? So that's what was going on between us. Kissing."

Mia blew out a breath, also expelling a self-conscious laugh. "I don't mean to sound like an asshole. I'm just...be careful, okay?"

"We're all adults here, Mia. We know what we're doing."

Her uncomfortable smile grew and she shifted from one leg to the other. "I know that—I know. It's just that you're leaving soon. And given your dating history..."

I blinked. Now Mia was singing the same song as Alex—*and* Helena! "The number of guys I've dated is irrelevant. Just because you never dated anyone before Adam—"

"That's not what I meant. I'm sorry. Of course you can date whoever you want and for however long you want, and you know that you'd get no judgment from me. At. All. I'm just worried about the whole dynamic going on here. What happens when you date and then break up? We're all a part of the same group of friends—"

"Oh, you're worried about that? Ross and Rachel did just fine." I shrugged.

Mia's jaw dropped. "Ross and Rachel aren't reality. They dated and broke up over and over again and hung out with their mutual friends with no consequences. Life isn't an episode of *Friends*, Jenna. If something like that happens...it could change everything."

And if anyone had learned lessons about the hard realities of life, it was Mia. She'd had a pretty horrible year last year, having been sick with a life-threatening disease. I looked into her dark eyes and saw the tiniest hint of something I hadn't seen before—an almost haunted look from unspoken traumas that I wasn't privy to.

"But I'm going away anyway." For some reason that I didn't examine too closely, my voice trembled.

Mia took a step toward me. "I'm sorry I'm being a pain. But...William means a lot to me, and I'm going to be the one picking up the pieces when you leave. Don't hurt him, okay?"

"I don't want to hurt him, Mia." And it was true. I had no desire to hurt him.

But I *did* want to be the one to pop William's very delicious cherry. Why not? He had to lose it sometime, and if the kisses we'd shared had been any indication, it could be very, *very* fun.

There was a tap at the door. Thinking it was William, I decided to end this awkward exchange. "Come in!"

The door open and another dark-haired man—who actually looked a lot like William—poked his head in. "You ready to go?" Adam said. "I really need to get home and crash."

Mia turned to him with a grin. "Oh, did all that beer finally catch up with you? Poor baby...even if you do fall asleep right away, you're going to be up half the night peeing it all out."

Adam's mouth curved in a lopsided smile, and he looked at her with sleepy eyes filled with love. "I love it when you talk dirty to me."

Mia laughed so hard she snorted, and Adam and I both teased her about it as we headed to the living room. It was as she said. Heath was passed out on the floor with drawings on every inch of his exposed skin. Someone had given him a wicked Victorian-style handlebar mustache and pointed goatee, along with Vulcan eyebrows and a pirate-style eye patch drawn over one eye. He had writing all over his arms, neck and even the part of his stomach where his t-shirt rode up and showed his belly.

I laughed. "Man is he going to be pissed when he wakes up and sees that."

"Meh..." Mia shrugged. "Serves him right for getting so hammered."

I studied Mia's best friend on the floor. "Connor's leaving to go back to Ireland soon, isn't he? Maybe Heath really needed to get drunk. Are they breaking up?"

Mia looked at him with concerned eyes. "I'm not clear on all the details of what's going on between them. Heath's not talking much. But we should make sure he's not alone for the next little while."

Adam rolled his eyes. "I officially want no part of babysitting him. Kat can do it. She's his roommate."

William walked in from the direction of the bathroom and stood quietly beside me.

Adam and Mia offered Kat a ride home, which she enthusiastically accepted.

"Can you make sure Heath makes it home all right tomorrow?" Mia asked her as they walked out.

"Yeah. I'll come get his hopeless ass."

They bid us goodbye and then left. With Heath passed out on the floor, William and I were the only two conscious people in the living room.

"So, um, will I see you tomorrow at the regional market?" I asked him, already knowing the answer.

William brightened. "Yes, I have to deliver some items to clan members. I've been in the workshop all week after work."

Suddenly, I envisioned him hammering away, biceps bulging and flexing, wearing nothing but his leather apron over those jeans.

"Would you like a ride there?" His innocuous question jolted me out of my lust-filled vision.

I swallowed, then glanced at him out of the corner of my eye. "Sure...how about we share some breakfast first?"

"How early would you like me to come get you for breakfast?"

I bit my lip, flummoxed by his oversight of my obvious hint. Then I stepped toward him, took his large hand in mine and said, "You could just...stay the night."

His reaction was subtle. With his eyes fixed on our interlocked hands, his dark brows lowered as if in concentration. "I'm not certain what you are asking, but I have an idea. And if it's the wrong idea..."

"You're not misreading me, okay? I want you to stay and spend the night with me."

He visibly—and noisily—swallowed, and his fingers closed around my hand. "Well, as I told you in the bedroom, I haven't been—"

"I know that. It doesn't matter to me." In fact, in some ways it made it even hotter. I found the idea of being his first powerfully arousing.

I took another step toward him so that my torso pressed against his. Angling my face up so that my lips were just a few inches from his, I said, "Did you feel it, too? When we were kissing?"

He exhaled, his breath tickling my nose. "Feel what?"

"That connection between us? The chemistry?"

"All I know is that it felt good." His hand tightened around mine, almost painfully so. "And I want more."

I brushed my lips against his. "Me too...so stay with me."

He stood stock-still for a long moment, and I brought my hand around to brush along his back as if to further my case.

"No." He said it with cold finality and completely divorced from emotion.

I frowned. "You don't want to?"

"Oh, I want to."

My lower abdomen brushed against him, and I felt it—he was erect again. I shamelessly used a little friction to sell him on the idea. "I want you, Wil."

His head bent to rest on my shoulder. "I don't want something temporary, Jenna. I want more than just once."

I froze. William lifted his head, his gaze not quite catching mine before skating away and fixing on the middle of my forehead instead. I cleared my throat. "Well, it doesn't have to be a one-night stand."

He sighed, stepping back and releasing my hand. "I won't have sex with you knowing that next week or next month you'll be with someone else. If I have you, I want it to be permanent. *Forever.*"

I shook my head. "I don't do permanent, William. *Ever.*"

He scowled. "I understand. Good night, Jenna."

My jaw dropped. Was this really happening? When had a guy ever turned down my proposition to go to bed? I didn't extend them often—I didn't have to—but the answer was *never* 'no.' Not until this minute. What the *hell?*

William turned to leave, but my voice seemed to be caught in my throat. His rejection was hitting a lot harder than it should. I grabbed his hand. "Wait. Don't you want to just...get it over with?"

He froze in his tracks, his body language stiff, but he didn't pull his hand away from mine. Slowly, he turned back to me and said, "I'm surprised you don't understand. You said in the bedroom that it means more to me than it does to other guys. Why would you think I'd ever want it to be something to 'just get over with'? I've had that opportunity before and didn't take it..." His voice died out and he shook his head forcefully. "Good night, Jenna," he said, tugging his hand gently from mine. "I'll pick you up at nine-thirty for the regional market tomorrow."

"Good night." I felt a weird lump in my throat as I watched him go. William was stubborn...resolved. I'd already worked those things out about his personality. But he was a man, and he was obviously attracted to me. How long could he hold out? He wasn't a superhuman, after all. I'd respect his wishes while secretly hoping he had a weak spot somewhere in there.

Alex entered from the kitchen moments after the door closed. She took one look at Heath spread out on the floor and said, "That doesn't look comfortable. Can you do me a favor and grab the extra pillow off my bed? I'm gonna get a blanket for him."

When I got back into the living room, she was crouched beside him, trying to roll him over. "Ugh, can you help me with this? I want to put him on his side in case he gets sick, but he's so damn huge."

Heath was at least six-four and extremely well built. He must have weighed two-fifty, at least. And Alex was a slight five-foot with a curvy build. I was taller, but stick thin. I had no idea how the two of us were going to move him, but somehow we managed.

"I'm exhausted," I said, stifling a yawn. "And I have the regional market tomorrow. I'm hoping to make some decent money doing readings."

"At twenty bucks a pop for fifteen minutes work, I'll say! I'd do it too if my mom wouldn't lose her shit about me playing with *cartas del Diablo*. Speaking of which...when do you start full-time at that? And when are you going to quit the refugee center? I bet they're bummed you're leaving."

Yawning loudly, I didn't meet her gaze when I said, "I'm about to pass out, cutie. Let's chat tomorrow."

I turned to go into my room, but Alex followed me inside. "They don't know you're leaving yet, do they?"

Reaching into my t-shirt, I unhooked my bra and pulled it out of my sleeves. "They will...soon."

"Still don't have the courage to break it to them?"

I shrugged. "They know I'm strapped for money and they can't give me a raise. I don't have the heart to even ask. They'll understand when I tell them I have to move on."

Alex cocked her head to the side. "It's not just about the money, though, is it? Are you really feeling antsy to move on, or is this all just some weird philosophy of yours? It's like you're that lady in the movie *Chocolat*. She always went where the wind took her, too."

I rolled my eyes. Romantic notions were Alex's bread and butter. "We've been over this before. I *do* need the money so I can make it back to Maja's wedding."

"Hopefully with the tiara."

My heart lurched. "Yeah, hopefully."

"So how's William coming along? Is he any closer to being able to win the big duel?"

I sighed. "He's getting there, but I'm hoping to take him to another crowded place. Problem is, it needs to be something entertaining enough to entice him. I'm thinking the movies or...I don't know."

"Why not Disneyland? It's five miles away."

I sighed dreamily. "You know how much I love that place, but...I don't have the funds to go to Disney right now."

She shrugged. "That's easy. I can still bum discount tickets off my former colleagues. I think you should go for it. After all, it *is* the happiest place on earth, right? Who could say no to that?"

12
WILLIAM

I SHAKE MY HEAD AS I GRIP THE STEERING WHEEL TIGHTER. "NO," I repeat.

"But it's Disneyland! Who could say no to Disneyland?" Jenna asks.

"I just did." I keep my eyes on the road and stop at the red light. Jenna is laughing, but I can't tell if it's at my answer or me. Maybe both.

"When was the last time you went?"

The memory of that visit flashes through my mind. I was six. My mother had started taking us for regular visits again but had insisted that she couldn't handle me for long periods of time. Things had gone all right until that horrible trek through Adventureland.

We'd been walking very close to the Jungle Cruise ride when shots were fired—from a cap gun. I was terrified by the sudden loud noise and unequipped to overcome my fear. I couldn't breathe, and when she tried to pull me along, I'd refused to walk, lying down on the ground while other park guests filed around me. I'd screamed and cried as she dragged me alongside her, cursing the entire time. Typically, when I had my episodes—my mom called them "meltdowns"—she became mean, yelling and calling me all the same things the kids at school called me.

"Why do you have to be such an idiot, Liam? I brought you and your sister here to have fun, and now you're ruining it. Britt's crying because of you. Stop it right now."

"Hey." Jenna puts her hand on my shoulder. "You okay?"

I tense and then shake my head. "I don't have good memories of that place. Especially the Jungle Cruise."

She turns and looks at me. "Well then, we could make some good memories. What about the Indiana Jones ride? Or the new version of Space Mountain? Were those there the last time you went?"

I shook my head. We'd never made it to Tomorrowland. My mother had called my dad and insisted he come get me. She'd spent the rest of the day there with Britt and hadn't brought her home until the next day. I'll never forget overhearing her telling my dad about how much fun they had together after I left. Or the words Britt said to me as she handed me candy that she'd bought with her very own spending money.

"I'm sorry, Liam. I wish you could have gone on more rides with me."

I'd always wondered why my sister was sorry. My mother wasn't.

She'd never tried to take me again after that, but continued to take Britt a few times a year. In fact, I was rarely invited over to my mother's house, and when I *was* invited, it seldom happened. Dad had tried hard to make me feel better, saying those were special father-son days. But he'd never succeeded. The only thing I felt was broken...so broken not even my mother could love me.

"I'm sorry, Wil. Do you want to talk about it?"

I blink, surprised by the realization that I do want to talk about it. "I had a bad experience at Disneyland as a child. And then my mother...she took my sister there often, but not me."

Jenna shifts her eyes back to the road, her hand slipping down my arm. "Oh. I'm sorry. Did she do that a lot? Favor your sister over you?"

"She didn't know how to handle me. It was difficult for her."

"You don't have to make excuses for her, William. And that statement makes it seem like you blame yourself for *her* shortcomings."

"I do. And how is stating the truth making excuses for her?"

"Because the way you state it shapes how you think—about her and about yourself. When the voice inside your head is saying negative things about you, then you have to find a way to change it."

"There are no voices in my head, Jenna. Just pictures. Lots of pictures."

"You have feelings."

I signal a right turn at the stop sign and follow through. "Yes, I have feelings too."

"You also have the power to rewrite your history, you know."

Her words run over me like a rushing river. I picture stacks of history books and an ancient parchment with an old-fashioned quill and ink. "I have no idea what that means," I say as I pull into the parking lot at the Yorba Regional Park—a beautiful, natural space situated along the bank of the wetlands of the Santa Ana River.

"It means you can change those negative associations and your attitude toward past events. You can change your perspective. Like...you can reprogram and frame those memories in the context where you're not blaming yourself, because you *weren't* to blame."

I turn to her, and for a split second our eyes meet. Her gaze stabs through me like a pointed lance. "Do you do that? If you did, maybe you wouldn't have to run away to a new place."

Her mouth drops open and then snaps shut, her blue eyes wide. I don't move a muscle while I wait for her answer. Her face flushes dark and she turns to gather her bag before climbing out of the cab of my truck then slamming the door—too hard. I slip out of my seat and go to the back of the truck. She faces me there, her arms stiff, her fists balled up, her face still flushed. She's just as beautiful as ever, and every time I notice, it makes it hard to swallow and sometimes hard to breathe.

"That wasn't nice of you," she says between her teeth.

"What?"

"What you just said."

"About how you run away? Why does the truth make you mad?"

"Because I'm *not* running away."

"So you're...walking away?"

She blows out a breath and her eyes roll up to the sky. "You make me crazy."

"I get told that a lot."

She licks her bottom lip with her small, pink tongue, and I immediately think about how it felt to have that tongue in my mouth. I've kissed exactly three women in my lifetime. One was a girl who said I was her boyfriend in high school, even though we never went on dates. Another was my roommate for a few years when I first moved out. She tried kissing me on different occasions and had made a similar offer to Jenna's last night. I'd told her no, too.

And now the third—Jenna.

But her kisses were different. It felt like I was drowning and waking up and suffocating and winning an impossible victory, all at the same time. It was overwhelming but also calming. My body felt like it was on fire and shivering in ice, standing perfectly still and also speeding incredibly fast down a racetrack.

I want that feeling again. I want *her*. And not just her kisses. I want everything. Everything she offered me...*and more.*

But I don't want it once. I don't want it for a week or a month, or even a few months. And that's what will happen, too. I'll be left here alone, burning for more of her.

I don't like that I feel like this already—that she has this much power over my thoughts and feelings. It makes me feel vulnerable. I don't like that feeling.

"I'm sorry you're angry," I say. And I really am. "I just speak the truth. I say what's on my mind, and I have no idea when it's appropriate or not."

She's looking down now, fiddling with something in her bag. I know she's brought her Tarot cards to do fortune readings for people who pay her. I wonder if she believes they are true. Maybe she follows what the cards tell her. Maybe *they* are what make her move on. "Is it the cards?"

She looks up at me. "What?"

"Do the cards tell you to move along? You've attended two different colleges, and you just dropped out of your Physics program without finishing. According to Alex, you've never spent longer than three or four years in one place. And you are leaving again soon. So if you aren't running away, then why do you move on?"

She shrugs and I start pulling items out of the back of my truck. Everything is meticulously labeled so that it's easier to deliver the goods. Shovels here, buckles there, gardening implements for Anita, our herbalist. She loves to use period-authentic gardening tools.

Jenna has her head turned, looking out over the park, when she begins speaking to me between clenched teeth. "I'm *not* running away. Maybe I've made it my life's goal to continue challenging myself to experience new things."

"Maybe? So you aren't sure?"

Her eyes close and she's muttering under her breath. It sounds like she's counting. Her face blotchy, she spins around and walks away, calling over her shoulder that she'll see me later when she doesn't feel like hitting me.

I doubt she could hit me very hard, or even that she really wants to. But I frown at the thought that I've angered her. As usual, I have no idea how I did it.

Once I've gathered all my items, I make my rounds, finding my friends from RMRA at various booths where they've spread out their wares. Among others, there's a spinner, a weaver, a seamstress, a woman who makes authentic woolen stockings and a silversmith who designs jewelry. Ann, an international student from Somalia, has ordered some new buckles for the leather belts she makes and sells. I'm still a beginner so it took me a few tries to get them right, but I'm pleased with the final results.

We've gotten permission from the city to spread our items out on tables in one corner of the park. The public wanders by to look at the booths, as do members of other RMRA clans in the area, who bring their own wares to sell or barter. I don't sell my items, since I don't need the money. I do it for the fun of learning how to craft things in an authentic manner. It makes my fellow clan members happy, and I don't have many friends so I take this seriously. They are friends I don't want to lose, so I try not to think about the possibility that if I lose this duel, I will lose them.

I see Doug in the distance. He's using a whetstone to sharpen weapons and tools. Like me, he doesn't need the money, but he charges anyway. He's stated many times that people won't value his work unless they pay him for it.

As I move from table to table, people ask me about the duel. Word has gotten around that I'll be banished from the community if Doug wins. Many are upset with him for demanding such unusual terms. But I've accepted it, because if I lose again, I won't count myself worthy to be among them anyway.

"Sir William!" says Thomas, our miller and baker, who has freshly baked artisan bread at his booth. He hands me a roll of sweet bread. "Break your fast with me."

"Good morrow, Thomas. I don't have time. Lots of deliveries today."

He nods and looks at me for a long moment. "Is it true what they're saying about the terms of the duel with Sir Douglas?"

I nod, unsurprised, as this is the third time I've been asked a variation of this question. "It is."

He begins talking and his words start to hit like waves on the beach, because I've just spotted Jenna's bright blond hair in a booth across the way. She's speaking with Agnes, our master seamstress, and admiring the gowns hanging at her booth. There are many beautiful, bright fabrics, but the dress that seems to have caught her eye is various shades of blue. It's the color of the sky at the top then gradually darkens into a deep cerulean, and eventually to midnight blue at the bottom. It has laces up the back and long, flowing sleeves in the style of a medieval lady's gown. The wind catches the skirt in the breeze, and I watch as Jenna runs a hand reverently over the fabric.

I picture her wearing it. How the cornflower shade at the waist of the skirt would match the blue of her eyes. How the sky blue near the neckline would make her skin glow. She's already beautiful, but in that gown she would look like an angel...or a fairy princess. I could paint her portrait as if she were wearing that gown, but it would be better to see her wearing it in real life.

She's laughing along with Agnes before she turns to walk away. After I finish my conversation with the miller, I make my way over to the seamstress's booth.

"Sir William! Well met," she says, giving me the typical medieval-style greeting.

"Well met, goodwife."

"I'm afraid I don't have any requests for you today. Those hangers and hooks you made for me a few months ago are working quite well. I think your craftsmanship is getting so good, you'll work yourself out of business soon."

Her words surprise me. "I would never do less than my best."

"Of course, of course. Now what can I do for you, Sir William? Are you looking for new garb? A doublet perhaps?"

I look at the exquisite dress that Jenna was just admiring. "I want to purchase this gown."

"I don't think it would fit you." Agnes smiles.

"No, it's not for me. I'd like you to tailor it so it fits Mistress Kovac."

Her facial expression changes, but I have no idea how to read it. "I'd love to do that. Would you want it to be a surprise? I could find an excuse to get her measurements."

I reflect on that for a moment. I don't like surprises at all, but I know that many do. And it might be nice to see what effect this surprise would have on her. Perhaps it might convince her to stay. Because ever since last night and the long hours I spent awake remembering the feel of her against me, I know that this is what I need. For her to stay. For her to be mine.

And I'll do whatever it takes to make that happen, even if I have no idea right now what that will be.

"I would like for her to have it in time for the Beltane Ball at the Festival. Is that possible?"

Agnes smiles widely. "More than possible. I could even make you something to match."

I think about that for a moment, unsure how Jenna would interpret such a gesture. Wearing matching clothing might make her think I'm claiming her. Then again, I *want* to claim her.

If she's going to try to run away and never come back, then it's up to me to make that decision impossible, or at least extremely difficult.

"Yes, that would be fine," I tell Agnes.

"Sounds wonderful. I'll take your measurements at the next meeting." I pull out my wallet and hand her two hundred dollars as a down payment. "I'll bill you the balance on delivery."

"Yes, ma'am." Before I leave, I remind myself to say, "Thank you."

I look down toward the end of the row and see that Jenna is now sitting at a table with her friend, Caitlyn, who traces people's silhouettes for a small fee. Jenna is flipping through her Tarot cards, but her eyes are on something else. I follow her gaze and see that she's watching Doug, who is speaking with a new member of our group, a dark-haired woman named Glynnis.

I wonder what Jenna is thinking. Is she angry to see her former boyfriend talking to another woman? Does she still have feelings for him? How strong were her feelings for him?

I decide that I don't want to find out—and that I will do everything in my power to make her forget him. Even if it means wiping him off the face of the Barony of Anaya. I won't risk losing her again.

With purposeful strides, I make my way toward her booth, sink down on the hard, wooden stool in front of her table and plunk down a twenty-dollar bill. I don't believe in fortunes at all, but I *do* believe in watching Jenna's every move and listening to her every word as she tells me mine.

13
JENNA

"WHAT IS IT YOU WISH FROM MISTRESS JENNA?" I asked, trying not to smile.

William's face was expressionless, but it also held somewhat of a challenge, as if to say, "Do your worst."

"I seek the answer to a question," he answered without hesitation. My brows twitched a little with surprise. He'd mentioned the night before that he was skeptical about this, and I was certain my brief answer explaining that the cards functioned as a meditative device didn't dispel his doubts.

I pulled out one of my older decks—the Rider-Waite. It was a classic, with bright colors and beautifully rendered pictures. It was one of the oldest and most well-known Tarot decks around. And something about William just screamed classic to me.

"Take this and handle the cards for a few minutes while thinking about your question. You can shuffle it, cut the cards, whatever. Just generally manipulate them and focus on what you want to know about."

I almost laughed at the expression on his face—clear and obvious disbelief—but he humored me and did as I asked. "Do I tell you my question?"

"If you want. But you don't have to."

After he'd shuffled the cards for a while, I took them back from him and laid out a classic Celtic Cross spread. The results were...extremely surprising. Hardly any Minor Arcana cards.

William's eyes glided over every card. "This is fine artwork." He reached out and traced the edge of one of them—The Hanged Man. A trump card. "Beautiful detail," he breathed.

"The deck is designed around a journey. It tells a very intricate story, but each part of the journey is marked by archetypes. It can be complex, but you can just look at them as...cues for things to think about in your own life. As you make your own journey through life."

His finger tapped the corner of the Hanged Man, which depicted exactly that—a man hanging from a tree upside-down by one leg with the other hooked over the branch, his hands behind his back and his hair hanging loosely toward the ground. "And what does he represent?"

"The Hanged Man is stasis, a rut, a need for change or to learn something new. In Norse mythology, the god Odin hung on the world tree for nine days in order to gain knowledge."

"So you're saying I need to learn something new?"

I shrugged. "Well, actually these should all be read in order, which I can do. But first, I want to point out that the only Minor Arcana card you drew is the King of Cups."

"There are suits? Like with playing cards?"

I nodded. "Yes, but instead of hearts, clubs, spades, et cetera, they are cups, wands, swords and pentacles."

"And why is the King of Cups significant?"

"Because in this spread and in that spot, it represents the querent. That's the person seeking the answer. *You.* And the King of Cups represents a man of emotional stability, a man who lives by honor— quiet, kind and trustworthy."

It was bizarre, really, that this card would come up in that exact spot, too. Was it Fate? Was She or He whispering something to me? "Goddess," I murmured at the realization that maybe this reading was as much for me as it was for William. The card might represent him, but right now it was speaking to me.

I reached out to touch the card at the exact same time William did, his mouth open to ask another question. Our fingers met and that electric jolt sent a shivering thrill up my arm again. Slowly, deliberately, William moved his hand over mine, not looking at me but trapping my fingers under his large, callused ones.

I could barely force a swallow through the heartbeat thrumming in my throat. "I take my honor very seriously," he said.

I drew in a shaky breath, unable to tear my eyes from the strong column of his throat where it extended from his period-style shirt.

"You take many things very seriously," I rasped, thinking again of my determination last night to get William into my bed. If possible, I wanted it even more now than I did then.

I trembled like I was cold, even though we were both sitting in the sunshine. "Oh goddess..." My eyes squeezed tight.

"Do you believe in a goddess?" I opened my eyes when he asked the question. "You say that a lot."

I cleared my throat. "If there's a higher being, I'd prefer to think of her as a female. Mother Nature. Mother Earth. I was raised Catholic and always thought very highly of the Virgin Mary. She was someone

I could relate to, so when I grew older and felt the need to pray, I prayed to her. As my beliefs strayed from the patriarchy, I kept thinking of deity as a woman. And mythology has always fascinated me. So my beliefs about a higher power kind of parallel the beliefs about the cards. Archetypes. Models and stories to look to for inspiration, courage... strength."

His eyes narrowed. "You have your own strength."

I blinked and sat still, thinking. I didn't know what to say to him in response, and even if I did, the sudden emotion clutching the base of my throat wouldn't have allowed it. By the time I was able to, I realized we were no longer alone.

"Sir William! Mistress Jenna," Caitlyn said. She smiled before grabbing a stool from her table, where she had been taking orders for silhouettes earlier. This time she had Ann with her. "What do we have here?"

"It's a run-of-the-mill reading," I lied with a shrug. I was still shaking off that weird feeling that those cards were speaking to me every bit as much as they were speaking to him. But what were they saying? What was my heart trying to tell me?

"So William," Caitlyn said, fluttering her dark blonde eyelashes at him. "How's your *sword*?"

"I didn't bring my sword. No fighting today."

"It's a nice, *long* sword though, isn't it?" She threw a playful glance my way. "Did you notice, Jenna? That William's sword is quite long? I bet it's longer than Doug's."

I sent her a death glare, which she handily avoided by fixing her gaze on William. Ann, however, was valiantly fighting laughter behind her fist.

"I'm taller than Doug so, yes, I wield a longer sword. They are custom made for us based on our height and the length of our arm span."

"Hmm. I *bet* you have a longer sword. Maybe I'll get to see how you wield it someday."

William looked at her like she was a Martian. "You've seen the sword. Both the long sword and the shorter one I use with the shield—"

"Then maybe you could explain the parts to me. There's a *shaft*, right?"

"Caitlyn—" I warned.

"Yes, the shaft is part of the blade." He nodded. "There's also the hilt, the cross-guard, the pommel—"

"And that knobby part at the very end... the peen?"

Ann doubled over, tears streaming down her face.

"Enough, Caitlyn!" I snarled. "I'm in the middle of a reading."

"Maybe Jenna has a sheath you can put your sword—"

I stood up and pushed her shoulder. "Go away before I have someone lock you in the stock and throw tomatoes at you."

"Well, well...so this is where the party's at," a familiar voice said just behind my shoulder. "Who'd have thought Sir William would be at the center of it?"

I refused to turn and look at him, but the other two women greeted Doug with cool politeness.

"Hey, Doug," said Caitlyn.

"Sir Douglas," Ann inclined her head and gave a very respectable curtsy.

There was an awkward silence, and I presumed Doug was waiting for me to turn and say something to him. I didn't.

"So what's up, Jen? Are you not speaking to me now?"

I folded my arms across my chest, still refusing to look at him. "Are you still holding my tiara hostage? If so, then you're correct. I'm not talking to you."

Out of the corner of my eye, I caught him gesturing dramatically with open palms. "Hey, we have a perfectly fair agreement. I think we can all be adults here."

"Too late for you," I ground out.

Doug stepped closer to me, and I detected more movement from the other side of the table.

"C'mon, Jen, do you have to be like that?" Doug's hand landed on my shoulder and I jerked away from the touch, rounding on him. But William was there first.

"Step away from her," he said in a quiet voice that was deadly as poison.

"Chill, Forrest Gump. I'm not hurting her. I have a right to talk to my girlfriend."

I stiffened, trying to keep a lid on the rage I was suddenly feeling. "*Ex,*" I corrected. "So *very* ex. And if you call him that again, I'm going to start talking about the *real* reason you need to overcompensate by acting like an asshole all the time." I held up my thumb and forefinger about an inch apart while both Caitlyn and Ann laughed.

His mouth thinned. "Whatever. So you've traded down I see. Hanging out with the Rain Man."

Caitlyn flushed beet red. "Fuck off, Doug. You're an asshole."

"I call it like I see it. And maybe I'm just concerned that Jen is making a big mistake."

"I already made a big mistake when I agreed to go out with you," I muttered. "Now go away."

"Wow." He held his hands up in mock surrender. "I see how it is. Treated you like gold for months, and now you just turn around and act all heartless. Believe it or not, I *do* have feelings that you seem to enjoy stomping on." He shifted his attention back to William. "Let that be a lesson to you, because she'll do the same to you. She'll lead you on like some small dog until she's done with you."

William looked him up and down.

"You do act like a little bitch, so why not treat you like a small dog?" William delivered the biting comeback so calmly that he sounded like he was discussing sword techniques.

Doug flushed dark red and opened his mouth, then shut it again like a fish. He turned to say something to me, but William pointed a finger right in his face before he could get a word out.

"Do *not* talk to her. She doesn't want to talk to you. And don't talk to *me*, either. Don't breathe my air."

Ann and Caitlyn both started laughing and Doug's head jerked in their direction. But instead of backing off, he crossed his arms over his chest and stared defiantly at William.

William did not meet his gaze, but he did take a threatening step toward Doug. I was *this* close to getting in between them and stopping the pissing contest when Doug stiffened, startled by William's threatening posture.

Doug stepped back, a distinct look of fear in his eyes, before waving a hand and saying, "Whatever. You're all a bunch of losers." Then he turned and walked off.

"Wow," Caitlyn said. "He's nutting up."

Fists clenched at his sides, William watched Doug retreat, his eyes following the douchebag's every movement. "Wil? Are you okay?" I asked.

186 | BRENNA AUBREY

His jaw clenched so tight that it bulged. I studied his posture, his physique. He was so goddamn hot it almost hurt to look at him for too long. And he was never hotter than when he was defending me.

"Hey," I said, laying a light hand on his shoulder. He immediately jerked away from my touch, and I remembered that he liked to be warned before being touched. "Sorry..."

He licked his lips. "I need to go for a walk and calm down. I'm very angry right now. If he comes back here, text me."

I bit my bottom lip. "He's not going to come back. But if he does, I will. I promise."

He frowned and looked at me intently—everywhere but my eyes, of course—as if inspecting me to make sure I was okay. Then he nodded, turned and left.

"Holy shit," Caitlyn huffed before swiveling on her stool. "A whole lot of testosterone flowing around here. What is up Doug's butt?"

Ann was staring straight at me, her head tilted. "Doug is jealous. I watched him while you were doing your reading for William, and he never took his eyes off the two of you."

Caitlyn frowned. "Is it true, then? Are you seeing William now?" She didn't seem entirely happy, and I remembered her comment from a few weeks ago.

Save some of them for us homely girls.

I'd suspected that she might have a thing for William. It wasn't out of the realm of possibility. He did have his own fangirl section, after all.

"I'm only working with him to help with his crowd issues. So he'll have a better shot at beating that twerp at the next duel."

Her shoulders relaxed a bit. *Uh-oh.* She might as well have just said, "Thank God."

Ann sat down in the seat William had vacated. I carefully scooped up my Rider-Waite deck and slid it inside its satin pouch. We passed the next few hours talking of other things, mostly work and Ann's new double major, African Studies and European Studies, at Cal State Fullerton.

I read for a few more people—clan members, visiting courtiers from other clans of the RMRA and "mundanes," modern park visiters who did not participate in reenactment. I made some decent cash by the time all was said and done.

And fortunately, William returned from his walk unscathed, as I saw him visiting booths again and talking with other clansmen as if nothing had happened. Ann caught me watching him right before it was time to close up shop.

"I don't think it would be a bad thing for you to date William," Ann murmured.

I didn't answer, throwing a surreptitious gaze at Caitlyn, who busied herself with tidying activities at her side of the booth. She laughed to herself after a tense stretch of minutes.

Ann's head swiveled in Caitlyn's direction. "What?"

"Just that I bet Jenna could date William and he wouldn't even know they were dating."

I stiffened. "He's not dumb."

"Oh no. Not even close. I just mean that he's...adorably clueless. For example, one time he brushed me off, and I don't think he even realized he did it."

I stacked my cards in the satchel along with the other decks and tucked my earnings from the day into my leather belt pouch. Though I normally might have asked Caitlyn to elaborate on her story, given the subject matter, I refrained.

Ann was still staring at me while I fiddled with the cloth covering on my table. "Why do those two hate each other so much?"

Caitlyn and I both brought our heads up to stare at her.

"Who? Doug and William?" Caitlyn asked.

I'd been curious about that, too. Ann nodded and we both stared at Caitlyn, waiting for the answer. Caitlyn had been a member of the clan for several years and knew all the gossip. She cleared her throat. "William has been one of the clan pillars since nearly the beginning. He's always supporting clansmen. Practically every member has mad respect for him. But things changed when Doug showed up. He knew how to schmooze and get into people's good graces quickly."

Including mine, I thought. Although Doug was a lot more charming and intriguing from a distance than he was up close. He'd been appreciative and extremely flattering, and I had been in a bit of a dark place so I welcomed the attention.

"So did he hate William from the start?" Ann asked.

Caitlyn shook her head. "No...not at all. He actually tried to kiss up to William, if you can believe it. But William doesn't respond well to schmoozing, and Doug ended up being particularly offended by William's blunt personality."

She tucked her art supplies into a cloth bag and stood up, gently tipping the folding table on its side so that it was ready to load onto the truck.

"I've always liked William. He's a great guy." She was silent for a moment before shrugging and continuing. "I have to admit that I kind of used that clash with Doug to get closer to him, you know? Talk to him, give him some advice. And one night, after one of our meetings, I offered to help him pack up his stuff in exchange for a ride home, which he took me up on. But when we got to my house, he was focused on getting home and not the least bit interested in coming up for a 'cup of coffee or a beer.' He said it was too late to drink either and thanked me. Then he drove off."

Ann snickered. "He really had no idea you were coming on to him?"

Caitlyn smiled ruefully. "I was offended for about five minutes, then I laughed and resolved to be more obvious. That didn't work either," she said with a neutral glance in my direction. "He was interested in someone else."

Ann followed her gaze to look at me, and I busied myself by grabbing a couple of stools. "We should get these out to the truck."

"Have you ever considered that that's the reason Doug asked you out?" Ann asked when Caitlyn was out of earshot.

"What?" I asked. She carried the third stool and we headed to the truck.

"A lot of people knew that William had a thing for you. I'm just wondering if Doug wasn't trying to get back at William by asking you out."

I raised my brows. "So what am I, chopped liver? He couldn't like me for me?"

Ann rolled her eyes. "No, that's not what I meant. Sorry. Of course he's attracted to you, but...you know how men get."

I sighed. "Men suffer from testosterone poisoning and it makes them do stupid shit all the time." Like challenging their arch nemesis to fight a duel when they have a phobia of crowds. Like going into beast protector mode whenever any type of threat to the meeker sex existed in the nearby vicinity. Like turning down perfectly sensible propositions to go to bed with a woman. *Okay, maybe not that last one...*

14
WILLIAM

URING THE RIDE BACK TO HER HOUSE, JENNA DOESN'T SAY A word. Perhaps she's still upset about the confrontation with Doug. He said some really mean things, and I wish there was a way she could unhear them.

But it could also be the things I said to her before the market. I wasn't mean, just truthful. It's unfortunate, because I have no idea how to read the subtleties in her mood.

"So…we need to talk about Doug's tendency to provoke you," she says, finally breaking the silence.

"What do we need to say?"

"Just that you shouldn't let him push your buttons like that." Suddenly, pictures are running through my mind—a control panel with glowing buttons, an elevator with lit numbers to denote the floors— "Oh sorry, that probably wasn't the best way to state that. What I mean is…it's obvious Doug is deliberately trying to get to you. You need to shake it off."

I blink. "I don't want to shake it off. If he offends someone I care about, I'm going to make him pay for it. Once someone is on my bad side, they are there forever."

"Forever? Really? You don't forgive?"

I think about that for a moment. "I see no reason to give a bad person a second chance to hurt me—or someone else I care about."

"Hmm. That makes you sound kind of stubborn."

"I am stubborn. And I'm proud of that fact."

She blows out a breath, muttering as she shakes her head. "Men."

I frown. "Women say that a lot."

"It's because men tend to annoy us quite often."

I signal and exit the off-ramp on the freeway. "Mia says that same thing."

"She's an ally, even though she's defected to the other side." She folds her arms across her chest.

"What other side? The man side?" I ask.

Jenna is looking out the window, but I steal a glance at her face. I can see she's smiling. "The relationship side. When people get into a relationship, they change."

I think about this for a moment. "Do you think it's because of the other person? That being with that person changes them?"

She frowns for a minute and her head turns toward me. My eyes are on the road, but I can tell she's watching my profile. My hands tighten on the wheel, and I'm so distracted that I almost take too long to hit the brakes at the red light.

"I think it changes attitudes and perceptions. I don't think it can change the people themselves. I guess it's different when you're with your soulmate, though. And no one can say that Adam and Mia aren't fated for each other."

"Souls can't mate. Only bodies..." I'm hit with the image of Jenna and I together on her bed, her body against mine. I wonder what her skin feels like. Is it as soft as it looks? I want to know.

"People can be fated for each other. They have their one true love," she replies.

I shake my head. "That sounds ridiculous. What if your soulmate was born on another continent? Or fifty years after you?"

She shrugs and then relaxes her shoulders. "That's just what I believe."

"And you? Do you think you would know if you met your soulmate?" I'm suddenly hoping—even though I don't believe in this— that she thinks *I'm* her soulmate. That would make things so much easier. That would give her the reason to stay.

"I already did...a long time ago."

A weight drops in my stomach. She loves someone else? Then why isn't she with him? Maybe he doesn't want her. No, that can't be right. I can't think of any idiot who wouldn't want Jenna.

But my throat's closed up. I can't ask. I want to change the subject, so I do.

"My dad and stepmother are having a family dinner tonight. It's a regular thing on Sundays, and I usually go alone. Will you come with me? Adam and Mia will be there. And you could meet my sister and brother-in-law and my two nephews."

She's quiet for a few moments. "We haven't gotten very far in our work, though. I'd like to try some yoga next."

"I know some yoga. My martial arts trainer uses it to warm up."

"Okay. I'll come to dinner on the condition that afterward we go to your house to try working on some new exercises."

"It's a deal. I'll pick you up at five-thirty?"

"That sounds good." I drop her off minutes later and drive home, trying not to think of Jenna and her *soulmate*. The impossible seems to be slipping out of reach, and if I let it, I will lose hope. I can't allow that to happen.

15
JENNA

ILLIAM PICKED ME UP RIGHT ON TIME—OF COURSE HE did. He was wearing a knit shirt and jeans, looking even more stunning than in his medieval garb.

We pulled into the driveway of a large home in the hills of North Tustin. I noted with surprise the butterflies in my stomach when I got out of the car and reminded myself that I was just meeting the family of a *friend*. Usually, I was pretty chill about meeting the parents. I'd been in enough short-term relationships that I knew it happened around the tenth date or so—maybe a month or two into the relationship. It was easy to measure a guy's enthusiasm by how quickly he dragged you out to meet them. First date? Hell no. The guy was potential stalker material, which meant cut and run *quickly*. If the guy waited too long or made vague excuses when the subject came up, then he had something to hide.

Fortunately, I had the perfect excuse—albeit a shitty one—to never return the favor. But at least I never had to disappoint my parents by taking a soon-to-be ex to meet them.

But this was...I didn't know what this was. William and I weren't *dating*. We were hanging out. Working toward a common goal. Okay, and kissing. There had definitely been kissing.

William led me into the house without a word, and I was greeted at the door by Mia's mom—William's new stepmom—Kim. I'd met her before and she gave me a warm hug.

"Jenna, so glad to see you."

"Great to see you, too. You look fantastic!" And she did. Marriage agreed with her.

Mia's mom met Adam's uncle, who was also William's dad, not long after Adam and Mia had begun dating. They'd fallen in love and married, beating Adam and Mia to the altar. Some of our friends—especially Jordan—liked to tease Mia and Adam about being "kissing cousins." But I thought the whole thing was wonderful. Seemed you could meet your soulmate at any stage of your life.

I wished my mom would be open to finding love again, but Papa had been her soulmate, and so for her, it was over. Why look for someone else? In that, I agreed with her.

Mia appeared beside her mother. They strongly resembled each other, both dark hair, brown eyes, tall and slender. But Mia didn't have a smile on her face—it was more like a frozen grimace.

"Jenna! What a surprise to see you here." Her eyes darted to William. She leaned over, and he stooped to bring his cheek to her level for a kiss. "William, you didn't tell us Jenna was coming. I'll go set another place at the table." Then without even looking at me, Mia spun around and left.

"So let's get you introduced to the people you haven't met. Peter's in the kitchen." Kim took my arm. "Liam, Adam wanted to talk to you, but he's on the phone right now. Something about work."

My eyes darted nervously around the room. All at once, I realized that it had been a mistake for me to come with William. Everyone here was going to get the wrong idea, and naturally, William could not have predicted that, with his myopia toward social situations. He was just imitating the rest of his family members, who'd likely brought their dates from time to time. Suddenly, the butterflies were buzzing wasps.

I entered the crowded kitchen, instantly assailed by the scent of cheesy, meaty, garlicky goodness hanging in the air. Mia had her back to me, pulling out utensils from a drawer. A tall gentleman in his early fifties was easily recognizable as a Drake, and there was another woman who looked to be about thirty years old.

Kim began making introductions. "Peter, this is Mia's friend, Jenna. She came with Liam."

Peter struck me as a quiet, stoic type, not unlike his son, though he did manage eye contact. Nevertheless, they were unmistakably father and son. "Great to meet you, Jenna. I've heard about you from Mia. All good things. Welcome, and I hope you like lasagna."

"Love it, thanks."

"Here's Britt, Liam's big sister," Kim continued.

"Please don't use 'big' to describe me. Good God," she said, placing her hands on her hips. "I'm already feeling self-conscious about these love handles. Still haven't made any progress on the new springtime diet!"

Unlike Peter and William, Britt was short. She had dark blonde hair and blue eyes, and I assumed she looked like her mother. She also talked fast and laughed loudly. A mirror opposite of her younger brother. "You're going to see two little hooligans around here somewhere, probably trouncing each other on the Xbox. They're mine."

"It's great to meet you all," I said to the room with false cheer.

Britt was wiping her hands on her apron. She smiled, but her eyes narrowed a fraction. "So you're the reason Liam's doubling down on the sword dueling?"

I blinked and my mouth opened, at a loss for how to answer that. "Uh..."

She waved me off. "It's okay. I'm glad. The fighting has been good for him, actually. All that training has pulled him away from his obsessions. I mean, he's so damn talented, but other than work, I don't think he ever has an excuse to leave the house. He's got his whole studio set up there and his blacksmith forge. Sometimes I go weeks and wonder if I still even have a brother."

"Well...I'm...glad to help. And that's all I'm doing, you know. Just helping." My face started to burn. *Oh, goddess.*

Three pairs of eyes were now staring at me. Oh shit. Now they were going to think I had no interest in William and get defensive or—oh crap.

This awkward family meet-and-greet seemed to have higher stakes than previous ones. I actually *cared* about what people thought of me at this one.

"I'm moving soon. Traveling with the Renaissance Faire starting at the end of June. We're moving up the coast to Northern California for most of the summer then up through the Northwest. The Faire travels all over the western states. I'm really excited about it." By now, I was getting radiation burns from my blushing.

Britt was nodding her head. "That's great... So, you don't go to college?"

Peter darted a sharp look at his daughter, but she ignored him.

"Uh, I did. I studied physics."

"Ah, so are you going on to grad school?" Britt asked.

"Um, I need to borrow Jenna for a minute," Mia said with a tug on my elbow.

Awash with relief, I followed her out of the kitchen and down the hall toward one of the bedrooms. "Thank you," I murmured quietly.

"You needed saving. Britt is awesome, but she can get brutal when she's in third-degree mode. She works for the Department of Justice."

"Cripes. It *was* like being grilled by the CIA."

"William doesn't bring a woman here every day. Or any day, for that matter."

I shook my head. "I don't get that. There's half a dozen girls in the clan who are in love with him."

"A couple in his department at work, too. But he doesn't date."

"Ah."

"Or...does he?" She turned to me with raised eyebrows.

Oh dear, talk about CIA interrogators. Mia was about to turn into one herself.

Not if I could help it. "So what's all this?" I asked, taking in an art table, paints and shelves. We were in a bedroom with no bed.

"This was William's bedroom. The three of them, William, Adam and Britt, all grew up in this house. When he's over here—especially for the bigger family gatherings—he sometimes dips into his old room and tinkers away at stuff to avoid the crowd."

"I see." I moved around the table to take a look at what was on it. A massive sketchpad and some watercolor paints. There were doodles and small renderings, but nothing major. What I did see showed the incredible talent that I'd heard so much about and the tiny glimpses that I'd seen for myself.

"Britt said something about William having an art studio?"

"Yeah, at his house. But I don't suppose you'll be seeing that anytime soon," Mia said meaningfully. She was not going to drop the subject about how the world would implode if William and I started dating each other.

I sighed. "I've already been to his house to help him with his crowd issues."

Mia opened her mouth to say more, but Adam appeared in the doorway, shoving his cell phone into his shirt pocket. Like his cousin, Adam was tall, dark and *very* good looking. The Family Drake had certainly scored big with the genetic lottery. "I've been sent as the messenger to let you know that it's dinnertime."

"Great," Mia said. Pressing up against him in the doorway, she snagged the phone out of his pocket. "I'll be right there after I throw this in the pool."

He laughed and kissed her on the nose. "Don't be grumpy. It *was* important. "

"You promised..."

He let out a long sigh. "Okay. Turn it off, then."

And he didn't have to tell her twice. She powered down the phone, then slipped it into her bra with a laugh and trotted down the hallway.

"I'm going to enjoy going after that later," he said, turning to follow her.

I brought up the rear, still marveling at what I'd seen on William's sketchpad. We were going over to his house after dinner, and I was going to make it my mission to see inside his art studio.

If I could make it out of family interrogation hell....

***

Hours later, William and I were sitting in the middle of the floor on the mat in his gym-slash-living room, ready to take on the art of meditation.

My plan was to get him so relaxed that he'd agree to go to Disneyland with me. I was convinced that if we could conquer the chaos of Main Street USA and penetrate Sleeping Beauty's castle without having to surrender, we'd have a very good chance of vanquishing William's phobia of crowds.

"You're a Dungeons and Dragons player, right?" I asked. "We're going to approach this like you would a D&D game." Again with that skeptical look on his face.

I caught a glimpse into his brown eyes that were the color of dark chocolate. He had amazing eyes fringed with dark lashes. Even if he didn't gaze deeply into mine, they were still enjoyable to look at. In fact, I never stopped appreciating William's good looks.

"How is this like D&D?"

I shrugged. "Well, you envision what the Dungeon Master is describing to you, right? *'You enter a room that is so dark you can only see a few feet around each torch. There's a musty smell in the air and the echoes of water dripping in the distance.'* Et cetera. It's all about creating the story in your mind as you experience it in your Dungeon Master's campaign. What we're going to do is similar to that."

"Only less fun and without the dice rolling," he said.

I laughed. "Right. But you can put your D&D skills to work when setting up a way to be in a crowd without allowing it to affect you.

Just visualize your preferred scenario, perhaps one where you are a hero fighting off evil."

His brows knit as he contemplated that, and then I replayed in my mind the words I'd just spoken. "And you know, that's really true. You really are a hero fighting off the evil ex." I laughed. "At least in *my* book, you are."

He focused intently on my fingers as I traced random shapes on the mat in front of me.

I straightened. "Now...take some deep breaths and relax. Just close your eyes and picture yourself in a room with five other people."

"What sort of room?"

"It doesn't matter. Any room. A large room."

"Okay...the dining room at Adam's house."

I inhale, reminding myself to be patient with him. "That will do. You're there with five other people."

"Do I have to tell you who they are?"

"No...just picture those people. You're standing around talking."

"I really don't like to stand around and talk."

Argh. I was starting to get a little hot under the collar. Gritting my teeth, I forced myself to relax. "Okay, you're standing in Adam's dining room with your hands in your pockets staring creepily at the other people in the room."

Silence from him. *Good.* If he'd asked me another question, I would have lost it.

"Okay, now another five people walk into the room."

"Do I know these people or are they strangers?"

Oh my goddess! I was going to stab him in the eye. "Does it matter?"

"It does to me."

Of course he would say that. *Calm, Jenna. You are in a wide-open field...* "Okay...um...you know these people. Now there are ten people in the room."

"Eleven."

"What?" I almost shrieked in frustration.

"There are eleven people in the room. Me, plus the original five, that makes six. Then five more. Eleven." He sounded supremely pleased with himself.

"Okay, whatever. Just focus, Wil. You're in this room with eleven—I mean, ten other people. How do you feel?"

"I'm okay. The dining room is big. It's not crowded."

At last we were getting somewhere. "All right. Now ten more people walk in. There are now..." I fumbled to figure it out.

"Twenty-one—"

"Twenty-one people in the room."

He hesitated. "The room is starting to feel full."

"Good...now focus. I want you to breathe."

"I have been. I'd pass out if I didn't." Or he'd pass out from me clobbering him, which I was kind of wanting to do.

"No, breathe in the special way, the good way—"

"The *right* way?"

"Yeah, picture yourself in this room with these twenty-one other people..."

"Twenty other people."

"You just told me there were twenty-one people in the room." Fuck, this was starting to sound like an Abbot and Costello comedy routine.

"There are. Me and twenty other people."

I opened my eyes and blew out a breath, flopping on my back to stare up at the ceiling. "This isn't working."

He didn't say anything for a long moment. "Are you angry with me?"

Deep breaths. In with the good, out with the bad. "No. I'm just frustrated. This obviously isn't going to work with your...literal way of thinking. We'll have to figure out something else that will work for you."

"It's okay. People have told me that I'm annoying before."

"I'm not going to tell you that you're annoying."

He stiffened. "You think I'm a lost cause."

I tilted my head to the side and looked at him. "I don't. I *never* give up on people that easily. I'm a fighter, remember? I was born in the middle of a war." I patted the mat. "Come lie down here next to me. Let's try something else."

He slowly complied until he was lying beside me on the mat. I could smell him again—that clean, masculine smell. It reminded me of the hot kisses we'd shared the other night on my bed.

I swallowed, suddenly feeling that sexual tension return, like a fist tightening just below my navel bringing a sweet ache. Maybe I needed to do a little grounding and centering myself. This guy was getting me all kinds of riled up—in more ways than one.

I turned to face him, bending my arm at the elbow to rest my head in my hand. "What is it about crowds that makes you upset? Is there a story behind it?"

He turned his head to look at me, but when his eyes met mine, he rolled back to look at the ceiling. "When I was in elementary school, I used to hate recess because of all the kids. They would pick on me. Surround me."

My mouth gaped in shock. "They bullied you? Why was that allowed?"

"They never hit me or hurt me—not then. They liked to freak me out, though. They'd stand in a circle all around me and yell, chanting different things. They thought it was funny to watch me get disoriented. When any adults asked what was happening, they'd say we were all playing a game—that I was fine with it. I used to have panic attacks whenever the bell rang and the teacher insisted I go outside for recess."

There was a sick feeling building inside me as I listened to his story, delivered with almost dispassionate neutrality—as if he were telling me about a story he'd read in the newspaper. I blinked, my eyes stinging as I felt that pain and confusion of a child trying to sort things out, overwhelmed by all the sensory input being forced on him. In a way, I could relate, having started first grade here in the US without speaking a word of English. It had been overwhelming for me, isolating. And I remembered months of panic and uncertainty. But it had faded as I'd adapted. I'd had the skills to pick up the language quickly. William hadn't been as fortunate.

"Shit, that's horrible," I said, my voice trembling. He continued to stare up at the ceiling but said nothing in response. On impulse, I reached out and touched his arm. "Hey...you're here now... not there."

He turned and looked at me, and this time he didn't pull his gaze away. It was almost as if he was unaware that his eyes were staring straight into mine. But *I* was aware of it and my breathing froze. Our connection sizzled silently in the space between us. Tears sprang to my eyes as I stared deep into that dark reflection of raw vulnerability, with a strong touch of self-loathing.

William was pure—and not just sexually so. His feelings, emotions, perceptions. Yet it seemed that all the darkness he had seen and experienced, he'd internalized to somehow be *his* fault. This warped logic was part of the misplaced burden he'd hefted onto his shoulders. And in this moment, I could tell he was troubled.

I placed my hand on his whisker-rough cheek. "They were wrong, what they did. You couldn't help your reactions. You are not lesser than them."

His cheek bulged under my hand, and he immediately pulled away and sat up.

I pushed up beside him. "What's wrong?"

"I don't need to be reassured like a child. I'm a man."

I paused, unsure of what to say. I felt like I was walking into a trap. "I was empathizing, Wil. I feel badly that you were bullied. No kid should have to have that happen. Just like no kid should live in a city that's being bombed."

He sat for another long moment, still tense. I shifted to rest on my knees and put a hand on his shoulder. He jerked it away. "I don't want to be touched right now."

"Okay. I'm sorry."

"War is a tragedy. Autism is *not* a tragedy."

I nodded. "I agree. Actually, in some ways, I think it's a blessing."

He looked at me sideways, probably trying to determine if I was being serious or not.

"I wish I could see the world the way you do sometimes," I explained. "I wish I could have your sensitivity, even when it's so intense it hurts. I wish I could focus my talents like you can. I'm sorry...I didn't mean to insult you."

He turned his head and looked at my chin, then my nose, then my mouth. His gaze stopped there. "Jenna," he said.

"Yes?"

"I want to kiss you."

"Help me visualize what you mean. Would you kiss me on the lips...or on the cheek?" I answered, unable to resist the urge to tease him.

His eyes rested on my lips with unwavering concentration. "On your lips. My lips and your lips."

Oh yes, please. I smiled. "For how long? Would it be for five seconds or closer to a minute?"

He hesitated but didn't tear his eyes away. I licked my lips, just to torture him a little.

"And would our mouths be open or closed? Or maybe halfway open? Would there be tongue? How much tongue?"

Another long pause. "You're teasing me."

"I was just trying to be cute... Are you mad?"

He growled, reaching over to hook his hand around the back of my neck, pulling my head to his. And this kiss. *This kiss.*

Wow.

His lips caressed mine, then pushed open my mouth. Without wasting a moment, his tongue slid in with confidence. Our previous kisses had been amazing, but *this* one...

He kissed me like he'd been doing it every day of his adult life. Our tongues tangled and writhed, and my blood pressure shot up about a hundred points. I was hot everywhere. Arousal blossomed wet and scalding in my center, radiating outward with each movement of his mouth, each swish of his delicious tongue. He was quickly, coolly enslaving me.

Despite the fact that he just told me he didn't want to be touched, I chanced that he might have changed his mind. I leaned forward, putting my hands against his chest, rubbing them down his front. His chest was hard, solid, strong—a blacksmith's chest. I continued to touch him firmly like I knew he preferred.

Suddenly, I felt his hand slide against my belly, stroking with that same deep pressure. My stomach somersaulted and I sat up in front of him so we were facing each other, my legs across his thighs.

He was still kissing me, his tongue exploring my mouth with the intrepidity of an astronaut on a new world, more driven by the urge to experience new things than held back by the need for safety.

As his hand continued to stroke my stomach, I noticed that each time it inched closer to the bottom of my bra before lowering again. I ran my hands shamelessly over his nipples, rubbing them through his shirt, and was rewarded with his quickening breath.

I yanked my mouth from his and began kissing his rough jaw, then his throat, all the way down to the neckline of his shirt before kissing back up again. His Adam's apple bobbed beneath my lips and his hands slid over my shoulder blades, holding me fast against him.

"Wil," I breathed. He didn't answer but continued kissing his way across my jaw to my ear, then taking my lobe into his mouth and lovingly caressing it with his tongue. "Touch me...touch my chest." My voice sounded shaky with my desire.

His hands on my back froze and his mouth found its way back to mine. We kissed again and his hand cupped my breast. Immediately, my nipple hardened under his touch. His palm rubbed against the already sensitive nub, sending shocks of heat from my breast clear down to my center, tightening that desire to a laser-thin focus.

"Wil," I whispered between follow-up kisses.

"Yes?" he said.

"I have another breast. And you have another hand."

I didn't have to tell him twice. His other hand slid around my body and began to lavish attention on the neglected breast. When he rolled both his thumbs over my nipples, my back arched, pushing my chest harder against his hands. Every nerve ending in my body was pulled so taut you could play a melody off them like a bow dragging across the strings of a violin.

I needed to feel the heat of his body next to mine—that heavenly feeling of skin on skin. My hands dropped to his waist, slid under his T-shirt and across his flat stomach. His eyes snapped shut and his hands froze. I wasn't sure if this would be the point where he'd pull back, so I pressed my advantage.

"Take your shirt off."

He opened his eyes, looking again at my mouth, and his hands left my breasts long enough to tug on the neck of his shirt and pull it up over his head.

That didn't take much coaxing.

I smiled, pleased at being one layer of clothing closer to the goal. "Now—"

But he was already reaching for my shirt, pulling it at the neck. I moved his hands to the bottom hem of the shirt instead.

"This is how girls do it."

"I'm not a girl."

I laughed. "But I am."

With a smile, he slowly took the hem of my shirt and drew it up and over my head. Then his eyes fixed on the knotted nipples evident through the thin material of my bra.

This was happening. This was *so* happening.

Without any further hints from me, William's hands returned to my breasts, cupping them over my bra. I pulled his head down to kiss me with one hand while caressing his very lickable chest with my other hand. Wow...who'd have thunk that a modern-day blacksmith-turned-warrior knight could be so hot and sexy?

"Jenna," he muttered against my lips when we finally came up for air. He spoke in halting syllables, so I knew he was trying to slow things down—which signaled to me that it was time to stomp on the accelerator.

I lowered my mouth to his chest, kissing my way down to one of his nipples and rolling my tongue over it. He tasted salty and sweet, like saltwater taffy.

His breath hissed through his lips and his fingers threaded through my hair.

"That feels so good," he whispered shakily.

I moved over to lick and suck the other nipple. He let out a satisfying groan, which I felt clear down to my toes. Every nerve and muscle in my body was now crying out for release.

"Wil, I want you," I said, kissing my way back up to his neck.

"I want you, too."

I reached back and unhooked my bra with one hand—a skill I'd mastered with some practice—and let it slide down my arms. His hands were on my breasts seconds after freeing them from my bra, and the rough and callused touch felt exquisite on my sensitive skin.

I rose up to kiss him. His kisses grew fiercer, his tongue plunging into my mouth, forcing mine into submission with the ferocity of his ardor. When we broke contact, I was breathing hard and so was he. His handsome face was flushed, his eyes dark with desire. I could tell he was about to lose control.

My plan to seduce the hot hunk of man-virgin? *So far, so good.*

Slowly, William lowered his head and enveloped my nipple with his hot mouth. "Yes," I breathed, urging him on, having already learned that subtlety was completely lost on him. "I like that a lot. I—"

My words died in my throat. There were no words. No thoughts even, only the piercing, intense pleasure of his mouth sucking my nipple. I think I might have even forgotten to breathe because, damn, it was overwhelming. Desire arced through me like lightning.

I grabbed William's head, threading my fingers through his thick hair to hold him where he was. Had I not done that, I may have collapsed into a helpless puddle of sexual heat on the floor. *Holy shit.* It wasn't just his kisses. It was his touch. It was everything. It was electric—and I was hooked.

"Oh, Wil, I want it. So. Damn. Bad."

His mouth froze for a moment, then he pulled away—mere millimeters, but it was enough to make my breath lurch with the deprivation. "What is *it?*"

"What?"

"You said you want 'it.' What is *it?*"

There I went again, assuming the obvious was clear to him. "This...us. I want to be together."

"We're together."

"No, I mean...together as in...as in having sex."

Another pause. His breath curled across the surface of my tender nipple, and I throbbed with the loss of his touch. I smoothed my fingers through his hair, then rubbed my thumb across his cheek.

"It's okay to want it, Wil."

He drew back and I noticed his face was flushed. Staring at my throat, he said, "Tell me you're staying and not traveling with the Ren Faire."

My head spun. "I—what?"

"I told you already that we are not going to have sex so I can just watch you leave. If we do this, I want your promise that you'll stay."

His voice was flat and cold, and it brought all my sexually-charged hopes crashing down. I fell back on my legs and looked at him. He turned, snatched up his shirt and slipped it over his head, but it was inside out. With a mild curse, he realized his mistake, and I was treated to another nice view of his chest while he straightened himself out.

I refused to call this an impasse. I knew he wanted it. I knew he was like any other red-blooded man in his mid-twenties. And he was clearly turned on... How resolute could he actually be?

I leaned back on my arms and pushed my breasts out at an attractive angle. I was rewarded when William fixed his eyes on my chest, then I watched the struggle cross his handsome features. Finally, he closed his eyes and sat back.

"Put your clothes on," he said.

I ignored his request. "Why don't you want to—?"

"I never said I didn't want to." And judging from the still obvious erection in his jeans, he could hardly deny it.

"Then—"

"But we aren't going to. Not until I have that promise. And if not, then we won't."

I'd change his mind—sooner or later. No man, no matter how stubborn, was *that* strong. Besides, he didn't realize the favor I was doing him by *not* committing. Bad things tended to happen to people who loved me...

I swallowed and shoved that thought aside.

"This isn't the Middle Ages, Wil. You aren't responsible or committed to someone just because you sleep with them."

He tensed. "If you think that's the reason, then you've completely misunderstood me."

I raised my brow, the challenge in his voice rankling me.

Reaching over, I grabbed my shirt and bra and put them on my lap. After a long moment, he opened his eyes, probably thinking that I'd dressed. When he saw that I hadn't, he didn't close his eyes again.

"So even though we could be enjoying ourselves..."

"It's not about enjoying. It's about you running away afterward."

There it was again. It had riled me up when he'd leveled that at me earlier today at the park, and now it just pissed me off.

"You don't know anything about me or my history, so it's rude to say I'm running away."

He shook his head. "People are always calling my honest statements rude. I didn't mean to be rude to you. But what is it, then, when you have people here who care about you, like Alex and Mia...like me. And you're just going to go away with no plan to ever come back?"

"I—" How could I explain this? I'd always thought about it as moving on to catch the next rainbow. To learn, to grow as a person. To experience life. To not grow stifled...attached. Because attachments could wound and murder parts of your heart, tearing those parts in the most painful manner possible when those attachments left you forever.

He wouldn't understand.

He *couldn't* understand.

And there was no sense in arguing about it, so I did what I was best at. I changed the subject.

Stretching out in a pose, I pushed out my naked chest. "Wil...I want you to draw me. Like one of your French girls."

His gaze slid down my body, warming the parts of me that it touched. "I have already."

I licked my lips and smiled. "Like this?"

He didn't answer, but heat crept across his face.

I sat up. "You *did?*"

His face was stoic. "I refuse to answer on the grounds that it might incriminate me."

"Pleading the Fifth? Hmm...now I'm going to have to see this. I'll make you a deal. I'll put my shirt back on if you show me."

He thought about that for a long time. "I could just hold out until you want to go home. You have to put your shirt back on for that."

"That's true. But until then, I'd be wandering around topless in your house, maybe even brushing up against you, falling against you. You know...being wanton."

He continued staring at my boobs as if he was mesmerized.

"You want to touch them again, don't you?"

He stood. "I'll show you some drawings if you put on your shirt."

With a small noise of triumph, I did as he asked. But in reality, I would have won either way. Having him grope me again with those big, callused hands certainly wouldn't be considered a loss by anyone's definition.

William gave me the succinct version of a grand tour of his large, ranch-style home. As he led me into his art studio, which interestingly enough was in the master suite, he explained that not only was it the largest bedroom in the house, but the lighting was the best there. He'd even installed an industrial-sized sink and drying rack in the attached bathroom so he could wash his supplies.

The room was equipped to the nines with special tools and items I didn't even recognize. The floor was polished concrete, and there was special diffused lighting with filters and shades at the ready to adjust the lighting. There were also blackout curtains that could be drawn on all the windows. It was a lovely room and would have made a wonderful bedroom, but as an art studio, it was amazing.

Cabinets and standing equipment lined the walls, along with a roll of different backdrops hanging from the ceiling. A large, high-end drafting table dominated the room, located just under the skylight. Upon that table were a variety of brushes, palettes, boxes of charcoal, pastels and containers of special pencils and erasers, all perfectly organized. I reached over to pick up a shiny metal ruler.

"Don't touch," he admonished. After a stern frown creased his brow, he added, "Please."

My eyes widened and I pulled my hand back. Apparently, the studio was sacrosanct. "I don't see any of your rules posted in here like in your smithy."

"That's because people are not permitted to come in here—besides me."

I blinked. "Mia said she's been here."

"She stands in the doorway, as does everyone else. I don't like having people in this space."

"Do you want me to go stand over at the door?"

"No. Just—if you don't touch anything, that would be good."

I was a bit overwhelmed at the special status of being able to enter the artist's temple when his closest loved ones could not. Did that reveal a certain level of special trust? A lump formed in my throat at the thought.

I fidgeted in my spot, then stuffed my hands in my pockets as if to reassure him that I would behave. "Deal."

He went to one of the easels and removed a blank canvas from it, setting it carefully on the ground. Then he opened up a big cabinet and flipped through a few boards without looking at them. It was as if he knew exactly what he was looking for and exactly where it was.

Moving from the cabinet back to the now-empty easel, he slowly, tentatively set a board on it. Once I got a look at what was on that board, I about fell over in shock. I most certainly couldn't breathe.

It was an absolutely exquisite acrylic painting of me... *Holy. Shit.*

Though he'd hinted that it might be lurid, in reality, it wasn't at all. The image was a close-up of my head and shoulders, depicting me staring over my bare shoulder. I had no shirt on, but as I was turned away from the viewer, there were no anatomical details. Even if he had chosen to be more explicit, I could not have felt more special in that moment than if Dégas himself had painted me with not a stitch of clothing on.

It must have taken him *forever,* and it was so lovingly detailed— the glint in my eyes, the strands of hair splayed across my shoulders, the curve of my earlobe. I labored to draw my next breath. "I don't ever remember you taking a photo of me. How—how did you do this?"

He seemed confused by my non sequitur question but answered anyway. "I don't paint from photos. Photos are two-dimensional. My memory remembers everything in three dimensions. And I've seen you enough to recall the details in order to create this image."

"So is that the reason you didn't do a full-frontal depiction? Because you haven't seen me naked?"

He looked away and shrugged.

I couldn't take my eyes off the painting. It made me feel strange inside—special, like a queen. *Janja, ti si kraljica.* Those words in Papa's voice popped into my head. Telling me I was a queen. I'd never felt like one again until this moment. I swallowed.

"Do you like it?" he asked.

I was blinking tears from my eyes. *Like it?*

"It's stunning. I'm just so..."

"What?"

"Overwhelmed..." I shook my head. "You're amazing, Wil."

He didn't reply, but he did turn back to look at the canvas.

"Would you paint me if I modeled for you?"

"Naked?" I laughed at his shocked face, which was good. It helped those strong emotions dissipate, and I welcomed that. Because with those memories came pain. And I didn't want to remember. Not now.

"*Yes*, naked... Clearly, you don't need me to be here for a head shot."

He looked from my shoulder to the canvas and back again. "I don't need you here while I paint."

I smiled. "Okay, shall I just model for you now then?" I reached as if to pull my shirt up again—mostly because I wanted to rile him up a bit, but also because I couldn't get over my sheer awe of his talent. He oozed with it, and I was confused and a little at a loss for how to act.

His brows rose in alarm. "Don't take your shirt off again. I just got things under control," he said with a glance at his crotch.

"I'm sorry...I'm just being goofy because I'm uncomfortable." I sighed, dropping my arms to my sides. "You know, it's really not fair."

"What's not fair?"

"That you're handsome, smart *and* mega-talented. I have no idea why you seem to be of the opinion that you need to prove your worthiness to *anyone*."

His eyes lowered, that same troubled look clouding his features. Would he finally talk about it or would he be tight-lipped again? And what did it all have to do with his mom and Disneyland?

I figured this was as good a time as any to spring it on him. "I have an idea...we should go to Disneyland to have fun while working on your crowds issue."

He stiffened, big hands curling into fists at his sides. "I'm not going to Disneyland."

"Hey, if you want me to help you, you've got to be open to my suggestions. We don't have to go anywhere near Adventureland or the Jungle Cruise, okay? To be honest, it would be no big loss for me. They tell dorky jokes, and I really don't need to see the 'back side of water' for the zillionth time." When he didn't say anything, I pressed it further. "Come on, Wil. It's the happiest place on earth. You can go with me there, can't you? We'll just go for a few hours."

He took a deep breath, then let it go.

"If you don't say 'yes,' I'm whipping my top off again."

He held his hand out. "Okay, okay. Yes. I'll go."

"Damn," I harrumphed. "I kind of wanted you to touch them again."

This time he rewarded me with a deep color on his face. "You like teasing me too much."

I laughed. "Well, you're going to have to learn to tease me back."

His stern expression dissolved into a soft smile that made my stomach flip. "When will we go?"

"I'd say next weekend, but I have to work all day on Saturday. A weekday would be better—and definitely less crowded—but *you* have to work."

"I can take a day of leave," he said. "They wouldn't say anything because I never take a day off. We can go on Wednesday."

"So we'd be disrupting your regular schedule *and* working on crowds. Two birds with one stone. I like that." Once again his face clouded, so I continued on. "I have to work in the morning at the Refugee Support Center. The group therapy session ends at ten. If you come to get me early, you could sit in, if you want."

He looked like he was about to say no, so I scooted up to him and—very slowly, so he knew what I was doing—put my arms around his neck. Then I rose on my tiptoes and kissed him on the cheek. "Please?"

He heaved a great sigh. "I'll be there. Just give me the address."

A little while later, he took me home, and after having spent practically the entire weekend with him, it almost felt like I had a William-shaped hole in my life. I was amazed and a little frightened at how much I really was looking forward to next Wednesday.

16
WILLIAM

AS JENNA ASKED, I'VE ARRIVED AT THE REFUGEE SUPPORT Center early. When I give my name at the front desk and tell them why I'm there, they are expecting me. Ann, her friend who I already know from the RMRA, comes out to escort me back.

"She's busy right now. Things got a bit emotional this morning, so while I think she originally wanted you to sit in on the circle, it probably wouldn't be best right now."

I have to admit that I'm relieved. I've been in a few group counseling sessions when I was a teenager and they did not go well.

When I enter through the door, I'm in a large room set up like a classroom with desks and chairs. There are computers along the wall, as well as groupings of couches and comfortable chairs near bookcases loaded with novels and nonfiction titles. In the back corner is a ring of seats with six people talking quietly.

Nearby, just opposite the support circle, Jenna stands beside a young woman, her head bent. They are talking quietly, and the other girl—a teenager, I think—is dabbing her eyes with a tissue.

Ann appears at my shoulder, speaking quietly. "Anchali is having some anxiety from some bad memories that were brought up in the session. Jenna is talking her down. It will be a little while."

I watch Jenna as she comforts the young lady, touching her on the arm much the way she does with me. I realize these things that I appreciate are things she shares with others, too. And while that might make me feel less special, it doesn't.

Jenna likes to help others. She's open-minded and sees things from different perspectives. Yet just last weekend, she told me that she wished she could see the world as I do. That thought elicits a warm feeling in the center of my chest.

As I watch her now, I can see that she likes to help people. And it can't be easy helping people here, in a refugee center, when she still has such awful memories of the war *she* lived through. But she listens to others tell their stories and helps them however she can.

Just like she's helping me. And though I know that it's in her best interest, I'd like to think that she'd help me anyway, without her tiara on the line.

Ann is speaking to me now. "Can you help me with Raul? Jenna asked him to make a sign, but I need to get the classroom ready for our next session." She points to a young man with black hair and bronze skin sitting at an art desk.

I'm wary of approaching a stranger so I walk slowly, trying to formulate what to say. What kind of help does he need? He appears to be drawing something. As I get closer, he glances up at me and then looks away.

"Hello. I'm William Drake. Do you need any assistance?"

Without looking at me, he shrugs. I stand there for a moment and watch him continue to work. He's creating rather complex lettering in a very modern, urban style, similar to some of the more artistic street tagging I've seen on random concrete walls and freeway overpasses. Ann said it's a sign for the support center, and it looks like he's doing the outline.

I stuff my hands in my pockets, unsure of what to do. I continue standing there before interrupting to offer a suggestion.

"You've created an interesting font. But if you are going to overlap the letters like that, then the bottom leg of the 'n 'should be on top of the 'g' instead of beneath it, as you have it. It's more aesthetically pleasing to have the letters overlap all the same way."

The young man sits back and studies the lettering for a moment, tilting his head. "I guess that might look good."

I bend over to grab a stray piece of paper and a woefully dull pencil, then quickly sketch out what I mean. "I'm not well versed in urban-style art, but it might look like this."

The young man is watching every move I make without saying anything. "How did you do that so fast?" He speaks with a heavy Spanish accent.

"It's just a mock-up, but you can also make sure you center your word on the page by counting the number of letters in the word. Then, pick the middle letter and start with that right at the center of the page. Like this." As I demonstrate, he puts his pencil down to focus on what I'm doing.

"Where did you learn that?" he asks.

"I just drew a lot—like you are doing. I was never any good at school besides art classes. I tried college and it wasn't for me. But the instructor there said I could study privately with her and a group of other students. You could study with friends and learn by critiquing each other's work. That's mostly the way I learned."

"I'm still in high school."

"Start with an art class there."

"But don't they just teach you stuff you don't want to do?"

"You have to learn the basic exercises in order to do the stuff you *want* to do. It's about building your skills and technique."

I pass along a few other tips, and then he pulls some sheets from his binder, showing me some of his previous work. It's impressive. I ask him about certain choices he's made and find I'm learning new things, too.

"I'm Raul," he says suddenly, holding out his hand. I stare at it for a few seconds then realize he wants me to shake it. I'm not a big fan of shaking hands, so I hold mine out as a high-five and he smiles and hits it.

"I'm William."

"Are you going to teach here?"

"I'm here to pick up Jenna. I'm not a teacher."

He tilts his head to the side. "You should be."

Something about how he says that makes me feel good. He turns back to his paper and begins working again on a new sign using my suggestions as examples. Then Jenna is by my side, watching him.

"Hey, R," she says. "Sorry I couldn't get to you earlier. I had to help Anchali."

Raul looks up. "That's okay, your boyfriend was helping me. He's pretty good. I just need to know how to spell some of these words for the sign you want."

Jenna looks at me out of the corner of her eyes as she bends to write down a phrase for Raul. She's blushing. I'm thinking about Raul's assumption that I am Jenna's boyfriend, and it makes me feel warm, too, right in my chest. Is Jenna thinking about it, too?

I watch her as she's bent over, the curve of her legs, her butt, her hips. I want her to be my girlfriend. I want it in every sense of that word. But it's more than just about kissing or having sex with a woman I find incredibly desirable. I want to spend time with her. I want to spend my days with her, along with my nights.

Suddenly, I want to hold her hand so I reach down and take it. Her head jerks toward me, then she smiles. Her fingers close around mine, and that warm feeling in my chest starts spreading.

"What do you think of our center?"

I nod. "It's a very interesting place. I bet they are sad you are leaving."

Raul's head comes up. "You're *leaving?*"

Jenna's head jerks sharply toward the boy. "No worries, R. I'm not leaving anytime soon."

"But—" I begin.

"Wil, it's time to go. 'Bye, Raul!" She's tugging me along and waving goodbye to Ann while giving her some instructions. Then she grabs her things, not speaking again until we are in the parking lot.

Letting out a breath, she says, "If you come back here, please don't say anything about my leaving, okay?"

Jenna is still holding my hand, so I tighten my grip. "They don't know?"

"They don't need to know. Not yet. I'll give them notice. The Faire doesn't even leave the area for two and a half months."

"You don't have the courage to tell them now?"

Her eyebrows bunch together. "It's not about courage. Jeez, William. Sometimes you can just be so..."

"Abrasive?" I've heard that one before.

"Judgmental of other people's choices. I have good, valid reasons for leaving."

Running away, I mentally add. "You also have good, valid reasons for staying," I say aloud.

She drops my hand and blows out a breath. "Let's just get in the car."

Sitting with her arms folded across her chest, she's silent most of the drive to Disneyland. So I begin speaking to her about the urban art that Raul was creating while pointing out some examples I see on our drive through Anaheim.

Some of it is just crude, ugly tagging, but there are some examples of truly beautiful artistic expression. It makes me hope the creators of that art will someday learn and push their craft to a professional level. I realize how good it felt to teach someone else a little of what I know—and for him to appreciate that knowledge I shared.

"I liked teaching Raul."

"Good. Teaching *can* be fun." She smiles, and I could swear the light inside the car grew brighter.

"Have you ever thought about becoming a teacher?"

She looks at me for a long time. "Yeah, actually. I think maybe, someday...when I'm done filling my need to wander."

I frown. The less said about that, the better. "I was surprised to see Ann. I'd forgotten that she worked with you."

"Yes. That's how we met, and when I started going to the RMRA, she got really interested in it, too."

"Is she also a war refugee?"

Jenna nods. "Yes. From Somalia. She and her family escaped the war there by fleeing to Kenya before making it to the US."

I think about that as we continue to drive. "And Raul? Where is he from?"

"Honduras. His mom was killed on their journey here, which was almost completely on foot, all the way up from Central America. It was horrible."

I picture Ann and Raul and their families walking through jungles or across deserts to find safety, and I'm suddenly sad that others have been born into such unfortunate situations. Like Jenna, for example. I can only imagine she saw more death and horror in the first five years of her life than I've ever seen—movies included. I realize how lucky I am, especially as I think about the news reports of the refugees from Syria who are escaping under similar circumstances.

"What was your journey like?" I ask.

"Huh? Oh, you mean from Yugoslavia?"

"Yes, was it like that? On foot?"

She pauses for a moment and glances out the window. "No, we were put on a truck in Sarajevo—my aunt, my sister and me—and driven to Zagreb in Croatia. There was a checkpoint along the way, and..." She shudders and shakes her head. "Anyway, it was not like Raul's at all. We had some family in Zagreb and stayed there until we could fly to America. I was lucky."

After hearing her story and some of the things she's been through, I don't think that she's as lucky as she feels she is. I just think she's strong. Incredibly strong.

And beautiful—not just on the outside, but all the way to the core of what makes her *her*. Jenna helps people and she's compassionate...it doesn't take a professional artist to appreciate that beauty.

I hope that in proving my worthiness, I'll win her over and she'll want to stay. Because the more time I spend with her, the more I want her with me for good.

But now my thoughts shift as we pull into the enormous "Mickey and Friends" parking structure that serves park guests. A weight drops into my stomach, my heart is racing and my breathing is coming fast. And though it's not even close to what Jenna has endured, I'm still filled with dread at the thought of reliving some of my own childhood horrors.

17
JENNA

WE OPTED OUT OF TAKING THE CROWDED TRAM FROM the parking structure. This way, as we walked, our transition would be more gradual, less likely to induce anxiety. Fortunately, there were fewer people as it was the middle of the week in April, and the park was not near as busy as it could be in high season.

But William still looked tense, so I decided to get his mind off of his fears. "So how come your dad and Adam call you 'Liam'? You don't seem to like it much."

"It's a family nickname."

"Ah, family *only*?"

"Family members and old friends called me Liam when I was young. They're used to it. But I prefer William."

"Oh, so I shouldn't call you Wil, then."

"Wil is fine—when *you* call me that."

I smiled. "So I'm the only one who can call you Wil?"

"Well, I can't exactly stop someone if they want to call me Wil."

"Would you want to stop me?" I tilted my head toward him with a cocked eyebrow.

"It depends."

"On what?"

"How you are saying it. If you're speaking in an angry voice or shouting, I'd rather you not use it at all."

I laughed and he smiled. Then he reached for my hand and I took it, squeezing it for reassurance—my silent way of saying, "You got this."

"Jenna is technically my nickname," I continued, noticing he was more at ease while he was talking to me. "But it became my legal name when I was naturalized as a US citizen."

He turned his head toward me, surprised. "Really?"

"Yeah, I chose it when I came here and started school. It's kind of close to my real name, Janja. People were mispronouncing it. It looks like 'Jan-ja' but supposed to be said 'Yan-ya.' I was little and it bugged me, so I changed it." I shrugged.

He frowned but didn't say anything.

"What's wrong?"

He shook his head as we walked along, his free hand stuffed in his pocket. "I just realized that there are so many things I don't know about you. And it made me sad realizing that there's so much more I'll never know."

I blinked, suddenly aware of a vague ache in my chest and the little voice at the back of my head that said it's better that way. It would hurt less.

"How do you say my name in Bosnian?" he said.

"Vilijam," I replied.

"And you'd shorten that to Vil? Someone might call me 'Vile' instead. I like it in English better."

I laughed, relieved by the levity. William could be a funny guy, a sharp contrast to his stoic, silent demeanor. I laughed more with him than I did with most guys I'd dated.

We were quickly approaching the park entrance. "Okay, the first hurdle is going to be the ticket stands," I said, squeezing his hand again. "It's a turnstile, so people will be lined up. There might be some crowding there."

As we exited Downtown Disney, William looked ahead of us, past the shops and restaurants, toward the entrance to the park. "First, they'll look through your bag over at that station, there," he said, pointing toward the bag inspection station. "Then they'll take our tickets at the gate. I looked up the entire procedure online so that I could be prepared and anticipate any outcome. I also memorized a map of the place."

I followed his gaze. "That's right. And after that, we'll pass the Mickey Mouse flowers on the front lawn just below the train station, then go through the tunnel to Main Street USA. There's usually a cluster of people taking pictures there."

He nodded. "You know this place really well."

"Alex used to work here. She snuck me in all the time. That is, after I told her the story."

"What story?" He cocked his head, clearly interested.

"When my mom and dad first told me they were sending my sister and me to live here, I didn't want to go." I shrugged. "So they sat me down and said I'd live near Mickey Mouse, and wouldn't that be a wonderful thing?"

"Did that convince you?"

You have to be brave, my little daughter. I gulped as Papa's voice invaded my thoughts. The Disneyland story was the story I usually told everyone. It was the truth. Just not the whole truth. As far as my friends knew, that was why I'd agreed to leave my parents and my country.

But it wasn't the full story.

"Sure, more or less." I shrugged again, suddenly wanting to change the subject. The thought of lying to William made me itchy and uncomfortable. But he was curious, I could tell, and we were about to make it through the ticket line without incident. So I kept talking. "I wanted to be a princess, like Ariel or Jasmine. Apparently, it was all I talked about, though I don't remember. Maja reminded me of it constantly when we were younger."

"So Maja lived here too. When did she go back?"

"We went back for a summer when I was sixteen and she was twenty-two. My mom asked us to stay and she did. I came back to the US."

"So your mom had to talk you into coming to the US when you were five, but she couldn't talk you into staying in Bosnia when you were sixteen?"

I darted a glance at him, impressed by his perceptiveness. "Yep. I was bound and determined to stay here."

"Why?"

"Well..." I glanced at him and then away, motioning for him to move ahead of me in line.

We were just about to go through the turnstile when William balked. The person behind me in line bumped up against me, and I, in turn, bumped up against William's well-developed backside. Not that I minded. He had a great butt.

"Sorry! Are you okay?" I asked.

"Um," was all he said. His hands began rubbing up and down his thighs. *Was he panicking?*

Quickly, I turned to the people behind me and directed them to the turnstile next to us, then I moved to William's side.

"Hey! You haven't heard the end of my story yet. I'm going to go through the turnstile, and if you want to hear the end, you'll have to follow me through."

He was frowning, staring at the turnstile. I handed the ticket lady both of our tickets and then slowly walked through. Then I turned back around and called, "Don't think about it, Wil. Just think about how much you want to hear my story."

He looked up and bravely met my gaze. I smiled and nodded to him, and he visibly swallowed. Then, he pushed through the turnstile without touching it with his hands.

We ignored the ticket lady, who was looking at us like we were aliens. William approached me, his eyes never leaving mine, and then he smiled.

"Now, tell me that story."

18
WILLIAM

"HIGH FIVE!" SHE SAYS, HOLDING UP HER HAND AND I SLAP it. Then she moves to hug me. I instinctively step back, not because I dislike hugs, but I don't take surprise hugs very well. It's startling when people reach out to grab me without advance notice.

Jenna's eyes widen when she sees my reaction. "I'm sorry."

"I prefer to be asked first."

"For a hug? Okay. Got it."

We walk toward one of the two tunnels that go under the train tracks and lead to the main plaza. There's artwork on the walls—stylized posters from the fifties and sixties advertising various attractions at the park. I stop to admire them for a moment and she stands beside me. "You could do better than that."

It's true, I could. But I haven't forgotten why I'd moved through that wretched turnstile in the first place, with the threat of getting stuck inside it still as strong as when I was six and being dragged through it by my irritated mother.

"So are you going to tell me why you decided to come back to the US?"

She glances at me. "Oh, well that's mostly the end of the story."

"But you said you were going to tell me why."

She nods and turns, indicating we should exit the short tunnel. It brings us out into the Town Square, which, despite its name, is a circular plaza. From here, a street leads toward the rest of the park. There's a horse-drawn trolley car rounding the bend, and I give it a wide berth as we walk. Horses also make me uneasy, especially big ones like that shiny black draft horse.

I take note of the buildings stretching down the short length of the "road," thinking I'd like to paint this scene some day. I wouldn't do it here, of course. So I memorize as many details as I can, in order to recall them later. Doing so also helps keep me distracted from noticing the people milling around. Thankfully, there aren't enough of them to be considered a crowd.

"I came back because I was in love."

I jerk my eyes to Jenna's face. It's hard to tell if she's joking, but she isn't smiling or laughing. I have to really know a person to know their body language and what it means. I can mostly read Adam, Britt and my dad, but Jenna is still about seventy percent mystery to me.

"Who were you in love with?"

She shrugs again. "A boy. Hey, we should go to the City Hall and find out what attractions have turnstiles so we can avoid them. Unless...you want to work on that today, too?"

I frown, picturing the turnstile again, reliving that fear of getting stuck or chopped in half. I shake my head. "One thing at a time."

"I'll be right back." Within minutes, she returns holding a list in her hand. "Apparently, you are far from the only person who has an issue with turnstiles! They had this list all prepared."

She's told me that to make me feel better, I assume. As if knowing that all those other people having the same fear should somehow make me feel better about my own. I think about it for a moment, surprised that, in a small way, it does. Jenna's good at putting me at ease, helping me to feel like less of a freak than I am.

Soon we're walking up one of the sidewalks on Main Street toward the famous candy shop. I can smell vanilla in the air.

"Did you know that Walt Disney designed this street to make it look longer than it actually is?" she asks.

"I did know that. And you changed the subject."

She darts a glance at me and then looks away again, stuffing her hands in her back pockets. "I did. Because really, there's not much more to the story. There was a boy. We met in junior high school. We'd been dating for a few years by the time I went back to Bosnia to visit. I decided to return to the US while my sister and aunt stayed there. When I came back, I moved in with him and his family. Two years later, he was killed in a car accident."

I frown. "That's sad. He was young."

"Yes." I study her face, trying to determine if she is sad. It's a strange thing, grief. It cuts like a knife for the short days and months afterward, eventually dulling into an ache, then a tiny flinch of memory and regret.

"What was his name?"

"His name was Braco, but in this country, he went by Brock. His family is from Serbia, but they live here. I'm still close with them. They're like my own family."

I don't know how to respond to this so I continue walking, and soon she continues. "In fact, I'm flying to Belgrade with them this summer and then traveling to Sarajevo for the wedding."

"But you'll come back so you can travel with the Ren Faire?"

"Yes." She points up ahead of us at the castle. "Look, Sir William, I do believe it's a castle to defend! Shall we go through and see if you can pull the sword out of the stone?"

I scoff. "That's for kids."

"Everyone's a kid at Disneyland, Wil. That's the beauty of it."

"Well, I don't do costumed people. They're creepy."

"The characters?"

I shudder. "Yes, we need to steer clear of those."

She laughs. I love the sound of her laugh. It's musical. And it's times like this when I wish I could paint or draw a sound or emotion— that I could record them as clearly as I can record the things I see.

We make it past the sword in the stone in front of King Arthur's Carousel and through the rest of Fantasyland without any incidents. And thankfully, no characters.

I find that my challenges with crowds are at their worst when we have to stand in long lines for the more popular attractions. Jenna uses those opportunities to practice visualization with me, and for the most part, I'm happy to say that it works.

One of the no-turnstile rides she found is Pirates of the Caribbean, and I end up enjoying this ride a lot. My favorite part about it is watching Jenna as she sits beside me, singing along with the music the entire way through. By the end of the ride, I'm happy that we came. It hasn't been nearly as bad as I thought.

We don't go anywhere near Adventureland though, and after dinner we resolve to do Space Mountain and Star Tours a few more times. I think she's getting exhausted.

We're coming out of the Haunted Mansion when everything changes in an instant.

There are sounds like lightning and thunder overhead. Startled, we both look up and I clap my hands over my ears. I'm grasping at anything to calm myself when, out of the corner of my eye, I notice Jenna collapse into a ball on the ground.

Is she sick? Hurt?

She's curled in on herself, hugging her knees to her chest. People exiting the ride file out past us, jostling us, but I'm too concerned about Jenna to worry about any of them. I bend down next to her and ask, "Are you all right?"

Shaking and whimpering, she rocks back and forth, tucking her head down.

My blood runs cold as my mind races, trying to figure out what to do.

19
JENNA

"JENNA..." EVEN WITH HIS MOUTH PRESSED TO MY EAR, I COULD barely hear William through the fog of my sheer terror.

My mind was frozen twenty years in the past, held hostage in the moments between each explosion. My eyes shut tight, I recoiled with each new sky-splitting boom, and my breath came so quickly I became lightheaded. Just as I thought I might black out, arms wrapped tightly around me.

"Papa! Papa! Pomozi nam!"

It's the third shelling this week. We haven't been able to take the trip to get water since last Thursday. Mama says we can't have baths until things calm down. We're almost out of candles, so every night at sunset I cry in fear of the dark. And this time, the bombing is coming in the dark...

Suddenly, I was on the move, but not under my own power. Those arms were still around me, holding me fast against a hard, broad chest. I could feel William's warm breath on my wet face.

"I'm sorry, sir. You can't go in this way—"

"We're going back inside," he said with fierce determination. "She's frightened by the fireworks."

The voices sounded so far away, and all I could think of was whether or not I was strong enough to draw my next breath. Amazing how sounds could carry you straight back to your worst nightmare, and when they did, that's all you could hear or see. It was like I was there again, in that small apartment, trying to call out to Maja, her not answering me. The smell of plaster and old wallpaper paste invading my nostrils.

"Follow me through the exit," a voice said.

The booming, cracking and popping continued, but the terrifying sounds were fading. I peeled my eyelids open just enough to see that we were once again inside the exit room of the Haunted Mansion.

William spoke quietly and kissed my hair. I nestled against him with a whimper, unwilling to be a grownup just yet. Closing my eyes, I pressed my cheek to his collarbone. "Wil..."

"Hold on to me for as long as you need," he whispered against my ear. I was barely aware of the crowd filing past us. The thudding of my own heart and the desperation of my own breath were the only sounds I could hear.

"Please don't let go," I said through my chattering teeth.

"I won't. I won't ever."

"Can—can we just stay here 'til they stop?"

There was some more discussion with someone I couldn't see, and then William was speaking against my ear again. "The fireworks should be over in about six minutes."

"Thank the goddess," I said.

"Do you want to stand now?"

"No...if that's okay with you."

"You're no heavier than my armor. It's okay with me."

"Thank you so much." I relished the feel of his solid arms around me, his hard chest pressed against my cheek. Relaxing, I closed my eyes.

I could stay here and let him hold me for a week, though his arms would surely break off by then. He would probably try it anyway. I smiled at that thought.

"I hardly did anything," he replied.

I forced a small laugh. "We were coming here today to help you, and *you* ended up helping *me*."

He paused for a moment, then asked quietly, "Are you okay now?"

I nodded, that foggy feeling of old memories fading away along with the panic. "I'd forgotten all about the fireworks show. I'm usually either inside a shop or attraction, or over in the other park, California Adventure, where the fireworks are farther away. It brings back a lot of memories. Bad memories."

"Is that what the shelling sounded like?"

Now that the booming had faded, I could think more objectively about what happened, talk about it like I always did—as if it had happened to someone else. "They sounded almost exactly like that. And I still hear them sometimes in my nightmares." I blew out a breath. "Every day we'd hear about a neighbor or friend whose house had been completely destroyed. It felt like you were a sitting duck, waiting for your own doom."

William kissed my hair again and I melted against him. And apparently, once I'd started talking, I couldn't shut up.

"And snipers…there were snipers too. One day we were at a park and Zora, my sister's best friend, was shot. Just out of the blue. Right in front of us. She was dead in minutes. I didn't even know what had happened, and Mama wouldn't tell me."

His arms tightened around me, and I realized in that moment that I didn't want him to let go, even though I was now past my initial panic. It felt too good. He wasn't saying anything, which prompted me to continue.

"One night, the building next to where we lived was bombed. The ceiling in the bedroom where my sister and I slept caved in. We were buried under plaster. It wasn't serious and we weren't injured, but it was terrifying. I just remember feeling like I was going to die. There was no electricity and everything was pitch black. All I could hear was my sister breathing and whimpering. That was the final straw for my parents."

"But you made it through," he said, kissing my hair again. "You're safe. You're here now."

I shook my head. "I can't believe how that one thing—hearing those fireworks—can take me straight back to that night."

"War is a terrible thing. Especially for children."

I looked up at him. The noise outside had died down, but we didn't move. Then I leaned forward and kissed him, long and deep. When we finally came up for air, his face was flushed. "You were my champion again, Wil. Thank you."

He was silent but smiling, looking very satisfied with himself.

I returned the smile. "If I give you the quest to take me on It's a Small World, would you?"

He frowned. "No dancing dolls. A man has his limits."

"Want to go home then?" I ask.

"Yes."

"Good. Your place or mine?"

"You're trying to seduce me, aren't you?"

I shrugged. "You'll give in sooner or later. A man does have his limits, just as you said. I'm not going to change my stance."

His arms tightened around me. "Neither am I."

My chin came up. I was rising to the challenge. "So I guess the person who is the most stubborn will win out?"

"It seems that way."

We left shortly after that and shared a quiet drive home. William pulled up to my curb, but I didn't get out right away. A half-hour—and a heated make-out session—later, I got out of the car, admitting temporary defeat in my quest to get him upstairs.

Normally, he would have walked me to my door, but tonight, I noticed that he didn't even offer.

Maybe I was getting closer than I thought.

20
WILLIAM

S HE REALLY HAS NO IDEA HOW CLOSE SHE IS.

I'm trying to hide it, but every time it's getting harder and harder to say no.

Because as I spend time with her, I realize that she's more than a beautiful face and a lovely body. She's strength and compassion. She's a fierce advocate for those who can't stand up for themselves.

And she cares. The last time I was at her house, I noticed a copy of *Thinking In Pictures* by Temple Grandin in her room. Grandin is a well-known spokesperson for people with autism, because she herself has Aspergers and has succeeded greatly in her chosen field. Without even saying anything to me, Jenna had obtained a copy of her book to read. I can only assume it's so that she'll have a better understanding of how my brain works.

But is it just a means to an end? Does she want her tiara back so badly that she's willing to do anything to help me get it for her? And if so, where does that leave me once I succeed?

These are a few of the questions I'm considering while training with my European martial arts instructor the following Saturday. As usual, Adam has come to help out. He usually stays for an hour, but today he's here longer because Jordan has decided to join us. And as much as I hate to admit it, Jordan is surprisingly good for a beginner. He has amazing balance from his years on a surfboard, and he is likely a natural athlete, whereas I am not. I've had to train and work hard to compensate.

We're taking a water break when Jordan asks me how things are going with Jenna. I shoot him a sidelong glance as I wipe my face with a towel. I have no idea what Jordan's motive is based on his tone of voice. Even though I've known him a long time, Jordan is harder for me to read than others.

I'm tempted to ignore him and tell him to go away because I'm still angry with him, but I remember the recent talk that I had with Adam.

"She's helping with my enochlophobia."

He frowns. "Ah," he says as if he understands, though I know he doesn't. "Hopefully her *help* involves multiple orgasms?"

I shake my head. "Nope, no orgasms."

"You, uh, need any help in that department?"

I grimace at him. "Not from *you*."

He starts laughing. "No, not—uh." When he looks at my face and likely notes my disgust, he starts laughing even harder. "I wasn't offering."

Adam rejoins our group after a trip to the bathroom. "What's so funny?" he asks Jordan.

"Just coaching our young protégé here in the ways of women."

Adam's eyes widen and he turns to me. "Don't listen to anything he says. His advice is shit."

Jordan flips his middle finger at Adam and turns to me. "So, you're interested in going there with her, right?"

"Going where?" I ask. Jordan and Adam exchange a look.

"He means sex, Liam."

"Oh. I'm interested, but it's not going to happen."

Adam frowns. "Wait, why not?"

"Because she'll be leaving to travel with the Ren Faire at the end of June."

"But that's over two months away. A lot can happen in that amount of time." Adam grinnes. "A lot of *fun* stuff."

"That actually sounds like the perfect starter set to me," Jordan says. "Get in there, get it done. Enjoy yourselves, and since there's a known expiration date to the whole thing, there's no baggage...no wondering if or when it's going to get serious or when to cut things off."

Adam shakes his head at Jordan. "Damn, dude, you really were jaded before you got yourself shackled down."

"Says the guy with his own string of friends-with-benefits lined up before he got *himself* shackled down."

"Shut up," Adam orders and turns back to me. "So, Liam, assuming you're not seeing this all as a strategic maneuver like our cynical friend here...she's bound to come back eventually, right? Or maybe if you start something good, she won't leave."

That had been my thought as well, but I wasn't about to have intercourse with Jenna before I got her commitment that she would stay. "You think I should *go there*, even if she hasn't committed yet?"

Adam blinks. "This isn't 1899, Liam. You don't need a commitment to go to bed with a woman, as long as she's willing—"

"And of age," inserts Jordan. We both turn and stare at him. He looks from one of us to the other. "What? Some of those young ones look a lot older than they really are."

Adam shakes his head and turns back to me. "*Anyway.* There's no harm in opening that door, you know."

I frown for a moment—images of a sliding glass door, the front door of my house, a screen door all flick my mind in quick succession. "I doubt I can be casual about this."

Jordan puts his hand on my shoulder. When I flinch and glare at it, he quickly slides it away. "You're a healthy, red-blooded, twenty-something male. You need to go there…and soon."

I look at Adam to see if he's shrugging off Jordan's comment, but he isn't. Instead, he's nodding in agreement. "If she's willing—and I'm guessing she is—you should go for it. Consider it a new life experience, if nothing else."

"Yes." Jordan nods. "Live in the now, William. *Carpe Diem.*"

A whistle blows and we return to the floor. We fight using metal practice swords and under-armor padding, but after a while we grow hot and sweaty, so we switch to lighter bamboo swords and take off our shirts. I'm getting a lot of good experience with Jordan, or "Southpaw" as Adam jokingly calls him because of his left-handedness.

I'm soundly beating him, getting in three or four hits to every one of his. He curses up a storm when I hit him in the ribs or waist, and Adam laughs until it's my turn to fight *him.* Then he doesn't laugh so much.

I'm doing great, as a matter of fact, not even distracted by the weirdness of my cousin and Jordan giving me sex advice. That is, until the women come back from wherever they've been to watch the end of training.

I'm embarrassed because we all have our shirts off and they're making comments about the "amazing view." April even whistles when Jordan flexes his biceps at her, then he asks, "Young lady, have you bought your tickets to the gun show?" Whatever *that* means.

As for me, I'm quickly getting red marks all over my chest as Adam and Jordan get back at me for clobbering them earlier.

"You lost your mojo, man," says Jordan.

"I'm just a little...distracted."

Jordan casts a glance in the direction where Jenna sits watching us. "Yeah, I picked up on that."

Later, as we are getting dressed in the locker room, Adam comes up to me and, with a warning, puts his hand on my shoulder. "You need to get laid, Liam. Get on that, okay? It might even help your fight." And with that, he places a wrapped condom in my hand.

Jordan, seeing this, nods. "Hey, I've got something for round two." He pulls his wallet from the back pocket of his jeans and extracts a condom. Then he unzips his gym bag and pulls out another one. From his sunglasses case, he removes yet another one, then hands me all three. "I don't need these anymore."

Adam scoffs at him and he shrugs. "April's on birth control now. But back when I was using them, I liked to be prepared." He winkes.

"Jackass," Adam mutters.

"You just hate it when I one-up you. Or in this case, two-up you." Jordan laughes all the way out the door.

I'm thinking a lot about their advice as I drive home with Jenna, aching and sore from the vigorous workout. She's coming to my house for the afternoon to strategize about more exercises to work on and places to go. I'm not happy about the thought—Disneyland was enough of a challenge—but I'm also determined to see this through.

I went from hardly knowing a thing about fighting to nearly defeating Doug at something he'd been working at for years. I could do *this*, too. I wouldn't rest until Jenna had her tiara back in her hands.

Which, come to think of it, she hasn't mentioned lately. So as we sit beside each other on the couch in my living room, I ask her why.

She shrugs. "I just don't think you need that added pressure."

I frown, thinking about that. "Pressure is good. It forces me to work harder."

She cocks her head, watching me. "Why do you insist on being so hard on yourself? Is it that worthiness thing again? You feel like you're not worthy? Because you seem incredibly worthy from where I'm sitting."

I smile. "My worthiness changes based on where you're sitting?"

She laughs. "You are a very funny man, you know that, William? A very funny, sweet, and gorgeous man."

God, how I want to kiss her right now. But instead, I settle against the couch, lean my head back and look up at the ceiling while letting out a groan.

"You okay?" she asks. "You keep rubbing your neck and groaning every time you shift in your seat."

I shrug, embarrassed to tell her that Jordan and Adam beat me down so much that I ache now. "Just a little sore."

"You're sore all over?" she asks. There's a look on her face that I think might be concern, but it's a weird sort of smile.

"Well, not *all* over—just in certain muscle groupings."

"Muscle groupings? Like where? Show me."

"Well, there's my right shoulder..."

Before I can point to it, she reaches over and brushes her fingertips on my sore shoulder. "Here?"

"Yes."

She leans toward me and I can't help but smell her. It makes my chest tingle whenever I smell that cinnamon scent, and before I realize what she's doing, she kisses my shoulder. My gaze drops as she pulls back to look at my face and says, "Is that all?"

Without thinking about what I'm going to say—like I've been warned so many times that I should do—I blurt out, "What are you doing?"

"I'm kissing it better." She appears serious, but sometimes she looks that way when she's being sarcastic.

"You don't seriously believe that that will make it feel better." She *must* be teasing me again. Kissing boo-boos is what mothers do for their small children.

She smiles widely, showing a row of even, white teeth. "It can't hurt, can it?"

I frown, confused. "Of course it won't hurt, but—"

"Wil, just show me. Where else does it hurt?"

I hesitate. "Well, my arm hurts, too."

"Upper arm?" Her fingers press against the exact arm in question. Then she bends and trails kisses from my shoulder down to my elbow. When she makes contact with my bare skin, it feels like icy fire. That's the only way to describe it. It burns and freezes at the same time. I'm completely aware of every cell of her soft lips that touches the cells of my skin.

My mouth is dry and the region below my belt is feeling uncomfortable.

"Does the soreness stop there?" she says, slowly raising her head to look at me. I notice her face is flushed, like that day we were in my weight room with our shirts off. The day when I touched her breasts and sucked on her nipples, and she made those sounds deep in her throat.

Now she's trailing more kisses across the inside of my arm, from my elbow to my wrist. She takes my hand in both of hers and brings my palm to her mouth, opening her lips to land hot kisses there.

I can't breathe. Well, *of course* I'm breathing or else I'd pass out, but it definitely feels more difficult to do so.

She peeks up at me. "Any other injured areas?"

I'm frozen because I really want to lie to her and make up injured areas. I want her mouth and her hands *everywhere*. I suddenly feel as if I *need* them everywhere.

"Um..." I casually point to the base of my neck, remembering how good it felt the last time she kissed me there. With a smile, she leans forward, planting a hot, open-mouth kiss, her tongue snaking out to lick my skin. My heartbeat speeds up. When she pulls away, the place where she kissed feels cold.

My hands move to her back, holding her in place. One of those little sighs escapes her lips and it streaks like lightning right down my spine.

I'm hard as cold-forged steel and have to adjust how I'm sitting in order to relieve the pressure. It feels good and painful all at once. I want this to last for hours, and I want it to end at the same time.

"Does your mouth hurt?"

I suddenly remember the famous scene from *Raiders of the Lost Ark* when Marion is trying to comfort Indiana Jones. She asks him where it *doesn't* hurt, and as he points out body parts, she kisses them. They're on a ship, kissing, and suddenly it fades to black, but you know that they had sex and it's not being shown to the viewer.

And even though I didn't respond, Jenna is kissing me on the mouth now, just like Marion kissed Indy. And just like Indy, I'm not pushing her away. Neither of us are idiots, after all. We both know a good thing when it's happening to our lips.

My mouth opens and her tongue slips in at almost the same moment, as if we'd agreed ahead of time that that's what we'd do. It's as if she knows all the entrance procedures and pass codes already. My barriers have deserted me.

She also seems to know how each stroke of her pretty pink tongue undoes me. I love how she tastes me, and I want to taste her, more and more. And the stronger this desire grows, the harder it is to imagine myself stopping what we're doing. Because it feels so good.

So good.

Jenna is now running her hands over my chest as she kisses me, but unlike last time, she's silent. I'm beginning to feel the danger of this, because if she's not talking, then she's not forcing me to concentrate on what she's saying and thereby distracting me.

Now her hand is on my stomach, moving lower and lower as her tongue continues to stroke mine. Her palm glides over my navel, dropping to rest on my thigh. And I can't help it. When she touches me *there,* no matter how lightly and how quickly, I suck in a breath.

Heat streaks through my belly, burning me up inside. I'm glad she can't see the thoughts inside my head—thoughts of her hands on me, her mouth on me.

She's hesitating, her hand stroking my thigh through my pant leg. I want her to touch me more, but I also want to push her hand away. This feeling is so powerful that it's threatening to control me, and the most frightening part is that I don't even care.

My hands are threaded through her pale hair, holding her head to mine. I have no memory of how they even got there. All I know is that I want her lips on mine and our tongues tangling—for hours. Then her hand moves, sliding back over my erection.

And it stays there. I freeze, unsure of what to do.

"Wil, please let me touch you," she whispers.

Let her. As if I could tell her to stop.

I lie back against the couch, pulling her with me so that our mouths are still connected. She's half beside me and half on top of me, and her hand is fondling me through the thin material of my khaki pants. I wonder if I can stop this before we actually have sex. I know I've drawn that line in the sand, hoping that it will protect me.

But for now, I have the overwhelming urge to touch *her.* I want to feel her breasts in my hands, feel her nipples harden beneath my fingertips.

When my hands find her breasts, she sighs again, and I rub her nipples until I feel that bead-like texture as they harden. I'm fascinated that I've learned this about her body after just one time. I know what she likes, and I want to learn more.

I want to know her body like I know the canvas of a project I've been working on for months—living with it, staring at it, aware of its textures and contours, of the colors and blending required to fill it up.

I want to fill *her* up.

I might not be able to tell when she's being snarky, but I can read these signs and know exactly what turns her on. And I wonder if this process is the same every time. I'll have to figure out what gets me the best results most consistently.

She's stroking me faster now, and it feels like the friction is starting the process of combustion deep within me. Each stroke of her hand is like a shock of electricity straight to the center of my being.

"I like touching you, Wil," she says. Her voice sounds different. Quiet and harsh at the same time.

I swallow what feels like a massive lump in my throat. *I sure like it, too.*

"Do you like it? When I touch you?"

"Yes," I groan.

Jenna's lips hover over mine. "Good. I want to make you feel good, Wil."

I reach down and pull up the hem of her shirt—like she showed me last time. She sucks in a breath and then lifts her arms so I can pull the shirt off, which I do with gusto. The lacy bra covering her beautiful breasts is the next barrier, and I haven't the slightest clue how to remove it. But I've been dying to taste her nipples again, so I push the lace aside and my mouth connects with one in seconds. She arches her back and threads her fingers through my hair.

"That feels so good, Wil. You make me feel so good." My tongue traces the outline of her beaded nipple, over and over again. I suck fiercely and she cries out. A good cry, I think? She isn't pulling away.

I slip my finger inside the other cup of her bra and toy with the other nipple. She's straddling me now, rocking against me. Each time her pelvis presses against mine, I become more and more aroused.

But I don't want to stop her. So I turn my head to suck on the other nipple and she continues to ride me, pushing against my erect penis in a way that almost hurts it's so intense.

"If you keep doing this, I'll climax," I finally choke out my warning. Shame is tangling its way into my chest and entwining with that heat that feels so good.

She pulls back to look at my face, and I'm almost afraid to look at her. When I finally do, she's smiling at me. I haven't shocked her. I haven't made her feel disgusted. At least I don't think I have.

"That's the idea," she says with a small laugh.

"You don't mind?"

"I said I wanted to make you feel good. What did you think I meant?"

I take in a deep, strangled breath and let it go. "I try not to come to conclusions about what people mean when they use words and expressions, because I'm often wrong about them."

"Well, you're not wrong this time." Her hand is on the button of my fly now and I stiffen. "May I?" She bites her lip.

I laugh. "Do you really think there's a remote chance that I'll say *no?*"

Her smile grows larger and she laughs. "You never know, Wil. You've surprised me before."

She slides off my lap, twisting her wrist to release the button on my pants. Then her hand slips inside and…

If I thought it felt good before, I was either wrong or had no perspective for how *this* would feel. Her skin on my skin, stroking lightly and then slowly increasing the pressure, is heavenly. I grasp a handful of her hair and roughly pull her head to mine. I need her lips melding with mine, our tongues together. This feeling as she touches me is almost more than I can handle, and I feel like I'm about to short-circuit.

As she continues, I long to put part of my body inside hers. I'm possessed with the desire to feel her wrapped around me, hot and wet. I want to roll us over right now and finally do it—push myself deep inside her. But I have to settle for pushing my tongue into her mouth while her slim, feminine fingers wrap around me.

"It feels so good," I finally let out between pants. I'm pleased to note that she's breathing just as hard as I am. "Jenna...you are..." I suck in a breath, and when I pull my mouth away from hers again, I murmur fiercely against her lips, "I wish I knew how it would feel to be inside you."

Her fingers slow and she begins to run her hot mouth along my neck. "I can show you what it feels like." When I begin to protest, she cuts me off. "No, it's not what you think."

Suddenly, she is kissing her way down my neck and then across my chest, sucking my nipples through the material of my t-shirt before pulling it off, with my help. Now she's licking my abs as she moves down to my navel. I take careful note of what she is doing because I'm determined to do it all to her, too. I'll kiss my way across her chest, her belly and her navel, then trace my tongue across the inside of her thighs and listen to her moan my name. And then I'll—

Oh, she's kissing me *there*.

Now I'm starting to feel self-conscious about what might happen—and *very* quickly, too. But it feels so good that I'm almost paralyzed by the intensity of the pleasure her mouth is giving me.

In spite of that, I think this might be the time to stop things before they go too far, though I'm really sick at the thought of stopping it. I try to gently remove her head, but she shoves my hand away. "It's okay, Wil. Please let me."

"But I might—"

"That's the point, Wil. It's okay." Her tongue snakes out to swirl around the tip and a hot rush of lust overwhelms me. "I've done this before."

Before I can say another word or even think about being jealous of her doing this for another man, her mouth opens and envelops my aching shaft. And that's it—every other thought in my mind is gone. All I can focus on is how good this feels.

My perspective of how good I can feel has just changed—*this* is the pinnacle. Until seconds later, when she slides her tongue along the underside of my penis and that perspective shifts yet again.

I know that it must feel even better to push myself inside her. To feel her muscles tighten around me, holding me there. To feel her soft thighs rest against my hips as I slip in and out of her. I'm imagining it all in great detail.

But if I think about it too much, I'll want to throw out every one of my principles and do it. In fact, I'm shaking with the need to do it. Like going for days without eating and *needing* food, or going hours through the hot desert without a drink and *needing* water.

I *need* to be inside Jenna.

And each slide of her tongue, each movement of her head, each shift of her mouth alters my perspective of what was amazing ten seconds ago. Sensations are being multiplied, intensified...magnified. Jenna's mouth is commanding my every thought—commanding *me*.

I'm gasping now, barely able to catch my breath. I try to pull away because I'm seconds from climaxing, but she won't let me.

"Jenna, I'm going to—" And it's all over because now I'm coming, and I don't want her to pull her mouth away. Even if she tried, I'd be tempted to hold her there. Fortunately, she doesn't.

Because *this*...

Incredible heated sensations wash over me—over my thighs, my stomach, my chest. My entire body stiffens, thick with pleasure, as I ejaculate. It goes on and on and I'm frozen, my mind numb to everything but *this*.

When my orgasm has played out, Jenna slowly pulls away from me. I can only stare up at the ceiling and bask in this stunning, glowing feeling as she gets up to go to the bathroom.

Minutes later she returns and lies beside me on the couch, leaning against me. I've barely moved. I'm covered in sweat and feeling drugged—or at least how I imagine it would feel to be drugged.

As one of the ninety-five percent of adult males that regularly masturbates, I have experienced numerous orgasms before. Some are very good and some are just okay. But what Jenna just did for me…it's almost like that word cannot be applied to all those other times. They don't even belong in the same lexicon.

I turn and gaze into those beautiful blue eyes, no longer afraid of invading her soul. "You have just ruined every orgasm I will ever have."

21
JENNA

I SAT UP, CONCERNED. "YOU'RE NOT SERIOUS, ARE YOU? WHAT'S wrong?"

His eyes still tracked mine, and it both pleased and disturbed me. It was so unusual for him to meet my gaze. It almost worried me.

"Nothing's wrong. It's just...I think every other orgasm will be a disappointment now."

I laughed, relieved. "It was your first time with oral sex, right? Or even with someone else giving you an orgasm? I almost always have a better orgasm from a partner than when I do it for myself."

His features clouded. "It's always better?"

"Well...yeah, when I actually get one."

"You don't always?"

I shrugged. "No. Sometimes I don't want one. Sometimes he just doesn't know what he's doing." *Like Doug*, I mentally add. Doug the Dud. "And sometimes I just fake it so it will be over."

William's face was serious as his gaze shifted to stare up at the ceiling. He threaded his fingers through my hair and said, "That doesn't sound very enjoyable."

"It's okay."

He shook his head. "No...it's not okay. Any man lucky enough to be able to touch you like that should do everything he can to make you feel good."

I smiled. No guile, no pretense. No pretty, honeyed words to try and get what he wanted. I could trust William because he'd always tell me exactly what was on his mind.

I rolled to my side and placed my hand on his scruffy cheek. "You're so sweet."

He was looking into my eyes again, and I wondered if it was a side effect of the orgasm. I didn't want him to look away. For the first time, I could tell that his eyes weren't as dark brown as I'd originally thought. There were lighter flecks of gold within his dark irises. I swallowed, touched that he was letting me gaze so profoundly at his secrets.

Suddenly, he rose up on an elbow and put a hand on my shoulder to gently roll me on my back. He lowered his head to press his mouth to mine, stealing my breath, invading my mouth with his tongue.

Then he pulled back. "I want to make you feel as good as you made me feel. *Better.*" His free hand cupped my breast, his thumb rubbing over my nipple through the bra. I let out a little squeak as the unfulfilled ache between my legs flared up again. My eyes rolled up into my head until my lids shut tight.

"Oh," I breathed, arching my back.

In seconds, he was tugging on my bra. "I'm not even going to pretend to know how this thing works."

I laughed and removed it for him, then watched his eyes darken as they slid over my bare chest. He flicked his fingers gently over each perky nipple. "Such a pale pink, like a winter rose."

"A winter rose...that's beautiful."

"Not nearly as beautiful as you are, Jenna."

He lowered his mouth to my chest, taking me into his heated, wet warmth. I let out a long, breathy moan, pressing myself deeper into his mouth. His hands tightened on my waist almost painfully, and it felt *so* good.

I really wanted to come, and I wanted it to be from William's touch. To that end, his hand was on my jeans, pulling open the top button as he continued to lavish attention on my chest.

His mouth returned to mine, his hand torturing my sensitive nubs as the other hand slipped inside my jeans.

I wanted my jeans *off*, so I unzipped them and kicked them off as quickly as I could. The moment my legs were free, William looped one of his legs over mine to anchor it in place and then put his hand right back where it had been, stroking me through the thin material of my panties.

"I've never done this before...but I have done extensive research," he murmured.

With a groan, I replied, "I'd say that, so far, you are getting an A-plus, Wil."

He pulled away and opened his mouth to ask for the inevitable explanation.

"I'll explain later. More mouth," I said.

He leaned in to kiss me again and the pressure of his fingers deepened. It burned right through me. I could feel that touch behind my eyes, under my rib cage, in my toes. With each movement of his hand, he was stroking me everywhere else, owning my body without even realizing it.

His mouth returned to my nipple and began tormenting me once again. I let out a tight breath as the tension between my legs increased. My desire thickened into husky moans.

"I can tell that you like it," he said.

"Yes," I said with a heavy sigh. "More."

He slowly slid the panties down my legs. Though I was in a hurry to have more of his hands on me, I didn't rush him. He'd likely never taken a woman's panties off before. This was a first for him in so many ways, and I wanted him to savor it.

"These look so delicate they might rip."

I smiled, thinking it might be a little sexy if he did decide to rip them off someday. After he pulled them off my ankles and carefully set them aside on top of my jeans, William turned back to me, scanning my body from head to toe.

Another first...me naked in front of him.

"Are you memorizing me so that you can paint me later?" I joked.

His brow twitched into a frown. "I'll always be able to recall what you look like in this moment, spread out on my couch with no clothes on."

I smiled, about to reply when one hand moved to the apex of my thighs and the other took my wrist and pinned it above my head. His fingers were gentle as they continued to explore, stroking lightly along the top of my sex before pushing deeper.

Then he found my clit and I almost jumped a foot. "Here? This is your clitoris..."

"Um, yes, that's right. That's a *very* good spot to touch."

"I know."

His mouth came down on mine and his fingers increased their pressure.

"Open your legs more," he whispered between kisses, and I readily complied. Now there were two—wait, make that three—fingers touching and stroking, taking turns, softly and quickly, then slowly, then firmly. All in just the right places.

He was a quick study at this.

Two fingers slipped inside me, exploring my entrance then sliding in deeper with consistent strokes. As if this wasn't enough, he clamped his mouth onto my breast again, sucking and grazing my nipple with his teeth. *Oh. My. Goddess.*

In minutes, I was a breathless slave to his fingers and his mouth. And he didn't stop.

"How will I know when you've climaxed?"

"Oh, you'll know," I said. "Just don't stop."

But he *did* stop. When I opened my eyes, he said, "I want to do what you did and use my mouth. Would that be okay with you?"

Would that be okay? That would be goddamn fucking heaven.

"Please," I said, and he instantly moved down toward the juncture of my thighs. He started with shallow kisses and then began licking my clit. At this same time, two fingers slipped inside me again, pushing deep.

Where the hell had he learned that? I thought in shock as my body arched obediently to the command of his hands. If he were any other man, I'd suspect he'd been lying about being a virgin.

My throat was now hoarse from my moans. Between what his mouth was doing to me and his fingers pushing deeper—not to mention how hot it was that he still tightly clasped my wrist with his free hand—I was experiencing nothing short of ecstasy.

Soon I was holding my breath as heated convulsions of pleasure washed over my entire body. He stopped a little too quickly, and I had to grab his hand and press it against my clit until the orgasm had faded. When it did, I collapsed on the couch, my skin glowing with perspiration.

He moved to lie beside me. "I pulled away because I wanted to watch your face when you had your orgasm. It may have been one of the most beautiful things I've ever seen."

I almost laughed but decided against making a joke about the infamous "O face." It would take too long to explain, anyway. Instead, I turned and looked into his eyes again. He held the gaze for a few seconds and then his eyes slid down to rest on my chin.

"That was amazing," I breathed. "Thank you."

A faint smile appeared on his lips, as if he was proud of himself, and I found that in spite of feeling sated, I really wanted to kiss him again. I wanted more of him. And now that he'd had a taste of what it could be like between us, and since I was already naked...

I rose up on one elbow and caught his mouth with a kiss. "No fair you got to see me naked and I didn't get to see you. But you know...we don't have to be done here."

He said nothing but returned my kisses with growing fervor. My hand slipped down over his crotch to, um, check the temperature, so to speak.

He was hard again.

"William," I said against his mouth, and he continued to kiss me. "I'm on birth control and I'm clean."

The kiss ended when he pulled back. "Why wouldn't you be clean? You shower regularly."

I grinned. "No, I mean I don't have any STDs. I get checked regularly. And since you've never...we won't have to worry about using a condom."

"I have condoms." My brows shot up. *Really...* "But nothing's going to happen unless..."

I fell back against the couch and looked up at him. He had a very determined look on his face, damn it.

"Say you'll stay, Jenna."

I licked my lips and remained silent. A niggling feeling of guilt rose up, causing me to question where the hell it had come from. When I spoke, my voice was barely above a whisper. "Life's too short to worry about things like commitment. We should just enjoy each other."

"Is that what you're afraid of? Life being too short?"

My eyes closed.

"People you've cared about have died. So that's why you think about life being short. That's why you have to run off and experience everything you can. That's why you let fear drive you."

Opening my eyes, I pushed against his chest, shoving him away from me. "Please get off," I said. "I'm no coward."

He sat back and watched me as I grabbed my clothes and slipped them on. "You're right. You aren't."

I blinked, suddenly feeling tears burning the backs of my eyes. He was closer to the truth than I'd *ever* admit in a million years. Life *was* short. People you loved died and left you all alone. I bit my lip and refused to allow those tears to escape.

"Jenna..." I was about to get off the couch when he hooked a hand around my waist. "I didn't mean to hurt your feelings."

"But you did."

He kissed my hair. "This is who I am. I say what's on my mind. I'm sorry."

I fell against his hard chest and his other arm held me close to him. Everything inside me ached. I wanted to be with him so badly it literally *hurt.*

And the scariest thing of all was that I was starting to seriously consider telling him I'd stay, seeing what this might become. But I had promises to keep—to others and to myself.

If it became *something*, then my beliefs and everything I thought I knew about the world would go flying out the window. I'd be in unchartered territory. No map. No plan. Not even my cards to rely on.

He was right. I *was* afraid. Terrified, in fact, of what this could become.

22
WILLIAM

A FEW DAYS LATER, MY WORKDAY IS INTERRUPTED BY AN unexpected text from Jenna. It's strange because I had just been thinking about her.

Mia and Adam invited us to go to Medieval Times w/ them. Wanted to check to see if ok w/ you.

I have never been there. From what I've gathered from advertising, it is a dinner and entertainment show involving knights and jousting—all with period-inaccurate armor and weapons.

I know that it would probably be best to follow up our progress from Disneyland with a setting of this sort, but I really don't want to. I'd much prefer to spend time alone with Jenna again.

But time alone would make for more frustrating circumstances like the other night—the night I really wanted to have sex and stopped it anyway.

Sometimes I think I'm not so smart.

Me: *I don't know.*

Her: *I'd love to see you again. And we could laugh @ the fake fighting. Might be fun & more importantly would help w/ crowd issues.*

Me: *Inauthentic fighting annoys me.*

Her: *I'll wear my low-cut medieval blouse & push-up bodice...*

Me: *Deal.*

As the days pass until the next time I see her, I spend a lot of time thinking about my convictions. I'm seriously considering letting them go. I've thought a lot about what Adam said—and even what that fool Jordan said.

So the next time Adam and I are alone together, I bring up the subject of sex and ask for more in-depth advice. I'm relieved that Jordan is nowhere near to interrupt with his plethora of condoms and bad advice.

It's just my surrogate big brother and me.

It's Wednesday night, and I'm working out in his home gym because he has weight machines that I don't have. He's choosing to use his treadmill instead of running out in the streets or along the beach, like he prefers. Afterward, we go up to his kitchen to take a water break and sit down. He pulls an apple from a nearby bowl of fruit, washes it and bites into it.

"What's on your mind, guy?" he says without looking at me.

I've been trying to figure out a way to ask, and he seems to have figured that out from how I'm acting. I envy that he can sense things based on my gestures and looks. I've seen that in his observation of others, too. We can be in the same room and both participate in a conversation, and yet afterward when we discuss it, he's come away with a long list of nuances and impressions that I have completely missed.

I've long since been thankful to have Adam as an ally. He is incredibly smart and always has been. So am I, but he is smart in different ways than I am. We complement each other because of that.

"I do want to talk to you about something," I say, confirming his inquiry. "But it might make you uncomfortable."

Part of his mouth slants up in a smile. "Are you going to nag me about setting a wedding date again? Because we're on the same side. I know what I want. Emilia is the one who keeps hedging." As usual, he calls his fiancé by her full name instead of Mia, like everyone else calls her.

"I'm not nagging you about that. First, a nag is an old horse. I'm neither old nor a horse." Adam grimaces at my attempt at a joke, then unscrews his water bottle to take a drink.

"I wanted to ask you about sex. I have a lot of questions, and the pornographic material I've been reviewing—"

Adam starts choking on his water. Perhaps it was the mention of pornography. But how else can I learn about sex if not by watching people do it?

"Do *not* use porn as educational material, Liam," Adam finally said, the redness in his face only deepening. "They do stuff in porn—even the vanilla stuff—that can't or shouldn't be attempted in real life."

I scratch my stubble. "Vanilla? Porn comes in flavors?"

"It means, um, regular sex. No kink. Anyway, a lot of what they do in porn videos is not real. There's a lot of acting involved, a lot of creative techniques. A lot of weird positions in order to maximize the camera angles."

I nod, absorbing that. "I understand the mechanics of it all. And I get that it's easier for a man to achieve orgasm. But what I want to know is what it's like if one of the partners is far less experienced than the other. Like how do they treat that person's first time?"

Adam took a breath and let it go, looking to the side. "Well, as long as each partner has some understanding of the other's sexual history—especially in a special case like that—"

"What about your first time?" I interrupt. "Was she more experienced than you?"

Adam blinks, his face reddening again. "Uh, yeah. She was older, and she'd had a few partners before me."

"How much older?"

"Six years," he answers, looking over his shoulder as if he's afraid someone might be listening in. We are alone though, since Mia is out with her mother tonight. Adam shifts in his seat and fiddles with his water bottle, cracking it loudly.

"Six years?" I repeat. "So Lindsay was your first partner? I thought she came later."

Adam's eyes widen. I know that look on his face means surprise. Likely he's surprised by my deduction. "I didn't realize you knew about that."

"It wasn't a well-kept secret, Adam. You both worked for my dad, and then when you went off to college, she drove up to Pasadena a lot to see you. It's hard to keep a two-year secret from all of your mutual friends."

His mouth thins. "I suppose so."

"I just didn't know she was your first. But that information is useful. Did she explain to you what she wanted? What she liked?"

Adam twists the stem of his apple and doesn't look up. "Uh, yeah, more or less. And I figured stuff out as I went along. I'm a quick learner."

He *must* have learned fast. I recall overhearing others gossip about him back in his single days, and he apparently never lacked for sexual partners.

"And Mia?"

Adam gets this strange look on his face that I cannot read at all. He shoots out of his chair, rubbing at the back of his neck.

After a long minute, I'm about to repeat my question—in case he didn't hear me the first time—when he finally speaks again. "What about her?" he asks quietly.

"Was she more experienced than you?"

His cheeks bulge, like he's clenching his jaw, and suddenly he's taking a lot of interest in rearranging the magnets on the fridge. "No," is all he says.

"Maybe I should talk to her. Maybe one of her previous partners wasn't as experienced as her."

That strange look crosses Adam's face again. "You shouldn't bother. Emilia was a virgin."

"Oh. Hmm." I scratch my jaw again. "So much for getting a woman's perspective, then. So she's never been with anyone else besides you?"

He's standing kind of stiffly now. "No."

"That doesn't worry you?" I ask.

He frowns. "Worry me? Why would it worry me?"

"Well, when you two get married, she will never have the chance to be with anyone else—presumably for the rest of her life. She doesn't feel like she missed out?"

Adam lets out a long sigh and turns around, picking up his workout towel. But he doesn't respond to me for a while. "I guess I never thought about it like that. She doesn't seem to mind."

"You should ask her."

"Or," he says, turning back to me, "I could just not bring it up. And neither should you—especially all that stuff about Lindsay."

"Why? Does she believe you have feelings for Lindsay? I hope you don't. But if you do, I'll fight the next duel against you." I'm joking. I know he doesn't feel anything for Lindsay, though they still see each other as friends from time to time.

"Emilia already knows the general gist of all that. But it would bug her to talk about it. People don't like to hear about their partner's former lovers."

"Well then, I guess you're lucky she doesn't have any that you might hear about."

Adam looks up at the ceiling for a few moments but doesn't say anything.

"Why is that?" I ask.

"Why is what?"

"Why don't people want to hear about their partner's former lovers?"

"Do you want to imagine Jenna with some other man?"

I picture it immediately—Jenna wrapped in Doug's arms. Holding his hand. Him kissing her. Suddenly, I'm inexplicably angry, my face flushing with heat. Adam notices, of course, because then he nods. "See? Now you get it."

"You're lucky you don't have to worry about that *ever*."

"I'm lucky for many reasons. I have the most amazing woman in the world. You can have the second best." He grins.

"It doesn't make sense, though, why that makes me mad. I know she hates Doug now. He was callous and rude to her. She won't even speak to him. I have nothing to be jealous about."

"But picturing them together, even if it's the past, is enough to make you angry. And maybe she was with other guys before that."

"That was before I knew her though. But even that makes me mad. I don't get it."

Adam smiles. "I think you've got it pretty bad."

"Got what?"

"I think you're falling hard for this girl. Just be careful, okay? Don't pin too much on this. Emilia says..." Then he cuts himself off, looking away.

"What does she say?"

Adam shakes his head. "Well, some people like being in long-term relationships and some don't. And you've mentioned that Jenna plans on moving soon."

I shrug and look away too. Adam's words are reconfirming my decision not to have sexual intercourse with Jenna. Even if it would be the most pleasurable experience of my life, the pain of her leaving afterward would not make it worth it.

"I understand. I'm not planning on having sex with her."

Adam gets that weird smile again. "You should just go with the flow, Liam. See where it takes you. Don't hold yourself back. Sometimes things happen that aren't in the plan."

"That never happens for you," I say. "You always have everything mapped out ahead of time."

Adam laughs, but I'm not sure why. "Some things in life are impossible to plan. Count on that for love—if, of course, that's what it turns out to be."

I wonder what he means and continue pondering this great mystery called *love*. Who'd have thought that something you can't see, hear or touch, much less even *define,* could rule your life so completely?

23
JENNA

I T WAS FINALLY THE WEEKEND, AND I WAS EXCITED TO ATTEND Medieval Times with William, Adam and Mia. As promised, I wore my medieval garb, complete with a bodice corset over my low-cut, off-the-shoulder blouse. Mia wore my other outfit—I'd bartered with one of our seamstresses to make it for me—but as Mia was taller, it ended up being a little short. She paired the dress with some boots though, and it looked great.

The boys had refused to join in on our fun, opting for boring twenty-first century clothing instead. However, Adam did say he approved of the cleavage that Mia's costume created and gave it two enthusiastic thumbs up.

I'd been pretty shocked when Mia had approached me with the idea of Medieval Times, saying she wanted to help William with his crowd issues. It seemed like this hard working, young power couple wouldn't have time for things like this. Adam was a mega-busy billionaire and Mia was just as overloaded with medical school. But apparently I was wrong. Adam even treated us to a limo ride and bought the tickets to the best seats in the house.

Medieval Times was located on the main drag in Buena Park along a stretch of entertainment venues not far from Disney's rival theme park, Knott's Berry Farm. The structure was large, like a big warehouse, but decorated with towers and other accouterments to make it appear like a castle. There were even fake turrets and a drawbridge, as well as brightly colored pennants flying above crenelated walls. The effect was ruined, however, by the flashing digital sign out front advertising the venue to passersby on the busy boulevard.

We presented our tickets and were given seating assignments and color-coded paper crowns that denoted we'd be sitting in the red section of the arena.

I sighed as we found seats along the walls of the entry hall. "What is with the male fascination with boobs, anyway? My eyes are up *here*, people!" I said after the fifteenth pair of male eyes fastened on my bust. Mia and I had both garnered a lot of attention in our period garb.

Adam shrugged, slinging an arm around his fiancée's shoulders and savoring an appreciative eyeful of her cleavage. "Be thankful men don't have boobs. If they did, they'd never leave the house."

William began berating him for how silly an idea that was, since male mammals do not have the need for mammary glands to produce milk for their young. It was amusing to watch Adam and Mia fight off the laughter from that mini-tirade.

The main hall outside the arena was a capitalist haven. Everywhere you looked there was princess swag, flowing pennants and medieval-style plastic play swords. Adjacent to the main hall were the stables where guests could admire the gorgeous steeds that the

knights would be riding during the jousts. Mia, having grown up around horses, took a great interest, commenting on how beautiful and well bred they were. We were also able to explore the mews for birds of prey—falcons and hawks with hoods and long leather jesses hanging from their legs.

As I walked beside William, I caught small snatches of the quiet chatter between Adam and Mia. I heard talk of some kind of "bet" along with the usual good-natured teasing between them.

Back in the front hall, William stood against the wall while we continued to wait. He scanned the room with arms tightly folded across his chest, breathing deeply—the way I'd shown him—and seemingly aware of every little thing that was happening. I offered him my ear buds and tunes from my playlist in order to drown out the sounds of the crowd, which seemed to visibly calm him.

Adam went off to buy us all some drinks.

"So...how are things going with you and William?" Mia asked.

"Good," I nodded. "We've been having fun."

Mia's head tipped toward me, her mouth twisted in a crooked smile. "Really...what kind of fun?"

I frowned. "The usual kind."

"Like the usual kind for two friends hanging out, or...*your* usual kind?"

"Goddess, Mia, you make me sound like a fallen woman, to use the medieval term."

She shrugged. "Just curious."

I narrowed my eyes. "So you've said. You're *extremely* curious. Both you *and* your future hubby." After our encounter on the couch, I asked William about the condoms and he said Adam had given them to him along with some advice.

Mia blushed and changed the subject. Which was good, because she really didn't need to know how much William had enjoyed playing with my boobs—or how much I'd liked it when he did. I'd keep that our little secret.

Nothing more was said until we were directed to enter the red section of the great arena. That was where we would be cheering for the Red Knight. The playing field was divided by six different colors: green, black, white, red, yellow and blue, each with its own corresponding "champion."

"This is our lucky night! Red is my favorite color," I said. "What's yours, Wil?"

"All of them," he answered with a straight face.

"Hmm...must be an artist thing, I guess."

He looked at the place settings. "There are no forks."

"We're at Medieval Times. We eat like the medievals did," joked Adam.

"This meal and style of eating is completely inauthentic. As is the term 'medievals,'" William said. "I'm not going to eat with my hands."

"How is it not authentic?" I asked.

"Well, look at the menu. Herbed potatoes and tomato bisque. Potatoes and tomatoes came from the New World. They were not available for European people to consume during the Middle Ages. And we won't even discuss the Pepsi."

Adam laughed behind his hand and Mia smacked his arm without even looking at him. "I'll ask for a fork for you, William. But I won't ask for one for Adam. He eats like a Neanderthal anyway."

"Hey," Adam replied, feigning irritation before letting a grin slip through.

ed through the doors and instantly heard the sound of
 whacking against hard plastic. Apparently, Adam had
word of his own and was fending off William's blows.

top the Inigo Montoya act before I really have to hurt
 said in time with William's aggressive thwacks against his
uple of times, Adam failed to block William's onslaught
 the flat of a "blade" across his thigh or shoulder.

are you!" William said between clenched teeth.

a joke. Shit. Fuck—that hurt, Liam. Goddamn it!" And then
an beating William back in earnest.

epped forward before I could say anything. Not that I was
 was completely bewildered by these two well-built grown
g at each other with all of their strength—with plastic
o less.

up!" Mia said, but they completely ignored her. I was
mostly because both of them adored her so I'd figured her
s the law. But they weren't listening, shoving each other and
g each other by turns.

le at the bar and the nearby gift shops had come out to watch,
e periphery of my vision, I saw a uniformed security guard
their way.

ys, you're about to get arrested—" I began.

ke this outside!" Mia yelled even louder than before. *That* they
 to.

d they even pay for those swords?" I asked as we pushed out of
s doors and into the parking lot.

hrew a bill at the guy when I grabbed the sword," Adam said
n gritted teeth as he glared at his cousin. "And asked them to
new one to the kid Liam swiped his from."

I took this opportunity to ask about something I'd been curious
about. "Do you two even get a chance to go out on dates much with
your busy schedules?"

The two of them looked at each other and Mia smiled ruefully.
"No, not really. We're like an old married couple already."

"Which is why we should just set the date already," Adam said.

She rolled her eyes. "You and your one-track mind. What
difference does it make?"

"We'll see, won't we?" he said, shooting her a mysterious look.
"When I get to name that date."

"In your dreams."

Puzzled by their cryptic conversation, I looked to William for
guidance, but he wasn't listening. He was casting a baleful eye over the
arena, particularly the horses and riders who had entered to "warm
up" by performing various feats. He muttered repeatedly how the
knights' games and contests were inauthentic. He used that word a *lot*.

We were served our meals—delicious, roasted chicken with the
afore-mentioned anachronistic potatoes, and even a yummy baked
apple tart for dessert.

After we ate, the knights started their tournament games in order
to please the "king" and the "princess," who sat high on a platform
above the arena. William critiqued the heraldry, the weapons and
especially the knights' "sham armor," saying, "If I wore armor like that
to a tournament, I'd be brain dead or physically disabled in minutes."

After the dishes were cleared, Adam and Mia sat with their heads
together in their own private conversation. I shamelessly attempted
to eavesdrop on them. Again I picked up the word "bet," which was
followed by a furtive glance in the direction of William and me. That's
when I put it together.

"Oh. My. Goddess," I exclaimed out loud the minute the conclusion jumped into my head. "You two made a bet about us, didn't you?"

William's head wheeled around and he looked at me. "A bet? What kind of bet?"

They didn't even have to answer my question. I could tell by the way Adam was looking away as if I hadn't said a thing, and by the fact that Mia was turning as red as a non-medieval era tomato. I was right.

"A bet?" Adam finally looked at me and said. "That's silly. What kind of bet would we make about you?"

I narrowed my eyes. "Well, I'm guessing that whoever wins gets to set the wedding date…and that you're betting about William and me sleeping together."

Adam's reserve slipped—just for a moment—but it was Mia's reaction that gave me all the information I needed. Her eyes widened and she had *guilty* written all over her face.

"*What?*" William said, shooting out of his seat to loom over the rest of us. He glared at his cousin. "Is that why you've been giving me *helpful* advice? You had a motive behind it?"

Adam held up an open hand to his cousin. "Sit down, man. We can talk about this later. The princess is about to get captured by the bad guy."

But instead, William grabbed a plastic toy sword—I had no idea where it came from—and pointed it at his cousin. Adam's eyes widened, but he grabbed the end of the sword and shoved it away. "Hey! Point that thing someplace else."

The tip of the play sword then returned right back in Adam's face. "Tell me the truth…what was the bet about?" William demanded of his cousin.

William shook his head, muttering. I fell into step beside him, looking at him closely. He was tense from head to toe. I caught Mia's eye and we placed ourselves in between the two men, who were still winded and glaring at each other.

"Are we going to be able to go home in the same car?" Mia asked the two of them. "Because I don't want to get caught between four hundred pounds of male bonehead going at it in the back of a limo."

"You two should really save all that pent-up energy for your practice tomorrow," I said, suppressing laughter at the thought of "Plastic Swords, Part 2" playing out in the martial arts studio. "You could wail on each other with real weapons then. And if things go your way, William, you'll injure him so badly that he won't be able to set a date for the wedding even if he were to win the bet."

"Why are you even making a bet to determine something as important as your wedding date, anyway?" William huffed. "This isn't the first time the two of you have behaved so childishly. You should let *me* set the date."

Mia's mouth dropped open.

"Well, that was kind of the idea," Adam cracked, and Mia elbowed him in the rib cage.

Awkward.

We rode home in silence. Mia finally got the nerve to say something before we got to my house. "I'm sorry, you guys. We didn't mean to make things weird for the two of you."

William and I glanced at each other. "It's not weird for *us*," he said.

Mia's brows rose. "Oh...well..."

He continued. "It's weird for the two of *you*, however. Adam wants to get married this year. He told me so. You want to wait until you're done with medical school. Even if he is being a dickhead, I agree with him."

Adam scowled. "Dickhead?"

I tried to hold back the laugh bubbling up in my throat as Mia stared at William, wide-eyed. The two of them had just gotten served and they knew it.

"Let's just leave it at that, okay?" I said before it could escalate again. "Maybe we should drop Wil off first."

"I think I'll be able to control these two for ten minutes," Mia said. "Especially since they get to beat on each other for real tomorrow."

Neither Adam nor William looked at each other, and thankfully my stop was first. As soon as we arrived, I beat it out of that limo like a bat out of awkward hell.

***

"And the lady behind the woman in the striped dress?"

William sat beside me again on the now infamous couch. I sat facing him with a large coffee table book open in my lap, propped so that he couldn't see the painting I was looking at. I hadn't mentioned the name or anything else about it, just the page number of the random book I'd pulled off his shelf.

His head was propped back against the wall, his eyes closed. "The one in the black, with the bonnet?"

"Uh, yeah, her."

His eyes squeezed tighter. "It's harder to do this with two-dimensional scenes, but...let's see. She has her hand on the shoulder of the woman in front of her. She's wearing a black gown, and her bonnet has blue and orange flowers. Around her neck she's wearing a black choker with a coral cameo pendant."

Holy crap, this was almost eerie. His recollection was both accurate and detailed. My eyes skimmed over the entire painting— *Dance at the Moulin de la Galette* by Auguste Renoir—a canvas that depicted hundreds of people in an outdoor dance hall gathering on a Sunday afternoon in Paris. The light and colors of the painting were exquisite.

"Did you want to know anything else? I can tell you about the dancing couples behind them if you want. Or the crowd further back."

I gently closed the book. "No, that's okay. I'm sufficiently intimidated."

He opened his eyes and looked at me. "Intimidated? Why? Because I have a good memory?" He shrugged. *Good*, ha! "It's nothing special. I still freak out in crowds."

"Not true. You did really well at the movie theater today."

"I had to take breaks," he said, referring to the multiple times he'd left the movie to take breathers.

"But the breaks were less and less frequent as the movie went on. I'm proud of your progress." He didn't reply so I nudged him. "I mean it, Wil. You're pushing yourself. You're doing great. There's no need to downplay all your wonderful accomplishments because you have a few hang-ups. We all do."

His brown eyes fixed on me, taking in my hair, my lips, my chin. "You have hang-ups? I thought you were perfect."

Heat flushed my cheeks. "Stop it. You know I'm not."

His dark brows creased, and he reached up to trace my cheek and my jaw with his thumb. "I *don't* know that. I see...a strong woman who is pure and good, and is determined to help others. Not just beautiful on the outside, but on the inside, too."

I licked my lips as my throat tightened. "Stop. You're embarrassing me."

He appeared truly puzzled. "You and I are the only ones here. What are you embarrassed about? The truth is not embarrassing, Jenna."

I placed the book on the floor at our feet. He promptly bent, scooped it up and replaced it in the exact spot where I'd removed it twenty minutes before.

"Why do you not like to hear positive things about yourself?" he said as he sank down beside me, closer this time.

I shrugged.

"Is that why you don't want to stay? Because you don't think you're good enough to deserve permanence?"

"Wil," I warned with a sigh. He was like a dog with a bone, unable or unwilling to let this go.

"Tell me, Jenna. I honestly want to understand."

I shook my head. "I don't think I can help you understand. It's just...my fate, I guess? My gut instinct that tells me this is what I need to do."

He thought about that for a moment, then reached up and ran his fingers through my hair. "Can your fate ever change? If you found someone...even if it's someone who's not your soulmate..." His voice shook with emotion and then died out.

I squeezed my eyes shut. "I don't have all the answers. I just know what I know...and it's not running away. I promise you..." I said the words, but my heart wasn't in them today. I just wanted him to hold me. I wanted us to enjoy being in each other's company. "I've learned the hard way that things are not permanent. That everything is temporary."

"They do end up being temporary if you move on before they can become permanent," he said. "It's a self-fulfilling prophecy."

"I can't expect you to understand."

"Maybe you should give me the chance to."

I leaned away from him, settling against the back of the couch, and his hand fell from my hair back into his lap. "You pretty much know it all...until I was five, I lived in a completely different country that got the shit bombed out of it. My sister and I were sent away. My papa made all kinds of promises, but they never happened. I never saw him again. The end."

William was watching me intently now. He shifted so that he was fully facing me. "He couldn't have known he was going to die."

My breath shivered. "He could have come with us. Then he wouldn't have died in that shitty, pointless war. Instead, he told me I had to be brave. 'Go to America,' he said. 'You'll be safe and we'll all be together again soon.' He was a liar." Sudden emotion rose up and choked me. I covered my face, not just to hide the tears from William, but to hide my utter shame at what I'd said. *I didn't mean that, Papa. Forgive me.*

I felt the weight of William's arms around my shoulders. I leaned against him, tears streaming quietly down my cheeks. With him this close, I felt the same sense of safety that I'd felt the night of my Disneyland firework freak-out. His solidness was comforting. Soon, I was telling him things I hadn't told anyone else...ever.

"And then we came here to live. We moved around in those days, stayed a year or two at a distant relative's home, had our own apartment for a while. Then we lived with family friends after we lost that place when the rent went up. And, as I told you, I met Brock and fell in love when I was a teen." I sniffed.

"Mama wanted me to go back—'come home, it's time,' she'd said. But I couldn't because it *wasn't* home. I'm no more Bosnian now than I am German or Canadian. Brock was *here,* and Mama was so mad that I'd give up the chance to live with my own family. But I was so dumb and young and in love that nothing else mattered. So I hurt my Mama and stayed here instead. Brock and I were going to be together. I was counting on that until..." My voice faded as emotions seized me once again.

"Until he died."

"Yes. People seem to do that around me." That darkness rose up, and it was blinding.

"What, do you think you're cursed or something?"

I took a deep breath and let it out in a shivery hiss. "I should have been the one driving him home that night. That was the plan. We'd gone to a party and there was drinking. But I was tired. We argued and I told him I was going home to sleep. I was sober. I could have driven him. Instead, he got a ride home later with a friend who'd been drinking too much. I...I wasn't there for him."

He shook his head. "That's not logical to blame yourself for something that you could not have predicted. No one can know the future."

"But I know my future. It's *change.* Always change. Once anything starts to become permanent, I get nervous...itchy." I stifled a sob and sniffed back my tears like a toddler. They clogged my throat just as quickly. "I lived with Brock's family for a while after he died. I was depressed, but somehow I finished high school. I didn't want to leave to go to college, until his mom said I must. That it would be the best thing for me to get on with my life. So I did...but moving on meant moving again." I sighed heavily. "There's a legend in my family. Baba—that's what we called my grandma—used to say we had Gypsy roots. The Roma are wanderers. They have no home, and sometimes I feel this connection to that part of myself. Like I was never meant to be pinned down in one spot. That these things in my life happened to teach me that."

He scoffed. "It's easier to move on and forget the past when things are painful. Or at least try to forget it."

I looked at him, wondering about that strange and accurate insight, so rare from him. Did he speak from experience? "So you still think I'm running away?"

"I think that sometimes a person can believe something about themselves so much that it becomes the truth."

My eyes narrowed at him. "Like being unworthy. A person can believe himself unworthy."

William blinked. "I guess you're right."

"Maybe we're more alike than you think." My mouth quirked into a semblance of a smile. "Despite the fact that I'm neurotypical."

"I don't hold that against you," he said with a sly smile.

In spite of the tears, I laughed. "Thank goodness."

He softly stroked my hair. "Maybe permanence is what scares you."

I shrugged. "Maybe." But if so, why did I feel empty inside? I was definitely lacking the usual excitement I felt just before moving on.

"I want you to stay, Jenna. I want you to be with me."

I raised a brow and looked up into his face. "You mean like, sex and stuff?"

"More than just that. We could...have a relationship."

I smiled. "My relationships don't last long, either. Doug was three months. That's about average." I looked away, disconcerted by the way William seemed to be studying my face without looking at my eyes.

"Are you always the one doing the breaking up?"

I thought about it for a moment, running through a quick inventory of past boyfriends. In every case, I had been the one to call things off. My jaw dropped. "Wow..."

"What?"

"I *have* been the one to break things off every time."

"After three months?"

I shrugged. "More or less." He turned away, but not before I saw the frown on his face. "What's wrong?"

He shook his head. "I'd rather not be with you if it's only going to last that long. I think in the end it would be too hard."

I swallowed, pulling away from him. He had a point. "You're an all-or-nothing sort of guy?"

"I'm all about absolutes."

My brows creased as I thought about it. Had I crushed those guys' hearts? I'd never let it get serious enough, and most of the times they'd shrugged it off and moved on. But I had a feeling that no matter what I told William and no matter how much I tried to prepare him for it, he wouldn't recover easily from me leaving.

He was right about this, and I had to stop pushing for it. He wanted something more than I could give him...and I couldn't demand that he expect anything less than what he wanted.

He wanted me. And as amazing and wonderful as that made me feel, I could not give him what he wanted. That was *my* failing, not his.

I was stuck in this endless cycle of momentary gratification. Of chasing the next shiny thing, following the wind. Of...*running away.*

24
WILLIAM

I'M FEELING MELANCHOLY AS I DRIVE HER HOME TONIGHT, UNABLE to shake the feelings we'd stirred up—a curious mix of happiness and sadness, of hopes and losses and strong desire.

This heaviness never seems to go away. Every time I look at her, the weight increases, twists and even makes me a little breathless. It's like I'm already losing something, and she's still right here. Not to mention, she was never mine to lose.

But I can't help it. I want her to be mine. And in those moments when I brought her to climax with my hands and mouth and tongue, she became my work of art. She became *mine*. For those few minutes when she surrendered herself to me, I'd readily claimed her. It felt powerful. And addictive.

The car is no longer moving, and neither is Jenna. She's looking out the window at her apartment building with her hands still in her lap. I keep my hands on the steering wheel at the ten o'clock and two o'clock positions as if I'm still driving. I'm staring straight out the windshield. I have no idea how to say the words I want to say.

"Are you worried?" I blurt suddenly.

Her head turns slowly until she's facing me. "About what?"

"About me losing the duel. About you not getting your tiara back."

She smiles weakly and places a hand lightly on my upper arm. I resist the urge to shrug off that touch, even though it's making my skin crawl. Because her touch is something I don't think I could refuse.

"You're not going to lose," she states. "I believe in you."

"The tiara is very valuable." It's not a question, but I have been wondering its worth for a while. Its personal worth.

She nods.

"Is it made of diamonds and precious gems?"

"Not diamonds, no. It does have monetary value, but that's not why it's important to me. It's more about sentimental value."

"What's the sentimental value, then?"

She licks her lips and looks at me for a long time. In fact, the silence stretches out so long that I think she's not going to answer.

After a long sigh, she clears her throat and speaks. "I've never talked about this to anyone outside my own family, so it's kind of hard to put into words. It's so rooted in emotion that I'm not sure you'll understand."

"I'm not a robot, Jenna. I have emotions."

She smiles. "I know you do." She winds a long strand of her bright angel hair around her index finger, then tucks it behind her ear. I'm transfixed by the gesture. Not only do I want to draw and paint that ear, I also want to feel that soft lobe in my mouth and between my teeth again.

"It's hard for me just..." She shakes her head and sniffs. "When I was little, I didn't want to come to the US. I told you that. It was scary, and my parents weren't coming with me. I also told you the story about my mom saying I'd live next to Mickey Mouse, but that isn't the real reason I agreed to leave."

I frown. "It isn't?"

"I mean, that actually happened, but what truly convinced me was my dad. He sat me down and made up this crazy story about how I was a secret princess and the tiara was my crown. It's true that tiara had been passed down in my family for a long time. It had been given to my grandma, who gave it to her only child, my father. My dad gave it to me on that day—the last day I ever saw him. He said he wanted me to be safe, so I had to hide in another country for a while and grow and learn and become educated so that I could come back and become the queen someday."

Now there are tears trailing out of the corners of her eyes, but she's laughing at the same time. I'm completely confused by this. Is she happy or sad? Or maybe both?

"You know how long I believed that story?" She hunches in her seat. "Far longer than I care to admit without dying from embarrassment."

"It makes sense." I nod. "When we are little, we especially want to believe everything our parents tell us."

I'm trying to picture the events as she recounts them to me. I imagine her father, a man in his thirties, perhaps as blond as she is, or maybe dark-haired with a strong jaw. He's stroking her beautiful angel hair and telling her she'll be a queen someday, but his face is serious and he doesn't want her to know that he's afraid.

And suddenly I'm even sadder.

"The tiara was his last gift to you?"

She looks down at her hands, still folded in her lap. "I don't think of it exactly like that, but yes, that is true."

"I assumed it was valuable to you, but I had no idea it had that kind of personal value. I don't understand something though."

"What's that?"

"If it means so much to you, why did you put it up for the loan?"

Her mouth thins. "It was a last resort. I did it for Maja, my sister. She wanted to get married, but her fiancé's family wouldn't allow it until the bride's family could pay for the wedding. She never asked for the money, but she also doesn't know what I had to do in order to get it. I'm never going to tell her. She is expecting me to bring the tiara with me to Bosnia so that she can wear it on her wedding day."

"Why didn't you tell her?"

She shrugs and leans forward, rubbing her hands over her face. "Why do you ask so many questions?"

"I'm sorry. I guess sometimes I just don't understand things that are easy for others."

She turns to me. "All this time you thought it was just some old, valuable piece of jewelry with no feelings attached to it. Yet you vowed to get it back for me without knowing why I did it or why it was important to me."

I have no idea what to say, so I don't answer her. It wasn't a question anyway.

"These past few weeks of training, of working with me..." She trails off and shakes her head.

I know she thinks these were unpleasant sacrifices for me, but I'd hardly call spending time with her a punishment.

"You must have thought I was so shallow and frivolous to have just hocked it like that."

"It didn't matter what your reasons were, Jenna. What mattered to me was that you wanted it back and it was important to you. I didn't need to know why."

A look crosses her face—I can't tell what it means, but she's biting her pretty pink lip with her white teeth. "You're sweet."

"You say that a lot."

She smiles. "Because it's true."

"It might be true, but I do have a very good memory. Repetition isn't necessary."

She laughs. It's that beautiful, musical sound I love. "So what if I'm saying it to remind myself?"

Now I'm really confused. "You have to remind yourself that I'm sweet?"

She throws her head back, laughing, and I can't take my eyes off that long stretch of pale neck that I want to taste again.

"I guess I do." She turns to me again and leans forward, kissing me on the cheek. I turn my head to capture her lips with mine.

At first her kiss is unsure, tentative. Like she's not sure if she wants to pull away or not. Before she can, I bring my hands up to hold her head to mine.

But she's resisting by keeping her mouth closed, and I get this weird idea in my head that if I can just get her to open up—open to *me*—that I can win her over and she'll be mine.

I need for her to be mine. I need *her*.

I'm tracing the line of her soft lips with my tongue, but she isn't opening fast enough for me so I decide to lay siege. To penetrate her defenses, my tongue pushes through the barrier of her lips with only little resistance. Then she sighs and relaxes against me.

I take her shoulders in my grasp and pull her against me. Suddenly, we are fused together, her heat and my heat. The feel of her against me is *so, so* good.

"Wil," she whispers. "Come upstairs with me."

I don't want to think about this or have this fight—and I know it will be a fight until she finally admits that I've won. Until then, I can't give in.

"Stay here and be my girlfriend," I reply.

I want to touch her again. All over her body. I want to make her moan. I want that painful tension in my body screaming for her to relieve it.

But more than anything, I want her to be mine.

Her hand presses against my chest and she pushes away, avoiding my eyes. Which is good because I really don't want to look into them. My stomach feels as if I've just swallowed eighty pounds of steel.

"I should go," she says breathlessly. Then she slowly leans back, opens the car door and then even more slowly climbs out, as if giving me the chance to change my mind.

I won't.

I can't.

Time is running short, but I can still make this happen

***

The following Sunday, Jenna and I go to the Santa Ana Zoo together in search of more crowds. Afterward, we end up at my dad's house for another family dinner. Kim has invited everyone she could think of, apparently. Along with our regular group, some of Mia's friends are here, including Heath—who mostly sits in a corner and drinks beer—Alex and Kat. Jenna is spending most of her time with the girls, and I'm stuck watching her from afar.

After a while, I feel the need to retreat, so I excuse myself to the bathroom and then slip into my old room at the back of the house. There, I take inventory of and dust my all-but-forgotten D&D figurines. It's been more than eight months since I've painted any. My job, blacksmithing and sword training have consumed the majority of my waking hours. I'm arranging the figurines on their shelf when Jenna enters and looks around.

"Mia was right! She said that you'd be back here."

"She knows me well." I point to the only chair in the room. "I was sitting in that chair when I first met her twenty-two months ago." Something I said amuses her because her smile grows wide and her teeth are showing. I can never tell if someone is finding me amusing or ridiculous, so I proceed regardless. "The night I met her, I knew that Adam was serious about her. It was the first time he'd ever brought a woman with him to family dinner."

"Well, seeing as they're getting married, I'd say you were right."

I turn back to the figurines. "I'm seldom right about stuff like that, but I'm glad I wasn't wrong about Mia and Adam."

"It seems you're not the only one. Not only did Adam find a fiancée, but your dad found a new wife when he met her mom. That's such a cool story. I think that Mia and Adam think so too—until Jordan brings up the whole step-cousin thing."

She watches me for a moment, then says, "I don't think you need to worry about them not getting married. They've been through a lot. If that didn't break them, nothing will."

"I just think it makes sense to make it official." I shrug. "I'm not an expert, but I like things finalized and settled."

"Well," she says with a small laugh as she reaches up to finger a button on my shirt, "there's always their bet—"

I tense, my face flushing with heat. "Do *not* talk about that bet!"

She laughs again but doesn't remove her finger. I grab her around the wrist and hold her hand there. She looks up into my eyes, and I have nanoseconds to escape her gaze.

"I don't like it when things don't go according to plan. Adam and Mia should get it over with if they know that's what they want to do. What's the point in waiting? I like to have everything figured out ahead of time. I like to be certain of the future."

She bites her lip. "Life doesn't always work out that way, Wil. I once thought I knew exactly what I'd be doing with my future, but..." Her voice trails off and it sounds sad again.

I can smell her hair as she turns to look at the figurines. I take mental note of the ones she admires. Maybe I'll give a few to her later. I realize that I'm still holding her wrist and she's not pulling away from me.

"Goddess, it's been ages since I've played D&D. I miss it. I never collected figurines like you do, but I have lots and lots of dice."

I glance at the dresser behind my worktable. "My old dice are in here too."

"Really? Can I see them?"

"You want to see my dice?"

She smiles. "Yes, like any self-respecting geek girl, I do have a dice fetish."

I move away from her to dig through the drawers to find my old bag of dice. Then I empty the worn velvet bag out onto my worktable. A pile of dice roll out across the scratched and stained surface. They are all different colors and—as they're Dungeons and Dragons dice—all different shapes and sizes as well.

By some weird coincidence, Jenna picks up my lucky d20. It's amber colored with black numbers on the faces. The twenty-sided die, the most famous of all the types of dice used in D&D, is an icosahedron—a symmetrical polyhedron with twenty faces.

She rolls it across the table and…a natural twenty. She laughs. "Nat 20. It's my lucky night. Too bad we aren't playing."

"You and I could play."

Her brows rise. "Right now? Like…we could role-play something?"

I shrug. "I wasn't a Dungeon Master—I could never come up with the storylines. But I could be an average character, perhaps a blacksmith who sometimes moonlights as a knight."

She looks me up and down. "You're far from average." She folds her arms across her chest in a way that makes her t-shirt tighten over her breasts. I instantly recall the vision of her spread out on my couch, making those noises of pleasure when I was touching and kissing her breasts. The memory alone makes me hard. *Painfully* hard.

I fight with myself to will that image away before it threatens to pull my attention completely away from the reality standing right in front of me. I tear my eyes from her chest, adjust the way I'm standing and hope she doesn't notice that I'm now sexually aroused when I shouldn't be.

"I could be a wayfaring fortune-teller and secret sorceress. We're at an inn somewhere, and we've run into each other in the pub. What do you say to me?"

I smile at her willingness to play the game. "I wonder what the chances are that you'll kiss me?"

Her brows rise again. *Good, I've surprised her.* With a smile, she turns back to my pile of dice and pulls out two ten-sided dice. A roll of these dice will determine a percentile score. If a character has a percentage chance of doing something, the score on the two dice will show their chance of accomplishing it.

"Let's say that right now you have a five percent chance of getting a kiss from me as a complete stranger. Do you wish to make that attempt?" she asks.

I think about that for a moment. "Can I do things to improve my chances?"

"Of course, we're role-playing!" She smiles. "But I'm not going to tell you what they are."

"Of course not. It wouldn't be a game worth playing if you did that. I'll offer to buy you a drink." I pause, thinking. "Then I signal the barkeep to buy the beautiful lady whatever she wishes to drink."

She considers that for a moment, handling the dice. "Okay...that's nice. Is there a limit on what you'll pay? What if I wish for the most expensive glass of champagne?"

"I'll order a glass of Dom Perignon for my lady," I say.

She smiles again, her teeth gleaming. "That has increased your chance by fifteen percent. You now have a twenty percent chance of getting a kiss from me."

I frown. "That's only one in five. I don't like those odds. I'd like to increase them. What if I tell you how beautiful you are?"

"Hmm. I'm waiting," she says, cocking her head to the side. "What do you want to say to me?"

"That your eyes are the same blue as the water in the famous Turkish salt flats called Pamukkale. The water in the travertine pools is a pure reflection of the sky—pale and pristine. They are the exact color of your eyes." She swallows and I continue, "And your hair is shiny and golden like angel hair. And your skin is soft—"

"Wait, how do you know my skin is soft? We've just met."

"Because..." I hesitate, trying to think of what to say, other than the fact that I *have* stroked that skin. I've run my hands across her smooth belly, her rounded breasts, her soft thighs. These thoughts aren't making my erection any easier to handle.

"It looks soft," I say. "Like silk."

"Okay," she says with a nod. "And I had no idea about those—those Turkish salt pools."

"Pamukkale. It means 'cotton castle' because of the white calcifications. But the water is powder blue. Like your eyes. I've seen pictures of it, and whenever I look at your eyes, I think of those pools."

She blinks. "Oh..."

"In ancient times, people bathed in the water because they believed it brought them special blessings."

"Are you saying you want to bathe in my water?"

I frown. "Umm..."

She laughs. "Never mind." She fiddles with the dice in her hand again. "Your chances are getting better. Fifty percent now. Want to risk it and roll?"

I prefer to weight the odds in my favor, so I reach out and take a strand of that celestial hair and tuck it behind her ear. Her big blue eyes widen as she looks at my face. Our eyes narrowly miss as I shift my gaze lower, to where that t-shirt is covering a chest that is moving faster due to an increased rate of respiration. "You are so beautiful that sometimes it's hard to breathe when I look at you."

She sways toward me for a moment, as if she's being pulled against her will. I steady her, my hand on her shoulder, and her eyelids droop.

She licks her lips. "Wow. You, um...you sure figure out what you're doing quickly."

We're standing very close now, and I can feel my heartbeat in my throat. Jenna swallows and clears her throat. "If you roll now, I'd give you an eighty-five percent chance of being able to kiss me."

I hold out my hand, palm up. I can do those odds. I rarely miss when given that chance. She places the two dice in my palm, and I promptly toss them on the worktable without taking my eyes off her. She turns her head to look, blowing out a breath. "Ninety-one. *Shit.*"

I look to verify. "No, it's the other way around. Nineteen. The blue die is the first digit."

She sighs. "Thank the goddess," she murmurs and reaches up to put her hands on either side of my face. I stiffen immediately, then pull them away and indicate that she should lace them around my neck instead. I snake my hands behind her back and pull her body firmly against me. Her breasts push up against my chest, her arms tightening around my neck as our mouths meet. Unlike the other night in the car, she immediately opens for me.

I'm tasting her and I'm drowning, but I'm also surging with power like a superhero. It's like dying and rebirth with each alternating second.

Her tongue moves and it stabs me with pleasure throughout my entire body. My hands slide down from her back to her shapely butt..

Our heads move together for long moments, but I know that my body wants more. I'm ready for her, and judging by the heat of her body against mine, she's ready too.

I really, *really* want her.

Basically, if people weren't in this house, I'd push her down on the ground right now and pull her clothes off. I'd ask her first, of course, but then I'd totally do it.

Although knowing her feelings about leaving, I know that it's a good thing people are in this house right now.

Jenna stands up on her tiptoes to press herself more forcibly against me and my hands cup her round butt, rubbing over the stiff denim of her jeans. She's making little noises that remind me of how she sounded when I brought her to climax.

Suddenly, I hear footsteps in the doorway. Jenna and I pull apart, and then turn to face the visitor. I'm now looking straight into the astonished face of my cousin, who takes a step back and is about to leave, but apparently he can't because he bumps into someone else right behind him—Mia.

Jenna ducks her head, wiping her mouth with the back of her hand, but I can tell that she's laughing. I don't know whether to laugh or be angry. The only thing that comforts me is that my cousin looks horrified.

Mia pokes her head around his shoulder and peeks into the doorway. She scans the room and then looks up at Adam. "What'd I miss?"

"Uh, hey," Adam says to me while ignoring her question. "Just wanted to, um, tell you that Mia and I have to get going. Wanted to say goodbye and make sure that, uh, things are good with us." His voice sounds funny, but at least he doesn't have that shocked look on his face anymore.

Jenna's face is now red and she's laughing really hard—so hard that her eyes are watering like she's crying. I know that she's not sad, though.

Mia gives her a look. "You okay?"

All Jenna does is nod. Now Adam is laughing as he's watching Jenna. "Well, I'd tell you to 'carry on,' but Liam might come after me with another sword."

"I think it's a good idea to keep your mouth shut," I warn, pointing to my old steel sword that is hanging on the wall for decoration.

Adam looks up at the ceiling for a moment, like he does when he doesn't know what to say to me. "Okay, Liam. See you at work tomorrow. Bye, Jenna." He turns and leaves, moving around Mia, who just stares at us with wide eyes.

"Well, I missed whatever *that* was, but just wanted to say goodbye and I'm cheering for you, William. I know your big duel is next weekend, and I'm not going to be able to make our breakfast date this week since I have that exam coming up."

I nod, troubled by the change in plans. "Okay. Text me later, then."

Mia is looking at Jenna now, who has finally recovered. The two of them seem to be communicating without speaking. Mia sends her a look and Jenna returns it, shaking her head, but suddenly the smile slides off her beautiful face and it actually transforms into a frown. I glance at Mia, who now actually looks upset or angry—those look just about the same on Mia. And suddenly I'm annoyed at her. Whatever she did made Jenna upset, and that bothers me.

For the hundredth time, I really wish I could read faces. "Well, bye now." Mia steps back.

"Yeah, bye," Jenna says, looking at me and then turning away from the door to study the figurines again. With that, Mia is gone.

I turn back to her and she's fiddling with the figurines, but I get the feeling she's not really looking at them. "What happened? Are you and Mia angry with each other?"

She looks at me and her brows rise. "No...no. It's just..." She shakes her head and then shrugs. "It's nothing to worry about, William. In a month, it won't even matter..." Her voice trails off and she frowns.

I clench my jaw, unhappy to be reminded—again—that she's going away. I turn and gather my old dice and throw them into the felt bag, then open the drawer to toss them back in.

"What's all that?" she asks over my shoulder.

I glance down to see that the drawer is full of sealed envelopes of different colors. Each one of them is addressed to me in familiar handwriting. I freeze. I *really* don't want to talk about this right now—or ever.

She bends closer. "Those envelopes are all sealed. You never opened them."

I shrug before slamming the drawer shut. "I never wanted to open them."

"What are they? Who are they from? If you don't mind me asking..."

My heart is racing and my stomach feels sick. "They're birthday cards, and they're from my mother."

"And you've never opened them?"

My fists clench and relax at my sides. "My mother and I didn't have a good relationship." I turn away from the dresser.

"Do you want to talk about it?"

"No."

"Okay."

There's a long silence. I shove my hands in my pockets, unable to think of a thing to say. Jenna moves close to me and firmly places a hand on my upper arm. "It's okay. We all have problematic parental relationships."

"*Had.* My mother died five years ago, when I was twenty-one."

"Oh. I'm sorry."

"Why are you sorry? You weren't responsible."

She shrugs. "It's just a thing people say. I'm sorry for your loss."

I frown, thinking about that. I wonder why I never knew that before.

All I can remember is *her* voice in my head. Her disapproving voice telling me she had no idea what to do with me, no idea how to even relate to me. *What mother tells her child that?*

My chest is tight and it's difficult to breathe. I refuse to let this overtake me.

To let talk of this—of *her*—ruin my moment with Jenna. Or has it already been ruined?

25
JENNA

I HAD NO IDEA WHAT TO SAY OR IF HE EVEN NEEDED COMFORTING. His lips were pressed tightly together and the muscles in his powerful arm were tense, like coiled springs.

"Wil. Maybe you *should* talk about it."

He jerked away from me suddenly and it took my breath away. He ran a hand through his dark hair over and over again until it was sticking up on the sides. But as he'd have to squeeze around me to get out from behind the worktable, I had him trapped. He rocked from one leg to the other instead.

"*Should* talk about it? Is that different than I *have* to talk about it or even *want* to talk about it?"

I sighed. "You're wound up and upset. Maybe I can help you work through it?"

He shrugged. "I don't get upset about my mother anymore."

I suppressed a laugh—I guess even autistic guys were into macho posturing when the opportunity presented itself. He could pretend all he wanted that nothing was wrong, but clearly the opposite was true.

"Everyone has an issue with their mother. I do...I told you about it, didn't I? We're okay now, but she was pretty mad at me for a while because I came back to the US to be with Brock."

He shook his head. "Don't talk about him." His fists opened and closed again.

"Okay," I whispered.

"I don't know why, but I feel angry when you talk about him. Like I'm jealous of him. I shouldn't be jealous because he's dead. But I *am* jealous and it's confusing, and I'd rather not think about it."

For some reason, his honest admission choked me up. *I shouldn't be jealous because he's dead.* Suddenly, my chest tightened and my eyes felt a little tingly. I couldn't put my finger on why—was it the reminder that Brock was dead, or was it something more?

Maybe it was William's heartfelt confession that he didn't even realize he'd confessed to. Sometimes he was so innocent that it pierced me to the core.

I leaned toward him despite his agitation, and, rising on tiptoes, I ran my fingers through his thick, dark hair, right where he'd done the same thing just moments ago. His eyes fluttered closed and his hands relaxed. "Wil, can I help you? Will you let me?"

"Just how do you think you can help me?" he asked quietly, without looking at me.

"Maybe by talking about it? We *all* have parent issues. I promise you. Yours might be more difficult because your mom has passed away and you can't talk to her."

"If she were alive, I'd have nothing to say to her. I never talked to her much."

"How old were you when she and your dad divorced?"

"Five." His voice held no emotion whatsoever. He really did sound like a robot, even though he'd claimed that he wasn't.

"And you and your sister lived with your dad when they separated?"

"Yes."

One word answers...*hmm*. It was going to take a while to get it out of him at this pace. I gave a slight push against his hard, thick arm, cueing for him to face me. "Wil, tell me about it. What was it like? Were you glad you were living with your dad instead of her?"

His face was as blank as his voice. A defense mechanism, maybe? "That was never an option. She left. She made it clear she didn't want to have a relationship with me."

I squinted, confused. "But your sister..."

"Oh, she saw Britt all the time. Every week. My mother even asked her to live with her when Britt turned thirteen, but Britt said no. I think my sister always felt bad for me and didn't want to leave me." He shrugged. "I told her she should go if she wanted. I love my dad and I was glad to stay with him."

I smiled. "Your dad is a pretty awesome guy."

His jaw clenched and then released. "Yes. He deserved better than he got." He shook his head.

"You mean your mom didn't treat him well?"

"I'm sure they were happy together once, maybe before I was born or before I got to be a handful."

Ah, *now* we were getting somewhere. "Wait, you don't believe you're the reason they got divorced, do you?"

He turned away from me slightly, directing his words at the wall. "It's a statistically proven fact that the parents of autistic children are more susceptible to divorce." I bit my lip, trying to think of what to say in response, but he kept talking. "Not that the divorce rate in the United States is all that great anyway, but it's higher among couples with children on the spectrum."

"So that's why you think they divorced? Because of some statistic? Wil—some people just freak out and can't handle parenthood, or even just being married in general."

He turned back toward me but still didn't look at me. "Her second marriage was just fine. She remarried less than a year after she left us and stayed married until she died."

"Well, then fuck her. That's *her* problem, not *yours*. You do not *ever* blame yourself for that. What kind of person abandons her children?"

"She didn't abandon us—"

I stepped up to him and took his arm in my hand again. I wanted to shake him—to show him how wrong and harmful his thinking really was. "Wil, she abandoned *you*. Maybe not your sister, but she did abandon you. She never realized or cared how much it would hurt you to favor your sister over you."

He swallowed but kept silent, looking over my shoulder. I put my hands on his cheeks. He jerked his head away.

"Not my face..."

"Okay." I moved my hands to his shoulders, pressing hard. "You *are* worthy of love. And you were worthy of *her* love. And the fact that she could not give it to you was *her* failing, not yours."

William licked his lips, and after a long stretch of seconds, his dark eyes finally met mine. I wanted to take him in my arms, hold him, kiss him, comfort him, but I had no idea if that was what he really needed from me right now. *I* needed to, but his needs in this moment were far more important.

His head fell forward slightly and his forehead touched mine. I could feel his warm breath float over my face as we stood there, silent. When I looked at his eyes again, they were closed, his long dark lashes lying calmly against his cheeks.

"You know what we should do?" I said in a small voice. He'd have never heard me had it not been so quiet here in the back of the house.

"What?" he asked without opening his eyes.

"We should open up those cards. We should read them and see what they say."

His eyelids snapped open. He looked almost sick at the idea, and slowly, he moved his forehead away from mine. "I don't want to do that."

"Why?"

"Because...because I'd rather imagine what I want them to say."

"And what is it that you'd want them to say?"

"I'd like to imagine that she was sorry. That every card was an apology that I had a chance to accept and didn't."

"Would that make you feel any differently about her?"

"I don't know."

"Can we find out?"

He was quiet again for a long time.

I turned and walked over to the drawer, gingerly sliding it open, giving him the chance to protest. He said nothing, so I fished out the cards—there were sixteen of them. I began to arrange the various colored envelopes in order of oldest postmark date to the newest, all stamped in the month of October. The first one was dated 1994. He'd been six years old.

"When's your birthday?"

"October fourteenth," he intoned flatly as he watched me arrange the cards.

"Ah, a Libra. That makes sense. Passionate, artistic, gentle and sensitive."

"None of that astrology stuff makes any sense," he responded.

"Okay, whatever. Here's the one for your sixth birthday," I said, holding the sunny yellow envelope out to him. "Do you want to open it?"

"I don't want to open any of them."

"Can I open this one, then?"

He slowly nodded. I slid a fingernail under the tongue of the envelope and tore it open. It was a garish, generic card for a young boy with pictures of trains and trucks in bright primary colors. It looked young, even for a six-year-old. When I opened the card, a bunch of dollar bills fell out.

There was a short note inside, which I read aloud:

For Liam,

Wishing you a happy sixth birthday. I promise to take you out for ice cream very soon.

Love, Mom

I turned to William. "So did she take you out for ice cream?"

He shrugged. "I don't remember. Maybe."

I placed a hand on his arm again. "You okay?"

He pulled away slightly. "Why wouldn't I be okay? That card said absolutely nothing."

"You want me to open the next one?"

He shrugged again. I set aside the six one-dollar bills—one for each year of his life—on his worktable and picked up the next envelope. The next few years were much like the first one. Always a cash gift that was equal to his age and a simple, quick birthday wish with a promise to see him or take him somewhere soon.

William grew a little more relaxed, if increasingly disappointed. Around his fifteenth birthday, he recalled that she attended some milestones, like his first amateur art show, but overall, her visits were infrequent. As he got older, she promised to take him out to dinner, and he made it a point to let me know that she never followed through.

As he stared at the last two cards in the pile, it was difficult to gauge his mood. But with a long sigh, he snatched up the second to last card, opened it with one quick, forceful tear and unfolded it without even looking at the artwork or formal message on the outside. A crisp twenty-dollar bill that had never been used slid out of the card. I added it to the orderly pile of cash on the table.

In a flat voice, he read:

Dear Liam,

I know it's probably too late to explain. I don't even know if I can. You are a man, now. A grown man that I don't even know... But I hope you'll understand someday.

With love,
Your Mom

He let out a long breath as if someone had punched him in the stomach. "She didn't know she was sick yet. I think she found out the following year."

"What did she die of?"

"Kidney failure."

I picked up the last one and handed it to him. "She knew by the time she sent this one, though. Maybe this one has what you're looking for?"

He glanced at me and then down to the card. "I doubt it."

"Well, let me just say this. She was not a perfect person. She had flaws, like we all do. And you can't mend fences with her anymore, but you can forgive her."

His forehead crumpled. "Why would I do that?"

"Because it'll make you feel better. The Buddha once said that holding on to anger is like drinking poison and expecting the other person to die."

He swallowed and tore open the last envelope without even responding. Then he opened the card, extracted the money and closed it immediately.

"You're not going to read that one?"

He breathed in and out. "Not yet. I'm not ready."

I nodded. "Okay. You need a hug?"

His brow furrowed. "No."

"Can I hold your hand, then?"

He nodded. I slipped my palm inside his rough hand and it closed around mine, holding tight—almost painfully so. I returned the pressure.

We both stared down at the pile of money. "That's two hundred and sixteen dollars," I said. "You should go blow it on something fun."

"Like what?"

I shrugged. "Oh, I don't know. How about the Fun Zone in Newport? Or we could go play video games at Dale and Boomers."

He froze. "It's crowded there."

"You still need to work on that."

He pressed his lips together. Pulling his hand free, he grabbed the money and tucked the thick wad of bills into his wallet. "Dale and Boomers it is, then. Will you go with me?"

"Of course. I'm your friend, right?"

His eyes fixed directly on mine. "I want you to be more than my friend."

He shoved his wallet back into his pocket and then turned his full attention on me, taking my wrist. The look in his eyes was so intense that I took a step backward.

He took a step forward.

I stepped back again and he followed.

"Jenna," he breathed.

"Wil—" But I was interrupted when I ran into the wall and his head descended on mine, the grasp around my wrist tightening, the other hand going into my hair.

He wasn't rough but he certainly wasn't gentle, and though I found it hot as hell, I had to wonder where this was coming from.

Still, as our tongues tangled and my body heated against his, I was all for forgetting everything but the heated night we shared a few weeks ago when I'd gotten naked with him. All I knew is that I wanted more—I hadn't *stopped* wanting more. I'd just stopped pushing for it.

Now, apparently it was *his* turn.

His chest pressed against mine, his head bent down to my level, his lips teasing and sucking at mine, his teeth nipping. He'd invaded my senses, capturing my desire and turning it against me like a foreign army seizing a fortress. The hand that was on my neck slipped down to grasp my breast, and my nipple rose in happy obeisance to his questing fingers. My eyes rolled back into my head as his whiskered cheek scraped against mine.

Oh goddess. This felt so good. His mouth slipped off mine and he kissed his way across my cheek and down my jaw. "Stay with me, Jenna."

My first impulse—it was almost on the tip of my tongue—was to say 'yes.' But I swallowed and clamped my mouth shut. By that time, my earlobe was in his hot mouth and he was scraping his teeth across it. I almost crumpled against him.

"Say you'll stay. Promise me."

"I can't," I whispered shakily. "But that doesn't mean we can't see each other 'til I leave..."

He froze, his body as stiff as if it had been carved in stone. Slowly, he pulled his mouth away from my neck.

"I need you to stay."

I swallowed. "You don't mean that."

His face flushed and his handsome features twisted with anger. "Don't tell me what I mean and what I don't. You don't know what's inside my head," he ground out between clenched teeth.

I laid a palm against his hard chest, easing him back, but he jerked his hand up and brushed away mine like it was an insect.

"Wil—"

"No, you're right. Why would I want someone who would just leave when things got difficult? You're absolutely right."

He may as well have slapped me. I blinked and my eyes stung.

"But—"

"No need to explain yourself. You've been honest from the beginning. You're here for one reason only. You need your tiara."

My mouth dropped open. "It might have been the reason at first, but—"

He held his palm up to stop me. "You don't need to spare my feelings. It's been a clear-cut deal from the start. I was wrong to expect more from you."

I frowned. "What do you mean?"

He stuffed his hands into his pockets. "It means that you don't need to waste any more time rehabilitating me. There's less than a week left. I'll either fail or succeed without you."

Blood drained from my face in the wake of his anger. "But I want—"

"No need to humor me either. I'll get your tiara back and then we won't have to see each other."

I blinked. "I'm not seeing you because I *have* to, and I know—"

He spun and walked away before I could finish... *I know you'll succeed, Wil. I believe in you.*

I felt like the floor had been yanked out from under me. "Wil— please don't be angry."

He shook his head. "It just...it hurts."

I ached at the thought of not seeing him again. I tried not to examine what this gaping hole-like sensation in the middle of my chest meant.

He stopped at the doorway and turned back to me. "I don't like this feeling, Jenna. I won't do it anymore. You say I'm worthy to be loved. But apparently not by *you*."

The air rushed out of my chest. "That's not true. You are...and I'm...but I *can't*. Because I honestly believe that I met my soulmate already. And he died so—"

"That makes it easy."

Suddenly, my face flushed hot. I tried to tell myself that he was acting out because of hurt feelings, but that didn't give him the right to lash out at me like this. "There's nothing *easy* about it, Wil. I'm resigned that—"

"In your mind, he's perfect. The perfect lover, the perfect partner. And nothing will ever contradict that because he'll never disappoint you—he *can't* disappoint you. But you'll be disappointed in your other relationships, and that just reinforces the ridiculous belief that there was only ever one person for you. Or one person for everyone on this planet."

"*Ridiculous?* Why are you being so mean? I've never said anything like this to you."

His jaw bulged where he clenched it, and his hand was gripping the doorjamb so hard that his knuckles whitened. "It's probably just as well that you believe that. Nobody could compete with a dead person and win."

I threw up my hands. "Why is anyone *competing*? Why are you even talking like this? Is it because of those birthday cards? You have a right to be mad at your Mom, but—"

William whipped out his keys from his pants pocket and abruptly turned. "You need a ride home." And he left the room. *Shit.*

I was still pissed at him as I followed him down the hallway. When I entered the family room, I saw Britt and Kim talking to one another on a couch, each with a glass of wine in hand. Peter was clearing the dishes from the table. "There's cake for dessert..." he began, but his voice faded out when he took one look at his son's face.

"I need to go. I'm taking Jenna home."

"I'll put a piece in a box for you both." His dad went into the kitchen, and William folded his arms tightly across his chest as he waited.

On the couch, his sister frowned, then looked directly at me. "What's up, Liam? You okay?"

"I'm fine," he snapped and then actually tapped his foot in an obvious show of impatience. My jaw dropped at his rude behavior.

Kim stood and walked over to us, setting her glass down. "Hey William, I've been wanting to get the details on your duel. The time and place and the directions, maybe? We'd like to come and cheer for you."

He shook his head but didn't say anything...he didn't even look at her. *Goddess, this was awkward.* "I'll, um, I'll wait in the car. Night all, and thank you for the wonderful dinner." I spun on my heel and walked out.

In the cool night air, I took some deep breaths and let the tears spill over onto my cheeks before quickly scrubbing them away. Part of me was seething with anger at him. But the bigger part of me was mad at myself.

This had started out as a simple and mutually beneficial situation for both of us. I'd needed to help him get my tiara back, he needed my help to deal with his crowd issues. It just so happened that I'd started to enjoy being in his company.

I'd started enjoying *him.*

And I wasn't ready for this to be over.

It was a tense drive home. William said absolutely nothing. With each passing mile, I felt more and more miserable. He stopped at my curb and kept the engine idling, not even looking at me.

I turned to him and put my hand on his arm. "Wil."

He yanked it out of my hold. "I'll see you at the Festival, Jenna. In the meantime, I wish you well."

My throat closed up with hurt. I would *not* lose it in front of him. But I couldn't just open the door and leave, either. "You're just like that Hanged Man, you know. That was the perfect card for you."

He scowled. "I told you I don't believe in that Tarot stuff."

"The Hanged Man is in stasis, and so are you. You're held back by your anger toward your mother. You let that be the tree you hang yourself on."

He was silent as he gripped the wheel tightly. And me, I was about to burst into tears again. So rather than let him see them, I scooted out of the car as fast as I could.

I managed to contain my emotions as I climbed up the stairs and even during my passing conversation with my roomie, who was in the middle of watching *The Walking Dead*. Then I slinked into my bedroom, dressed for bed and sobbed myself to sleep when I couldn't hold it in any longer.

Sometimes a good cry was cathartic, calming. But this wasn't. Into the gaping hole that had just been torn into my heart, the salty tears flowed, only increased the sting instead of lessening it.

***

"What's going on, Jenna? You seem so out of it this week," Alex said to me. It was a few nights before I was to leave for the Beltane Festival, and yeah, 'out of it' might have been a good way to describe how I felt. Off-kilter was another one.

I missed William terribly. Since we'd started hanging out together, I'd spent a week without seeing him, but never without texting or a short conversation on the phone. This felt worse than a breakup—at least those breakups that I'd cared about, anyway.

And the more I thought about his words, the more I started to wonder about this flaw in myself. Specifically, whether I'd hurt other people because of my own shortcomings. My own fears.

Fears I'd hidden behind my beliefs.

And speaking of hurting people...I gave my notice at the Refugee Support Center, choking up when I saw the look on my boss's face. *Shock. Disappointment. Sadness.* But in the end, she wished me well.

So yeah...I was out of it. I had reasons.

I shrugged at Alex, picking at my food. Reheated leftover spaghetti, along with ramen noodles, had become a staple of my diet.

"Are you nervous about the duel?" Her forehead creased. "Do you think William will lose the tiara?"

I shook my head. "I think he'll win. He's worked very hard."

"Then smile!"

I put my fork down and stared at my plate, blinking back sudden tears as my hands shook. "What am I doing, Alex? Where am I going?"

She slapped her textbook closed—unlike me, she was actually doing homework—and set down her pencil. "Sounds like you need to hit the advice booth."

Our little joke. Alex liked to counsel people and give them advice. My friends and I had started hinting that she should have a booth, complete with a tin can for change like Lucy from the *Peanuts* comic strip.

"Talk to me," she said when I looked up.

"I don't know...I just don't... Up until last week, I was so sure of what I wanted."

Alex's dark brows rose. "But you're not anymore?"

I knew Alex would never say she told me so. It just wasn't in her DNA. So I didn't fear sharing this change of heart with her. Leaning forward, I massaged my forehead with my hand. "I'm so confused."

"The rest of the population our age is confused most of the time. It's okay. No one knows all the answers."

I sighed. "I was trying to be more excited about this move, but—"

"But the reality of what it will mean to leave everyone has sunk in?"

"I..." My gaze drifted away as I thought about what she'd said. Then I nodded. "Yeah."

"Jenna, my *abuelita* had a saying. She said that the oak tree has the deepest and strongest roots, and that when the Santa Ana winds blow, those live oak trees are the hardest to blow over. On the other hand, the eucalyptus trees that grow all over the place around here...you know, those really, really tall ones? They're always in danger of getting blown over by the very same winds, and that's because their roots are shallow."

I played with the food on my plate, listening intently.

She continued. "In other words, the deeper the roots go, the less likely you are to be blown over. And if you uproot yourself and move around every so often, there's no way your roots can go deep."

I smiled. "Why do I have a sudden urge to climb a tree?"

She shrugged. "You asked for my advice."

"I didn't, really, but thank you. Your *abuelita* was a wise lady."

"She was." Her wide, dark eyes grew solemn. "She taught me lots of things."

I laughed. "You aren't going to try and read my head bumps, are you?"

She snorted. "No. But maybe *you* should read your cards."

That was an excellent idea...

And later that night, that's exactly what I did. I pulled out my trustiest deck—the same one I'd used to give William his reading—spread a cloth out on the floor and sat cross-legged in front of it. I let my thoughts drift as I shuffled the cards, but every time I closed my eyes, *he* was there. His handsome face, his big hands holding my head as he kissed me, the feel of his body against mine.

I swallowed the lump in my throat and pulled a simple window spread—nine cards in three rows. The top row represented the past. The middle, the present. The bottom row, the future. I saved my more elaborate spreads for when I was reading for others. Either way, the cards in front of me all at once seemed to help clear my mind and whisper new stories to me.

Sometimes the cards "spoke" to me, and sometimes they just didn't. Tonight, it almost seemed like they were shouting. The first row hit me squarely between the eyes: the Page of Pentacles, the Tower, the five of Cups. Wow, it was almost like my very own biography in three simple cards.

My hands trembled as I fingered the Page of Pentacles—*Brock*. The card represented a young person full of potential, practical, dutiful, reflective and conscientious. I smiled. Yes, that was him.

That card was followed by the Tower—the universal shit-hits-the fan card. It was always hard to have this card come up in a reading, but I comforted myself knowing that it was about the past. That the terrible event—the loss of Brock and all that I'd planned for our future—had taken place long ago. Six long and painful years ago.

Which brought me to the Five of Cups. The loss and my reaction to it. The impact that sent ripples of pain into the present and the future. My throat thickened so that I couldn't swallow.

The suit of Cups represented all that was tied to emotions. And there were so many tied to that loss and the events that followed. Losses that went even deeper than the loss of Brock. *Papa...*

The image of three cups turned over, two cups still filled depicted three cups' worth of water lost—mourning. And yet...two cups remained full. For the first time ever, I saw it as a card of hope. What a strange notion...

Taking a shivery breath, I moved on to the next row—my present. The three of Swords—the classic card of emotional turmoil and conflict. *So true.* Everything was mixed up, boiling over.

I tucked my straggly hair behind my ears. *Wil...* His words—that bare naked honesty. *It hurts,* he'd said.

Blinking back stinging tears that prickled my throat, I realized how right he was. It *did* hurt. It almost seemed to be the legacy of living on this earth, breathing this air, existing. There was no happiness without pain.

But did losing something you'd once pegged your hopes on mean that you could never be happy again?

Was that what I was doing? Punishing myself for living while Brock was dead? And Papa?

And there it was...the next card in the middle row, staring me in the face. The eight of Swords. *Fear. Blockage. Prevention.* I swallowed. And it was followed by the Moon card—a warning of dishonesty, deceit or confusion.

Maybe all of the above. I *was* confused. Had I been deceiving myself? Had I been convinced that it was my fate to wander...to never love? To never *be* loved? I'd often seen the card that most represented me as the Fool. And maybe in more ways than one, I *had* been a fool. A fool who lied to herself.

Tears streamed down my cheeks and I blinked to see through blurry eyes by the time I made it to the third row—the future. My throat was tight and it was hard to breathe, because...

That first card.

The King of Cups.

I remembered my words to William at the regional market. *The King of Cups represents a man of emotional stability, a man who lives by honor—quiet, kind and trustworthy.*

William...sitting right there at the start of my future.

Biting my lip, I snatched up the entire stack, suddenly overcome with emotion. With no desire to examine the deeper meanings, I tucked the cards inside their bag and then stuffed it in my bottom drawer. I vowed not to touch them again for months. And maybe I'd smudge them with white sage smoke for good measure and take other decks with me to the Festival.

It took me hours to fall asleep, and when I did, I dreamt of giant cards the same size as me, chasing me everywhere but never catching me.

26
WILLIAM

I'T'S BEEN ONE WEEK SINCE I SAID GOODBYE TO JENNA, AND EVERY day after I've been single-mindedly continuing my training. I've lifted weights, run and gone to the martial arts studio. I've even meditated and practiced Jenna's crazy visualization crap.

The hardest part has been forcing myself to spend time in crowded areas. Britt and Mia took me to the mall, but Adam deserted me, saying that even helping me wasn't worth having to go shopping. As we walked through the area between the stores, I tried the visualization technique again—instead of a river of people flowing toward me, I pictured an actual rushing river and a bubbling waterfall. It took work, but eventually I felt myself entering a zone of calmness, able to look at the situation as if outside my body.

And as much as I don't like it, I've eaten lunch every day in the crowded lunchroom at work. Instead of people hunched around circular tables and booths, talking and clanking dishes, I started to picture them as animals in the wild—a herd of zebras or gazelles in the African veldt. It was weird, but it worked.

But despite the progress I've made, what I haven't been able to do is stop thinking about Jenna. I've missed her, and I've wanted to tell her that things are starting to click. That I'd hear her voice in my head—the way she encouraged and believed in me—and when I butted up against an obstacle, I remembered the way she helped me around it.

We worked together so well. But that isn't the reason I've ached every time I've thought of her. Or why my heart speeds up whenever I think of the next time I'll see her. And though the festival means the inevitable rematch with Doug—and with that, the uncertainty of the outcome—I've found myself counting the days, hours and minutes until I see her again.

There are 1,440 minutes in a day. We haven't seen each other since Sunday night at approximately nine o'clock, and I'll see her again on Friday night at around six o'clock. That means there are about 7,020 minutes between the time we parted on poor terms and the time when I can try to make it better.

And things *will* be better. They just have to be.

Because Friday marks the beginning of the Festival, and once the Festival ends, the Renaissance Faire will begin operation on the same site until the end of June. And once the Renaissance Faire moves on, Jenna will gone for good.

On Friday, we traveled to a small community just north of "the Grapevine" in Kern County, about a two-hour drive from where we live in Orange County. It is an area of Southern California where there is *lots* of open space. We congregate yearly at a large campground nestled amongst rolling, dry and mostly plain hills that surround our lightly wooded site. I had nothing to bring with me this time but my armor and fighting equipment, as well as my hand-sewn, period-authentic tent and living essentials.

Our clan has set up at the southwest edge of the campground, which we essentially take over for the week. Everyone stakes places for their personal tents, cook areas and booths, where they'll set up their wares to sell. To the north and tucked into a small side canyon, there's a great oblong arena with concrete stands climbing up each side. It is there where the battles will take place—teams fighting it out, in addition to one-on-one duels like the rematch I am scheduled to fight with Doug.

I'm walking the length of the arena and looking up at the empty stands, trying to work out a strategy for visualization. As I'm attempting to picture what it will be like when we face off in two days, I notice another person at the opposite end from where I'm standing. From her height, body style and coloring, it's easy to determine that it is Jenna.

I can suddenly feel my heart pound in my throat and my mouth is dry, like I really need a drink. What's confusing is that, at the same time I want to avoid her, I also urgently want to see her again. These feelings are pulling me in two directions like a huge tug-of-war.

And she's here watching me, which means she's clearly *not* avoiding me. She might have even sought me out. Slowly, I kick at the dirt clods at the edge of the arena and make my way toward her, my heart speeding up the closer I get. She doesn't come forward to greet me, but she doesn't turn and walk away either. And with each step I take, I realize that I'm craving the chance to see her face again, to talk to her, to hold her, to kiss her.

But when I finally make it to where she's standing, I come to a stop and watch the ground between our feet. "Hello," I say.

She takes a deep breath and lets it go. "Hi."

"I'm glad to see you made it here safely."

"I caught a ride with Caitlyn and the girls."

I nod, unsurprised by this information. "It's good to see you."

Her mouth curves in a small smile. "I missed you."

I missed her too. I wanted to see her every day. And thinking about that now makes me remember how much it's hurt *not* to see her. I don't know what to say.

"Wil—" Her voice trembles and she turns away. I watch as her hands curl into fists at her sides.

"Yes?"

"Can we be friends again? *Please?*"

I close my eyes and open them. "We're friends, Jenna."

"I've hated not being able to talk to you this week."

I think about it for a long moment. "I've hated it, too."

She takes a step toward me. And then another.

"Can I hug you?"

I step forward and fold her into my arms. There's this sharp stab of pain and then this feeling of rightness. Like we fit together.

Her head shifts and I smell her hair—cinnamon. A rush of feelings and impulses rise to the surface. Without realizing it, my arms tighten around her, pulling her fast against me. That one small whiff has brought back memories—holding her, shaking in my arms, at Disneyland, kissing her on her bed when she was crying, the feel of her small hand when she slipped it inside mine.

I swallow what feels like a boulder in my throat. "Let's spend some time together tonight," I say.

She sighs, and I feel her warm breath rush past my arm. She's rubbing her cheek against the cloth of my shirt, causing tension in every inch of my body.

I want her. And *not* just as a friend.

Our time away from each other hasn't helped in that respect. Those feelings are as strong as ever. *Stronger.*

We have dinner together—soup and dark bread—and then I set up her booth for her. She decorates it with glittery scraps of cloth and a big banner that says *Mistress Jenna's Fortune Readings*. We talk about what each of us did this past week, and I tell her about my progress with the visualization. She listens intently and asks me questions, but I'm feeling apprehensive.

What if I can't win her tiara back?

I'm worried I'll disappoint her if I don't win. But I've never been more ready than I am now for this fight. And I *have* to win, because I can't disappoint her.

I have to show her that I'm worthy of her love.

27
JENNA

"ID YOU DO ANYTHING FUN THIS WEEK?" I ASKED, stuffing the last corner of bread into my mouth. The corn chowder soup was spicy and delicious.

He shrugged. "Just a minor art project. Helped me relax." As William polished off his second bowl, my eyes traveled up his finely sculpted arms—not a trace of excess fat anywhere. The veins crisscrossed his muscles like a contour map under his skin, and I wanted to trace every one of them with my fingertips...followed by my tongue.

My eyes darted to his handsome face. "What project? A painting?"

He was quiet for a moment, his thumbs twiddling against each other. Finally, he said, "It's something for you. A sort of apology for the way I acted on Sunday..."

I straightened. "What? You made something for me and I can't see it 'til we get home? How—"

"I brought it. It's not very big. I didn't have a lot of time."

I stand up at the picnic bench where we've been sitting. "You brought it here? Why am I not seeing it right this minute?"

His eyes widened, and he was staring at me like I was a crazy person. "Calm down."

I shook my head and playfully slapped the picnic bench between us. "I'm not calming down. You made something pretty for me. I want to see it!"

"You don't know if it's pretty."

I put my hands on my hips. "William Drake, if you made it, then it's pretty. I already know that. I *have* seen your work before."

Slowly, he rose from his seat, a satisfied smile solidifying, but he shook his head as if exasperated with me and my excitability.

"Well, you brought it up, so now you have to show me," I said with a smile, holding out my hand to him. "Come on...."

I knew he wanted to show it to me but he was being modest, so I gently took his hand and urged him along. William led me to his tent, a pavilion that looked a lot like something a medieval nobleman would inhabit while off in the field of war. The floor was lined with a big, thick Middle Eastern-style carpet, and there were cushions and bedding on the floor to one side, with a table and some wooden boxes and crates on the other. His armor was on a stand in the corner next to a small weapons rack.

It was after sunset, so William lit a modern propane camping lantern. It was generally agreed upon that modern nighttime lighting was needed in our campsites. If we were to go for anything authentic, such as candles or torches, we'd be exposing ourselves to fire hazards and other safety concerns. And though the rest of his tent looked straight out of the medieval time period, the lantern he hung on a hook at the top of the tent did not.

William pulled out a leather poster tube, and from it he extracted a rolled-up canvas. His actions were slow, halting, as if he feared my reaction. Maybe he'd decided to do that naked picture of me after all...

But no, the picture that he unrolled across the top of his patchwork silk and satin bedspread was not a naked picture at all. It only took seconds for me to absorb what it was, and once I did, my heart stopped and my eyes clouded with tears. I had no idea how or when I'd catch my next breath.

Outlined in black and filled with gorgeous watercolors was a view of Main Street USA in Disneyland. But instead of a crowded street, there were only two figures. They were holding hands as they walked down the street toward Sleeping Beauty's castle, their backs to the viewer. There was no mistaking Mickey Mouse, who was holding the hand of a little girl with white-blond hair—me.

That story I'd told him...from my childhood. He'd remembered. And he'd rendered it in such loving detail that it made me ache just to look at it.

Tears streamed down my face, and I wasn't even self-conscious that he could see them. In fact, he stood next to me and, with his big fingers, reached up to sweep them away.

"I didn't mean to make you sad," he said quietly.

I shook my head and sniffed, not even sure what I was. Was this *happy*? Was this *sad*? Was this *so incredibly moved*?

"It's beautiful, Wil. You didn't make me sad. But I've gotta warn you that I'm going to hug you so hard right now—if that's okay."

"That's okay," he said and opened his arms.

I grabbed him around the waist and held on tight. This meant that he'd been thinking about me during the week that we'd been away from each other.

We continued holding each other for a long time, and then I turned to look at the painting again. Crawling onto the bed, I spread it as flat as I could—the corners kept curling up—and took in every detail. "You're amazing, Wil."

He sank down on the bed beside me. "So are you."

I shook my head. "No, I'm not..."

"You are. You've been through so much hardship, and yet you're still a positive person. You help others. You're strong and brave, and you care about other people. You've cared about me, Jenna. You're like a ray of sunlight cutting into darkness."

I turned and lay my head against his shoulder, and he reached up to cup it in his large hand. We lay like that in silence for a while. And then, as my lids grew heavy, with sleep-slurred speech I asked him if I could spend the night here.

William sat up and I helped him pull the bedspread down. Then I kicked off my shoes while he extinguished the lamp. We crawled onto the fluffy bedroll, where I promptly curled in beside him as he held me in his strong arms. And I slept so peacefully—more so than I had in a long time.

The next morning I woke in William's bed. He was sleeping on his side, facing away from me, but he'd taken off his shirt sometime during the night. I studied the muscles of his back, the way his rib cage slowly expanded and contracted. I wanted to lean over and kiss him, to run my hand down his solid back.

But I restrained myself—barely. I didn't want to start something I knew that he would stop. The fundamental disagreement between us had not been resolved.

I swallowed a sudden lump in my throat. *Would it ever?*

With stealthy movements, I crept out of bed and slipped on my shoes. I needed to go to the tent I shared with my friends so I could change for the big day.

It was the first day of May—May Day, or within our reenactment group, the first day of the Beltane Festival. In ancient times, this day marked the beginning of the summer season and honored fertility. There would be feasting, folk dancing and a celebration around the Maypole. After dark, the Beltane Ball would be held around a raging bonfire.

I couldn't wait.

When I got to my tent, a few of my friends gave me curious glances. Caitlyn, of course, asked me where I'd been all night.

"I, uh, well it's not as exciting as you think. I was with William—"

Her brows shot up, and once again I got that weird feeling from her—something like vague jealousy. "Then it *is* as exciting as I think. Sir Hottie MacFine likes women after all."

I had no desire whatsoever to rub salt into her wounds. Caitlyn was a good friend and I didn't want to hurt her, so I chose my words carefully. "He does...and it would have been exciting if our clothes had come off, but they didn't."

Her mouth twisted. "Well, that sucks." But I could tell she wasn't all that disappointed by the news.

I turned away to put my bag on my cot, distracted by the box sitting there. "Who left their stuff on my cot?"

"That's for you, apparently. Johnny came by doing deliveries for Mistress Agnes last night. Said that one was for you."

"The dressmaker? I didn't order anything from her."

"Yeah, we thought you'd won the lotto or something," said Ann with a wide grin. "Or robbed a bank."

"That's what it would take for me to afford her gorgeous dresses..." My eyes skimmed the box. It must have been a mistake.

"Open it up and see what it is," Ann said.

But I already had the top off the box, and what I saw literally took my breath away. I pulled the pile of gorgeous blue cloth from the white tissue and held it up. Starting with the palest blue—almost white at the shoulders—there was a gradual ombre from sky blue to cerulean and every shade of blue in between, until it became a deep, dark midnight blue at the hem. The dress was decorated with gold embroidery at the neckline that extended down the long, flowing sleeves. The garment looked like it had been woven from the sky, the clearest blue lake and a midnight starfield.

"Holy shit," Caitlyn uttered in a harsh whisper. "That is gorgeous."

"I know," I said in a trembling voice. My eyes flew up to the pale blue at the shoulders—pale, pale blue. Like the Turkish pools. Some long name that I couldn't remember, even though I'd searched for Google images the night he'd told me about them. This dress could not have come from anyone other than William.

And not only was it beautiful, but it was such a thoughtful thing to do. I sank down on the cot next to me and passed my hand over the exquisite material. It was too much. I shouldn't accept this.

"I think I can guess who had this sent to you," Caitlyn said in a low voice.

I looked up, biting my lip. She was smiling. A very small smile.

Ann sat on the cot beside Caitlyn and put an arm around her shoulder.

I took a breath and released it. "Caitlyn, I'm—"

She held her hand up. "Don't say you're sorry. You have nothing to be sorry about. But please, for the love of God, don't break his heart.

William is hard enough to reach, but it doesn't take a rocket scientist to know that he's got it bad for you. I think I've mostly just been in denial. Honestly, Jenna, you're the sweetest person ever. You deserve him."

Don't break his heart.

Yet as I looked at her and then down at the dress, I felt that strange knot of emotion twisting in my chest. I had to wonder—whose heart was breaking, exactly?

My chest physically hurt. Like someone had sunk a grappling hook deep inside and was tugging it in the direction of William. And the harder they pulled, the deeper it went.

I was so confused. I was *so* attached. Since seeing him again, I couldn't deny that feeling of my heart leaping in my throat. What did this mean? What was my heart telling me? What had the cards told me? And that talk with Alex? And...just...everything.

With each passing minute, the thought of leaving with the Renaissance Faire became less and less appealing.

My nose started to sting as I swallowed more tears, and soon I was surrounded by the other ladies in the tent—Caitlyn, Ann, and even their friend Fiona.

"Hey," cooed Caitlyn. "What's wrong? You don't want him? Because you already know that I'll take him," she added playfully.

I shook my head and patted the dress again. "I'm just confused."

"But do you want him?"

Fingering the delicate glass beads sewn into the bodice of the gown, I knew I didn't really have to think about it. As much as I hadn't wanted to admit it to myself, I did. I *totally* did. So I let out a breathy, "Yes."

But…did he still want me? Or had he already mentally tucked me into that group of women who would just hurt him and leave him? Just the thought of being in the same category as his mother, who essentially abandoned him, made me feel ill.

But then I thought about the way he'd held me last night as we lay next to each other. How his thumb had caressed my wrist, my hand. How he'd laced his fingers around mine and hadn't let go.

And somehow I knew, deep down, that he *never would.*

"I need to go for a walk." I got up and carefully stored the dress back in its box. "I'll be back to help with lunch and to set up for the Maypole."

"Have some breakfast first?" Caitlyn said.

"Not hungry. But thanks! I just have some thinking to do."

And that's exactly what I did as I made my way along a dusty path that led to the amphitheater where William and Doug would face off tomorrow. I wound up the trail amidst dried-out brush, various types of high desert flora, darting lizards and the occasional beetle. I kept my feet on the ground and my eyes locked on the distant bluish Sierras that cut into the horizon in the east. The sun wasn't that bad yet. As it was still spring, it would be warm today, but not unbearably so.

I hugged myself as I stood there, feeling small and insignificant amongst all the natural beauty. My doubts and fears felt so insignificant in the face of the massive universe all around me.

I thought about Brock and me, two tiny specks in that universe. I thought about how much I still loved him. How much I'd held fast to the belief that he was the one person for me. Now my feelings for William were tearing that belief to shreds, and I had to come to terms with that.

I couldn't help but think of that reading I did days before, specifically the Moon card. The Moon and Earth, two more specks in the universe—albeit much larger specks. The Moon pulled and tugged the tides of the Earth, causing movement in the tides. Causing confusion, uncertainty, untruth. That card was a warning that I'd been deceiving myself.

Deceiving myself with my own misguided beliefs.

The realization took my breath away, and I blinked as I tried to catch the next one, knotting and then unknotting my sweaty hands.

"I don't know what to do," I said out loud to the Universe. The breeze seemed to carry my words away into the distance. My eyes closed, and suddenly I heard a voice in my head.

Go to him. Be with him.

My heartbeat sped up, and yet...I couldn't help but feel that pang of disloyalty.

"Brock, what should I do?" I said to the air, hoping the breeze would answer me.

Be happy. I want you to be happy.

Whether it was a spirit or my imagination saying the things I knew Brock would say, I'd never know. But that message was clear in my mind, followed immediately by another.

Stay, stay. Stay, stay.

Brock was my past. And how very blessed I was to have known him and to have loved him. But William...William could be my future. If I'd just let him in.

***

I had no chance to speak to William before lunch, as we were both so heavily involved in the set-up for the Beltane celebration. And at the center of it all was the Maypole—a smoothly cut log that had been buried a few feet into the ground by some of the stronger men in our group. At the very top, colorful ribbons were attached, radiating out like the spokes of a bicycle wheel. The end of each green, yellow, red, pink and purple ribbon was staked down in the ground in a circle around the clearing. This was where we would be dancing.

All those who were unattached circled the ring, alternating men and women. We each pulled up the end of the ribbon nearest us and took it in hand. When it was time to claim our places, William was reluctantly pushed into the fray by a group of the unavailable women, who cheered him on from where they stood outside the ring, waiting for us to start the dance. I marveled at how far he'd come. Months ago, he never would have participated in an event like this.

William faced me across the circle, sending me a smile that could only be described as a slight upward curvature of his lips. I smiled back until his head ducked and his eyes sank away from my gaze. My heart danced—and not necessarily in anticipation of the music.

I sucked in a sudden breath at the obvious but beautiful thought that William made me happy.

But what did that *mean?*

Doug stood beside me, throwing dirty looks at both William and me. But William did not notice or even look at Doug, so I followed his example and ignored Doug too.

Suddenly, the music started—a lute, a drum and a fiddle all playing a simple period melody for the Maypole Dance. We began the straightforward trip around the Maypole according to ancient custom: a step, a hop and a bow or curtsy to our neighbor. A steady breeze blew as we wove in and out amongst each other, our ribbons growing shorter by the minute. Soon, the Maypole was clothed in a beautiful intertwined pattern consisting of a multitude of bright colors.

I passed my friends, mystified by their awkward smiles, winks and laughs as we acknowledged each other. At first I thought nothing of it, then slowly I started to get the feeling I was the butt of some joke. Maybe they were silently teasing me about William.

I studied the pole without realizing how often I was weaving in and out of my neighbors and dancing partners. I didn't even make an extra effort to meet William's eyes each time we passed each other. I kept my eyes on that pole until I realized that my ribbon was growing *very* short.

And as the person with the shortest ribbon, I was the one who got tied to the pole by everyone else's ribbons, which made me the official May Queen. It wasn't long before my fellow dancers pressed me up against the pole, using their extra length of ribbon to tie me there, as was custom.

As the first to run out of my ribbon, Fate had chosen me to be the May Queen. My friends circled closer, offering me congratulations with huge grins on their faces. Eventually, when they reached the ends of their ribbons, they pressed kisses on my cheek.

For a quick, stressful moment, I thought Doug would be the last man standing. But when he faced me with his ribbon, instead of bending to kiss me, he grimaced and walked away, leaving the person behind him in plain view to me. The last man holding a ribbon end was now the May King.

William stood soberly in front of me as people whooped and hollered their congratulations. When my gaze met his, I blushed to the roots of my hair as everyone around us clapped their hands in time to the music and chanted, "Kiss her! Kiss her!"

He smiled down at me, clearly pleased, and I, equally pleased, grinned back at him. Finally, after a few more seconds of goading, he bent his head just as I tilted my head back, more than ready to meet his mouth.

When at last he kissed me, it was *delicious.* The moment my lips parted, his tongue was there, tasting me, and I felt it flash like lightning through my body. His hands rested on my hips, and gently he tried to tug me toward him. Though, tied down as I was by the ribbons on the pole, I couldn't go to him.

"Huzzah!" called our baron, Lord de Bricasse. "The Fates have now chosen our May Queen and King. All hail! Let us open these Beltane festivities with their coronation!"

I was released by Caitlyn, who hugged me while whispering in my ear that the group of ladies had rigged the dance to work out the way it had by ensuring that I started with the shortest ribbon, and William, the longest. I gave her a stern look, suddenly understanding their snickering and cheeky looks. But then my face melted into a grin, which she quickly returned. I thanked her, and in the next second, I had a crown of beautiful wildflowers placed on my head with ribbons streaming down the back.

I turned to watch as they crowned the May King, taking a moment to marvel that the crowd during the dance had hardly appeared to faze him. William's crown was much more Spartan, made of laurel and ivy vines woven together in a masculine style.

At the crowd's request—and much less required this time than before—we kissed again as they sang and cheered. I murmured against his mouth, "I have to get dressed for the feast and dancing."

His hold only tightened and his mouth continued to move over mine, claiming it again and again, leaving me breathless.

"C'mon, Wil, you have to let me go." I reluctantly pulled back from him.

"I'm the king. I don't have to do anything I don't want to do," he responded, kissing me again, even as the crowd started to dissipate in preparation for the evening celebration.

Thrill surged through me and my eyes fluttered closed. I'd wondered if he still wanted me like I now knew I wanted him. I guess I had my answer.

Intense joy crackled within, hot as sunlight. The only thing that could make this more perfect was..."But I want to wear that gorgeous new dress you bought for me."

He froze and slowly, ever so slowly, pulled away. "Even though I've pictured it clearly, I'd love to see you wearing it."

"Thank you. You shouldn't have done it."

"But I did. And I'm the king, so I can do whatever I want."

I laughed. "You're really loving that new title, aren't you?"

He smiled, lifting a hand to brush his thumb across my cheek. "It's good to be the king."

"Maybe tonight you'll get to see me...*not* wearing the dress, too."

His brows pinched and his eyes grew intense. "I don't have to imagine that, because I've already seen it. I just have to remember it."

And maybe look forward to it. If I was very, *very* lucky.

"Wil, there's something I need to tell you—"

He kissed me again. We were now alone in the empty clearing, as everyone else had gone back to their tents or to circulate amongst the booths.

"Tell me in between kisses," he said, his voice raspy with a harsh edge to it. That edge dragged across my senses, the scratch made by a lover during a passionate moment. I swallowed my thready heartbeat and suppressed the vertigo of someone about to step off a precipice into the unknown below.

"I want to stay, Wil. I want us to be together. I want to see where this takes us." He froze, his eyes on my shoulder, his features revealing no reaction whatsoever.

Had he heard me? Oh no...maybe he'd changed his mind. "If—if that's what you still want, of course...." I added, hating how my voice squeaked when I said it.

He let loose a gruff laugh. "You have to ask me that?"

I shrugged, self-conscious. "People change their minds..."

"*I* don't," he said, his voice as hard as the granite rocks in the hills around us. "But I need to be sure that you are certain."

I nodded. "I am...I've been giving it a lot of thought." *Nonstop, obsessive thought at that.*

Slowly, tenderly, he kissed me on the cheek. "And your job?"

"I plan on asking for it back."

He kissed my chin. "And what about school?"

"I want to finish, once I've saved up the money."

He kissed my nose. "And what about the Renaissance Faire?"

"I'll tell them they need to find someone else to read—" I was cut off by his mouth landing on mine again, his strong hands pulling me to him. As our bodies pressed together, my breath hissed out of my chest. And when he finished the kiss, he pulled away, only to lay his forehead against mine. "You've made me very happy, Jenna. *Very happy.* But that's not even a fraction of the way I want to make you feel."

I smiled. "Wil, you already do..."

We hugged and then I excused myself, reminding him that I could hardly contain my excitement to wear the beautiful blue dress. He reluctantly let me go with still more kisses to punctuate our breathless sentences.

Caitlyn snatched up the hairbrush the minute I entered the tent. "*There you are.* You weren't answering your text messages!"

"Sorry, I was, um...tied up."

She smirked. "Funny. Come on, Ann and I are going to braid your hair."

And that's exactly what they did. They braided my hair along my crown, threading in the matching ribbon that had come in the box from Agnes. After that, Ann helped me put on the dress and carefully laced my corset up my back. It was definitely one instance where I wished I had a full-length mirror to admire myself.

Because I felt like a princess. Papa once told me that I was a princess—and that someday I'd be a queen. Now it wasn't a lie. He'd been right. I was the May Queen.

And William was my king. Every time I thought of him, pictured him, remembered the taste of him on my lips, my stomach fluttered. And with each minute that passed until I could see him again, that excitement grew.

The evening started with the feast. Roasted chicken and bread with boiled vegetables by candlelight—the one exception to our open-flame rule, and only because the candles were all covered by glass lanterns. We did *not* eat with our hands.

Picnic benches had been lined up, and I sat at one end and William at the other in our places of honor. We talked to our neighbors, occasionally catching each other's eye before William's gaze stole away like an elusive ninja. It became somewhat of a game, to try and catch his eyes on mine. He caught onto me, I think, because he started to smile whenever I caught him watching at me.

And then he turned the game around on me, piercing me with his dark stare that reflected the golden candlelight. When our eyes locked, everything else around us seemed to vanish. It was only us.

My throat tightened and I swallowed, admiring him in his fine new tunic, which—not coincidentally, I'm sure—matched my dress. Despite everything going on around me, I could only think of later tonight when I hoped that we'd have time to spend together.

Alone.

28
WILLIAM

A FTER LEAVING JENNA, I DRESS QUICKLY, RETURN TO THE clearing to wait...and wait. Almost an *hour. Late again, Mistress Kovac!*

One of the clanswomen tells me to be patient, that Jenna is busy "prettying herself up." Completely unnecessary, in my opinion. How can you improve on perfection? The features and hair of an angel, the glowing skin and body of a goddess. And a heart of pure gold.

My heart speeds up as those thoughts lead where they usually do. What if I'm not enough for her? What if I can't get her heirloom back tomorrow? What if I'm not ...worthy?

I'm dressed in my new tunic, finely crafted by Agnes. Our clan seamstress has done an excellent job with the stitching on the sleeves, especially. And the embroidery itself is a work of art. Knowing what kind of effort it takes to produce an item of beauty, I'm always appreciative of these efforts in others.

My tunic matches the beautiful gown that Agnes made for Jenna. When she finally enters the clearing, all heads turn in her direction.

It's not difficult to understand why. The shades of blue next to her pale skin look as beautiful as I knew they would. In fact, they look *better*. And she walks in like the queen that she is, graceful, her chin tilted up a little—probably conscious of the crown of flowers in her golden hair. *Beautiful.*

I can't draw the next breath, and I'm pretty certain I've completely forgotten any hunger I had for the food in front of me. She flashes me a smile and apologizes for being late, but says she wanted to do the dress justice. I watch Jenna's lips as she talks, remembering how she tasted just an hour ago. Sweeter than ever, because she told me she would stay. And right now, all I want to do is take her in my arms and make her mine—for real.

Everyone around us is admiring her and Lord de Bricasse speaks up. "We haven't had a May Queen this beautiful since…"

Never. I mentally complete for him, though he's joking that it's been since the previous Beltane.

After our feast, the fire is lit in the specially designated area for a campfire. And it's a massive bonfire, the heat singeing our faces and hands. Everyone is clapping and cheering as the flames reach higher and higher. Lord Ryleigh, or "Joe," as he is known in his mundane life, breaks out his fiddle, and we begin to assemble in the space around the fire.

In the past, I made it a point to leave before the dancing began, because dancing inevitably meant crowds. But tonight nothing will stop me from dancing and holding my Jenna—her body close to mine. My face next to hers. The smell of her hair and skin in my nostrils.

We start with easy formations based on English country dancing. Lady Ryleigh, Joe's wife, is an expert in recreational European folk dance and has taught most of us how to do it. I've been brushing up with videos and Youtube.

Without question, I'm paired with Jenna, and I wonder at the lucky coincidence that brought us together as King and Queen. I'd almost start adopting Jenna's belief in fate if I didn't find it so silly.

As I watch her, I imagine the tiara on her head instead of the May crown. Determination steels me. Tomorrow, I'll get it back for her and I'll humiliate Doug in the process. I don't care what he thinks of me or what he's said. I don't even care that the stakes are high for me, too. Because if I lose, I won't be able to come back here and be with all my friends. That concerns me, but it's not the worst thing that could happen.

No, all I care about is getting that tiara back for Jenna. Making her happy. Being worthy of her.

Her thin hands in mine feel good as we clasp them together and spin slowly first to the left and then to the right. Stepping back, I bow and she curtsies ,then we execute the complex but repetitive steps. I find myself looking down at my feet often, which not only helps me avoid tripping over my own feet but also to evade accidental eye contact.

I don't want to make a wrong move, and I definitely don't want to step on her toes. I want this night to be perfect. I've run everything through my head a thousand times and it should be perfect. We'll dance. We'll kiss. And more.

But what if I can't get her what she needs? What if I can't be her champion tomorrow? What if I disappoint her? That thought sets my heart beating faster than it should based on this light physical activity. Because now my fears are taking over and they're all I can see.

It's getting hard to concentrate. A tightness in my chest is intensifying, and when I look up and feel the crowd around us, I get lightheaded. I squeeze my eyes closed, suppressing a wave of nausea.

My eyes snap open when I'm suddenly jolted in the back. The breath is knocked out of me and cold fear seizes me, making my gut churn. I spin, looking all around me, but see only a blur. People close in around me, loudly talking and clapping. Heads are moving this way and that.

I stop, but the whole world keeps moving. It feels like everyone around me is closing in, and I can't breathe.

A hand grabs my shoulder and I'm knotted with dread. I tear away from that hold with all of my strength. "Watch your space!"

I see that it's Ronald, another clan member, and he's now staring at me, eyes and mouth wide open. People near us are stopping and staring.

"Whoa, friend," Ronald says, laughing. "The duel isn't until tomorrow."

My palms are sweaty and the fear in my throat is cold.

I can't lose this for her. I can't. I can't lose her just as I've finally won her.

I squeeze my eyes shut, trying to take a breath, when he pounds on my back. I turn and shove him away so hard that he falls to the ground. The music screeches to a halt, but I'm already running, already moving, pushing through the cluster of bodies.

I need to get out of here. This is a nightmare made reality.

But it just might be that the nightmare won't start until that duel tomorrow, when I could lose everything.

29
JENNA

I GRASPED WILLIAM'S UPPER ARM TO STOP HIM, BUT HE PUSHED violently away from me before tearing the May King crown from his head and flinging it to the ground in the process. I turned and muttered my apologies to the stunned group of people in our vicinity.

"Go back to dancing. He'll be all right."

But he was already gone, disappearing into the darkness beyond the glowing ring of the bonfire. And like a little girl, I chased after him, my own crown bouncing off my head and tumbling to the ground behind me.

The music started up again and I assumed people resumed their dancing, but I was already wading into the darkness, willing my eyes to adjust quickly.

"Wil?"

Silence. I couldn't even hear footsteps. Crickets chirped in the distance and coyotes howled, too. The only light out here was that of the nearly full moon above.

A group of people off to the left spoke in hushed voices, laughing occasionally. As I made my way toward William's tent, I heard another sound. A groan, followed by a gasp. Remembering that it was Beltane, I realized that people had paired up and peeled off to go and celebrate in a private—and much more enjoyable—way.

I swallowed, immediately turned on. It had been months, and I'd been lusting after William for far too long. The unrealized sexual tension that lived in my belly was now infiltrating my vital organs.

But I was too worried about him be concerned with that at this moment. I'd attack him later, when I knew he was safe and calm.

I was just outside his tent when a hand reached out of the darkness and latched onto me just above the elbow. Startled, I jerked away.

"Wil! You scared the—"

But my words were swallowed in a gasp when the hand tightened painfully on my arm and the eyes I met were not William's.

I drew back. "Doug, what the hell? Get away from me."

"What's got you so upset, *your majesty*? Did your freak wander off into the woods without you? Maybe the coyotes will eat him."

I tilted my head toward him and spoke with faux sweetness. "Shouldn't you be off trying to convince yourself that you have a hope in hell of winning your duel tomorrow?"

His jaw clenched, eyes narrowing. "You're mighty confident in your new boyfriend, aren't you?"

I grinned at him, with a faux gloat. "I sure as hell am. Now get out of my way."

Instead, he stepped forward, blocking me fully. "Someone needs to warn that poor bastard about you—how you play with men and use them for your own purposes, then dump them when you don't need them anymore. I'm sure you're just fucking him to get him to fight for your little princess crown."

I held out my hand, middle finger pointed straight up. "Bite me, asshole."

Doug laughed. "Wow, such a lady."

"If a man can say those words, then so can I. Especially when it's deserved. Got a problem with that?"

He smirked, and I honestly wanted to smack that smirk off his face. I didn't get violent feelings often, but I had to prevent the sudden urge to charge him knee him right in his inadequately sized junk. I contented myself with the thought that William would be doing plenty of smacking him around on my behalf in the morning. It would be sword against sword—and preferably William's sword on Doug's helmet a few hundred times.

"And here I was going to be all magnanimous and offer you your little tiara back, no duel required."

Sudden tightness formed in my throat, but suspicion laced any hope that rose in my chest. "And the catch?"

He shrugged and looked away. "I'll hand over the tiara right now if *Sir William* forfeits the tournament tomorrow."

I hesitated, picturing the tiara. Then I was assailed with a vision of my sister's face when I showed up at her doorstep without the tiara and had to tell her she wouldn't be walking down the aisle with Papa and Baba's blessings on her wedding day. The disappointment in her eyes as she fought back tears. My gut tightened.

I was tempted...*so tempted*. That tiara could easily be mine if I talked William into forfeiting. And I knew I probably could.

I cleared my throat and spoke in a tiny voice. "If he forfeits, that counts as a loss for him. And—and your conditions would still apply?"

He shrugged again. "Yup. He forfeits, he goes. Full exile."

I shook my head, folding my arms across my chest. "I can't ask him to do that."

"He's scared of people anyway. You saw that freak show just now. You'd be doing him a favor to give him an excuse to go. Just give him a really good blow job tonight as a reward."

My arms stiffened and I was awash with true disgust. "You really are gross, Doug. Truly disgusting. And William has more courage, manliness and honor in his thumbnail than you do in your entire body and one hundred clones of yourself, if, goddess forbid, they existed. You're a shameful, spiteful man. William is a true knight."

Doug's face flushed during my speech, but he offered a slight shrug. Nevertheless, I could tell that I'd gotten to him. "We'll see how it all shakes out in the morning, then."

"I already know how it's going to go. William's going to beat you down like the bitch that you are. And deep down, you know that too, because you never would have offered this 'out' if you thought you could win. Now get out of my way."

He stepped aside, and as I passed him, he turned and said, "Go enjoy your retard while he can still associate with the clan."

I raised a fist and spun toward him, getting right in his face. "Call him that again, you fucker. I dare you."

In the low light, he actually looked afraid. Not so brave without his armor, to be frightened by a woman roughly half his size. I really wanted to box his ears or stub his nose. Or something else *really* painful. My palms were almost aching to slap the shit out of him.

He flipped me off and then disappeared behind the nearest tent.

Making rude gestures at his back didn't help my frustration. With a weary sigh, I continued my search for William, that deep worry settling over me again.

He probably wasn't in his tent. I would have seen the glow from his propane lantern. Lifting the flap anyway, I peeked in, but couldn't see a thing. I was about to go search elsewhere when I heard a movement from the bed.

William had been lying down, but his strong silhouette in the dim light was easily detectable as he stood up.

"Jenna," he said in a hoarse voice.

"Wil!" I breathed, awash with relief. I pushed into the tent. "I was so worried about you. I didn't see where you ran off to."

He took another step toward me without saying anything.

Worried, I kept talking. "You didn't, uh, you didn't hear all that shit Doug said..."

He took another step and nodded, hands rubbing up and down his pant legs. I bit my lip. *Shit.* Was he angry with me? I had responded to Doug's offer without consulting William, not giving him a chance to choose whether or not to forfeit. Maybe that annoyed him.

He moved forward again until he was standing right in front of me. My eyes latched onto the strong column of his neck and the bare part of his chest where his doublet was unlaced.

He smelled of sweat and soap and William. My breath caught.

"You turned down his offer." He sounded incredulous. "But you need that tiara. I would have done that for you. I would—"

Without giving him a warning, I reached up and pressed two fingers to his lips to shush him. "I *believe* in you, Wil."

His eyes flew to mine and his hand reached up to smooth my cheek. My eyes fluttered closed, and in seconds his hand slid around to the back of my neck. With a firm tug, he pulled me to him and our mouths met with enough force to shock me.

I was stunned at the power in this kiss, like a physical electric shock. And after that brief moment of surprise, my body fell against his, soft and pliant against his male hardness.

His free arm slid around my waist, holding me tight to him, and his kiss intensified, stealing my breath. I opened for him and he readily pushed his tongue into my mouth with enthusiastic vigor that I happily matched.

Eventually, our heads separated—just barely, though. And when I looked up at him, he was breathing hard, his dark eyes cloudy with desire, like a storm just about to break over the mountains. He was moving in for another kiss when I spoke.

"Wil, I—" But I never finished, because he pulled me to him again and kissed me so ferociously that I forgot my own name. I couldn't think, but I could feel those warm, firm, delicious lips on mine. Those hands, which tightened and became more insistent with each passing minute. That solid chest under my questing hands. That body, which hardened against mine, leaving me fully aware of his arousal.

I began to unlace the rest of his doublet while he was feasting on my neck, caressing it in all the right places with hot, demanding, sandpapery kisses. He seemed determined to cover every inch of the sensitive skin there, and I certainly wasn't going to argue with his need to be thorough.

When his chest was fully exposed, I started to kiss him there, and at that point his mouth moved away from my neck. I could feel his hurried, steamy breath in my hair as my lips skated over his rough, whiskered neck, sliding down the solid neck to caress his collarbone. One of his hands threaded through my hair, massaging my scalp, while the other went to the neckline of my dress, tugging at it as if trying to figure out how to get the dress off.

"Wil..."

"What?" he answered tersely, apparently consumed by his current goal of figuring out the puzzle of my dress.

"I need help getting this off..." I said.

"I *really* want it off."

I laughed a little. "I, um, figured that out. I really want it off, too. As beautiful as it is—"

"It's not as beautiful as you are," he said, and then he continued to kiss me, taking an earlobe between his lips, caressing it with his tongue. My eyes rolled back in my head as a sizzle of pleasure zapped down my nerve endings straight to my core, heating everything in its path. Everything ached for him now.

I'd been aching for him for a while, in fact. And hopefully what was about to happen would satisfy that ache.

Slowly, I pulled away from him. It wasn't easy. It was like walking against a windstorm, with resistance every inch of the way. But the moment he saw that I was turning around, he let me go.

"It's laces, just like your doublet. Only they're in the back," I said, trying to catch my breath, knowing there was no way I could calm my racing heart.

Without a word, he tugged at the laces with abrupt, sharp movements. At first his movements were hurried, but gradually he slowed. Each time he pulled a lace from an eyelet, his hand touched my bare back and I shivered. He caught on quickly, making sure he touched me as he removed the laces.

My eyes drifted closed again and my awareness centered around his breath on my neck. He ran a rough index finger along the exposed part of my spine, seeming to enjoy the shivery reaction his touches evoked from me.

When the lacings were done, and before I could turn back around to face him, he tore off his doublet and pressed his hard chest to my back. "I like making you shiver."

"It means I really want you."

He was kissing me at my temple, my ear, my jaw. "I know what it means, Jenna."

I laughed. Of course he did. "Wil, I want to have sex with you."

"I know that, too."

"I hope *you* want it."

"You already know that I do."

"Then why are we still talking?"

He angled his head to capture my mouth with his and I tilted my head back as his kiss deepened. His hands were suddenly inside my dress, sliding around to cup my breasts. When he rubbed his hard, calloused palms across them, I almost shrieked with pleasure right then and there. My sensitive nipples were now taut peaks and he stroked them with his thumbs, as if plucking strings causing vibrations down to my deepest depths. I fell back against him.

This was happening. *Finally.* And I hadn't even had a chance to tell him about my feelings. Slowly, I pulled away and turned back to him.

"Can we—?"

But he shook his head and pulled the front of my dress down to my waist. "No more talking," he said roughly before ducking his head to suck one of my nipples into his mouth. The contact was like fireworks—the good kind, not the kind that made me scream in terror. No, these fireworks were brilliant, scorching, overwhelming.

His mouth and tongue were doing wicked things. I let out a small grunt of surprise when his teeth ever so lightly grazed that sensitive point. I thought it was an accident until, seconds later, he did it again. My back arched, pushing more of my breast into his mouth.

He responded by gently taking my shoulder and gently lowering me to his plush mattress without ever stopping what he was doing. Soon he was lying beside me, still covering my chest with hot, wet kisses. When he shifted, his thigh pinned mine to the bed and my hands gravitated to his hard chest.

And then I knew—just as I'd been suspecting for months—this was going to be *so good.*

30
WILLIAM

JENNA IS MAKING SOUNDS—SMALL SIGHS AND GASPS AND A FEW louder moans that increase in volume the more I caress and taste her. And the more she does, the harder I get, until it hurts almost everywhere. I'm so tense, I feel like I'm going to explode.

I *want* to explode. Inside her. Right now it's what I want more than anything. Almost more than breathing. It's like...being hungry and then eating, but never feeling full. The more I taste her, the hungrier I get.

I reach down to pull the rest of her dress from her body and she helps me by lifting her hips from the bed to let me remove it. Her hand is still stroking my chest in the way that I like, with firm, hard strokes instead of that tickling light touch that I can't stand.

Jenna is not wearing a bra under her corset bodice, but she has a pair of modern women's underwear on. I'm glad she didn't go with more period-appropriate underclothing, because these are small, lacy...sexy. They're low-cut and a pretty shade of lavender that looks gorgeous next to her skin under the silvery light from the moon above my tent. The next time I paint her, she'll be wearing that shade of lavender. Or nothing at all.

I'd prefer nothing at all. I'm so desperate to have her that when I grab the panties to pull them off her, I'm a little too forceful. She lets out a shocked breath and I mutter my apology.

She smiles and shakes her head. "No, it's good. It's sexy. Pull them off as hard as you want."

That's all I need to hear. As they come off with a vicious yank, she makes that sound again...almost like a sob. But she's not crying.

She's smiling and luminous.

She's naked.

And she's on my bed.

I'm fumbling with the lacings on my breeches, almost willing to cut through them to get them off as quickly as I can. Unlike Jenna, I opted for period-style underwear, which look weird by modern-day standards. They're, loose and falling almost to the knee with a drawstring at the top.

But I'm out of the breeches and the underwear in less than two-thirds of a minute. And, for the first time ever, we're both naked.

Just a few seconds after registering that fact, I cover her warm body with mine, skin against skin. My mouth finds hers again and then all rational thought becomes like a stick floating in the middle of a rushing river, being torn this way and that by vicious currents. This desire is the most powerful force in my head and my heart.

At last. I'm naked and Jenna's naked underneath me, touching me, kissing me. Her sighs and moans are like music to me. And they are like a blacksmith's bellowes to the desire burning inside, fanning it even hotter.

She's giving herself to me, and I'm taking what I've wanted for so long.

In the distance, there are people talking, laughing, throwing more wood onto the pile to feed the bonfire. And the drums. They are beating, pulsing, thumping, a primal, rhythmic beat.

It's Beltane—the mating season.

And like an ancient, powerful magic that I don't actually believe in, it's taking me over.

My hands move over her soft skin, insistent. In theory, I know what to do. I'm sure instinct will probably take over, but I want it to be good for her. I may have done extensive research, but that may not be enough.

I shift so that I'm lying on her, but I brace myself on my elbows so as not to crush her. Then I pull my mouth away from hers and she looks up at me. Slowly, she opens her legs...and I hesitate.

I swallow, feeling again like I'm unworthy. Like I might be unable to give her what she wants. She reaches up to touch my face. Her lids are heavy over her heavenly blue eyes. "Can I show you what I like?"

I don't move and she cups my shoulder with her hand. The touch burns and my eyes close. "I want to make you feel good, Jenna."

"You are, Wil. You are."

She pushes against my shoulder so that I'm now lying down beside her, and then she straddles me. Her firm, beaded nipples are against my chest, and the heat between us is expanding into a scorching furnace. Every surface of my skin that touches her softness is on fire.

She starts by kissing my chest, taking my nipples in her mouth as I have done to her. Her hands are roaming my thighs, slipping between my legs to explore me. My hands are smoothing down her back, cupping her butt, cinching her waist to mine.

We're burning like a molten star. We're generating a new type of heat, a fusion, that particular nuclear reaction found at the center of a star, that incomparable heat and light extending out for billions of years.

"Jenna, I need—"

"I know what you need."

"Then let me inside you."

She moans. "*Yes.*" She pulls back and my eyes once again fixate on those perfect, radiant breasts. They look as if carved from marble by the master hand of Michelangelo. Every shape, every curve, every peak in perfect proportion. A masterwork of art.

She is art.

And then I can't think anymore because with a shift of her hips, she slides over my erection and I slip against her wetness. It's a shallow connection but one that has me singed with powerful pleasure. I haven't even gotten inside her and yet I'm about to collapse upon myself, like the star that eventually forms a black hole.

Jenna reaches down and grasps me at the base, slowly angling my erection so that I can enter her. I hold my breath, unable to feel anything else as her impossible heat and wetness envelop me.

She lets out a long sigh, then pauses, but I'm not all of the way in yet. I can't wait another second. With a quick intake of breath, I grasp her hips and slide them forward, pushing myself into her.

She gasps, her eyes widening, and I hesitate. "Did I hurt you?"

She beams a smile as she opens her eyes. "No...not at all. You feel good, Wil. *So* good inside me."

I need to move, but there's a conundrum, because while I want to push forward toward that ultimate release, I also want it to last. *Forever.*

I want to lie here connected with Jenna, our heat multiplying, fusion adding to fusion, burning hotter and brighter for an eternity.

Slowly, Jenna rocks her hips against mine and a hiss slips out between my lips. The world moves in conjunction with those slim, round, feminine hips. She's got me in her grasp with every bit as much force as a star's gravity. And I'm sinking into her powerful, primal well.

Without realizing what I'm doing, my hands clasp around her hips, pushing her to move faster. I can't get enough. But she gently puts a hand over mine and stops all movement. "Not too fast, Wil. Or this is going to be underwhelming."

In my research, I'd read that often a man didn't perform well his first time and that often that was due to climaxing too quickly. I slowly release my hold of her hips and she bends to kiss me. Her mouth opens over mine and I slip my tongue inside without a moment's hesitation.

The thought of multiplying that connection to her consumes me. I wish there were other ways we could cleave to each other besides just these two. My hands travel around her back to reinforce that desire, holding her to me.

Her hips move again. I thread my fingers through her hair, holding her mouth to mine. She touches my chest, rubbing over my pectoral muscles, followed by my lateral muscles. Her hands are appreciative, reverential.

"You're so gorgeous, Wil," she breathes as she picks up the pace. I release her and she pulls away with a brilliant smile.

I can't tear my eyes from her breasts. I bend forward and catch one of those pale pink nipples in my mouth. She like that, a lot. Her pace falters, and her breath jerks with startled irregularity.

"You are precious. Beautiful," I murmur. My voice sounds strange. Heavier, thicker. I feel myself surge inside her along with that familiar climb to climax. Jenna feels it, too, responding with a long sigh.

She has not yet climaxed. With a purposeful quest, my fingers slip between her legs, right where we are joined, and I find her clitoris, like a pert, prominent button. She gives a little yelp of surprise but doesn't stop moving. If anything, she moves faster.

So I rub her there, and everything shifts and changes again. She feels tighter around me with her own building excitement. And as I focus more on what I'm doing for *her*, I try to forget—at least just a little bit—what she is doing to me so that this will last longer. It's an interesting challenge, attempting to find that balance, but Jenna is so soft and giving as she envelops me, cushions me. Surrounds me. Owns me.

She's all-powerful. Like a goddess.

My goddess.

She stops moving her hips about a half minute before I come, so I drag her hips over mine and she tightens around me, gripping me with the rippling pulses of her own orgasm. Then she throws her head back and shouts.

We may have been heard, but I don't care. Because right now, my entire world is *her*. There is no one else in it besides us.

And I'm finally coming, everything straining to an impossible apex. I go completely rigid under her and she keeps moving, but I can't breathe, can't move, can't think as my release shifts everything from unyielding tension to warm, haunting bliss.

I grab her hips and hold them still as I push into her as deep as I can go. Pure pleasure—more forceful than I've ever felt before—consumes me.

My eyes drift to hers and our gazes lock. And I'm not afraid anymore...to look into her soul, to connect with her on that level.

She leans forward, lying across my chest to kiss me. When our mouths connect, I roll us over so that we're lying on our sides, facing each other. Then I smooth my hand over her silky hair, relishing the feel. I love the texture and wish I could do this all night and day. But it's not all I wish I could do all night and day.

I swallow, my eyes drifting to the ceiling. Jenna's sweaty body sticks to mine and suddenly we are cold and she's shivering against me. I reach over and grab the extra blanket, pulling it over us. She's cradled in the crook between my arm and my body, her head resting on my shoulder.

"Well..." she finally says. "That was amazing." She shifts against me to look into my face. "You aren't a virgin anymore. What did you think?"

I lick my lips. "It was good."

She laughs, but I have no idea why.

"Just good, huh?"

I nod. "There's no *just* about it. It was...not even comparable to anything I've ever experienced before."

She ran a hand over my chest and smiled. "Okay...I'll take it."

I blink, not understanding what that means, but too relaxed to ask her to explain. My arm around her back tightens around her.

"William, I...I think I'm falling for you."

I mull over her words, picturing several different scenarios—tripping over something, slipping off a cliff, frantic, terrified. My heartbeat speeds up. But she's *not*. "You're not falling. I'm holding on to you."

She laughs again. Clearly, I haven't understood her. But I don't mind it when *she* laughs. At least I know that she's not laughing at me. Or if she is, it's not in a mocking, derogatory way.

"No, I meant that figuratively. I meant *falling* as in...falling in love." I frown. She hesitates, scanning every inch of my face. I'm guessing that she's trying to gauge my reaction. But that would be hard, since I don't even know what my reaction is. She clears her throat and continues. "I mean—"

"You think you're falling in love with me?" I ask. They are wonderful words, but I don't want to believe them until I'm sure— until *she's* sure. She said "I think," which means she's uncertain of it.

And besides, it defies her very own logic. "But that's not possible. You said that wasn't possible."

She opens her mouth to answer and then shuts it again. She's thinking of what to say. Finally, she shakes her head.

"Let me be more clear, then. I love you, Wil. I'm not sure how or why it happened...just that it did."

I love you, Wil. Those words hit me like a forge hammer between the eyes. I know exactly what they mean, but they slip off me, unable to gain purchase—like a climber on an icy cliff. These words are too dangerous.

A spot in my chest tightens and starts to hurt. "What about Brock?"

She frowns. "I'll always love him. But that doesn't mean I can't love you."

I swallow a suddenly large lump in my throat. "You *do* want to be with me?"

She smoothes a hand across my cheek, smiling. "I told you already that I did. I haven't changed my mind since this afternoon."

My fingers comb idly through her hair as I study the pattern of shadows on the ceiling of the tent, backlit by the moonlight. If I could draw this feeling—this moment—those patterns would be the background.

"And what does that mean? We'll date?"

She hesitates, her finger tracing a light pattern over my chest. The touch distracts me, so I stop her by cupping my hand over hers.

"Sure...like we have been. Even though we haven't been calling it dating."

"I want you to live with me. So we'll see each other all the time."

She's silent for a long time. "Let's just...see what happens."

I turn to look at her. "You don't want to live with me?"

She nestles deeper into my side. "I'm not saying that at all. I'm just saying...one thing at a time, okay? For right now, let's enjoy this. It's been a long time coming."

Yes, it has. But that doesn't mean I don't want her with me all the time. I wonder if this is her way of getting close...but not too close. I shut off that fear. She's here, right? And she's changed her plans so we can be together.

She's right. We should just enjoy this.

But I can't—not just yet. There are still so many unanswered questions, and in order to know what to expect in the immediate future, I need more information. So I ask the next question on my mind. "And what about soul mates? You still believe Brock is yours."

She sighs. "I'm in the process of revising that belief, actually."

I pull away and then run a hand over my jaw, trying to allow this to sink in. My thoughts are racing, full of *what ifs* and *whys*. "But I haven't proven myself worthy yet."

She rises up on her elbow to look at me more directly. "Yes, you have. A dozen times over, you have."

I'm silent. I don't believe her.

Her hand caresses my face, my neck, trying to get me to look at her. Finally, she sighs again. "You were my champion, Wil. With Doug. You didn't have to volunteer to fight another duel, but you did. And you've worked so hard to overcome everything that held you back the last time.

"You were my champion at Disneyland when I panicked because of the fireworks. You're—you're just an awesome human being. There is so much about you that is worthy, and I'm pissed that you ever believed you weren't. Because *nothing* could be further from the truth. You're the worthiest person I've ever had the privilege of knowing, and I believe in you."

There it is again. That phrase, grabbing me like a vise around the throat. I'm in the grip of some complex emotions with no hope of being able to sort them out.

But it was the same exact phrase she'd uttered when she entered the tent. I had been so overwhelmed with the need to have her that I'd grabbed her and hadn't let her say anything else.

Part of me is doubtful, wondering if she's just saying these things now because of what just happened between us. Like she's telling me what she thinks I want to hear. That possibility does not make me happy.

But when I turn to look at her, my eyes catch hers and our gazes tangle together, as if connected by fishing lines that are knotted and twisted round each other. And the more I look into her eyes, the deeper I go. It's like looking into her soul. Now I want to see it all.

After a few minutes, she blinks and draws back, but I put my hand to her head, preventing her from withdrawing from me. "Jenna...you're the most beautiful woman I've ever met. And I'm not just talking about the outside. That's what I noticed first, of course, but I've seen beautiful women before. And many of them end up not being good people inside. But you..." My voice dies out, so I clear my throat and continue. "You're beautiful in every way...how you act, how you think, how you comprehend the feelings of others, how you help them."

Her eyes become inexplicably round and her lip trembles. She bites it to keep it still. When she says nothing, I continue. "You once said nothing in your life is permanent—that everything becomes temporary. I couldn't stop thinking about those words because of how unfair that is. You deserve permanence, and I want to be the man who gives it to you."

She turns to kiss my shoulder. "I want you to be that man, too."

My heart surges into my throat, buoyed by hope.

"So are you going to get that wander-thing—"

"Wanderlust."

"—and just pack your bags and leave like...like with your other boyfriends?"

She studies my face. Placing a palm along my cheek, she smoothes her fingers over my prickly whiskers. I'm suddenly sorry I didn't have a chance to shave before I kissed her all over her face, her neck, her chest. Maybe it didn't feel pleasant for her, but she didn't want to tell me...

Her lids droop and she leans forward, placing her forehead against mine and looking into my eyes. This time, however, I'm finding it difficult to return her gaze. I'm afraid she's going to see my doubt there.

"Something's different this time, Wil. I never felt for any of them the way I do for you. Is that enough? Can you trust me?"

I slip my arms around her waist and pull her fast against me. She closes her eyes and trembles. A strange feeling comes over me, threatening to smother me like a quilt. It's confusing and thrilling and frightening all at the same time.

"Are you cold?" I ask, already knowing that she isn't.

"No," she whispers. "I'm just...affected."

"By what?"

"By *you.*"

I bury my mouth and nose in her hair, inhaling deeply, savoring her smell. Savoring the feel of her skin pressed to mine. I want to touch and taste her soft, curvy body again as soon as possible. Even as I'm thinking this, I'm getting hard for her once more. I run my hand down the supple skin between her shoulder blades to the base of her spine and back.

"Jenna, I need to ask you something very important..."

She tilts her head back, pulling that heavenly smell away from my nose. "Yes? What is it?"

"How long should we wait before having sex again?"

Her face breaks into a brilliant smile. "Not another minute longer."

She moves her face to mine, kissing me from above, and as we kiss, she's moving to straddle me again. But that's not how I want it this time.

I grasp her shoulder with one hand, her waist with the other, and roll us completely over so that now I'm on top of her.

31
JENNA

I T DIDN'T TAKE LONG TO DISCOVER THAT WILLIAM WAS A QUICK learner. Sex was no different. So when he rolled me over and pressed his desperate kisses onto my mouth, I was delighted.

While his tongue tasted liberally, his scruffy jaw was scratching me everywhere—my neck, my chest, my breasts. Though the previous time had been no chore, it felt good to be able to lie back and let him steer this ship. I was anxious to see where he would take us.

And despite the fact that we'd had sex just a half hour before, William was just as driven and deliberate this time. No inch of skin was left uncovered by his hot mouth, no surface left uncaressed by those rough hands. He spent a lot of time lavishing my breasts with special attention—likely having been so desperate the first time to get inside me. As desperate as I had been to have him there.

But these touches were building that urgency anew, like nothing had been satisfied the last time. I arched up to meet him as his mouth slipped slowly over my nipples, his tongue rolling over them, his teeth grazing until I was shivering with anticipation.

"William, I need you *now*."

He didn't budge, continuing his quest to drive me crazy with his tongue and teeth.

"Wil—"

"I've been dreaming of this since the moment I first laid eyes on you almost two years ago. I'm not going to rush it."

My spine relaxed on the bed and I sighed. He was right. We had all night. And I'd resolved to leave this in his hands—his capable, talented, maddening hands. So despite the fact that I was aching to have him again, I closed my eyes and let him on his course.

"Beautiful, beautiful Jenna," he whispered against the sensitive skin of my belly. It quivered under his warm breath. I licked my lips and swallowed. Everything inside me was throbbing with renewed need.

He ran those working hands from my knees up my thighs, first the outside then along the sensitive inside, before resting at the center of my need for him. His fingers slipped into my wetness, rubbing against my sensitive clit, and everything tightened inside me. In minutes, overwhelming waves of pleasure washed over me. I was shocked with how quickly it had happened.

I lay back, awash and glowing, when he pressed a light touch to my mouth with his warm lips. With slow, deliberate movements, he settled himself between my legs, his chest lying over mine. And in the dim, bluish light under the full Beltane moon, our bodies joined together once again.

As it was our second time, it took William longer to get where he had already taken me in minutes. Therefore, I began to climb that mountain with him again, feeling remarkably spoiled. I ran my hands down his hard chest, smoothing over his nipples, sliding to his back, clasping my legs around him when I needed him to slow down.

But he was having none of that. He pushed through my hold, gently pulling my legs away from his hips, his breath bathing my neck with ragged puffs. I came again just as he pushed in deep and let loose a hoarse moan, my name on his lips.

He surged inside me and, despite his earlier protest, I clamped my legs around him again, pulling him tight against me. He released his breath, resting his sweaty forehead to mine. He carefully smoothed back of my hair.

And then..."I love you," he whispered.

Tears sprang to my eyes. Those words I'd never thought I'd hear again brought such joy rushing into my heart that it ached. Soon those tears were streaming down my temples as he rolled to the side, watching me carefully.

"Oh no," he breathed, wiping them away with his hand. "Why are you sad?"

I shook my head and sniffed. "Not sad, Wil. Happy. Very, very happy."

He frowned. Tears of happiness obviously confused him, but I didn't want to explain so I kissed him to stave off the inevitable questions.

Eventually, we drifted off to sleep. The last thing I said to him was that he needed his rest so he'd be ready to kick ass in the morning. And we slept peacefully, wrapped in each other's arms all night, too exhausted to even move.

When I woke up, bright early morning light slanted into the tent, and William was gone. I felt for him first, before even wading through the layers of sleep. When I came up empty, I contemplated how natural it had been for me to reach for him. Like I'd been doing it every morning for months.

And that weird echoing ache when I found him gone—that wasn't lost on me, either. It was scary and thrilling at the same time. I rolled over and buried my face in his pillow, inhaling his scent.

For the first time since I was a teen—a child, really—I'd told a man that I loved him. And I'd *meant* it. I swallowed in a thickening throat, suddenly terrified of the ramifications of that admission. I was changing my plans to be with William, but it wasn't *just* about being with him.

I was starting a future, setting down roots. Trusting myself to find happiness again instead of running away from the possibility of it.

I hurriedly got dressed and wove between tents toward the campsite I was *supposed* to be sharing with the girls. I tried not to focus on the possibility of clan members seeing me in the same dress I'd worn last night, only minimally laced to avoid indecent exposure.

It was my own medieval reenactment of the infamous walk of shame. But I didn't give a crap who saw me. I was too buzzed by this high. What a night...

The girls practically pounced when I got back. "Ohhh, hmm, well look at that. Her Majesty has just-fucked hair. Her royal dress is rumpled and looks like it's falling off, doesn't it? Ann, what do *you* think Queen Jenna was doing last night?" Fiona, Caitlyn's BFF said.

I rolled my eyes and dug into my duffel bag to pull out some proper twenty-first century clothing. "The Queen does not have to be accountable for her actions," I sniffed haughtily.

Caitlyn twisted a strand of honey-colored hair around her index finger and studied me. "Girl, I spent a long time on your hair and makeup yesterday. You better spill what's going on with you and Sir Hottie MacFine."

I smiled. "Or else...?"

"Or else I'm going to take your crown, which I picked up off the ground last night when you went running after William, and I'll give it to Doug. I'll tell him you told me to give it to him as a favor."

I raise my brow at her. "I know Roma curses, you know. I can make your toenails ache."

She plopped onto my sleeping bag and lay back, folding her arms under her head. "Spill."

"I don't kiss and tell."

"Do you fuck and tell?" said Fiona.

I rolled my eyes. "Goddess, you are all so crude."

A Cheshire-style grin spread across Caitlyn's face. "Oh, I'm sorry. Should she have asked if you *make love* and tell?"

My face flamed instantly, and they both shrieked and clapped their hands. Caitlyn sat up. "You did! Jeez, Jenna. People are going to hate you—and by people, I mean *me*. Do you know how many have been trying to crack that nut over the last two years?"

I raised my brow. "Interesting choice of imagery."

"He's totally going to win your duel for you because you put out," she retorted.

If those words had come from anyone but Caitlyn or Ann, they would have pissed me off. But as I knew they were completely joking and meant nothing untoward, I merely stuck my tongue out at her.

"The duel's in an hour. Are you going to give him your, um, *best wishes* beforehand?" She added air quotes, just to be extra obnoxious. "And what about a lady's favor? Do you have a scarf or a ribbon or something?"

I hesitated as I was changing from my gown to my regular clothes. "That's actually a good idea, to give him a favor."

"Just give him your panties," Fiona said, snickering.

"He already got into those last night," Caitlyn cracked.

"Ladies!" I reprimanded as I pulled a brush through my knotted hair, scanning the small tent for something to give him. A hair ribbon? A handkerchief?

"Have you ever deflowered a virgin before?" Caitlyn asked.

"What makes you think William was a virgin?" I evaded.

Brock had been a virgin, too, so William had not been my first. But I'd been a virgin right along with Brock, as our first time together was our first time ever. It had taken place more than a decade ago, so I only remembered a lot of awkwardness and that it had been disappointing. Last night with William had been pretty darn good, actually. He may have been a virgin, but there was no doubt he'd done his research.

"What about a ribbon from the Maypole?" Ann said, pointing to the red one on the floor by my sleeping bag as I pulled on my jeans.

"Oh yes, I'll take him that."

"You don't think he'll want to ask you for it in front of everyone— like what Doug did last time?" Ann asked.

I shook my head, adjusting my clothes. "Nope. That's not Wil." I smiled at the thought.

"Well, off with you, then. Go wish your man luck!" Ann said.

I found him in a clearing at the edge of our encampment. He was warming up in his under armor padding—gambeson, it's called. He continued to stretch his muscles and practice his swings even when I was pretty certain he'd seen me arrive. I assumed that this was all part of some routine that he'd established for warm-up, and he wasn't about to interrupt that routine—not even for me. I was okay with that.

I patiently watched him work, and about ten minutes later he stopped and unscrewed a bottle of water to take a long drink. I walked up to him then. "Hi."

His eyes flew to mine and then away. "Good morning," he said with a small smile that made my heart zing just a little bit. Seeing him again after last night and all that had happened between us was thrilling. Like I couldn't get enough air fast enough. I bit my lip, hoping he felt the same.

But it was highly unlikely that anything could have changed from the night before. So he likely *did* feel the same. He was constant, permanent. He'd told me last night that he loved me and my guess was that he probably didn't see the need to repeat it. I'd have to clue him in that I liked to hear it anyway, whether or not he thought it worth repeating.

I smiled and took his free hand, twirling the red ribbon in my other hand. "Do you know what this is?" I said without preamble.

His eyes narrowed, taking it in. He removed the bottle from his mouth and squeezed my hand. Then he freed it in order to replace the cap. "It's a ribbon from the Maypole," he answered.

"Nope. Not today."

He frowned, clearly confused. "It is a Maypole ribbon every day."

"Today it's much more than that. It's my favor. And I choose to bestow it upon the worthiest knight I know."

His gaze floated to the ribbon again, and his expression was so serious that I almost laughed. Without another word, he took up his sword and presented it to me, hilt first. Just as solemnly, I tied the ribbon around the grip, just below the cross-guard. He took the sword back and adjusted the ribbon. Then he hefted the sword to try it out.

He murmured in an almost reverential voice, "Thank you."

"Kicking his ass will be all the thanks I need," I said, grinning.

"There's no kicking at these tournaments. It's difficult to kick someone while wearing plated greaves."

I laughed. "I meant it figuratively. You'll be thanking me by winning soundly."

His brow trembled. "But if I lose—"

"You won't. Now come here and give me a kiss before I leave you to get all suited up."

I didn't have to tell him twice. He set down both the sword and the water bottle and then put his hands on my waist to pull me against him. Our mouths met in a long, passionate kiss, and a group of our closest friends found us right in the middle of that steamy kiss, where I'd locked my arms around him to keep his lips on mine.

To his credit, William kept kissing me even though they stood there, and even after someone cleared their throat loudly. We finally pulled apart when a wolf whistle interrupted us. I looked up and there were our friends all around us.

"Who could say 'no' to a good luck kiss like *that*?" Jordan said with a cocky grin. William did not look amused and Jordan clued into his obvious annoyance. "If it hadn't been for my advice—"

"Your advice is shit," both William and Adam said at almost the exact same time. April immediately doubled over laughing while Jordan's smile slid right off his face.

Eyes gradually turned toward me and Mia asked a question with her eyes. I studiously avoided her gaze. Alex handed me a cup of coffee in an insulated cup and I thanked her.

Then we all turned to look at the man of the hour.

And if all went well in the next little while, the man of the day, of the week. Of my future...

32
WILLIAM

S O IT ALL COMES DOWN TO THIS.

Months of training, to include fitness activities and specialized exercises to build stamina. Refining my fighting style and customizing my armor. Weeks of working with Jenna—not that I minded *that* in any way.

But for all my pre-fighting focus, I'm upset that she came to watch me warm up. Because now all I can think of is her, and all I want to do is look at her. Our friends are all around us now, wishing me luck. My mind is distracted from the fight, and that's bothering me.

My cousin stands at my shoulder and puts a hand there. I turn to him as he speaks. "Hey, guy. You okay? You're looking…intense."

I look around again, trying to keep my eyes away from Jenna, though they are pulled to her bright blonde head like a magnet. "This isn't how I normally warm up, with all these people around."

He nods. "Right. I'll see if I can clear them out for you," he says quietly.

A few minutes afterward, he suggests that they all go claim a section in the bleachers and save seats for the others who are coming to support me, including my dad and Kim. Jenna goes with them, but not before giving me another kiss on the cheek. "I'd say good luck, but you don't need luck. You've got this."

I smile and watch her as she goes, not realizing that Adam and Mia have lingered behind. Mia steps forward and gives me a hug. "Just wanted to get mine in real quick. I'll leave Adam to help you warm up." Adam has offered to be my squire today, and I've accepted that offer.

"Okay. Thank you." I briefly return her hug. As she turns to go, I say to Adam, loudly, so that she'll hear, "Adam, you can tell Mia later what date you've decided on for your wedding."

Mia comes to an abrupt halt and spins around to look at me. Her mouth and eyes are round. Adam's dark eyebrows scoot up his forehead. "That's, uh, great news," he says, and then one of his sly grins creeps across his face. He and Mia exchange a look, but I have no clue as to its meaning.

"I love winning," he mutters. Mia's eyes roll up toward the sky and she lets out a big sigh. Then she turns around and stomps away while Adam watches her, laughing loudly.

I'm smiling when Adam looks at me. "*I'm* the one who won, dickhead. You're just benefitting."

Adam's eyes narrow and he grabs one of my spare swords. "I'm here to help you warm up. Don't make me use this for real."

I bring my sword up to meet his, Jenna's red ribbon fluttering in the breeze below the cross guard. "Just don't be an idiot and waste this chance," I tell him. "You need to marry her as soon as possible."

Adam gets that sneaky look on his face again. "So you sacrificed for the greater good?"

I swing and our swords clash against each other. The morning sun glints off his blade. "It wasn't a sacrifice."

Another swing, another crash. "I was being sarcastic."

"All wasted on me." I bring my sword around in a series of moves meant to throw him off his guard.

"Easy, tiger," he says after the onslaught. "I don't have armor on."

"I'm not going to hurt your pretty face. You still need to look good for wedding pictures."

He laughed. "It's important to you that we get married, huh?"

"You almost lost each other once. That should not happen again. So don't squander the opportunity."

"But you said deciding our wedding date on a bet was dumb."

"It *is* dumb, but you might as well take advantage of it since you won."

We continue to warm up without saying anything further about the wedding. Twenty minutes later, he begins helping me strap on my full suit of plate mail, draping my black and silver tabard over the breastplate. Then he carries my swords, shield and buckler to the arena.

When we get there, the bleachers are full, not only with people from our clan but from other clans who are attending the Summer Festival. There are also those who've come ahead of time with the Renaissance Faire, which starts up as soon as the Beltane Festival is over. In addition, there are many dressed in modern clothes, indicating they are here as visitors, some of which are in my "cheering section."

The minute I see the crowd, my heartbeat starts to race, my blood chilling in my veins. My mind starts to go down that same thorny path that it always travels in situations like these.

I try one of Jenna's Jedi mind tricks—a little controlled breathing. But the breathing is only making it hotter inside my helmet, even with the visor up. The crowd is yelling and cheering and stomping, and

Doug is over there encouraging them by raising his sword in the air and walking back and forth in front of them.

He stops in front of Jenna, who is sitting in the front row, and I freeze. He's obviously trying to get her attention, but she folds her arms and looks away.

Taking a deep breath, I'm suddenly regretful that she didn't accept the deal he offered her last night. It would be a certainty that she'd get her tiara back, had she accepted.

And I'm not certain about this. Not at all. I know my skills are on par with his. I know that I'm in the best physical shape of my life. I also know that I'm capable of defeating him in perfect circumstances.

But I'm not certain.

The referee waves a triangular yellow flag mounted on a short, striped pole as he calls for the first bout to begin. Our squires begin handing us our equipment, and then Adam places a hand on my metal-encased shoulder. Looking at me through the grill of my helmet, he says solemnly, "Good luck, Liam."

I nod to acknowledge his words with a thumbs-up, and then I turn away to face Doug. With narrowed eyes, he says, "This time I beat you cleanly. You're a goner, Drake, you hear me?"

"I do hear you. But you're wrong. You've already lost the girl, and now you're going to lose the duel."

His face flushes a deep red and then he slams the visor down, muttering to himself. I know there are probably obscenities peppered amongst his rant, but he can't say them too loudly. If the referee hears him, Doug could be penalized for unchivalrous language.

I don't want him to, though. He's done so much to hurt Jenna that I really want to hurt him. I want to beat him down, and I'm going to do it under the watchful eyes of the tournament judges. No losing or winning on technicalities...not today.

Our first bout is long swords only, which we both wield two-handed. As is customary with European martial arts, we both hold our swords high, two hands gripping at the hilt in order to chop downward. We must hit with what would be the sharp edge of the blade—the side closest to the opponent—in order to score a hit. Each bout is played until one contestant gets three hits.

In our previous duel, I won this particular bout. But this time, the minute the yellow flag is lifted, Doug comes charging at me like a ferocious bull. I bring my sword down just in time to block his first onslaught.

The crowd is loud and distracting, and I can't help but look over at them. I decide to go on the offensive, knowing in the back of my mind that it's too early. I know Doug's fighting style well enough to know that he's long on aggressive tactics in small bursts, but short on stamina. Last time I just tired him out that first bout, blocking his onslaughts and letting him come at me until he got winded. My plan was to do the same thing this round, but I can't curb these anxious feelings for long.

I continue glancing at the crowd, trying to catch a glimpse of Jenna. She's leaning forward intently, her hand tightly gripping the railing in front of her. And that's when Doug charges and clips me on my upper arm pauldron with the outside edge of his blade.

The flag comes down between us. The ref watching for hits raises his hand and points to Doug, indicating that the first touch has gone to him.

Gritting my teeth, I narrow my eyes and swing—hard—the minute the flag lifts again. Before Doug can react, I clip him on the top of his bracer, just below his elbow. He shouts the f-word and the whistle blows. My hit is registered, and Doug is warned about his language.

Meanwhile, I'm noting that I hit him on his left arm. In this first bout, where we are both wielding a weapon with each of our hands, it's not an issue. But I wonder if I clipped him enough to cause some pain for the next bout. He swore, so that tells me that it hurt. He'd never risk a warning otherwise—not even in anger. So it likely came from pain.

I'll use that to my advantage.

But while I'm working it out, Doug comes at me again, pushing me back. I'm beating off his blows, but he's not relenting in his offense. Soon he's scored another hit, this time on the greaves of my armor, which covers my upper thigh. I note that he's left a slight dent, though my padding underneath has protected me.

After the flag lifts again, Doug starts with a low feint, pointing the tip of his sword directly at my codpiece, like he wants to chop my dick off. *Asshole.* I think it without actually saying it, fortunately.

I swing low to push his sword away from my crotch, and he starts laughing loudly behind his helmet. This just pisses me off more, so I swing around in a wide arc to land on his favored arm, but he deflects it just in time.

I've studied Doug's style. Due to my ability to recall things in great detail, I can slow things down in my memory and analyze them. Therefore, I have a good handle on his strengths and weaknesses. His advantages are speed and short bursts of energy, while mine are stamina and consistency. Also, my hits land harder than his, so I beat him in the strength department, too.

But my overanalysis of his approach has worked against me. I have anticipated a move and he makes a very convincing feint, only to quickly shift and swing up, landing a hit squarely in the middle of my chest piece. That's his third, and now this first bout is over.

Doug has won. *For now.*

I inhale and close my eyes, taking a moment while Adam switches out my long sword for my buckler and one-handed sword. I don't want to look at Jenna right now. I know what her worried face looks like, and I don't want to see it. She's thinking she might lose her tiara—that she shouldn't have put her trust in me to win it for her.

Doug is trying to rile the crowd again under the pretense of grabbing a drink from his water bottle, just like last time. Adam, on the other hand, is muttering encouragements to me. Neither one of them is helping the situation.

I wish that I could erase the crowd—I don't even want to look at them. Then I recall being at the mall last week, imagining the people as a rushing river of water. I imagined people in the lunchroom at work as a herd of animals, munching popcorn like those zebras or gazelles munched on dry savannah grass.

It occurs to me that I *do* have the power to erase this crowd. I can tune them out and picture something else in their place. So instead of a roaring crowd, they suddenly become a roaring dragon. An evil beast that threatens to destroy the countryside. Doug is the dragon's defender—a dark knight. And I have to get through Doug in order to defeat the dragon and save everyone. It's actually a lot like playing D&D, except I have a sword in my hand instead of dice and a character sheet.

With every bit of concentration and imagination that I have, I visualize that dragon, steam rising from its nostrils, claws scraping the air, wings generating a mighty wind that threatens to blow me back, were I not the strongest, bravest knight of the land.

Pretend isn't just a game for kids. I can do this, too. And I have to. Because *she* believes in me, and I will not let her down.

I finger the red ribbon tied just below my cross-guard and focus all my attention on Doug as I wait for the referee to start the second round.

I *will* prevail.

When the fighting starts again, Doug becomes more and more winded and is practically wheezing through his helmet by the time I land my first blow. I've let him dance around and swing wildly for almost two full minutes, staying just out of his range. I step around him like a boxer and fend off his blows; I've become an impenetrable wall.

When I finally land the blow—on his left elbow again—I can tell by the way he sucks in his breath that it hurt. This time, he at least has the self-control to curb his tongue. But I've struck his wielding arm with two good blows, and it's going to weaken him. I wonder if I can sweep this round. I just need two more hits...

Doug's sword crashes down on my buckler the second the yellow flag between us is moved away. I shove it back toward him, forcing his arm at an uncomfortable angle, and he gives an audible grunt about a millisecond before I catch him on the side of the breastplate. *Another hit for me.*

He does manage to get one hit in on me just before I land my third on him. I take the buckler round with ease, noting the minute it's finished how he immediately drops his left arm and hands his sword off to his squire while we re-equip for the last round.

I have a full-sized oblong shield—harder to wield due to weight, but provides more coverage. Doug wields his round shield, which looks much like his buckler, only bigger—complete with the heraldry, a rampant black lion on a field of red, poorly painted on it.

I also note that he's switched to his lighter sword for this round. It will be easier for him to maneuver, but that sword doesn't have as long a reach. Therefore, I calculate that if I keep him at a distance, he will have difficulty reaching me in order to make a hit. So not only is my sword longer, but my shield's coverage is superior. Together with the fact that he's obviously favoring his wielding arm, I estimate that I have at least a three-to-one advantage on him. Possibly more, if I play this smart.

Doug is no longer playing to the crowd as we face each other for the last time. We stare through our visors, yet are unable to see each other's eyes. I briefly muse that it would be great if everyone wore helmets and visors in real life so that eye contact wouldn't be as important to neurotypicals as it is now.

The flag comes up and Doug charges at me with a roar. He gets close enough to crowd me, so I leverage my big shield against him, giving him a mighty shove. He's thrown off balance, and having difficulty finding his footing, so he falls to a knee. I'm allowed to get in one hit in a case such as this—when the other knight has fallen. So I take the opportunity and sweep down on his shoulder with a harder-than-necessary hit. He rewards me with a grunt.

That was for making her cry, douchebag.

And I have plenty more where that came from. For making her worry about her tiara. For making her doubt herself and believe those horrible things you said to her.

This third round will be all about payback—Doug has it coming to him.

The yellow flag is again lowered between us, and I step back as Doug lumbers to his feet. He's dropped his shield, and his squire scrambles to pull it out of the dust and settle it back on his right arm. Something occurs to me...since we are mirror opposites—because he's left-handed and I'm right-handed—I can shove my shield against his to upset his balance again.

The minute the flag comes up between us, I test this maneuver out on him. He is visibly shaken by it and steps back, lowering his weapon-bearing arm just slightly. Then he hesitates as if he's trying to figure me out. So I use his uncertainty to my advantage, pushing forward again with a burst of speed he hasn't seen from me before. I give him another shove, and this time, before he can find his footing, I acquire another hit.

Doug throws down his weapon and the flag comes down again. One more hit and I will have swept him in the third bout. More importantly, the duel will be mine.

His squire is pressing the sword back into his gauntlet, trying to encourage him. I can't hear what they are saying, but Doug's voice sounds tight, like he's talking through his teeth. He's no longer bothering to rile up the crowd.

Oh yeah, the crowd. They're still there, but I've completely forgotten about them. I'm in the zone, a place I never could have imagined attaining—that place of ultimate focus, like when I'm painting in my studio or working at my forge.

As the flag comes up again, it's obvious that Doug's anger has gotten the best of him. He's swinging wildly, every way he can, chopping through the air, probably hoping to overwhelm me. In my focused state, I block each hit with either my shield or my sword, and in seconds I see my opening and take it, slamming the blade down near where his collarbone would be under his armor. *My third hit.*

I've swept him in the final round, but suddenly the chinstrap on my helmet is feeling very tight. As the flag comes down and I'm declared the winner, I yank the chinstrap free to alleviate that feeling. I'm coming back from "the zone," and I'm all too aware of the crowd again.

Everyone is cheering loudly, waving their hands and stomping their feet. "Huzzah!" they shout, and the ground starts wavering beneath my feet. I turn toward Jenna to find her gaze, and our eyes meet through my visor before her head jerks to the side. She's looking off to my right and her eyes widen. Before I can even guess what's happening, a weight slams into me from behind, knocking me to my knees. *"Stupid fucking retard!"* I hear Doug yell, just as he lands a blow on my head, one that knocks my helmet completely off.

I turn to see what's happened, and now the refs and my cousin are on top of Doug, wrestling him to the ground as he continues to shout obscenities. I make a wobbling attempt to get back on my feet, but suddenly the world goes fuzzy and the ground feels like it's buckling.

There's stickiness across my forehead and moisture running into my eyes, stinging them. I'm overheated, but it's too much to just be sweat.

And before I have another thought, everything goes black.

33
JENNA

T HE WHOLE CROWD GASPED AS WE WATCHED WILLIAM GO down. Instead of shaking hands and walking away like a gentleman, Doug had charged William the minute his back was turned...to look for me.

My heart stopped as William fell over, lifeless, like a bag of sand. Blood streamed down his forehead and into his eyes. *So much blood...*

And he wasn't moving. He was as still as that bag of sand.

With a curse, Mia jumped up from her spot beside me and hopped the short fence to run to him.

But I couldn't move. I was frozen where I sat, aware only of the racing heartbeat in my throat, the ice invading my limbs, the shallowness of my breathing.

Absurd. That word once again invaded my thoughts, and I almost laughed—*laughed*—to stave off the cold panic.

I tried to get up and follow after Mia, because somewhere in the midst of this strange, outside-of-myself sensation, I knew that's what I should do. But my legs wouldn't obey and my arms were like dead wood. The sounds of everyone around me echoed as if from a vast distance.

I was in the middle of a dream—no, *a nightmare*—willing myself to wake up. Every cell in my body weighed more by a factor of at least a hundred, or maybe even a thousand.

Mia and Adam crouched over William's unconscious form. People in the crowd were on their feet, watching it all, discussing amongst themselves what had just happened. Mia cupped a hand around William's neck and gently rolled him onto his back while checking his vital signs. Adam pulled out his cell phone, presumably to call 911.

And all I could do was sit here and stare, as if I was watching a news report on TV.

"Holy crap, what the hell just happened?" Alex said at my shoulder as the two refs dragged Doug out of the ring. Several people from the clan council quickly crowded around him just outside the arena.

Someone ran up to Mia with what looked like a first aid kit, which she quickly sifted through before pulling out a package of gauze. As I watched her tend to William, saw the blood begin to soak through the white bandage, my numb fists knotted so tightly that my fingers cramped.

I closed my eyes as a massive shudder wracked my body. My throat constricted at the recollection of that horrible night when Helena woke me up, sobbing, telling me there'd been an accident. That Brock had been killed.

I wanted to cry, but no tears came. Everything within me was lifeless and cold as the Moon.

Was it happening again? Could Fate really be this cruel?

When I was six, Aunt Beti sat my sister and I down next to each other on the couch of the tiny apartment we lived in when we first came to the US. Mama and Papa were due to arrive next month, so I couldn't imagine why Beti had tears in her eyes. I recalled her gripping her hands so tightly that the skin turned white, and I'd focused on them as she told us she had news.

Papa would not be coming. He'd been hit by a sniper's bullet on his way back from getting the water for the week. Beti said he'd been pulling the big tanks in a wagon behind him, like he did every week since the beginning days of the siege. There hadn't been running water or electricity in Sarajevo for months—*years*.

But I was six and I didn't understand any of that. What I *did* understand was that I was never going to see my papa again. I'd never again hug him around his neck and feel his whiskers tickle me when he kissed me. I'd never listen to him tell me another one of those wild and outlandish bedtime stories. I'd never sneak another piece of *halvi* from him when Mama wasn't looking. I'd never again get to look in his eyes.

And I couldn't even go back for his funeral.

That night before bed when I said my prayers—the way Aunt Beti always told us to do—I told God I wouldn't speak to Him again after that day. That I would always be angry at Him for taking my Papa away.

But I wasn't just angry at God. I'd polished that tiara and cried as I thought about Papa's words to me—his promises that we'd all live together in America and be a family again.

Lies.

And here I was in the present, watching my future threatened yet again. As always, a helpless observer of my own life.

I couldn't breathe. And I couldn't cry. I could only sit and stare, tracing the scattered threads of thought as they slipped through my mind.

William was not coming to, despite Mia's best efforts. In the distance, I picked up the faint sound of a siren. *Paramedics.*

The blood was pooling around William's head now. Mia applied pressure to the wound and appeared to be giving instructions to Adam.

Alex nudged my arm. "They'll let you ride with him to the hospital, I'm sure."

My nails dug into my palms, drawing blood. Adam was on his feet calling to Jordan, who hopped the fence and was beside them in seconds.

By this time, the ambulance was already pulling into the parking lot, red lights ablaze.

"Wow, they got here fast," Alex said. "There must be a fire station nearby. The closest hospital is in Bakersfield, about thirty minutes away. I just checked it on my phone. We can follow them over."

I didn't move. I didn't answer her.

I couldn't take my eyes off the prone figure lying on the ground. After conferring with Adam, Jordan took off running toward the paramedics while Mia and Adam stayed with William.

"Jenna, are you okay?" Alex asked, her voice squeaking.

I shook my head, my hands clamping tighter around the seat beneath me. The paramedics wheeled in a stretcher and surrounded the figure lying in the dust. Everyone crowded the railing, gawking as they worked on William. Soon, they were strapping his head and neck to a board and putting him on the stretcher.

"He's coming to...I think he's conscious!" Alex said. She stood up on tiptoes to look over the rest of the crowd. I buried my face in my hands, unable to look.

I could hear Mia at the railing, calling up to her mom, informing her that she and Adam were going to ride in the ambulance to the hospital. I looked up as Adam threw his keys to Jordan. Then they were gone, following the stretcher to the parking lot and the waiting ambulance.

The bleachers around us started to empty, everyone talking excitedly about what had happened. As far as I knew, there were more events scheduled, but they had either been canceled or postponed to deal with William's emergency. I even heard someone mention an impromptu clan council meeting, probably to address Doug's asshole move. Maybe I should attend...or maybe I'd grab my stuff to—

"Jenna!" Alex said loudly. I stood up, brushed off my skirt and started for my tent. She called out again, but instead of turning to face her, I kept walking in the opposite direction of the parking lot.

A breeze blew and my cheeks were cold and wet. I marveled at that. Was I really crying? Tears trickled out of my eyes, but it didn't feel like I was crying. I just felt freezing cold. *Numb.*

Alex's arm wrapped around my shoulder, attempting to redirect me toward the parking lot. "William will want to see you. Come on, we can follow them."

I shook my head, my unsteady legs pulling me back on my intended path. "Can you wait for me? I'm going to pack my bag and I'd like to go home."

She frowned at me. "Uh, did you two have a fight or something?"

I shook, from my scalp to my toenails. But I remained silent, unable to talk about this with her...or anyone, for that matter. This pure, icy terror pulsing through my veins was muting everything. It was all I could think about, all I could feel.

This powerful sense of loss. This pain. This *panic.*

Brock can't be dead. He's not even eighteen years old! This isn't fair. It's not!

I remembered the day they put him into that cold, hard ground at the cemetery. I'd fallen to my knees at his graveside and wept, wishing they could put me in there, too. It had been my fault. *My* fault. I hadn't driven him home from the party. Josh had—and Josh had had too much to drink.

And now here was William, injured and possibly permanently impaired because of *me*. He would *never* have been fighting the second duel if it hadn't been for me...

What if he had a concussion, or worse, a brain injury? What if he was hemorrhaging? What if...

But William won the fight. It's not fair. It's not!

I sucked in a breath, alarmed at the parallels. And I was devastated that I felt every bit as helpless today as I did then.

This was all my fault. It was true. *Be a man and love me, and you'll end up dead.* I really *was* cursed.

A sob escaped my lips. "I can't handle this." My voice was tight, strangled.

Alex's arm slid tentatively around my shoulders. "*Dios mio,* you are shaking like it's twenty below."

"Please, Alex...I want to go home."

She was silent as we walked to my tent, then she stood nearby watching as I shoved all my stuff into my bag and cinched up the top, occasionally wiping my face with the back of my hand or my sleeve to dry the tears. But the moment I did it, more trickled down to replace them.

The moment the bag was full, I was ready to go. I tried to suck in another breath, but it wouldn't come. My chest wouldn't cooperate...it wouldn't expand to inhale again.

I doubled over, falling to my knees.

"Jenna!" Alex shrieked, crouching down with me. "Okay, you are *really* freaking me out, girl."

I shook my head, sobbing so hard I couldn't catch my next breath.

"William will be fine!" She rubbed my back. "I'm sure of it. We'll go to the hospital. You'll see. Head wounds naturally bleed a lot."

But I wasn't listening. I just kept shaking my head, and then I curled in on myself, pressing my cold, wet face to my bag.

"Take me home, please," I finally managed.

Alex's eyes widened. No doubt she thought I was insane. Or heartless. Or both. Maybe I was. Maybe I didn't deserve to be happy. I'd already blown my chance.

I couldn't do this again. Not for the third time. Fate had spoken.

On shaky legs, I followed her out to her car. I shoved my things in her trunk, and then we wordlessly drove the hour and a half home to Orange County.

My phone chimed repeatedly the entire way.

Mia: Hey, where are you? You okay?
A few minutes later...
Mia: W is asking for you. Are you coming? What do I tell him?

I swallowed hard before turning off the phone. The tears began pooling again and the terror came back with a vengeance. I remembered reaching out and touching Brock's face at the viewing. His skin felt like ice. Like how I felt inside.

Maybe that was it? Maybe I *was* dead inside.

34
WILLIAM

"**C**ALL HER AGAIN," I SAY TO MIA. I CAN TELL THERE'S something she wants to say but doesn't.

"I will. I'm just going to give it a few minutes. Lie back, William. They aren't done."

I stare up at the holes in the acoustic ceiling. We've been in this stupid little room in the ER for *hours,* and there's no cell reception in here. Whenever Mia needs to make a phone call, she has to walk outside the hospital in order to do it. We may as well be back in the Middle Ages with our lack of ability to communicate. Worse, actually, because we have no carrier pigeons, either.

I'm starving and my head hurts, but other than that, I'm fine. They've already sewed me up and glued me shut. And now all I want is to see Jenna.

"Maybe Alex's car broke down and Jenna's phone is out of charge," I say. "They could be in danger."

Mia looks across the room at Adam, who rubs his jaw and turns to me. "I'm sure she's okay." Then he turns back to Mia. "Maybe you should try texting Alex."

Mia's eyes widen, and then she looks at me and jerks her head back at Adam. I have neither the energy nor the desire to figure out what all that means. My head is *really* hurting.

"Uh, good idea," she mumbles.

411

She's staring at Adam and then looking at the door, then back at Adam again. I close my eyelids and rub my eyeballs through them. Everything hurts, and this stupid hospital gown I'm wearing is itchy and leaves my back completely exposed. I hate hospitals. *Hate* them.

I open my eyes when both Adam and Mia stand up. "I've gotta hit the bathroom," Adam says.

"I'll show you where it is. It's kind of hard to find." Mia takes his arm and they head to the door.

I frown, recalling that we walked right by a bathroom on the way to this examination room.

"It's just down the—"

"Be back in a minute, guy," Adam says, holding the door open for Mia. They're gone for about five minutes, and then the door opens up again and it's just Mia.

"Adam's going to go check in with your Dad and my Mom in the waiting room as soon as he's done in the bathroom."

"You could have just texted to tell them I'm all right. I wish I had my phone. I have *nothing* with me."

"Well, some of your friends from your clan were here while you were getting sewn up. They offered to pack up your tent and belongings then load them up in your truck. Your dad is going to go to the campsite so he can drive it back to your house. I think they were hoping you'd have gotten the MRI by now."

I scowl. "I don't want the MRI."

"It's not about what you want. The doctors are not going to release you 'til they know you're okay. You were knocked out, William. It's a given that they're going to do an MRI. I'm sure it will be soon...okay?"

I stare at her, folding my arms over my chest. "Has Alex replied to your text yet? I'm very worried about Jenna."

Mia hesitates and looks toward the door, but she doesn't answer me.

"Are you waiting for Adam to come back so he can give you permission to tell me whatever it is?"

She gives me her mad look. "I don't need Adam's permission. Yes, Alex texted me. They're okay. They, are, uh, back in Orange County."

I sit up, more questions pouring into my mind. Why hasn't Jenna checked to see that I'm all right? Why hasn't she even answered her damn phone?

I open my mouth to start asking when suddenly Adam returns holding various objects he didn't have before. Mia, however, is watching me closely. "You okay?"

"No," I reply.

Adam steps closer to the bed. "Your dad and Kim just left to go get your truck, but they gave me some stuff your friends brought from the campground. Your phone..." He brandishes it, and I reach up and snatch it out of his hand. I check the text messages.

Nothing. Nothing from her at all.

He sets a weird-looking lacquered box on the meal tray in front of me. "That isn't mine," I say.

Adam gestured to it. "Sure it is. It's your prize, Sir William. They got Doug to cough it up."

I picture Doug coughing and things coming up—and gross as that image is in my mind, I can't see him coughing a box out of his mouth.

I give Adam a look and he laughs. "It's the tiara. The council required Doug to produce it, according to the terms previously agreed upon. Once he did, they voted to exile him on the grounds of his cowardly attack on you. You can also choose to press assault charges on him."

I look at my phone again. "The only thing I want to do right now is talk to Jenna." I start to get up from the gurney, but Mia stands in front of me, placing a hand on my shoulder.

"No, you don't, buster. You can't get up right now. The doctor hasn't cleared you. In fact, I'm guessing that they're going to admit you for the night."

I push her hand off my shoulder and stand. "No, they fucking are *not*," I say.

But Adam's there and he pushes me back down on the gurney. "Down, boy," he says. "And be nice to Mia, please. She took good care of you while you were knocked out."

I mumble my thanks and move to stand up again. "I'll just step out to call—"

At that exact moment, the doctor walks in to check for a head injury. I have to do lame things like squeeze his finger, then follow his finger with my eyes as he waves it in front of me. After that, he looks into my eyes with a small flashlight, which I *loathe*.

"I am *not* staying here," I say before he can speak. He's inputting things into a tablet—my chart.

"We need to run an MRI and ideally keep you for observation. We'll have this discussion after I have that MRI in my hand. How's that?"

"I need to make a very important phone call!" I say, attempting to get up.

"Mr. Drake, you can't get up and walk around. You're a patient here until you're released."

"Then I'm releasing myself. I'll just—"

Adam's at my side again, resting a heavy hand on my shoulder. "You're *not* releasing yourself. You're staying right here 'til you have your test."

I shove his hands off me. "Stop touching me, damn it! I want to know where Jenna is and why she's not here."

The doctor is looking from Adam to me and back again. Mia steps forward. "I think the sooner we can get his MRI, the better."

The doctor nods. "I'll see what I can do to bump him up in the queue." He steps out shortly after that, and I try one more time to stand up. Adam prevents it and I take a swing at him.

"Jesus, Liam, calm the fuck down!" He bats my fist away before it can connect.

"No, stop this bullshit. I need to talk to Jenna. I need to know why she's not here. She's probably very worried about me."

"She's okay." Mia steps forward. "She's, um...well, she's with Alex, who told me that Jenna was really shaken up by your injury. She may be blaming herself. I'm not sure exactly what's going on, but she insisted that Alex take her straight home instead of coming here."

Silence.

None of us say anything for a long time. "But why wouldn't she come? Why wouldn't she want to be here for me? I've been there for her...through *all* of this."

Mia shakes her head, and I know her well enough to know that the look on her face is her sad look. "I'm sorry, William. I just don't know what's going through her mind right now. But she's safe and she's not in any danger. I'm sure that she cares about what's going on with you and would want you to get this test."

"Fuck the test," I mutter.

"I promise we'll take you straight over to her house when we get you out of here, all right?" Adam says. I glare at him, a ball of rage starting to burn in the pit of my stomach. "You can take her the tiara..."

"Right now, I want to shove that tiara up your—"

"Boys!" Mia holds up a hand. "Adam, why don't you go grab us some food? I think William's feeling a bit *hangry* right now. I'll keep him company, and maybe he'll calm down."

Adam leaves, but I *don't* calm down. All I can think of is that Jenna is at home, going about her day, not even considering that I'd want her to be with me.

I put my face in my hands, aware that the headache is still there but dulling gradually.

"I'm sure she'd be here if she could."

That sounded familiar. I'd heard that from Dad and Britt a *lot* when I was growing up. Almost word for word.

And I'm reminded...reminded of those times when Mother had arranged to come get me and something would come up—sometimes days in advance, sometimes at the last minute. Our plans for dinner, or the park, or the museum...

She never came through for me. Those shifts in plans, which already made me uneasy to begin with, created a wall of frustration and anger, solid as a brick barrier. It took weeks and months and years before I got over the anger and the resentment. To this day, I'm not sure I ever really have.

Disappointment sits in my stomach like a blacksmith's anvil, weighing everything down. It makes me feel like *I* am the problem. I am the reason.

I am not worthy.

It's the same thing. It's *always* the same.

I'd foolishly hoped that this one moment in time, this victory, would make me deserving of admiration, of respect...

Of love.

Jenna told me she loved me, but she's not here by my side showing me that love when I need her most. I close my eyes, trying to imagine her standing here next to me in this cold, horrible hospital instead of Mia.

But I can't. Instead, I only burn with hurt and rage. I try to breathe through it so I can make it through these next few hours before I'm out of here.

Mia sits down and is talking, but I'm not listening. And once Adam returns, the only thing I can do is sit here and wish that Adam and Mia were Jenna instead, and that she's sitting beside me and holding my hand. But reality is a cold harsh distance from that fantasy—as cold and harsh as this hospital room, where the only thing I have to warm me is my burning anger.

35
JENNA

I T WAS JUST PAST LUNCHTIME WHEN WE GOT HOME, BUT INSTEAD of grabbing a bite to eat, I poured a shot of tequila left over from our drinking night escapade and chased it with some juice.

"Jenna—"

I jerked my hand up to stop Alex from whatever she was about to say.

"No, Alejandra. I don't want to hear it."

I grabbed the bottle of Cuervo and took it into my bedroom. Then, divorced from all emotion—and all logical thought—I calmly started packing up my stuff.

Everything went into boxes. The two suitcases would go with me, and I'd ask Alex to store a couple of boxes at her mom's house. The rest I'd give away...to friends, to charity, whoever. As long as I could get rid of it all.

Old things just brought back old memories—and I didn't want any of those. They hurt too much. My heartbeat raced with fear and misery with each box I packed up, so I'd take another drink and continue, my hands working as if independent of my feelings.

Fate was calling. It was time to move on. But every time I had that thought, my heart hurt like it had been scraped by a piece of glass.

I heard Papa's voice in my head...*"Budi hraba, kci."* *You must be brave...*

It had been chilly that April morning as he loaded me up on the refugee truck in the outskirts of Sarajevo, along with my sister and my aunt. We'd finally had the opportunity to pass safely through the warzone to Zagreb. That day he'd pressed the tiara in my hand, assuring me it would be safe inside the beautifully lacquered case. Explaining how my grandmother had worn it on her wedding day, as her mother had before her. "You're a princess and you need to be kept safe. I'll see you soon. *Obecavam.*" *I promise.*

He'd broken that promise. Mama told me he'd died in minutes, bleeding out in the gutters on a street we'd walked down nearly every day of my young life there.

Papa...I can't do this anymore. It hurts too much. Please take this pain away.

Even in my tequila stupor, everything was too tight—my clothes, my chest, my fists. The doorbell rang and I glanced out my bedroom window, astonished to see that it was dark. The entire day had passed me by in my heartache-induced daze.

"Hello?" I heard a familiar voice call into the apartment. *Helena.*

I'd used all the tissues in my room, so I bolted out the door and toward the bathroom, but she was standing in the hallway, blocking my progress.

"Oh Janjica!" she said, taking my face in her elegant, long-fingered hands. "What are we going to do with you?"

Instead of answering, I sniffed and hiccupped, my lip quivering. I thought about the tragedy that linked the two of us, and how fitting it was that she was here right now. Helena pushed the hair from my face back behind my ear. Over her shoulder, I could see Alex watching us, and I knew then that it was Alex who had called her.

"Don't be mad at Alex," Helena said, reading my mind—as usual. "She's worried about you. And so am I."

I shivered and the tears came in a rush again. Helena pulled me into a hug, and I pressed my face to her shoulder and sobbed. "I can't forget that night, Helena. I can't."

She knew what I was talking about without even having to ask. "You never will...and neither will I," she said, switching to Bosnian. "That night changed us all forever."

She gave me a little nudge toward my bedroom. As soon as we'd entered, Alex handed me a fresh box of tissues and then shut the door behind us.

Helena sank down on the bed beside me as I rocked back and forth, fisting my hands. She gave the bare room a onceover, her eyes landing on the boxes lining the wall. In mere hours, my life had been condensed into those boxes and I was ready to move on.

"Tell me what happened..."

I inhaled a shuddery breath and let it go. "There's a boy...and..." My voice trembled, and I glanced up at her before quickly looking away. "He's a man, actually, but..."

Helena placed an arm around my shoulders, watching my face carefully. "Go on, Janja. Tell me about him."

My cheeks heated and I glanced at her out of the corner of my eye, feeling oddly guilty. Like I was cheating on her...and Brock.

"Last night I, uh...I told him I loved him."

She nodded. "And it's the truth? *Do* you love him?"

That shard of glass scraped over my heart again and the air hissed from my lungs. I doubled over. "*Yes.* I love him. I love him so much. So much it hurts. Oh God, Helena. I'm sorry."

Her arm tightened, pulling me back to a sitting position. "Love is nothing to apologize for. And we are not meant to love only one person in our lives. You loved Braco. And now you love this man, too. That's not a betrayal."

My pitiful sobs started up again, drowning out her noble speech. "He'll die, Helena. He'll die, just like the others. Like Papa. Like Brock."

She inhaled sharply and reached to push my hair back from my face. "Stop this. Right now. You have the right to love a man, and you have the right to be loved. Stop hurting yourself because you lived and Braco didn't."

"How can you be so nice to me? I didn't drive him home that night—"

"We're not going through this again, Jenna," she said, switching to English with a stern tone. "You spent two years utterly depressed, crippled by your guilt. I don't blame you, because it was not your fault. It happened. You went home early. He got another ride…"

Her voice faded out in a sob. That sob stabbed me to the core. I squeezed my eyes shut and buried my face in my hands, but Helena pulled them away just as quickly.

"Stop hiding. Stop running away. Listen to me!" She squeezed my hands. "You are like my own daughter. You know that. I tell you all the time. The only thing worse than losing Braco would be to lose you, too."

"But—"

"No *but*. You get up. You wash your face and you go to this man. You tell him how you feel, all right? You tell him you love him and want to be with him. Be brave, Janja. It takes courage to get through this life, because if you aren't brave, then life and circumstances will grind you up into dust."

Be brave, Janja.

My breath stung in my lungs and tears clogged my throat. My eyes were so impossibly sore, yet tears continued to pour out. I had no idea where they were coming from.

I shook my head. "I'm so scared."

She stroked my hair. "We all are. Every day we are here, we never know what is going to happen. But life is meant to be lived. Do you think if I had the choice that I would choose to go back in time and not have a son, just so I could avoid the pain of losing him? No. *Never.* I carried that baby and raised him and held him in my arms and kissed him and loved him. And I remember the wonderful boy that he was. Yes, I think about the amazing man he would have become, but I'm grateful for every day that he was on this earth. I'll never regret it. And you shouldn't, either."

I rubbed my eyes, hearing the truth in her words, and suddenly an inexplicable calm settled on my shoulders. The soreness and grief were still there, but there was comfort, too. There was love. The love I felt for Helena. The gratitude for having her in my life.

And she was right. If I had the choice, I'd go back and relive everything again. I'd be more than grateful for the time I had with Brock. The memories. My relationship with his amazing parents. All of it. No regrets.

No regrets.

Helena must have sensed the change in me because she just stroked my hair and spoke comforting words in our native language. Soon, my head was on her shoulder and she was singing an old folk song that my mama used to sing when I was little.

I was exhausted and depleted, but also fraught with worry about William. After ten minutes of silence, I slowly rose from the bed and went to my dresser to retrieve my phone.

When it bloomed to life, there was a stack of text messages and notifications of missed calls. *Shit.* Everyone was probably sick with worry about me while I was off having my pity party. When I should have been there for William...

Just as I was about to open my text-messaging app, the doorbell rang. I took a deep breath, and Helena rose from the bed, grabbed my hand and said, "Let's go see who it is, okay? And then after that, you'll speak to your young man. I hope I will meet him soon. In fact, I *expect* to meet him soon."

Nodding, I wiped my face one last time with a tissue. Helena opened the door and together we walked into my front room. There, Alex stood talking with Adam, Mia, and a somber and dazed-looking William, whose head was heavily bandaged.

Joy infused the blood pumping through every vein the minute I laid eyes on him. I couldn't suppress the goofy smile or the warm, overpowering relief I felt when I saw that he was okay.

I rushed to William, stopping myself just before taking him into my arms when I noticed him visibly stiffen. "Wil," I breathed.

His jaw tensed and he stepped away from me, then held out a familiar lacquered box. *My tiara.* But the expression on his face was glacial. That brought me up short, and I stared at him over the box instead of taking what he offered me. His eyes dropped to the floor.

And the tension...you couldn't have broken through it with a jackhammer. Adam and Mia shared a long look. Then she turned to William, placing a hand on his shoulder, which he promptly shrugged off. "Uh, Adam and I are going to wait for you outside by the stairwell." She threw a significant glance at Alex.

"Oh, yeah...Mia, I have to talk to you two about something. I'll go too."

The three of them filed out. Beside me, Helena put a hand on my shoulder and squeezed it before following the others, gently closing the door behind her.

The minute it closed, William spoke in a monotone even flatter than normal. "I came to deliver this to you. I won the duel and I am giving you the tiara, as promised." He thrust the box toward me again. This time, I took it from him, flipping it open to make sure the tiara was inside and then setting it aside on a nearby table.

"Thank you. I'm so—"

But he had already turned away and was heading toward the door.

"Wil, wait!" I said and grabbed hold of his arm. He jerked it away like I'd burned him.

My gut twisted in panic. "William! *Please.* Please let me explain. I'm sorry."

He hesitated, then slowly turned toward me. "I waited for you. Mia texted you. I called. You didn't answer. All day I sat there worrying about *you.* I was in a hospital—I *loathe* hospitals. That's a fact you don't know because you never bothered to get to know me well enough to know that. I had to sit there and go through every stupid test without you. They had to sedate me to get me in that fucking machine to do a scan on my head."

I gasped, realizing the depth of his anger in the simple use of that curse word. I'd never heard him say it before, and it sounded more venomous coming from him.

I felt like garbage. Less than garbage. And yet all I could choke out was, "I'm so glad you're all right."

"You weren't there for me," he repeated.

"I know. I'm sorry. I was..." My voice died before I could complete the sentence. *I was selfishly freaking out and thinking about myself instead of you.*

"Please, William. Can we talk?"

He blinked. "We *are* talking."

"You're mad at me. And you have every right to be. But please, can I explain what happened? I—I freaked out when I saw you go down. There was *so* much blood. I thought I was going to lose you, and I started to relive losing Brock—"

He jerked away from the door and started pacing across the small living area, hands rubbing over his thighs. "You still love Brock."

"Yes, I told you that already. But I love you, too."

He paced faster as he shook his head. "But you weren't there for me."

"Wil, I screwed up. I'm sorry."

"I can't depend on you. How do I know you won't just leave?"

I swallowed. "I don't want to leave. I want to be with you."

He dragged in a ragged breath and let it go. "So last night you tell me you want to stay with me. Then we had sex. After the duel was over, you were nowhere to be seen. Was that a coincidence?"

I frowned, trying to wrap my head around what he was implying. I shook my head.

Then he stopped pacing so abruptly that it looked like the momentum might knock him right over. I'd left my door open and William was staring directly into my bedroom. At the bare walls, the stacked boxes, the open, empty dresser drawers.

I swallowed a hard lump in my throat.

"You *are* leaving," he said between clenched teeth, fists tightening at his sides.

If I could have sunk into the ground and melted through the floor in that minute, I would have. While he'd been in the hospital, badly injured yet still worried about *me*, I'd been guzzling tequila and packing everything up.

And William was all about absolutes—everything was either black or white. How could I translate this for him?

"I was afraid..." I began, but he turned away from me as I spoke, his eyes scanning the rest of the apartment, probably searching for other clues pointing to my imminent departure. *That was me. Jenna Kovac, permanent flight risk.*

William was having none of it. He turned back to me, fists balled at his sides. "*I* was afraid, too. Afraid to go into that duel and fight Doug again. Afraid I'd be defeated and lose all my friends *and* your tiara. I was afraid, but I did it anyway. I showed you how I felt with my actions, not just words."

I closed my eyes, the tears welling inside their sore depths yet again. "I'm not perfect, William. I'm just human. And I have failings."

"Yes. You do."

That hurt. In fact, it felt like more glass just scraped across that tender organ in the center of my chest. I took a deep breath and tried not to get defensive. He had the right to be hurt. But then again, so did I. And his words *did* hurt.

"Can we talk about this when you aren't so angry?"

He tightened his jaw, cheeks bulging. "I'm not angry. I'm disappointed. I need someone I can count on, and you aren't that person. I need someone who will back what she says with actions, who won't just say something to get her way. You weren't there for me." He stuffed his hands into his pockets. "Just like you weren't there for Brock."

I gasped, feeling like he'd slammed his buckler into my stomach. My knees gave out and I landed on the couch, covering my face with my hands. His words cut me to the core, confirming every single doubt I had about myself—about the night Brock died and my role in it.

"How could you?" I choked out between sobs, the pain overwhelming me. It punctured me through every pore, like needles in my skin.

William said nothing. He didn't even move for a long time as I tried to gain control of myself—and failed.

"This was a mistake," he finally said in a shaky voice. I pulled my hands away from my face to look up at him. A few beats after that, he turned toward the door.

I popped up off the couch and sped to the door, blocking it so he couldn't open it. "Don't do this," I sobbed. "You know damn well that I didn't use you. You know..." My voice faded with a squeak.

His features were just as placid as when he'd entered. He looked as unmoved as that robot he'd often been likened to. "I *don't* know."

I tried as hard as I could to look into his eyes, but they deftly eluded me. "You know that I love you, Wil. I *do*."

His lips thinned. "Those are the words you used, but they don't match your actions. You abandoned me the second something got difficult. You won't commit to any course of action. You'll find a reason to run away again."

I sucked my lip inside my mouth and gnawed on it, new tears burning like acid, pouring from the wells of my eyes and down my cheeks. "And you'll never forgive any mistake I make."

He closed his eyes for a good long time, took a deep breath, and when he opened them again, he looked into my eyes. But instead of replying, he turned the knob of the door. "Please move aside."

I shook my head, refusing to accept what he was saying. "Wil," I sobbed.

And for a split second, I saw it because he was looking directly at me. Pain streaked through his eyes. Then he blinked harshly and turned his head away.

I decided to chance it. What did I have to lose? I reached up and put my hand on his face, my fingertips brushing his scratchy face.

He jerked his head away from my touch. "Goodbye, Jenna," he repeated in a low, trembling voice.

Slowly, quietly, I did as he asked, and he wasted no time before turning the knob. Then he opened the door and left the minute I was free of it.

I slid down the wall beside the doorjamb, curling into a ball, my face against my knees. I thought I had no tears left to cry. I was wrong.

Because even though I'd been prepared to throw everything away in my panic and fear earlier today, I was not prepared to lose this.

But ready or not, it was happening. And there was nothing more I could do.

36
WILLIAM

WALKING AWAY FROM HER APARTMENT IS THE MOST difficult thing I've ever done. It's a piercing type of pain that starts in the middle of my chest and makes it hard to breathe. I feel like I'm being poked and prodded from within by sharp objects. It hurts...but that hurt, along with anger, burns like a fire.

And I couldn't look at her anymore.

My friends stand in a cluster near the stairwell, but I don't want to talk to any of them. I want to go home, to my orderly house and my comforting routine, where nothing is a surprise and everything happens as it should. There, I never have to rely on anyone else, and I'm *never* disappointed.

I can't handle being disappointed again. Not like this. It hurts too much.

Casting a glance at the group, I note that they are tightly bunched together and talking in low voices. Except for the older woman who was with Jenna when we arrived. I have no idea who she is, and I don't want to know.

I want to go home and forget about all of this—forget about *her*. I'll use the visualization techniques that she taught me to visualize her right out of my mind. Out of my heart. Out of my life.

Passing them, I make my way down the stairs without stopping or even acknowledging anyone. My heart thumps, each beat hurting my chest a little more. I wonder if this is a symptom of the head wound. As I'm still feeling out of it from the medication, I grip the railing to make sure I don't fall over.

Adam and Mia follow closely behind. They've let me know that they do not want me spending the night alone, but when I refused to go to their house, they invited themselves over to spend the night at mine instead. Worse, they'll be driving me to the local hospital for another MRI in the morning.

Just what I need...as if this crappy situation wasn't bad enough.

I'm tired and hurting, and I just want to go to sleep and forget about this day.

Yes, I won—but I lost, too. *So, so much.*

***

I've been forced to take time off from my job for the first three days of the week. Sometimes it's a real disadvantage to work for your annoyingly overprotective—and bossy—cousin.

I spend my spare time at home completely overhauling my art studio and repairing my forge tools. It's the perfect opportunity to hone my skills by working on the damaged practice armor.

I return to work on Thursday, but I don't go to family dinner on Sunday. And ignoring the phone is easy to do, since I've turned it off completely. Jordan and Adam both check in with me at work, but I don't meet Mia for our usual breakfast the following Wednesday morning, mostly because she has a lot of studying to do.

Routines have once again become my comfort. But they don't help me forget. And though I continue going about my regular pre-Jenna routine, it hurts too much to attempt to forget her now.

It hurts too much to attempt anything.

I want to talk to her. I want to hear her voice. I want to feel her touch, smell her smell. I want to lie beside her, our skin touching while I listen to her breathe.

And it's driving me insane. Because I don't *want* to want her as much as I do. I want these feelings to go away. I want things to go back to how they were before it hurt so much.

So I occupy myself with every mundane task that needs to be accomplished. Adhering strictly to my schedule, I keep myself so busy that I hardly have any time to let my mind wander to thoughts that I can't control.

The following weekend, I spend the entire day in my shop. I can't create art when my mind is like this, but I can hit things with a hammer just fine. In a strange way, it makes everything feel better.

The forge is going at full force and it's hotter than an oven. I'm blowing through my supply of wood at an alarming pace as I keep working the bellows. I hear the doorbell when it rings, having rigged it to ring back here, too. Nevertheless, I decide to ignore it.

Minutes later, however, my dad appears in the doorway of the shop, maintaining the distance I request as he watches me work. I continue on, ignoring his presence for a quarter of an hour before dropping my work in the slag bucket. The heated metal hisses on contact.

"Hey," he says when I finally turn to him.

I remove my goggles and my leather apron, then wipe my sweaty face with a clean towel. "Hi. Why are you here?"

His brows twitch. "Do I need an excuse to see my son? We missed you at dinner last week."

"I didn't feel like being social." Not that I ever do, but even less so than usual.

He frowns. "Okay. But I can still check up on you, right?"

"I'm an adult, Dad," I remind him as I power down the forge. I'll have to come back out here to clean up once it's cooled, but it's safe to leave for a short time.

"You have anything to drink? It's hot in here," he asks.

"There is beer, water and juice in my fridge."

"Well, then take a break and let's sit down for a minute."

I try not to sigh too loudly as we leave the workshop and head through the backyard to the kitchen. It's obvious Dad wants to talk. We haven't had many of these one-on-ones lately, but I recognize one when it's coming.

And I don't want to push him away. I know he's worried about me—they all are. It's better if I just do my best to sweep his worries aside and then things will get back to normal soon.

Normal is key. I need for things to go back to normal.

I reach into the fridge and pull out two bottles of beer, since I know what he likes. I cut a lime and offer him a wedge to squeeze inside. It's the best way to drink Mexican beer.

Dad thanks me and squeezes his slice of lime into his bottle before cramming the entire wedge down the long bottleneck so that it floats inside the beer—a habit that drives me crazy. I scoff at him and he smiles. "I'm not going to change at my age, Liam. You should know better."

I take a pull from my beer without answering. We drink in silence for a few minutes before he finally clears his throat. "Adam says you're back at work already. I wonder if that's a good idea. How's the injury?"

Instinctively, I raise my hand to my hairline without actually touching the injured area. It's still sore, but it's survivable. "I'm fine. The injury is minor. I get the stitches out on Monday, and that's the part that's the most annoying. They are starting to itch."

"So you'll be right as rain, physically. How about emotionally?"

I don't answer. I continue sipping my beer while thinking about how odd that expression is. Dad uses it a lot, but I have no idea how "right" rain can be.

"Liam...do you want to talk about it?"

"We are talking about it."

"About Jenna." He's giving me his serious look.

I sip my beer some more. I don't know what to say. I don't know how to describe what it is I feel. I'm living the same life I've always led, but now it feels like there's a giant hole. Like a huge part of me is missing. During that week before the Festival—when I chose not to see her—I'd missed her deeply. But now...

It's a little bit like how I imagine missing a physical part of me that I can no longer see, feel or touch. Like having a limb removed. It's like that.

"Why did you and my mother divorce?" I suddenly ask, shocking myself even more than my dad. That's saying a lot because, with raised eyebrows and an open mouth, he appears pretty startled.

"Uh..." He leans back and sets the beer down, rubbing the dark stubble along his jaw. People say I look like my dad and I take that as a compliment, though I'd be more proud to be as good a man as my dad is. "We didn't communicate very well...and I was spending a lot of time getting the firm up and running. She had two little ones at home. It was a lot of stress with me gone so much."

Even now he won't blame her—like couples who break up usually do. But not him. That's my dad.

"And having me. I'm sure that was additional stress."

His brows come down sharply. "No more than any other young child."

"Statistics say that parents of autistic children—"

He makes a sharp chopping gesture with his hand. "I don't care what statistics say. It wasn't your fault, Liam. There are a lot of different factors that determine whether a marriage will work or not. We just weren't as good a fit as we initially thought we were. Things change when you start your adult life. We were young and ambitious. We took on a lot—parenthood and a new business, among other things. It was no one's fault, Liam. Or if it was anyone's fault, it was mine and your mother's. You were just little when we split up."

"But—"

"Is this what you've thought all along? That she left because of you?"

I shrug and sip my beer.

His shoulders are rigid as he rocks in his seat. "Your mother's relationship with you—or lack thereof—had nothing to do with the divorce," he states. Then, he gets out of his seat and starts walking around the room. Mercifully, he knows better than to pick up my things and put them down. That really bothers me.

He shoves his hands in his pockets and says, "I wish I could have done more to make things better between you and her. I thought I was protecting you."

I think about that for a minute. "There's nothing you could have done."

"I could have not interfered." He hung his head for a moment before straightening to look at me. "I saw what it did to you the few times she made plans that fell through, so I...discouraged her from making plans after that."

I'm silent for a moment, trying to recover from my shock before he notices. But he's watching my face and he's almost as good as Adam at sensing other people's feelings. He starts talking again before I can think of anything to say. "I screwed up, and the damage was done by the time you were old enough to understand. I think I was hoping things would get better between the two of you when you got older, but..."

"But you didn't know she was going to die."

He was studying a painting on the wall, the signed and numbered Meyers print that I'd purchased last year. "It wasn't all her fault, Liam. I share the blame in that, too."

"Don't blame yourself for her failings as a person."

He turned back to me. "We all have failings, Liam. We're human. Yes, she had hers, but I have mine, too."

I blink, thinking how much those words sound like what Jenna said to me. *You'll never forgive any mistake I make—any human failing I have.* It bothers me and I don't know why. Tipping my bottle back, I finish the last of the beer.

A half hour later, I escort my dad to the door. He stops and asks for a hug, which I concede. "Love you, son," he says as he grips my shoulders.

"I love you, too."

"Liam," he says, pulling back and looking at me directly. My eyes lower to his shoulder. "Try to forgive your mother. It will help a lot. I know she's not here anymore, but...she's your mother. She deserves your forgiveness. And as for your life, well... You should talk to Jenna. Sort this all out. She seems like a very sweet girl."

"She's a woman."

He laughs. "Yeah, you know what I mean."

I do, but it's easier to correct him than to address the rest of what he said. It's true, I could talk to her...but would she only hurt me again?

***

Another week passes. Another week of my comforting, regular routine. It's during our usual Wednesday morning breakfast meeting that I finally summon the courage to bring up the subject with Mia.

"How is Jenna?" I say as quietly and as blandly as I can manage. As if my next breath isn't hanging on the answer. But my voice still sounds like it's strangled.

She stares at her breakfast plate for a long time, cutting everything up into smaller bites than she usually does. Then she sits back, suppressing a yawn with the back of her hand. "Sorry, I had a bad night last night. Up late studying."

I fork a bite of sausage and pop it in my mouth, waiting for her answer.

"So, um, Jenna left."

Suddenly, the sausage tastes like ashes in my mouth. I stop chewing as everything inside me tightens. And yet—I knew it. I *knew* she would leave. But somehow it still hits me like a ton of bricks.

"The Renaissance Faire doesn't move on until the end of June, though," I say once I've managed to swallow that dry lump of sawdust.

Mia looks away with a sigh. "No, I mean she left the country, William. She went to Bosnia early to spend time with her mom and sister before the wedding."

"Did she say when she'd be back?"

"She didn't, William. I'm sorry. She said that...there's a possibility she might stay there permanently with her family."

Suddenly, I'm done with my breakfast. I sit back and push my plate away, then quickly excuse myself. I do have lots of work to do, but I can't think about anything else the rest of the day. Not that Jenna was far from my thoughts before this, but now she's halfway around the world and I can't stop thinking about how permanent this is. I've lost her forever.

I can't explain why, but that night when I get home, I open the drawer that holds the stack of cash and birthday cards from my mother. After opening them at my dad's house, I brought them to mine. They are still arranged in order from my sixth birthday to my twenty-first. I read through them in that order until I reach the last one—the one I didn't read the night I was with Jenna.

The one Mother sent me only months before she died.

Liam,

It's too late. I know that. I wish I could go back and change everything between us, but by the time I was in a place to try, you were too old and too hurt by things that happened when you were a child. I'm sorry I wasn't a good mother to you. I regret that every day. But I was young and human and imperfect. Your dad was so much better with you than I ever was. He did a good job raising you and I'm proud of all you've accomplished, though I really have no right to be.

Someday, perhaps after I'm gone, I hope you will forgive me.

I love you. I always have.

Mom

There it was—the one I'd been looking for. The message I'd doubted she ever penned. And had I opened it the day I received it, there would have been time. Time for me to pick up the phone and call her, to meet with her, to forgive.

But because I'd let my anger and resentment rule me, that opportunity had been lost. *Forever.*

As I stand in my bedroom, my face is wet. I'm crying while thinking about how much I wanted her love when I was young. About how she didn't love me because I was broken...different. All the words that had been heaped upon me during childhood—*spaz, freak, retard, Liam the Loon.*

In the middle of my room, I stand there and cry like a baby for almost an hour. Because I've realized that my stubbornness has caused me to miss out on the opportunity to forgive my own mother while she was still alive.

The Buddha once said that holding on to anger is like drinking poison and expecting the other person to die.

I remember Jenna's words from the night we read the birthday cards, and I know then that I've been judging Jenna based on what my mother did. That I've been expecting her to run away from me, and in so doing, I pushed her away.

With my face in my hands, I picture Jenna the last time I saw her, pressed against the door, her face wet, her eyes red and swollen from weeping.

And my words...so cruel. So heartless. *Just like a robot.*

But what can I do?

Jenna is gone, and she might never come back.

Have I lost her for good? And if I find her again, would she even want me back?

The only thing I can do is try.

37
JENNA

MY STOMACH CHURNED AS THE BUS MADE ITS WAY ALONG twisting mountain roads. Only two hours remained of the lengthy trip from Belgrade to Sarajevo.

Just five hours before, I'd said goodbye to Helena and Vuk at the bus station. It had been a quick and exhausting few days in Serbia, meeting their family members and touring the city. And now here I was—alone—once again, with only my thoughts and no possibility of escaping them.

The past few weeks were a blur—a sore, painful, and then numb blur. Helena had been worried about me, checking in like a concerned mother several times a day. She'd kept her distance until Alex spilled the beans when I didn't get out of bed one day. That's when Helena decided to make arrangements for us to fly out a week earlier than planned.

Yet despite the whirlwind surrounding a trip overseas, I missed William terribly. I'd wake in the morning after dreaming of him, feeling his ephemeral kiss on my lips. And as the Dream Wil faded and reality set in, I'd die a little when I realized that he hated me still. That I could never erase the image of his face when he left my apartment weeks ago. Pain and disappointment. *Disgust.*

I shook my head, fixing my eyes on the beautiful, green and hilly countryside of the land of my birth. Bosnia-Herzegovina was a

443

country of rugged, verdant beauty. And until darkness fell, I lost myself in the gorgeous views while trying to forget the slowly dulling heartache.

I'd decided it was time to find some permanence, and there was a strong possibility that my real home would never be in Southern California. Maybe my destiny lay here after all. I'd decided to give it an honest chance, anyway. Maybe the reason I'd never set down roots in the US was because I truly *was* Bosnian. After all, I had family here who cared about me deeply.

Maybe Bosnia was my future.

Seven long hours after boarding the bus in Belgrade, I finally arrived outside of Sarajevo. The last time I'd been here was nine years ago, and I'd let my older sister handle everything. But now it was just me...all alone.

I'd exchanged some money before leaving Belgrade and thus was able to negotiate a cab ride. The driver flirted with me and called me "American Girl," despite the fact that I spoke to him in fluent Bosnian.

I supposed I had an accent now.

This only emphasized that feeling of never fully belonging in either place. Maybe because I hadn't allowed myself to belong? Maybe it was time to let myself do just that.

You deserve permanence, and I want to be the man who gives it to you.

Maybe I did...but apparently, I didn't deserve *him*.

Twenty minutes later, I handed the cab driver my money and popped out of the taxi. He unloaded my suitcase and set it beside me on the sidewalk. "*Hvala*," I said, thanking him.

"You speak Bosnian very well, American Girl."

With a sigh, I picked up my suitcase, entered the apartment building and then climbed the steps toward Mama's apartment.

Mama and Maja were both home, having taken the day off from work to wait for me. When I showed up at the door, Mama and Maja pounced on me immediately with screaming, crying and kisses. Mama, with tears in her eyes, smooshed my cheeks together and said I was beautiful but way too skinny.

Maja introduced me to her fiancé, a tall, thin, dark-haired man with crooked teeth and a sweet, soft-spoken voice. They told me Sanjin was a beautiful singer in the church choir, which reminded me that I probably needed to attend church while I was here. It had been ages.

"Janjica, I can't believe it. I can't. You've come back to us at last," Mama said.

Maja smiled at me, tugging playfully on a lock of my hair. "Sanjin has four brothers. We should introduce them. Maybe we'll find you a Bosnian boyfriend, Janja, so you won't go back to America."

That sharp pang in the center of my chest made it a little harder to breathe. I sighed. "No boyfriends for me. But I do want to stay for a while." Sanjin grabbed my suitcase and carried it up a floor to Maja's room, where I'd sleep in the extra bed they'd borrowed for me.

That night, we stayed up way too late drinking wine, eating amazing food—*ćevapi* and *somun,* kebabs and flat Bosnian bread—talking and laughing. It felt so good to be here.

I spent my days exploring Stari Grad—the oldest district of the city, dating back to the fifteenth century—along with the *Baščaršija,* one of Europe's most ancient bazaars. I also ran pre-wedding errands for my sister while she was at work. In doing so, I discovered that my Bosnian vocabulary was painfully lacking, so I attempted to relearn my own language and culture.

One night as Maja prepared to turn in, I lay on my bed flipping through one of her books I'd pulled off the shelf. It was a children's book written entirely in Bosnian-Serb-Croatian, and I struggled to read it. After ten minutes, I slapped the book shut.

"You have anything to read in English?"

"A few old books. I don't read in English anymore."

I smiled. Maja now had an accent when she spoke English. Probably the way I had one in Bosnian, I imagined. And yes, everyone in the neighborhood referred to me as either Maja's American sister or Silvija's American daughter.

I smiled as I watched Maja rubbing moisturizer into her face. "You're going to a beautiful bride."

She glowed. "And you, my beautiful bridesmaid! Wait 'til you see your dress." At the mention of the dress, I pictured the beautiful blue gown that William had given me. I blinked, frustrated that no matter how hard I tried, I couldn't get him out of my mind.

Maja watched me. "Are you homesick?" she asked suddenly.

I guessed I would be, if I actually *had* a home...

But I was starting to question what "home" meant for me. Was it people or a place? My people were scattered on opposite sides of the earth. In Bosnia, in California...

"Not really. I'm glad to be here," I hedged.

"There wasn't someone special you left behind in California?"

I rolled over on my back to look at her. "You are so madly in love that you look at everything through love glasses."

She gave me a strange look. "You're as silly as ever, Janja."

My eyes wandered up to the ceiling. "I sure am...silly."

"But you're also sad."

I frowned. "Yes."

"If you're not homesick, then what is it?"

I sighed. "There *was* someone. But it's over now. And...it still hurts."

She came over and sank down on the edge of my bed. "Oh, *draga moja.*" She pushed my hair back from my face. "I'm sorry. It didn't end well?"

I shook my head, suddenly and inexplicably close to tears. My lip trembled and I bit it. That ache returned with a vengeance.

"Come here," she said, waving for me to sit up, which I did. Then she took me in her arms and held me tight. "Do you want to talk?"

Now I was sobbing—for the first time since the day William walked out the door, declaring us a "mistake." I expelled a long breath, letting the tears flow this time instead of holding them back. I was with my big sister and it felt good. It felt safe.

"Maja, I love him so much. I just want it to go away. I can't help but wonder if it will ever feel better."

"It *will* get better with time. It's still new and raw. I know it's hard to believe that now."

Like with Brock. I still loved him, but that crippling pain I felt after his death had eased with each passing year until he'd become a sweet, aching memory.

Would it be that way with William someday? More importantly, did I want it to be? Wishing for the pain to go away was a double-edged sword, because it would be wishing for these feelings to fade, too. And these feelings, though they hurt—they *stabbed*—they also made me feel alive.

Weeks passed and the wedding approached. Maja and Sanjin would be married in a cute little sixteenth century church not far from the neighborhood where my family resided. Their humble apartment was located in a middle-class section of Sarajevo amongst a mixed population of Serbs, Croats and Bosniaks. As such, there was a Roman Catholic church, an Eastern Orthodox church and a mosque all in close proximity.

The night before the wedding, I visited the church where Maja would be married. It was quiet, serene and aglow with flickering candles. It smelled of old incense, desperate prayers, crumbling stone and ancient dust that no doubt remained untouched in high places that no cleaner could reach.

As I sat on the pew staring up at the glittering altar, I wondered about my belief in soulmates. Was Maja about to marry hers? Had I lost mine seven years ago in a random car accident?

Was I destined to go through this life alone?

Maybe William was right. Maybe our coming together *was* a mistake. But if so, it was the sweetest mistake I'd ever made. And though I ached every time I thought of him, I'd never regret the time we spent together.

I just hoped that there'd be a way to start over again. Because right now, it was looking pretty bleak.

Our relationship had flared, burning bright and hot for a short period of time. It had blinded us. Blinded *me* from reality. And now here I was sitting in a cold church halfway around the world, pondering if I'd ever see him again.

My sister was a beautiful bride. The morning of the big day, our aunt fixed her hair and make-up, and afterward, we helped Maja into her exquisite dress. When Baba's tiara was placed on Maja's head beneath the veil, it gleamed in her dark hair.

But damned if I couldn't look at that tiara and not think of William and all he had done to get it back for me. The emotions clamped around my throat, choking me as I dressed in my own beautiful gown to stand up with my sister.

I wore seashell pink satin and was the only bridesmaid, with our little cousin wearing a darker shade of pink and acting as the flower girl. As we walked to the church—a short distance down the street— neighbors called out their well wishes, and I held up Maja's train to keep it clean.

Several hours, and one very thorough wedding mass later, Maja and Sanjin were husband and wife. And I was exhausted. After handing my sister her bouquet, they began to walk back down the aisle and everyone clapped and cheered.

I immediately fell into the nearest pew to take a load off my feet. The guests had all been able to sit down during the mass, whereas I'd had to stand and kneel repeatedly.

From the pew, I lifted my head to stare at the painted murals on the ceiling of the church while it emptied of people. I'd join them in a few minutes, after I'd had a chance to catch my breath.

"Janjica? Are you coming?" Mama asked.

I continued to stare at the ceiling. "Yes, I'll catch up. Go, enjoy! And make sure you get in some of the pictures, Mama!"

She grumbled something about not wanting photographs taken of her and then turned and followed the remaining stragglers. Just as I heard her nearing the exit, I sat up suddenly, remembering that I'd left my gift in a bag at home.

I turned. "Mama, can you—?"

I froze, certain my eyes were playing tricks on me. There was a tall, handsome man standing behind Mama who was a dead ringer for William. Though I knew it was some sort of illusion, my heart started palpitating anyway.

Mama turned to follow my gaze and then looked back at me with questions all over her face. "Do you know him?" she asked.

"I think so..." I squinted, hoping that would provide some clarity. "I'll be along...I promise."

The man—William, it *had* to be William—watched Mama walk out of the church before shifting his gaze back toward me. When his hands began rubbing down over the material of his thighs, my throat tightened.

I moved toward him at the same moment he approached me. The stone floor echoed our footsteps, and no other sound could be heard besides the cheers and congratulations for the couple just outside.

Soon we met in the middle of the aisle. I couldn't breathe, couldn't swallow—and I most certainly couldn't talk. William watched me with solemn features, perhaps trying to guess what I was feeling. I wished him all the luck with that, because I sure as hell had no idea what I was feeling.

He looked so remarkably handsome in that suit—which was obviously new—even if he didn't look comfortable wearing it. And by some miracle, he'd matched the shirt and tie.

William scanned every inch of my face without meeting my eyes, while I studied his chiseled, masculine features and the curve of his mouth, which reminded me of his passionate kisses.

And these *feelings.* Going from the dark places I'd explored in the past few weeks to this rush of euphoria at the sight of him was like stepping onto an already moving tilt-a-whirl.

Finally, he cleared his throat. "*Zdravo,*" he greeted me in perfect Bosnian.

I blinked, barely able to reply. "What? How? *When?*" I shook my head, wishing I could make some sense of *something.*

"I found out you left. I decided to come get you."

I decided to come get you. I wavered where I stood, in danger of swooning like some corseted woman from the nineteenth century.

"How did you find me here?"

He looked at me like the answer was obvious. "You saw me read the wedding invitation in your bedroom."

I blinked. "You glanced at the invitation for a minute, two months ago..."

He shrugged. "I remembered the date, time and location of the wedding, so I knew exactly where you would be on this date at this time."

Of course he did. I shook my head. "But why come all this way? You said—"

He startled me by lifting a finger and pressing it to my mouth. "*Volim te,*" he said.

I love you.

My heart leapt, but the rest of me could not forget still-fresh hurts. It was strange, this feeling of flying and being anchored to the earth at the same time. "Wil, you were so angry with me, I—"

"I'm not angry anymore. I forgot to remember that we all have our flaws. I have lots of them too."

I smiled—a tremulous, shaky thing, like a newborn puppy. "You forgot to remember?"

He smiled too. "Yes." His brow creased. "My flaw is that I don't forgive those in others. And that's just as bad or even worse."

I thought about that for a long moment. I wasn't angry at him, but I *was* incredibly hurt and still nursing those wounds.

His eyes skimmed me from head to toe, taking in my dress, my braided hair, my fancy make-up. "You are beautiful, Jenna. The most beautiful woman I've ever seen." His eyes scanned my face again, his posture straightening as if he was suddenly self-conscious. "But as gorgeous as I find your face and your body, they're nothing compared to your heart...your gentle, loving heart. I was wrong, and it was unchivalrous to hurt that pure heart of yours."

I bit my lip. "Wil—"

"I'm not done," he said. It sounded as if he'd practiced this speech many times before—which he probably had. "I'm a knight, and you are the woman whom I hope might become my lady. And a wise man once told you that you were a princess and someday you would be queen. He was right. You're my queen. The queen of my heart." He took my hand and bowed deeply, much like a medieval knight giving courtly obeisance to royalty. Then he gently kissed my hand. "I am your humble servant. Please, will you grant me your forgiveness?"

I exhaled a long breath as he held his position, bent over my arm. Then I reached out and stroked his soft, thick hair.

"Of course I forgive you. Arise, Sir William. You are my noble protector, and I thank you for all that you've done for me. *Volim i ja tebe.* I love you, too."

He straightened, a wide smile on his handsome face. "Jenna, I—"

"Hold on, William," I said. His face clouded, and I rushed to clarify so he'd understand. "I mean, I need you to wait for a minute while I say what's on my mind." I sighed. "And why I think this can't work between us."

He blinked as if I'd slapped him, but said nothing.

"I need to be here for a while...spend time with my family. Find out where my home is."

He shook his head. "I don't understand. Your home is where you've been living for the past twenty years—"

For once, it was *me* avoiding *his* eyes. "It's not that easy, William. You helped me understand that I needed to stop wandering. That I need to establish roots, find permanency. I need to know where my home really is." His eyes narrowed on a point just over my shoulder with laser precision. "Do you get it?"

He nodded. "I think that home is the place where you are at ease. The place where you feel safe and secure. Where you know that you are loved."

"Yes." I nodded. "And I need to find out what that looks like for me."

His eyes flew to mine. "I've had some lessons in visualization from a very good teacher, so I can help you with that."

My brows rose. "Oh you can, can you?"

He gave one quick, decisive nod. "Close your eyes, Your Highness." I laughed. "No, you can't laugh. You have to take this seriously."

I pressed my lips together. "Okay. Lay it on me." I cleared my throat, remembering that I needed to speak plainly. "I mean— proceed."

"Take my hands and close your eyes. Begin to breathe deeply and relax." I did as he asked. "Now listen carefully and envision what I describe. You've come home from a long day at your job—a job you love where you work with people who are kind to you and appreciate your contributions. You get out of your car, which you bought with money you've been saving up. And you live in your own place that you decorated yourself. A place where you are safe and calm and happy. You're at your front door right now. Do you see it?"

I was amazed at how easily I could picture a door made of dark wood with a polished brass handle. "Now you take your keys out of your bag and put the key in the lock. After you unlock the door, then you slowly turn the knob. You see the entryway. You see your pictures and art pieces hanging on the walls, your rug on the floor, your furniture in the living room. You walk inside, just like you've been doing for weeks, months, *years*. And your home is a place that you love."

He was quiet for a long moment, so I went with it...picturing what he described and then some. I let myself walk around in that imaginary space, feeling relaxed, allowing the stress of the day to melt away from me.

"You notice that something smells different," he continued. "The smell is coming from the kitchen. A delicious aroma of cooked vegetables and meat and spices."

A self-cooking kitchen? Not bad. Or maybe a housekeeper? I bit my tongue and didn't ask because I wanted him to continue.

Fortunately, he did. "When you enter the kitchen, you see that there's soup in the slow cooker."

"Who put it there?" I couldn't help asking that time.

"I did. I made the soup for you. I make very good soup."

I opened one eye to look at him. "How come I didn't know that?"

He smiled. "You didn't ask. Close your eyes," he murmured and I obeyed.

I started hoping that somewhere in this imaginary house, my personal soup chef would show up wearing nothing but his apron. Because he stood close to me and *his* smell was making my nose tingle, I was starting to crave his arms around me.

"Do you smell the soup?" William asked.

"Yes. My stomach is growling."

"Good. Because when I come into the kitchen, the first thing I'll do is kiss you and ask you how your day was. Then, I'll spoon you a bowl of soup and cut a slice of fresh bread I bought at the bakery."

"Do you live here, too?"

There was a long pause. "That's for you to decide. This is your exercise, not mine."

I swallowed. "Hmm. Maybe...maybe if you hug me while I'm visualizing? That might help."

Seconds later, William shifted closer and then his strong arms were around me. I gulped, overpowered by emotions as he held me.

My domestic vision was suddenly replaced by powerful, protective arms holding me while the park fireworks terrorized me. A soft voice whispering in my ear, telling me I'd be all right. That he would never leave me. Keen eyes that noticed everything, even my chipped fingernail. Long, deft fingers sweeping away my tears, telling me my heart was as beautiful as my face and my body. Lips that caressed mine slowly but could also possess me fiercely. A man who stood up for me against a bully—more than once—while subjecting himself to ridicule and a potentially devastating loss.

I pressed my face into William's suit jacket and inhaled him. And I felt that jolt, followed by a deep, warm sensation in my chest—of safety, of security, of unconditional love. *Home.*

Because there are many things you'll do for the ones you care about—sacrifices you'll endure, risks you'll take, obstacles you'll overcome. But for the one who's become the air you breathe and the home you crave, you'll forgive any flaw, brave any challenge and even plan a new future.

And I was ready—*so* ready—to plan a future with him.

"Wil, I want to kiss you."

He hesitated for a moment then tilted his head toward me. "On the cheek or on the mouth? With tongue?"

I growled, grabbing the back of his head, and after his initial shock, he complied readily. And we were kissing...just like that. As if we had never stopped.

His tongue slid into my mouth, scorching me. His hands curled around my shoulder blades and he hitched me to him. Heat streaked through me and powerful desire burned like a wildfire up and down my spine.

Suddenly, it was feeling very warm in the little church and it wasn't even summer yet. I could hear footsteps near the altar— probably an altar boy or even the priest. William must have heard too, because he paused and slowly pulled his mouth away.

Our damp foreheads pressed together. "Jenna."

"William," I replied.

"Say you won't go away again. Not unless you take me with you."

"I won't go anywhere without you if it makes me feel as miserable as I have been these past few weeks."

His arms tightened around me. "Let's not be stupid like that again," he said. "We belong together."

"Come on...your crowd skills are going to be tested once again, at least for a little while. We need to go to the wedding party. And I need to show off my handsome American."

He laughed. "I've been listening to recordings to learn how to say key phrases in Bosnian."

"Well, I like the ones I've heard so far..."

"Želim te."

I sucked in a breath, warm desire blooming in my center. "Mmm. I want you, too. Tonight. After the party."

I took his hand, and we walked out of the church and into the square. I couldn't wait to show him around and explore new places with him beside me.

But first, I wanted to introduce him to my family. I was certain that they'd love him. Maybe not as much as I did, but that was okay.

Because now I understood what being home truly was. With William's help, I'd finally found it.

And it felt incredible.

38
MIA

L OS ANGELES INTERNATIONAL AIRPORT

Jenna: In Customs now. Will meet you at curb outside baggage claim?

Me: Yes! Will be there ASAP. Can't wait to see you!

I notified the driver to pull out of the cell phone waiting lot near LAX and head to the curb of the Tom Bradley International Terminal. We had plenty of time because William and Jenna would have to pass through Customs and then claim their luggage. So I decided to while away that time by wheedling Adam some more.

It had been almost two months since the duel, and he still wouldn't tell me when this wedding was going to happen. And he was loving every minute of stringing me along. I'd laughed along with him at first, but as time passed, I was ready to stage a revolt.

We sat in a rented limo—part of the service we sometimes used. Though Adam still preferred driving himself most of the time, *no* one—not even him—liked circling an airport. Thus, I had the benefit of him being a captive audience with no distractions. I was prepared to use that benefit to get my way.

"Let's see…how about Star Wars Day?" I asked.

"What?" He frowned.

459

"May 4th?" At his blank expression, I elaborated. "May. The. Fourth. As in 'May the fourth be with you.'"

One dark brow rose. "Stupidest pun ever. Besides, we're already past that date."

I shrugged. "That date comes around again next year..."

His smile grew shrewd. "Oh no you don't. I told you already, we are getting married *this* year."

"But you're not going to tell me what date."

He shrugged. "Surprise parties are always fun. Why not a surprise wedding?"

I scowled at him. "Surprise parties are always fun? You threw a surprise party for me once that was definitely *not* fun. And you've warned me never to throw one for *you*. Not that I'd attempt it. Your prescient genius brain powers would sniff out the secret long before it ever happened."

A slow, smug grin crept across his handsome face. "That's right. *I'm* the one who does the surprises."

My mouth twisted with faux frustration. "You missed your calling, Adam Drake. You should have worked for the CIA."

He grabbed me around the waist and pulled me up against him. "Maybe I already do."

I shook my head. "If you make this a surprise wedding, I promise you it's not going to go down any better than that surprise party did."

It was good that we were finally in the place where we could joke about one of the dark points in our life—the night that Adam had asked me to marry him for the first time—and for all the wrong reasons. The night I'd refused him and then walked into the most awkward surprise party ever. Yes, we were light years away from that night. And when you got to the point where you could laugh or smile about painful memories, then you knew you'd arrived at your happy place—at least for the time being.

The smile slid off his handsome face and he looked away, rubbing his jaw dramatically with his free hand as if he were a cartoon villain.

"C'mon, Adam, I need a date," I whined.

He leaned over and kissed my temple. "I promised you a date. I'll give it to you. I just didn't say *when* I would give it to you."

I got up and moved to the opposite bench seat to avoid his groping hands. "You don't want to at least tell William we have a date? He helped you win that bet. "

"Oh, I could tell him. He'll keep my secret."

My mouth pursed. "Just make sure that secret isn't too well kept or the bride might not even know when to show up."

His smile widened and he patted the seat next to him. I shook my head at him, refusing to risk getting within reach of his all-too-convincing hands. I stuck my tongue out at him before saying, "You're enjoying this way too much. I might have to get violent. *Or* get you drunk."

"*Or...*" He held his hand up his mouth to mime a blowjob.

I folded my arms across my chest, and then a brilliant idea popped into my head. Adam studied me with a wary look on his face. *As he should.* "What?"

I gave an exaggerated shrug. "Sadly, I'm not even sure I'll be able to get freaky with you." For effect, I sighed dramatically. "At least not until my mind is alleviated of the burden of worrying about when I'm getting married."

His eyes narrowed. "Are you saying what I think you're saying?"

My devious grin widened. "Probably."

"I feel the need to warn you that I do have legendary willpower."

I laughed. And laughed. And snorted. And then laughed some more. That may have been the case once, but it *hadn't* been the case for quite a while now. Nowadays, he had the willpower of a frat boy on viagra.

He frowned. "It wasn't *that* funny."

The car pulled into the loading zone outside the terminal. I spotted William and Jenna standing on the curb beside their baggage, holding hands and waiting. They both looked utterly exhausted. After a fifteen-hour trip, I couldn't blame them.

I turned back to Adam. "I can't wait to test that legendary willpower." And with that, I reached under my skirt and yanked off my panties. Then I tucked them into a ball and leaned forward to stuff them in the front pocket of his khakis. "Here, hold these for me, will you?"

I saw his eyes widen just I hopped out of the limo. Immediately, I gave William a hug—after warning him first—noticing Adam was slow to get of the car. "Here are our world travelers!"

"How are you?" Adam slapped his cousin on the arm while I moved to hug Jenna.

"Hungry and tired," she said. "Neither of us could sleep on the plane."

"We have dinner ready for you at our house, and a guest room made up if you want to stay. Or the driver can take you home after we eat. We weren't sure what you wanted to do."

"Dinner would be *awesome*," said Jenna.

"William, how was Sarajevo?" I asked.

"Busy," he said. "Beautiful. Old. And crowded."

Once the driver had loaded the luggage, we all piled into the back of the limo. I smooshed in next to Adam even though it was completely unnecessary. There was a ton of room back here, but my seduction plans were in play. I'd have to press my body up against his as much as possible. Not that *that* was really a chore. The man was too damn sexy for his own good.

William sat facing us on the opposite seat with his arm around Jenna. I was thrilled to see them so happy after having seen them both positively miserable when they were apart from each other. And I couldn't help being proud of William for taking the risk to travel halfway around the world when he hadn't even known how she'd receive him. That had taken major balls. *Good on him.*

However, my efforts at seducing Adam on the way home were hampered because the two of them could see every move I made. The panties had been just the opening salvo. But as we all talked during the hour-long drive from LAX to our house in Newport Beach, I laced my fingers between his, resting both our hands atop my lap—*very* close to where the panties would have been. I was also trying to figure out a way to flash him some boob when the other two weren't looking.

Adam, of course, was not taking this lying down. While his hand rested on my lap, his fingers ever so subtly traced circles on my upper thigh, and as usual, his fingers evoked tingles and raised the perceived air temperature in the car. He knew damn well that there was only one thin layer between his hand and the goal. This was war.

Challenge accepted.

"We got you Licitar!" Jenna was saying.

Adam and I looked at each other. "What's that?"

"Gingerbread," William replied. "And not the kind you actually eat. It's too beautiful to eat." A few days after arriving in Sarajevo, William had called Adam to let him know he had found Jenna and that he would be staying for a month. Adam, who was his boss as well his cousin, had to remind William of his current unfinished project. But given the circumstances and the fact that William hardly ever took a day off or a vacation, he couldn't say much—project or no project. So instead, Adam had Fedexed him a special computer to use, and William had been able to get some work done between touring the city and spending time with Jenna.

But I imagined that a month away from the familiar and the routine would be hard for anyone—and for William, even harder. My eyes zeroed in on the way he held her, sweetly caressing her shoulder. And the way he looked at her. Like she was his everything.

Jenna reached into her carry-on and pulled out a box. "I didn't want it to get crushed in the luggage. But look! We got your names written on them."

"But we had to leave your wedding date blank because I had no idea what it was." William shot an accusatory look at his cousin. "Adam never told me before I left."

"That makes two of us, William." I smirked. "He hasn't told *me* the date, either."

Jenna produced two beautiful heart-shaped cookies that were, as William said, exquisitely decorated in brilliant colors and patterns. They were definitely much too gorgeous to eat. "It's a Croatian art form," he explained. "We purchased these during our trip to Zagreb."

We were then treated to a detailed description and history of the art of Licitar in Croatia. All the while, I tried to sneak my hand further and further up Adam's thigh without them noticing. It's not an easy business, this stealth seduction. Adam may have been CIA material, but I most certainly was *not.*

Luckily, I was wearing my best push-up bra and made sure to lean in every chance I got—under the guise of admiring his gingerbread. "Adam likes cookies," I said, nodding. "A *lot.*"

He laughed and looked out the window. Jenna was digging through her carry-on for something and wasn't listening. William carried on, having completely missed the innuendo.

The limo dropped us off at end of the bridge that led to the little island on the Back Bay where we lived. Adam instructed the driver to hang out until William and Jenna were ready to go home afterward. William had said he was anxious to sleep in his own bed again. Apparently, Jenna hadn't yet decided whether or not she was going to move in with him, but they had agreed to try it out for the next few days at his house.

Walking across Bay Island to our house, the two of us fell into step behind William and Jenna. I cozied up to my prey, ready to take on a new role—Emilia the Huntress. "If you play your cards right, you can eat some cookie for dessert."

Adam promptly slid his hand around to my ass, copping a feel. "You're sounding very confident. Maybe I need to prove that I can outlast you."

Ha! I ran my hand quickly down his crotch, cupping him, and he sucked in his breath before sidestepping out of reach. "Evasive action!" he said as we made it to the door and unlocked it to go inside.

We had a nice, pleasant dinner. Chef stayed to serve us appetizers and the main course, leaving once the meal was underway. She'd already given us instructions for dessert, which she'd put in the fridge.

Adam and I continued playing host together, dipping into the kitchen for more wine or to clear plates after the main course. Each time we passed, we took the opportunity to torture one another just a little bit more. I grabbed his ass with my free hand, carrying a wine bottle in the other. He brushed a hand across my breast when he made his way to the sink with the dirty dishes.

I spooned the chilled vanilla mouse into fancy dessert cups and lined the four of them up on the counter, waiting for Adam to come back in the kitchen.

Still in stealth-seduction mode, I unbuttoned my blouse and pulled my bra down to expose and also push my breasts up, providing him a perfect view. Then I propped myself against the counter, posing like an erotic model, as I waited for him to round the corner.

Unfortunately, the person stepping into the kitchen was *not* Adam—thankfully, it wasn't William either. Jenna stopped cold as I, mortified, scrambled to pull my blouse together and cover myself up.

Jenna openly laughed at me. "I didn't know you cared for me like that, Mia."

"Shut up," I snapped, buttoning up my shirt again.

She walked up to the counter. "I offered to help with dessert and Adam was fine with it. I'm going to assume he'll be upset when he finds out what he missed."

"Damn it! I'm trying to get the wedding date out of him. I want to get him all horny and then tell him I'm not putting out 'til he gives me the date."

Jenna snickered and grabbed two dessert cups. "Try going commando," she said as she took off around the corner again.

I picked up the other two desserts and glared at her back. "Uh, thanks. Good idea." *That I already thought of two hours ago.*

Once I sat down next to Adam, however, another idea sparked. When he wasn't looking, I dropped a small spoonful of mousse on his pant leg. Jenna saw what I did and had to cover her mouth to keep from exposing my nefarious plan.

"Oops! Sorry. I spilled some of that..." I grabbed Adam's hand and used his finger to pick up the glob of mousse. He looked at me like I was a freak, apparently too surprised by my action to anticipate what I would do next. Bringing his hand to my mouth, I sucked the mousse right off his finger, not hesitating to get my tongue in on the action.

Then, as the pièce de résistance, I gazed deeply into his beautiful eyes as I finished my tongue flourish. I was rewarded by that unmistakable glow of arousal deep in those shining black eyes.

Thank God. I was beginning to think I was getting rusty in the art of stealth seduction.

Jenna was full-on laughing her ass off across the table. As I pulled Adam's finger free, I kicked her under the table.

"Hey!" she whined.

William just watched the scene while enthusiastically spooning his vanilla mousse into his mouth as if it might disappear if he didn't move fast enough.

Fifteen minutes later, Adam drove the pair in the golf cart back to the bridge, where the limo was waiting to take them to William's house. When Adam reentered the house, I was at the sink rinsing off the dishes while mulling over my next plan of attack.

My hands were sopping wet, the sink water running, when he came up behind me and grabbed my hips, pulling my butt flush against his obvious erection. "Shameless vixen," he muttered against my neck as I shivered.

"Mmm. Is that a lightsaber in your pocket or are you happy to see me?"

He devoured me with his lips, teeth and tongue. Tingles shot all the way down to my toes. At this rate, he was going to get me to give in without spilling the info, the fucker. I couldn't let him get away with that—irresistibly sexy as hell or not.

I leaned my head back to rest on his shoulder at the same time I felt his hands slip under my skirt and skate up the back of my thighs. "No fair. You're too good at this," I choked out.

"You've never complained about me being 'too good' before. I'll take it."

I turned off the faucet, but couldn't reach the dishtowel to dry my hands, and there was no way I was moving out of his reach. Giving one last halfhearted attempt to get my way before conceding defeat, I wiggled my ass right against his crotch. He rewarded me with a husky groan while his maddening mouth wrapped around my earlobe. His hands slipped around to my front, holding me against him.

I licked his neck. "Do you want me enough to tell me when we're getting married?"

"I might. But you ought to know by now, I never, *ever* like to lose."

His fingers slipped lower and my breath stuttered. I arched against his solid chest. "Oh, I guarantee you, Mr. Drake, this is definitely a win-win for both of us."

"Mmm," he breathed against my ear, one hand pulling away for few seconds. The next thing I heard was his zipper and the crackle of a condom wrapper. I bit my lip. He'd come prepared.

"Brace yourself, Ms. Strong—or should I say, the future Mrs. Drake?"

A jolt of elation instead of what normally was fear. "I like the sound of that. If only I knew *when*." I turned my head to kiss him, and his mouth claimed mine with strong, possessive lips, followed by fierce strokes of his tongue.

God, I loved this man.

Even when he was driving me bonkers. And not just with his maddening tongue.

"So when will that be? Tomorrow? Next week? I need a dress, at least."

"You could wear rags and still be the most beautiful bride on the planet. Because you'll be *my* bride."

"Mmm. You're getting better at that flattery thing." His hands were rubbing now, in all the right places. I shifted against him. "And you're still pretty damn good at the hands thing."

"So, let's call this a draw, then?" I could feel him pressing at my entrance, and my grip tightened on the edge of the counter.

"I think I could do that."

Just before he entered me, he leaned forward and whispered a date in my ear. After that, it was a mad, passionate blur of ferocious kitchen sex. We hadn't done *that* in a while. And by the end, I wasn't quite sure I remembered the date right, so I had to ask him again.

Meh, so I'd had to seduce it out of him, but damned if hadn't been fun.

That was just how Mr. Drake and I rolled. *Win-win.*

But, of course, being a man—and being *Adam*—he had to ruin the moment just as I was gloating that I'd gotten the intel from him.

"Sure, you know *when*...but I didn't tell you *where*, now did I?"

Men.

ABOUT THE AUTHOR

Brenna Aubrey is a USA TODAY Bestselling Author of contemporary romance stories that center on geek culture.

She has always sought comfort in good books and the long, involved stories she weaves in her head. Brenna is a city girl with a nature-lover's heart. She therefore finds herself out in green open spaces any chance she can get. She's also a mom, teacher, geek girl, Francophile, unabashed video-game addict & eBook hoarder.

She currently resides on the west coast with her husband, two children, two adorable golden retriever pups, a bird and some fish.

CPSIA information can be obtained
at www.ICGtesting.com
Printed in the USA
LVOW10s1812021017
550899LV00004B/692/P